TRUST ME

KRISTIN MAYER

ISBN-13: 978-0-9899913-0-8

OTHER BOOKS BY KRISTIN MAYER

THE TRUST SERIES
TRUST ME
LOVE ME
PROMISE ME

DEDICATION

This book is dedicated to my husband, Paul, my daughter, Makaela, and my best friend, Sarah. I love you all dearly.

Contents

CHAPTER
1

I'm rushing around my apartment, trying to do some last-minute packing before my trip, when my phone rings. It's my best friend, Sam. We've been best friends since we were in diapers, and our parents had been friends since they were in school. Neither of us has any siblings, so Sam and I have basically been sisters all these years.

We live in Waleska, Georgia. It has that wonderful Mayberry aura about it. I think the population sign says around six-hundred people reside here. Sam and I will both be seniors this fall at Reinhardt University. My true love is photography, but I've always been scared that I wouldn't succeed at it.

Holding the phone between my ear and shoulder, I answer, "Hey, Sam. Are you on your way?"

"Yes. Are you sure you want to do this? Alone? For a week? I'm just not sure if that's the best idea."

Since my parents died, Sam's been my rock. She's afraid I'm using this trip to withdraw from life again.

I zip up my bag. With as much sincerity in my voice as possible, I respond, "I need to do this. I have to do this. It's long overdue. It's been planned since spring break. I know you don't want me to go off the radar for an entire week, but it will be fine."

"I know. It's just that I worry about you. If I didn't have my presentation this week for the sorority, I'd insist on going with you. Just promise me that you will call if it gets to be too much for you to handle. I'm here for you. I know you're strong, but this is going to be a tough week."

Smiling to myself, I can picture her animatedly talking with one of her hands while she's driving. "I know, and I appreciate it. You just have to trust me on this. Everything will be okay."

"Okay, Allison. I don't like it, but I support you."

"You're the best. I don't know what I would do without you."

"You'll never have to find out. I'll be there in five, girl."

And that's why she will be my best friend for life. "Okay, honk when you pull up, and I'll be right down."

I dash over to the kitchen island to make sure all my camera gear is safe and secure in my bag. I breathe out a calming sigh as I prepare myself for this journey. Over this last year since my parents' accident, my small two-bedroom apartment has been my sanctuary. Just like at my parents' place, it has that cozy-home feeling that makes me want to curl underneath a blanket while drinking hot chocolate.

Before I can think too much about the past, I go through my mental checklist again to ensure I have everything for my weeklong hiatus from the real world. Nothing but room service, sandy beaches, pools, and sleep are in my near future.

A honk sounds from outside, and I dart down the stairs. A beautiful May day welcomes me as I walk out of my building to Sam's black Toyota Camry.

Sam is one of those people who just instantly attracts friends. Her personality makes anyone she meets want to adopt her and take her everywhere they go. She is a sports fan through and through, which is the exact opposite of me. She's that person who screams at the TV, encouraging the players or telling them how to play. She's naturally gorgeous with green eyes, a curvy figure, and long nearly black hair that has a natural sheen to it. Sam is currently single, and it is not for the lack of trying from the opposite sex. She just doesn't do relationships.

"Hey, Sam. Got a hot date after you drop me off at the airport?"

She's wearing cutoffs and a cute little green halter top that sets off her emerald eyes surrounded by smoky makeup, and her hair is flowing freely around her face.

"Um, yeah, Carmen asked me to lunch. Since I'm going to be in Atlanta, I figured, why the hell not?" Her voice goes a tad tense.

"Whoa. You mean Greg's sister, Carmen? That Carmen? Doesn't Greg play football for the University of Georgia now?"

Sam and Greg had been secretly hot and heavy at the beginning of her senior year in high school, but it abruptly ended after New Year's Eve of the same year. Sam gave some stupid excuse and refused to talk about it to anyone. She just kept saying it was time to move on. After several attempts, I stopped asking for the full story, knowing she would tell me when she was ready.

I've never been the type of person to force information out of someone. Sam has to be ready to tell me, regardless of what it is, and she just isn't there yet.

My Carmen inquiry has earned me one of those don't-go-there looks. Giving her a moment to calm down, I focus on watching the cars pass by on our way to the Atlanta Airport.

"Yes, she wants to catch up. And, no, there's no chance that Greg and I will end up together. There's nothing between us anymore. Please drop it."

Whatever happened between them hurt Sam deeply. The tone in her voice tells me I might receive bodily harm if I continue down this road.

"Okay. I'm just surprised is all." *It's definitely time for a subject change.* "How's living in the house with the girls going? I haven't heard about the latest fiasco."

Sam and a few other juniors are trying to start the first sorority at our college. I think she's crazy for taking this on, but Sam loves a challenge.

"Allison, I swear that if I wasn't so involved with this project, I just don't know if I would keep forging ahead. I hope we were never this incorrigible to live with when we were back home. We have fifteen girls living in a house right off campus, and sharing the space seems to be a foreign concept. Last night, we discussed labeling food in the refrigerator and the amount of time each person should be allotted in the bathroom. I mean, come on, give me a break. Can't we just be a little more grown-up? Why did I ever think it would be a good idea to move out of your cozy apartment?"

The fake irritation in her voice says otherwise. Deep down, she loves those girls.

I laugh. "Oh, Sam, you know you love it. Hopefully, your charter gets approved, so you guys can become the first official sorority of the university."

We pull up to the terminal, and Sam puts the car in park.

"Damn straight. It better happen before the end of our senior year." She's recovered from the earlier mention of Greg.

After grabbing my luggage from the back, Sam meets me at the curb to give me a hug.

"I promise to email you the moment I get checked in at the hotel. Don't worry about me. I'll be fine," I reassure her.

"You better."

I can tell she's still not pleased with the idea. She worries about me too much.

As I am heading inside the airport, Sam yells, "Hey, Allison!"

I turn back to face her.

"Don't forget to find some cute-ass guy while you are there."

I smile wryly and shake my head at her as she winks and blows a kiss. I watch as she hops into her car and drives away.

I board the plane, and I'm ready to go. Excitement is beyond me. A change of scenery is just what I need, and I am practically bouncing in my chair in anticipation of heading to the beautiful beaches of Miami, Florida. It's just a state away from Georgia, but it feels like I am traveling across the ocean to a secluded place where I can sit and process all my thoughts.

As I hear the flight attendant go over safety instructions in the blandest voice possible, I lay my head back and think about how my life has changed so drastically in just a year's time. In three days, it will be a year since I received the worst news of my entire life.

Sam and I just finished our sophomore year of college.

There was an art show in town, and Sam had talked me into showcasing some of my photographs that I had taken through the years. My parents had bought my first camera for me at the age of six, and from that day forward, photography became my passion. I'd devoured any book about photography I could get my hands on, so I could learn about all aspects of it. I'd even won a few contests during my high school years. At the end of the show, a writer from a local magazine approached me to tell me he was impressed with my natural talent.

Heading home to our town of Homerville, I say to Sam for the hundredth time, "Can you believe it? They actually liked my photographs."

"Yes, and they want to offer you an internship. I told you." She gives my shoulder a nudge as I drive.

"I know. I know. Tell your parents that I'm sorry I can't stay and chat. I'll come by tomorrow. I'm too excited to tell Mom and Dad my news." I'm bouncing in my seat with excitement.

"Will do. Mama's gonna want to have you guys over to celebrate at some point."

We start screaming in delight as we pull into Sam's driveway. Looking disheveled, her parents, Dean and Chandra, run up to the car. As I roll down the passenger window, I notice the smell of freshly mowed lawns.

With Dean standing solemnly beside her, Chandra says, "Hey, girls. Can you come inside? It's important."

Her tone alone makes me automatically obey her request.

After we walk inside, Sam and I head straight for the couch and take a seat next to one another. Chandra sits on the other side of me. Dean sits in a chair across from me on the other side of the coffee table. Seeing Sam's parents' sad faces, I immediately have that sinking feeling in the pit of my stomach.

A tear slips out of Chandra's eye, and she wipes it away before putting an arm around me. "Allison, there has been a terrible accident, and—"

I know what she is going to say before she has a chance to finish. "No, no, no. Please no. Tell me they are okay. Please." I plead with her as my tears start falling faster and faster.

She grabs me and hugs me against her. "Honey, there was an accident at the four-way intersection in town. The semi couldn't stop, and it hit them."

I just sob and sob and sob.

As Chandra and Sam sit there, hugging me, the only thing I can think about is the terrible fight I had with my mom last week. It was about me not pursuing my dreams of photography.

Life is a bitch at times.

Later, I was told my parents had never had a chance in the little car they were driving, so they hadn't known what hit them. Every day, I pray that was the case.

If it wasn't for Sam's family, I don't know what I would have done. They helped me get through everything—the funeral, the will, and the never-ending paperwork. A lot of it seems like a dream. I couldn't be sure how much I truly functioned, but I went through the motions. Sam was there for me every step of the way. No one could ever have a truer friend.

Decisions regarding the farm had to be made quickly. Animals needed tending, fields needed plowing, and crops needed planting. Selling the farm was the second hardest thing I had ever done. The first had been burying both my parents on the same day.

Within two weeks, it felt like my whole life was completely ripped from me. My heart had been savagely torn out, and each passing week, the hole in my chest kept growing and growing. The pain never ceased.

I became a recluse. I stopped seeing all my friends, and I spent all my energy just getting through the day. Eventually, my friends stopped calling me, and as horrible as it seemed, I was relieved. Sam never gave up on me though. She kept after me and kept after me and kept after me. If it wasn't for Sam's persistence, I don't know where I would be now. This last

Christmas, I slowly started to go out to social events. I mainly went to give Sam her social time since she refused to leave me by myself.

My hermit status was one of the main reasons she objected so much to this solo trip, but what she didn't know was that I had knowingly picked a time when she couldn't come.

I open my eyes when the plane wheels squeak as we land. This moment feels right, and I know I have done the perfect thing by coming here alone. I was so persistent with Sam about going on this trip because something kept telling me that I had to go find myself.

I'm hoping to clear out all the old cobwebs from the past year. My fear of not letting anyone in because I'm absolutely terrified of losing someone again will hopefully be a thing of the past. Even though I'm frightened, I pray that I have the courage to put myself out there again.

CHAPTER
2

My taxi pulls up to the hotel in the early evening. *Oh, I am in heaven.* Walking up the long blue welcoming carpet into the hotel, I am greeted by shades of golds and blues. Along the perimeter, the floor has an intricate gold swirl design outlined with blue. Tropical plants are strategically placed to further give that paradise feel. The hotel is fairly empty for a Saturday.

The woman at the front desk with a double French twist updo is impeccably dressed in her light blue suit accented in gold. "Hello, and welcome to the Miami Beach Resort. How may I help you?" she asks in her perfected business manner.

"I'm checking in. The reservation is under Allison Scott." I hand her my credit card. I'm ready to see my room and relax.

"Thank you. We have your reservation for four nights, five days in an oceanfront room. You are in room 717. Here's your room key. Elevators are down the hall and on the right. Do you need any help with your bags?" Her smile is small as she waits for my response.

As I take the room key off the counter, I respond, "No, thank you."

"Please enjoy your stay with us and let us know if you need anything else."

After grabbing my suitcase, I head anxiously to my room.

The sound of the hotel key card opening the door is music to my ears. Taking a deep breath, I cross over the threshold. As the door closes, I take a cleansing sigh of relief and look around with a smile. The royal blue curtain valances remind me of the ocean, the yellow walls make me feel warm, and the taupe furniture and bedding provide me with a peaceful ambience. Immediately, the tension begins to ease out of me while I'm surrounded in this sea of tranquil colors.

Approaching the balcony, I cast my eyes out to the aqua sea. *Breakfast out here tomorrow and each morning after will be a must.*

Remembering my promise to Sam, I grab my phone and head out to a chair on the balcony to email her. *If I text her, we will never stop going back and forth.*

From: Allison Scott
To: Sam Matthews
Subject: All in One Piece

Hey, there! I made it here all in one piece! See? There was nothing to worry about, my friend. Have a great time this week. Good luck with your presentations. I will call on my way back.

Miss you lots!

Oh, I can't wait to tell you about this guy I met. Just following your departing orders.

xoxo

I giggle as I turn off my phone. She's going to kill me for that last line when she finds out I was screwing with her. She's constantly trying to set me up with some of her guy friends. Brad, in particular, has been the most tenacious in asking. He probably just feels sorry for me since I never go out. However, he does nothing for me. He never has.

I want that inexplicable connection I've read about—the feeling that consumes my heart, searing the love in forever. Anything less just seems like a waste since I would be giving a piece of myself to someone forever.

I decide to call it a night, and I settle into my room. The crashing waves against the beach lull me into a peaceful deep sleep.

∞∞∞∞∞∞∞∞∞∞∞∞∞∞∞

Squinting from the early morning light coming through my balcony doors, I throw off the covers, ready to embark on my day.

As I sit on the balcony, letting the sun penetrate my pores, I think about one of the last meaningful conversations my mom and I had when I was at home during spring break of my sophomore year. That was the last time I saw my parents before their accident.

In our small farmhouse kitchen, my mom and I are making breakfast before my dad comes in from his early morning chores. The smell of eggs and bacon cooking on the stove fill the house. I look at my mom, wearing a blue plaid apron as she walks around the kitchen, and I think about how much I treasure these moments because it's when we truly talk.

"Mom, do you think it's weird that I haven't really started dating yet? I keep thinking there's something wrong with me."

She opens the oven and checks on the biscuits. "Sweetie, nothing is wrong with you. You're like me. I never dated anyone prior to your dad."

"How will I know when I've found the one?" I come up beside her as I get glasses out of the cabinet.

She pulls the food off the stove, and then she turns to me, giving me her full attention. She does this when she wants to tell me something important. "How do you know when the peaches from the tree out back are ready to be eaten?"

My brows scrunch together. What in the world do peaches have to do with anything? *"Um…the color, smell, feel…and the stem gets a little loose, making it easy to pull it from the tree. I don't know. I just know when it's right."*

"Same thing will happen when you meet the right one. Your instincts will take over, and you'll know. Just follow your heart, sweetie. It'll never lead you astray. You just haven't found the one yet. Be patient." She gives me a hug just as my dad walks in from outside.

Those morning chats are now so precious to me.

After finishing breakfast, I go to change into an ivory one-piece swimsuit with a matching sarong wrap trimmed in black. Looking in the mirror, I critique my appearance. I am average-looking with blue-green eyes, slightly tanned skin, and dirty-blonde hair that reaches the middle of my back. At five foot six inches, I'm neither tall nor short, and from my days on the farm, I suppose I am toned. I put my hair up into a French twist, grab my things, and then head downstairs for some pre-lunch sun-soaking.

The large rectangular pool is surrounded by blue-and-white mesh lounge chairs with matching umbrellas. I walk over to some empty lounge chairs sitting next to a few palm trees in the corner, and I settle in. I crack open my latest mystery novel, and I begin to get lost in the book. Every once in a while, I get a whiff of someone's suntan oil, giving off that perfect beach aroma. The warmth from the sun causes my eyes to close slowly.

Screech.

I stir.

Screech.

Metal being dragged across the concrete is making an awful racket, like nails scratching on a chalkboard. I look over to see who in the world is creating that noise, and I see a guy pulling over a chair, making himself at home right next to me. *Damn, I wish he had picked one of the other many chairs available.* I notice he has a nice toned body. Sam would push me to talk to him, but it's the same as always. Something is just lacking.

He lifts up his sunglasses, and I keep mine in place.

"I hope I didn't wake you," he says.

"I was just dozing in and out." Immediately, I pick up my book as I try to send the not-interested vibe, but he doesn't get the message.

"Can I get you a drink from the bar?" He steeples his fingers under his chin as he looks me over.

Cocky bastard. Indifferently, I respond, "No, thanks."

"Are you here on business or pleasure?"

This guy is not taking the hint. I hate to be bitchy, but I just want to be left alone. "Please don't take this the wrong way, but I came down here for some alone time." Being blunt isn't normally my style.

He sighs, getting the message, and heads to the water.

Good.

After I go for a dip in the pool and have a quick bite to eat, the area is exploding with people. I head toward my room to take a relaxing bubble bath. As I near the bar area, I see a waiter wiping off a vacated table.

"Excuse me. What time does the sun set here?"

He straightens up. "Right before eight, ma'am. If you're thinking about catching it, I suggest coming down around seven thirty. Make sure to bring your camera if you have one."

"Thank you. Have a good day." I start to get excited about using my camera. Taking pictures is one of the only things that still soothes me and gives me peace.

"You, too, ma'am," he says as he finishes cleaning the table.

I continue my way up to my room. As soon as I enter, I head to the bathroom to start my bath water. The hotel room comes with a complimentary bottle of chamomile-scented bubble bath. The smell relaxes me, and I add a generous amount to the steaming hot water. Anxious to get into the tub, I strip and ease myself in. Turning off the water, I decide to close my eyes for a bit.

Lying there among the foaming bubbles, I randomly pop them with my fingers while listening to the consoling voice of Michael Bublé. I think about what my next steps might be. *What would Mom and Dad think of what I've become in the last year?* Sometimes, I feel like I don't even recognize myself.

If I were to ask my mom for advice on this, I could hear her saying, *Advice is what we ask when we already know the answer but wish we didn't.*

It's so true. They would be sad to see how I have quit living life to the fullest and have resorted to just existing. I do want to start living again, but I am so afraid of what will happen after the loss I have suffered.

As I climb out of the tub, I ponder about how I'll start reclaiming my life. I've let the pain of my parent's death consume me, and if I'm not careful, it'll continue to devour me until nothing is left.

I decide to take a quick nap before the sunset, so I open the balcony doors and rest as the distant sounds of seagulls and the ocean play me a lullaby.

A few hours later, I emerge from my room, wearing a light blue T-shirt and comfortable black yoga pants, with my camera in hand and my bag on my shoulder. During the elevator ride down, I rummage through my bag for a hair tie, and after finding one, I throw my hair up into a haphazard messy ponytail to keep the hair out of my face while I'm taking pictures on the beach.

Once in the lobby, I head outside to the beach, and a clean, salty scent greets me and wraps around me. After removing my flip-flops, I squish the sand in between my toes. The scenery brings happy memories, and I welcome them as I remember when my family used to head to the beach for long weekend getaways. It's good to think about the memories and not feel like I am being swallowed up by the sadness that normally accompanies the thought of my parents.

Making my way down the shoreline, I enjoy the peaceful feeling of having no expectations. It's just the crashing waves, my camera, and me. In the distance, I see some dolphins tormenting a seagull. They seem to be playing a keep-away game. I prepare my camera and adjust the settings. It's a professional digital camera with a wide-angle zoom lens that my parents had bought as my birthday present after I finished my first year of college.

I begin taking shots from different angles as I try to capture contrasting lights from the sky. There's something magical about taking an image that will help me remember all the smells, feelings, and thoughts I had in that exact moment of time. It's like freezing a piece of history that can never happen in the same way again.

As I start walking, I think back to my apartment, which is covered with pictures I've taken, memories I have made, and moments I will cherish.

"Ow!" *Oh my gosh!* I got so captivated in the moment that I almost ran someone over in the process. My eyes automatically shut from the impact. I decide not to open them as I take stock of how hard this guy's body feels. *Crap, my shoulder hurts from hitting him.*

"Shit." The voice is deep, raw, and powerful.

Now is when I have to face this total stranger and admit that I made a total idiot of myself because I was distracted. *Um, yeah, I totally rock.* He did not sound pleased either. *Well, who would be when some crazy person rams into you out of the blue?* It's time to face that inevitable moment when I wish I could just fast forward, so I don't physically have to live through it.

"I'm so sorry. I was gazing out at the ocean, and I didn't see you." When I look up into the eyes of the stranger, I am immediately frozen into place from the deep blue eyes gazing back at me. They are the purest blue pair of eyes I have ever seen. *Thank goodness I got that last sentence out.* Right now, my brain has completely stopped working, and I am not even sure I can process anything of sound mind.

Mr. Blue Eyes has black hair flopping in that sexy way. My fingers want to run through it as I pull his mouth down to mine. His lips look to be firm yet soft. His angular jaw is something I could spend hours—

Holy shit! I shake my head to stop my train of thought as I turn ten shades of red. *Did he just ask me something?* "Um, sorry, what did you say again?" *Oh, kill me now.*

"I said, do you always go to such extremes to get attention from guys you're interested in talking to?" His eyes are dancing with amusement.

Just then, I realize that he hasn't let go of my upper shoulders from when he reached out to grab me. My skin is on fire at the spots where he's touching me. I'm confused by my reaction, and it causes me to completely miss what he said…again. "What?"

"Are you seriously asking me to repeat myself for a third time?" He's says jokingly.

Oh, that smile. Would it be weird to start fanning myself? "Um, no…I mean, um…"

Damn him. He is now smirking as I remember his previous question. He's caused my brain to run on a ten-second delay. It's time for a little payback as I play along. "Actually, I was vying for that hot guy's attention over there. By irritating a brute like you, I was hoping that I could play the damsel-in-distress card. Then, he would come to my rescue, and voila, you would be out of the picture, and I would be with someone who deserves my time."

He gives me a once-over, and the heat in his eyes feels as if he is devouring me.

"I think that guy would actually need to be paying attention to your damsel-in-distress act to be able to rescue you."

On a cellular level, my body reacts to the sound of his voice. We are still standing close, and my body is not listening to my mind telling it to take a step back. It doesn't want this feeling to end.

I must remain outwardly unaffected. "Oh, he is, trust me. He's just playing it cool. He's waiting for the best moment to make the biggest impression, so he can ensure never-ending gratitude."

"Have dinner with me," he says, his voice serious and seductive.

All I can do is blink at the sudden change in conversation. It makes me feel like I'm on a rocking boat, and I'm trying to keep it from swaying too much. For whatever reason, I am drawn to him like I have never been drawn to anyone in my life.

"What?" I want to facepalm myself for saying that again to him.

He's on the verge of chuckling. *Gah!* He's so infuriating and intriguing at the same time.

"I think you like the sound of my voice. Is that why you keep asking me to repeat myself?"

"Um...no?" I just want to die. *Seriously, why did I respond with a question?* My cheeks begin to heat again as I get a full megawatt smile, but then he looks confused.

"No, you won't have dinner with me? Or, no, you don't like the sound of my voice?"

My brain is on overload, and honestly, at this point, I am not even sure what my *no* meant. I don't want this moment to end, but he's a complete stranger. *Didn't I learn about stranger-danger in school?*

He interrupts my thoughts. "Hey, listen, a perfectly crowded restaurant is right over there on the beach. Please join me for dinner, and if you want to leave at any time, you can. Plus, I think you owe me after trying to use me," he says as he winks at me.

Oh geez. My heart starts to beat faster. I don't think I could say no even if I tried. My body is obviously refusing to obey my mind. I can picture it now. After saying no, he would start to walk off, only to have me hanging on, not letting him go. *There's only so much humiliation a person can take in a day.* "Okay, sure."

He lets go of my shoulders and rests his hand on the small of my back. That strange feeling is pulsing at the place where he is now touching me, causing an unfamiliar deep ache to grow within me. *I have got to get a grip.* His effect on me is crazy.

He leads me to a restaurant called The Beach Hut. The place has a thatched roof and is open on all sides. When we arrive at our wooden wicker table, the arm pulling out my chair is toned and defined. Every attribute about him is mouthwatering. My mental swooning has to stay in check before I lose all control. He takes a seat in front of me.

The sun has begun to set behind us, casting magnificent orange and purple rays across the sky. Seagulls are flying circles over the ocean as they try to bring in one last snack for the day. A slight breeze blows from the north, and the smell of mesquite coming from the kitchen fills the air. It's perfect. A waiter delivers two water glasses.

"So, what should I call the beautiful damsel in distress?"

He takes a sip of water as he watches my every move, making me feel self-conscious.

Beautiful. Did he call me beautiful?

The waiter comes and takes our order. I pick out the first thing on the menu, not even processing what I requested, as this stranger in front of me continues to fry my circuits.

"Alli," I finally answer him. *Alli? What the hell? I never go by Alli. Why did I use the nickname I have fought against my entire life?*

I am completely taken off guard. I am drawn to this guy, like a bug is to one of those zapper things. I cross my fingers, hoping that whatever this is doesn't end up shocking the hell out of me.

I should go. No, I should stay. Wait…calm down. I feel like my mind is going in never-ending circles because of this guy. *This is crazy. I am crazy.*

When he reaches out and touches my hand, my eyes shoot up to his. There's an undeniable connection between us.

"Don't go. It's just dinner," he says softly.

I look down at our hands and then back into his eyes, and for some unexplained reason, my nerves instantly settle. "Okay."

He lets out a small breath as he releases my hand, and I immediately miss his touch.

He continues on his quest for information. "What's your last name?" He looks at me expectantly.

I get the feeling this guy is used to getting what he wants and when he wants it. *What could he possibly see in me?*

Before I have a chance to answer, our dinner and beers are delivered. It looks like I ordered a burger and fries.

Thinking back to the question I was just asked, I try to answer sincerely. "Can we just have dinner and only exchange first names for now? I need to get to know you a little bit more before I give my last name." It sounds stupid and naive, but if this guy is a creepy stalker and my intuition has completely evaded me, I'll feel a tad safer.

"Okay, Alli. I'm not trying to make you nervous. I'm Damien." He sits back in his chair and lifts one of his eyebrows as if he is trying to make a decision.

His white linen shirt paired with khaki shorts are doing wonders for him. His clothing hangs perfectly on his body, accentuating all the right parts. He has quite a calculating temperament.

I want to crawl over to him, straddle his legs, and kiss him. *Crap.* My mind is being a total traitor right now, causing my libido to make a surprise appearance this evening. *What is wrong with me?*

"So, what happens when I want to see you after tonight?" he asks.

"After tonight?"

What started as an accident has now turned into a potential second date. When he laughs at me again, I realize that he's caught on to when I'm flustered since I just keep repeating what he says. *Damn it.* Luckily, he gives me a minute to redeem myself.

"I guess we can set up something to meet again," I say.

"Whatever works for you, Alli. How many dates do you think it will take until you feel comfortable enough to tell me your full name?"

Part of me wants to be honest and say now, but keeping my last name a secret seems to keep a barrier between us. I don't want to get engulfed in the tidal wave I'm sure Damien can create. Plus, giving him my last name now would put me in the insane category since I just said we should stay on a first-name basis.

Hell, I have no idea how to respond. It's Sunday, and I consider the fact that I'm leaving on Wednesday. "How about three dates?" The likelihood that he'll still be interested by that time is slim, and if he is crazy, I can just disappear back to Georgia.

"Does tonight count as date one?" He takes a sip of his beer as he waits for my response.

"Sure."

He nods as if he is solidifying something in his head. "I'm looking forward to the third date."

When he takes a bite of his sandwich, I watch in awe as his strongly defined chin moves as he chews.

"So, besides trying to get my attention for a dinner date, what were you doing out on the beach this evening?"

I just shake my head and raise my eyebrow. Finally, I respond, "A waiter told me about the sunsets. I love photography, so I came down, hoping to freeze a moment from this trip to remember it always. What were you doing down there before I practically ran you over?"

"Just enjoying an evening stroll on the beach while unwinding from a busy day. Are you a photographer for a living?"

That makes sense. He seems like the business type. "No, I just finished my junior year in college. Photography is really just a hobby at this point." I shrug as I take another bite. My mind wanders to the interview I have scheduled shortly after my return. It's with the same magazine that was interested in me prior to my parents' death.

"Well, I would like to spend some time together tomorrow. Would you be opposed to riding in a car with me?"

We have finished our meals, and we're both sitting back in our seats, sipping on our drinks.

I check my creepy meter, and I'm still not getting anything. "I know this is going to sound a little crazy and a lot naive, but you're a normal guy, right? I mean, not some—"

He cuts me off before I have a chance to continue. He looks at me seriously and honestly as he speaks, "Alli, what do you need to feel safe? I just want to get to know you. If at any time you feel uncomfortable, I swear we'll leave, and I'll take you wherever you want to go. Just give me a chance."

His words strike me hard as he lays it all out there. I know I shouldn't, but I really do feel safe with this stranger.

"What do you have in mind?" I ask.

"I thought lunch and the beach would be good. How does eleven sound? I can pick you up here if it's not too far for you or just let me know where I can meet you."

The intimate way his blue eyes are penetrating me makes me feel as if he can see deep inside me.

"Here at eleven will work. Is there something I should wear or bring?"

The waiter comes and delivers the bill.

"Dress casual and bring a swimsuit. I'll take care of everything else. It will be about a thirty-minute drive if that's okay with you." He pulls out some cash and pays for our dinner and drinks.

I'm momentarily distracted as I watch him put his wallet back in his pants, and then I realize I've taken longer than necessary to respond. "Sounds great. Thank you for dinner. However, I should be the one buying since I rudely ran you over."

As he stands, he grabs my bag off the floor and then reaches for my hand, and I oblige.

"Alli, it's been my pleasure." He looks like he is about to ask me something else, but he seems to change his mind at the last second.

We leave the restaurant and walk toward the beach. He moves his hand to the small of my back as we pass a couple coming from the opposite direction. Those tingles return. Our time is drawing to an end, and it saddens me.

"I'll meet you here at eleven tomorrow morning. Here's your bag. Thank you for taking a chance on me."

I take my bag from him and look up into his blue eyes. I am once again captivated, and I want to lean in to feel those lips, but I quickly pull back. It's still too soon to kiss him. "I'll see you then."

From the way he is looking at me, I can tell he knows that I find him attractive. *The bastard.*

As I begin to walk off, I decide to give a bold exit line. "Oh, and Damien?" I wait for a few seconds until I know I have his undying attention. "I'm glad fate had me run into you tonight." I give him a wink before I turn and sashay down the beach without looking back.

Even if I make a fool of myself here, no one back home has to know. Reveling in the feeling of being on cloud nine, I decide I'm ready to live.

CHAPTER
3

When I wake up the next morning, I replay my dinner with Damien as I turn over to face the breathtaking view outside my balcony. Last night felt so good because my old self was starting to reemerge as I let go of those chains holding me prisoner. For once, the suffocation that has been ever-present since last year is gone.

The surprising part is that this happened because of a guy, a total stranger I feel a strong connection with. Damien is an utter mystery to me. I have no idea why someone of that caliber would be interested with a country girl like me. *Just enjoy this as it comes. You're here to start living again. You don't have to declare your undying love and fall into bed with him.*

I can't explain what is drawing me to Damien. It's as though an electric current has encapsulated and tethered us into our own little world. Obviously, I was so surprised by the sudden feeling that I couldn't even focus on what he was saying.

This has never happened to me before. I feel powerless around him, but I also feel empowered to be the person who has been missing over the last year. The likelihood of nothing coming from this eases my tension, but at the same time, it leaves me feeling hollow.

Looking at the clock, I decide it is time to start getting ready for the day. If I'm going to be in a swimsuit around Damien, I want the extra time to buff and shave. *No prickly legs for this girl.*

∞∞∞∞∞∞∞∞∞∞∞∞∞∞

I have about thirty minutes until it's time to see Damien. I slowly head toward where I am supposed to meet him, and I stop to take a few pictures along the way. It's a warm day in

Miami, and the city is alive. The beach is covered in people soaking in the rays. I am wearing a light blue sundress that comes just above my knees. I accented it with silver jewelry and some comfortable semi-dressy strappy sandals. Arriving just in time at the front of The Beach Hut's parking lot, I see a candy-apple red sporty convertible pulling into a parking space.

Damien easily extricates his body from the car. As he gracefully makes his way toward me with a smile on his face, I take in his mirrored aviator glasses, blue polo shirt, and cream linen shorts. My heart rate quickens at the sight of him.

My mind is going places as I imagine what I bet is one hell of a body in a swimsuit. *Shit.* Just thinking about him half-naked in the ocean builds a desire between my legs that has me instinctively wanting to rub them together. It's almost embarrassing how my body reacts to him on that level. I haven't even spoken to the guy, and I'm ready to tackle him here in the parking lot. *Classy, Allison. Get it together. This is not like you. Geez!*

He comes up to me and puts his hand on my arm. "Good morning, Alli. You look even more beautiful than I remember."

The way his lip is quirking to the side gives me butterflies in my stomach.

"Th-thank you," I stutter nervously. My brain needs a good slapping for continuing to evade me in my time of need.

He knowingly smiles at me as he leads me to the car with his hand on the small of my back.

Like a true gentleman, he opens the door for me and waits for me to be seated. After closing the door, he gracefully strides to the driver's side of the car. The interior is all masculine with chrome accessories and black leather. I imagine it's what the inside of a race car would look like. He starts the vehicle, and it roars to life.

"So, where are we going?" I ask.

"A little beach house up the way."

I know I should feel uneasy and scared about going to an undisclosed location with an almost complete stranger, but I don't. The wind has started to pick up, and I realize it's going to do a number on my hair. I quickly grab my hair tie from my bag and pull my hair up into a ponytail.

"Is this what you do on all your second dates?" I ask curiously.

The smoldering look he gives me has me getting all hot and bothered all over again. Despite my embarrassment, I consider asking him to turn on the air full blast because I am having a heatstroke in the mere presence of this man. *What is happening to my body?*

He doesn't answer my question as he pulls into a gravel driveway. I want to ask again, but the scene I'm suddenly in has completely taken me off guard. The beach house is beautiful with its white brick and blue shutters. The front door is framed by a trellis with flowers and vines winding around it. The tropical plants in a variety of colors surround the house and permeate the air with a floral scent. *I wish I could bottle this smell and keep it forever.* The ocean is behind the house, and I can hear the waves crashing against the shore. We have entered our own bubble, and I never want to leave.

Absentmindedly, I grab my camera and get out of the car. While taking a few shots, I murmur, "Wow, this place is mesmerizing." Lowering my camera, I cannot take my eyes off this picture-perfect scene in front of me.

His hand grabs mine and gives it a slight squeeze. "I was hoping you would like it. I rented it for the afternoon to give us some time together without interruption. If you're ready, lunch should be waiting for us out back."

As we start to make our way, he stops suddenly and pins me in place with his sincere gaze. "Alli, if you start to feel uncomfortable at any moment, just let me know, and we will head back to do something else. Okay?"

"Okay. I promise I'll tell you."

He constantly surprises me at every turn, and I can feel myself being drawn to him, craving him more and more. I'm scared shitless because I have known him for less than a day.

When I follow Damien around to the back of the house, I am greeted by a pergola trimmed in sheer white curtains swaying with the gentle ocean breeze. In the center is a white wicker table set for two with large wicker chairs placed beside each other, adding that romantic touch. The food on the table looks decadent. There appears to be a crab dip with baguettes, salmon drizzled with a sauce, some type of pasta dish, and asparagus. A variety of fruits and chocolate petit fours adorn a tiered platter stand.

"Damien, this is lovely, but I think you have gone to way too much trouble. I just don't know what to say." I'm motionless as I take it all in and realize how much work this must have been.

"I wanted us to have a peaceful afternoon. Come, let's eat. This is a private area, and we have it all to ourselves." Putting his arm around my waist, he guides me to the table.

My body is starting to thrum with that electrical current, and my heart is beginning to thunder in my chest. *How can this guy be real?*

We eat lunch in companionable conversation, and the food is even better than I could have imagined.

"So, tell me about yourself, Alli."

"What do you want to know?"

"Everything, absolutely everything. You're intriguing."

"I don't know about that. Let's see…I love drama TV, mystery books, photography, and a good love story. Oh, and I grew up on a farm. Um, I listen to eclectic music. I hate sports with a passion. Honestly, I'd rather watch paint dry on a wall. I'm just an average girl, I guess." *Wow, that sounded super exciting. Subject change.* "What about you?" I ask, trying to get the attention off of me.

"You're anything but average."

He penetrates me with his gaze, and I nod, hoping he'll just drop it.

"Okay, let's see. If I'm watching TV for pleasure, which is rare, it's usually a history show. I tend to read biographies or things that will benefit me in the business world. My music preference is also eclectic. Sports is my passion."

He seems comfortable and laid-back, but every once in a while, he shifts as if he's regaining control over what seems to be an internal struggle. It seems like we are both dealing with putting ourselves out there in one way or another.

"Would you like anything else to eat?" he asks.

"Oh, I'm good. If I eat anything else, I think you'll have to roll me out to the car. Thanks for lunch."

"You're most welcome. I'm not one to beat around the bush, and I need to put this out there. I want to continue to see you. I don't want there to be any misunderstandings on where I stand on that, Alli."

Oh, good grief. At the tone in his voice, that spot between my legs is absolutely throbbing. My body is aching for something, but I just don't know what it is. *He wants to continue seeing me?* I am staring at him with my mouth hanging open. He grabs my hand, bringing me back down to reality.

"Breathe, Alli, breathe. This is going to be good. We are going to be good."

He pauses, waiting for me to respond, but I just stare at him like an idiot. *Super suave, Allison.* I nod, trying to take in that action-packed declaration. *Did he just say what I think he said? We are going to be good?* My heart is saying to go for it, and my mind is trying to process a list of pros and cons with what could happen.

"Why don't we put on our swimsuits and go for a swim? I have a business dinner engagement, but I'm going to cancel. If it's okay with you, I want to spend more time together this afternoon."

For the time being, I'm just going to exist in the moment with this beautiful man. "Okay," I say as I grab my bag before I head indoors.

The inside of the beach house is absolutely adorable. It's done in a classic seashell beach theme, reminding me of scenery I've read about in books. The place is decorated in cute cottage wicker furniture and conch shells of all sizes. Shades of blue adorn the pillows, curtains and rugs within the different rooms. I try to mentally catalog every detail to imprint it permanently into my mind.

I change into my red bikini with silver accents. Sam insisted that I buy this, and when she sets her mind on something, there is no arguing with her. I laugh, thinking about when I tried this on with Sam.

When I came out of the dressing room, she did her little diva-snappy thing. "Girl, you gotta drop it like it's hot."

Leave it to Sam to keep it real.

As I put on the slightly sheer matching swimsuit cover, I remind myself to give Sam a huge hug for making me buy this.

I walk out the back, and I freeze. *Holy hell.* His body is even better than what I could have possibly conjured up in my wildest dreams. His muscles are perfectly formed. They are just the right amount without being too bulky. His perfectly tanned skin against his black boardshorts is mouthwateringly delicious. And for all that is holy, he has a six-pack. *A six-pack!* Over his left pec, he has a symbol tattoo done in black ink.

I would love to take my tongue and trace that symbol. Stop it, Allison. I cannot sleep with a man I don't even know. Oh, I am going to lose total control of myself if I don't get a grip. I'm sure he would love to be mauled by the crazy lady from the beach just because he has a body for sin. That would be so attractive.

He walks right up to me with purpose and puts both hands on each side of my hips. He slowly pulls my body to meet his front, which is all hard male, and our eyes lock.

"You take my breath away. I can feel your need for me. My need is just as bad as yours. I don't want to rush this, Alli, because I want you to get to know me. I won't be a one-night stand for you."

Shit! That was the single most alluring thing that anyone has ever said to me. Part of me wants to let him have his wicked way with me, right here and now, but I refrain. I swallow hard and continue to get lost staring into his deep dark blue eyes. I feel his erection growing against my belly, and— *holy Hannah*—I don't think it's going to stop. I'm scared to death of where this is going, but I'm so excited at the same time. Damien has awoken something in my body I didn't even know existed.

I have to know if this is his normal behavior with women before I go too far down this road. "Is that what you say to all the girls?"

"No, Alli, you're different. Come on, let's go for a walk."

It's not a request but a command in order to keep us from going down a path I'm not ready to tread yet. I grab his hand to give my assent.

We are walking along the beach as the water comes in and splashes around our ankles.

Wanting to know more about him, I start with a simple question. "So, can you tell me something crazy about yourself?"

He rubs his chin in thought. "I love fast cars."

I stop walking as I start laughing. "Really? I mean, really? You consider that crazy?" My voice goes all sarcastic as I finger quote the word *crazy*.

Looking at me innocently, he shrugs as he replies, "What? They're crazy fast."

"That's just so guyish of you." I roll my eyes dramatically to drive the point home.

"Okay then, what's something crazy about you?"

I think about it for a minute and decide on the one thing my dad never understood about me since we lived out in the country. "I have a crazy fear of crickets. I loathe the little beasts." I shudder, thinking about how they just keep jumping with those nasty little antennae things. *Ugh.*

He starts chuckling at me.

"Hey, no laughing. This is a judgment-free zone."

He chuckles harder.

Finally, he gets out, "I thought you grew up on a farm."

"Hey, I said, no judging."

I give him a good playful push just as a larger wave is coming in. He loses his balance, and pulls me with him to the ground. We land in the water with me lying on top of him. The waves rush around us, and Damien's strong arms hold me above the influx of seawater as he pulls himself up.

At that exact moment, I realize I'm straddling his hips. He shifts, and I gasp at the small pleasurable feeling it brings me. We are both starting to breathe heavily as I lean down to taste his lips. Just then, another wave crashes and breaks the intense connection. I scramble and stand up. As I grasp how forward I was being, I blush. Neither one of us says anything about what just happened as we resume our walk.

⊂⊃⊂⊃⊂⊃⊂⊃⊂⊃⊂⊃⊂⊃⊂⊃⊂⊃

Early evening approaches, and we return to the house to grab our belongings. After heading inside and changing, I come out the back door and run right into Damien. He immediately puts his hands on my arms to steady me. Images from earlier this afternoon and the feeling of that tiny movement when I was on top of him come to the forefront of my mind. He must be thinking about the same thing as we say nothing for a few minutes while staring into each other's eyes, completely lost in one another. The energy between us continues to charge to unprecedented levels.

After swallowing hard, I murmur, "Today has been perfect. Thank you." I lick my lips as my eyes dart to his mouth.

"Fuck," he mutters, moving his hands to my waist.

Leaning in, he swiftly comes down on my lips with a crushing force. His lips are as divine as I imagined. Lifting me with ease, he backs me up against the door. His tongue is asking for permission to enter my mouth, and I grant it to him without hesitation. Our tongues begin that sensual dance with each other, exploring all we can in this new, uncharted territory.

The desire I felt on the beach comes back full force. I am drenched with want between my legs, and I can feel his erection growing against me as he continues his assault on my mouth. I have never been kissed like this in my life. His hands grab my hips possessively and pull me even closer to him. In response, my hands wrap around his neck as if I am holding on for dear life. He tastes wonderful. His kiss is like a drug, and I'm not sure I will ever be able to kick this habit.

He pulls back slightly and rests his head against my forehead as we rapidly breathe, trying to calm ourselves down.

"Alli, what are you doing to me?"

I don't know what to say. Without another word, he sets me down, grabs my hand, and leads me to the car.

The car ride back to The Beach Hut's parking lot is silent as we both seem to be deep in thought. I try to process everything that just happened. My world just flipped and tilted on its axis. I feel so vulnerable with Damien, like my heart is there for the taking, and it scares me.

After we pull into the parking lot, he turns off the car and looks at me seriously. "I need to ask you something, Alli."

"Okay." I'm a little nervous by the intensity I see on his face.

"Do you feel comfortable with me?"

His gaze makes me feel like he can see into my soul. To give myself some distance from him, I look at the hem of my dress and play with it between my fingers.

"Um, yes. I'm not sure where you're going with this."

From the corner of my eye, I see him rake his hand down his face as he thinks about his next question.

"Do you feel comfortable enough with me to give me your full name? And tell me where I can find you? After what just happened today, I can't take the chance of never seeing you again."

Oh, wow. Just wow. I have so many emotions running through my mind, and I take too long to respond.

Damien continues, "There is something strong between us, and you know it. We can't deny that, especially with how we both responded to each other at the cottage. I'm afraid you are going to disappear on me because of how intense this is."

He's right. Whatever we have is intense. From his last comment, I'm guessing he must sense how scared I am about relationships.

Without even thinking, my mouth spits out, "Scott."

I want this to be real, but I have to face that my luck this last year or so has not been stellar. I feel raw from putting myself out there.

"Scott?" He sounds confused.

I look his way. "My last name."

In the dim light, I can see him smile. When his hand reaches out to grab mine, I'm reminded of the intensity between us.

"When can I see you tomorrow? I will clear my schedule for whenever you are available."

Laying my other hand on top of his, I respond, "Damien, I'm not going to lie. I am a little overwhelmed right now. We have known each other for about a day, and I need to process all of this. You're obviously busy, and I don't want you to clear your schedule for me."

"Spending time with you today took precedence over all that shit. The world will survive."

I blush a little at his words.

"How about breakfast? I'll give you my cell phone number, and you can call me when you're ready."

The earnestness in his voice stirs something within me. I need to think, but I find myself wanting to see him as soon as possible, too. "That'll work."

"Great. Do you want to tell me where I can drop you off tonight? Then, I'll be able to pick you up properly tomorrow morning."

He gives me a smile, and I cannot help but answer his smile in return.

"Miami Beach Resort."

He turns the car back on and starts heading toward my hotel. He appears to be processing the night's events while I'm trying to get my head wrapped around what has just happened. *Oh hell, this is absolutely nuts.*

The roads around my hotel are blocked due to some construction for maintenance. Damien pulls into a lot across the street, right next to the crosswalk, and then he shuts off the car.

"Thank you," he says.

I look at him quizzically, not understanding what he could be thanking me for.

He continues, "Thank you for trusting me enough to give me your name."

As I lean across the car to kiss him on the cheek, I can see a muscle twitching in his neck. Right as I am about to make contact, he turns his head and connects with my lips. His lips are soft, and the kiss is sweet. He smells all male with a mix of some erotic spice. He pulls back and puts a hand on my cheek.

I whisper, "Damien, I'm scared of how intense this has become, but I can't bear the thought of never seeing you again. Please...let's just take things slow and see where it goes, okay?"

"Baby, I feel the same way. I can live with that for now. I'm not trying to scare you off." He gets out of the car and walks to the passenger side to let me out.

I grab my bag, and I start to make my way toward the sidewalk when he grabs my hand. He brings me back to him and gives me another kiss. With this one, he makes me feel as if I am the most valuable thing to him. As he is cherishing me, the walls around my carefully guarded heart continue to crumble. He slightly pulls away from me, and our breaths mingle.

"Let me walk you to the hotel."

"Not tonight, please. I'm not sure if I'll be able to turn you away, and I'm not ready." I need some space and control pronto to think about everything that has happened.

He starts to protest, and I do the only thing I know to hopefully win this little impasse.

"Waleska," I say quickly.

"What?"

"My last name is Scott, and I live in Waleska, Georgia. I currently attend Reinhardt University. I am not running, Damien. I just need to process. Please."

The sincerity in my voice causes him to relent. He runs his finger down my cheek, and I automatically lean into it as we continue to gaze at each other.

"Thank you. My last name is Wales. Now, please go to your hotel and straight to your room. I'll call the front desk in a bit and have them connect me to your room to make sure you made it safely. I will be counting down the minutes until I see you tomorrow morning. Good night, baby." He gives my face one last caress.

I smile at Damien and turn to walk away. I am both elated and scared shitless about everything that has come to pass since running into him. *What is happening? What is going to happen?* I look both ways and start to make my way across the road. After a few steps, I turn to give Damien one last wave good-bye, and then I blow a kiss to him.

"ALLI!"

That's the last thing I hear before everything goes black.

CHAPTER
4

What a night! How does this kind of stuff happen to me at the most inopportune times?

I'm waiting for the X-ray results to come back while lying in a hospital bed in one of those awesome gowns they insisted I wear. *Who designed these things to be almost sheer with only ties to hold it together? That person must have been a serious pervert. Who in his right mind would feel comfortable like this in front of total strangers?*

The blankets are drawn up almost to my chin because the guy that I think I am kind of seeing is in the room, and I am not ready for him to see any of my unmentionables at this point, especially at a hospital of all places. The room is a harsh white with all the normal things a hospital room would have, including that antiseptic smell. *Ugh, I hate hospitals.*

Damien has been incessantly worrying over me since the incident. He has not stopped moving since we got here. With how he is reacting, I would think that I had been in a serious accident.

"Please, Damien, can you sit down and turn on the TV? You are going to wear a hole in the tile if you keep up your pacing."

Paying no attention to my request, he rubs his forehead. "What is taking so long?"

"This stuff takes time, Damien, especially with all the tests you asked to be run. I'm not even sure if this could be classified as an accident. Be patient," I say, trying to be as calm as possible even though I find this all to be totally over the top.

Incredulously, he responds, "Alli, you were basically run over."

"No, I was clipped on the elbow by a moped."

"You fainted."

Ah, this is getting me nowhere! "I have a low tolerance for pain. I was hit on my funny bone. I've fainted before for similar reasons. For the record, I am not disclosing those other incidents to you as I would like to keep some of my dignity intact."

I give him a playful smile and receive a level look in return. *Good grief.* I reach for the remote, turn on the TV, and start to flip through the channels. His repetitive motions are making me a nervous wreck. He's pacing continuously—ten steps across the room, turn around, ten steps back—and then he rubs his forehead three times. Repeat, repeat, repeat. I need a distraction, so I continue flipping through the channels. *What do you know?* The only thing on is sports, sports, and more sports.

"Ugh."

He stops and looks at the TV. "Sports can't be that bad. It's all strategy and skill."

"Or a bunch of little men chasing a ball in meaningless circles."

He gives me his first semi-smile since the *accident.* Hopefully, I am finally making way with Mr. Overreaction.

"Are you hurting? Do you need more Tylenol?"

"No, I'm good. Thanks for asking for the millionth time." *Oh, and now, I am back to receiving that level look. At least the damn pacing has stopped.* I decide to recant. "I'm just cranky and ready to go."

Finally, the doctor strolls into the hospital room. He's a stubby man with a receding hairline and a five o'clock shadow.

"Good evening, Miss Scott. All of your X-rays and test results are good, just as we expected. We are going to work on discharging you. Your elbow will be sore, so we will send an ice pack with you to use as needed. I am going to prescribe a low dosage of pain medicine for your head. If you have any sudden dizziness or intense headaches, please come back immediately. Take it easy for a couple of days. Do you have any questions?" His voice is really soothing, like a grandparent reading a bedtime story.

"No. Thank you, doctor."

Damien, of course, has some questions, and I laugh internally.

"Did you run all of the requested tests?" His tone has completely changed. It's distant and businesslike.

"Yes, and all came back normal." The doctor remains professional, but I wonder what he's making out of all of this. "Is there anything else either of you need prior to me discharging her?"

"No."

Damien's dismissive tone catches me off guard. The doctor looks at me, and I can see that he thinks my date is a little overprotective. I couldn't agree more with him.

As he is leaving, he adds, "Remember to look both ways before crossing the street next time, Miss Scott."

Seriously, the doctor also finds this comical. *Ha-ha.* I give him my best salute and glance over at Damien. He is emitting a death glare at the good ole doc.

I just want to go. Trying to give an adorable smile, I say, "Hey, turn that frown upside down. We get to leave."

"I'll be out in the hall…unless you need some help?" His voice has turned warm and is laced with hope.

"I think I'm good." *There is no way in hell that he's going to see me naked for the first time in the hospital. Is he crazy?* He walks out of the room as he pulls his phone out of his pants pocket, while giving me a semi-worried look. I give a warm smile in return, hoping to placate him. I just want to go back to my hotel room. After I finish getting dressed, I walk into the hall.

Damien is standing there with the phone up to his ear. "Take care of it. He needs to remember that I'm the one paying his fucking check." That cold, distant voice is back.

When he looks over to see me, he hangs up, and his demeanor immediately softens as he walks toward me. "Hey, let's get you back to your hotel room."

"Sounds good."

He puts his hand on the small of my back and escorts me toward the exit.

It's just after four in the morning when he starts the car and exits the hospital parking lot. I lay my head back and close my eyes.

His voice comes through the space between us, enveloping me and making me feel cherished. "Are you comfortable? Do you need anything?"

"I'm okay. I'm sure I'll be a little sore. I just want my pillow." The growling from my stomach makes another need known. My cheeks feel hot from the embarrassing noise. "And I guess maybe a snack."

"Are you hungry? Shit, we didn't have dinner."

I crack my eyes open and look toward him to see genuine concern on his face. "Yes, but no worries. I'll get room service."

"Are you up for some breakfast? We could stop somewhere. I think there's a Pancake House up here."

I'm so tired, but I don't want to leave him. Part of me is afraid all of this is a dream, and I'll wake up at any moment. My stomach growls again. "Geez, I think you have your answer."

He laughs, and one hand goes to my thigh. "I like that answer."

We pull into the parking lot at the Pancake House moments later. The smell of batter and bacon greets me as we walk in through doors. *Mmm*. Breakfast is my favorite meal since it's the start of a fresh day. We are escorted to a booth in the back of the restaurant. A young brunette waitress saunters up to our table. No doubt she has already gotten an eyeful of Damien.

"Can I get you anything to drink, sugar?" Her hip is cocked to one side.

"Alli, what would you like to drink?" He has not taken his eyes off of me since she walked up to the table.

"Orange juice."

"Two glasses of orange juice." He holds up two fingers as he still maintains eye contact with me.

The powerful intensity between us is building again.

The waitress huffs and leaves. She's obviously disappointed that she has not received any attention from him.

He casually lays his hands on the table. "I noticed your hospital bracelet said Allison, but you asked me to call you Alli. Which name do you generally go by?"

Wow, he's really observant. "Normally, I go by Allison. In case you were unhinged, I improvised."

I shrug as he smiles.

"I like Alli. Allison is a beautiful name, but I prefer Alli. It makes it special for us."

The fact is that I like the way his voice turns possessive as he says it. It's just too soon, too fast for me to have these thoughts, but the way he says the word *us* does things to me.

"Alli it is then," I agree.

The waitress comes back to deliver our beverages. She has definitely taken the time to spruce up. I notice she has unbuttoned the top two buttons of her uniform. *Can we say desperate?* I suppress the urge to roll my eyes.

After we place our order, I hear a frustrated sigh from the waitress as she saunters off.

"Our waitress is upset that you're not paying attention to her," I say.

"I am interested in only one person. No one else compares. You said you live in Waleska. Believe it or not, I'm in Atlanta. When are you heading back?"

The fervor of his voice causes me to blush. He's so open with his feelings for me, but I just can't bring myself to tell him that I feel the same way. However, it doesn't stop my heart from doing a happy dance.

"I head back late Wednesday evening. You?"

"Next Tuesday. What brought you to Miami?"

My entire world suddenly closes around me. I cannot believe that it has slipped my mind. Today is the one year anniversary of my parents' death. Damien and the moped incident have completely distracted me. *How could I have forgotten?* All of a sudden, I feel sick as the waitress approaches with our food.

I slide to the edge of the booth and stand. "Excuse me," I mutter, not waiting for a response.

I dodge several trays of food on my way to the restroom before I push through the doors. My heart hurts at how I could have forgotten them. I feel like I betrayed my parents. I rinse my face with water and take deep breaths in and out, trying to calm myself down. This is not the place for a breakdown, especially in front of a man I just met.

I walk out of the restroom door in a fog. Damien gently grabs me by my shoulders and brings me to the corner of the hallway. He's searching me all over.

"Alli, what's wrong? Are you okay? Do you need to go back to the doctor?" The concern and distress in his voice are clear.

"No. Can you take me back to the hotel? I need to rest. I'll pay for breakfast." I hear myself talking, but right now, I feel so disconnected from my body.

He continues to peruse me as if he's missed something from his initial scans. "Don't be ridiculous. What's wrong? What happened?" He's not letting me go.

"Please, Damien, can we leave? I need to leave. I can't talk about it right now. Please."

He studies my pleading face for a few seconds, and then he begins to escort me quickly from the hallway to the front of the restaurant. I feel so protected when he is around. He pulls out some cash from his pocket to cover our bill and gives it to the hostess before we leave the restaurant. He opens my car door, helps me inside, and then makes his way over to the driver's side. As we drive to the hotel, I stare out at the streets of Miami in a trance.

His voice makes me jump. "Alli, what's wrong? Did I say something? You just all of a sudden shut down, and I don't know what to do."

He pulls into the same parking lot across the street from my hotel, and he shuts off his car. I know I need to give him some explanation, but I am too tired to have this conversation right now. I know I would only break down into an absolute mess. Whatever it is we have going on, being the blubbering girlfriend with out-of-control emotions just seems a little too fast.

"Can we talk about this tomorrow? I am so exhausted, and I don't have the energy right now. It has nothing to do with you. I just need sleep. I'll talk to you later, okay?"

I go to get out of the car, but Damien puts his hand on my shoulder.

"I'm going to walk you to your room. There's no leeway for discussion on this. Please let me do this because I need to know you're safe."

I nod because I'm too tired to argue. He exits the car, opens the passenger door for me, and extends his hand to help me out. He pulls me into his side, and we walk across the street. I love the feeling his protectiveness brings when I'm in his proximity.

We walk through the lobby of my hotel and into the elevator.

He asks, "What room are you in?"

"Room 717."

Pushing the proper button on the panel, the elevator begins its ascent to the floor. After we leave the elevator and reach my hotel door, he brings me in for a hug. He seems like he's trying to figure out what's going on, but I can feel my blank mask is in place. Over the last year, I have perfected it to keep people from knowing how not okay I was.

"Get some rest and call me as soon as you wake up. I'm trying to give you the space you asked for, but it is taking every ounce of willpower not to keep you close to me. Here's my card with my cell phone number on the back. Call me if you need absolutely anything. What's your cell phone number?"

Robotically, I give him my number as I pull out my hotel room key. Besides the sadness I feel from the loss of my parents, I have so much to process from my time with Damien. Right now, the spark is out of me.

Bringing his head down to my eye level, he looks me squarely in the eyes. "Alli, I mean it. You can call me for anything. At least, just make sure to call me as soon as you get up, okay?"

I nod. "Thanks, Damien."

He leans down and gently kisses my lips. At a time like this, it's amazing that my body still responds to him. All too soon, he pulls away just enough to break the kiss.

"I'll talk to you this afternoon when you get up. Sleep well, baby." He kisses my forehead, takes my room key from me, and opens my door for me. "Good night, Alli," he murmurs.

"Night." After I close the door, I put the dead bolt in place. Laying my hand on the door, I think about how badly I want him in here with me, but sleep is what I need to clear my head.

After putting on my pajamas, I take some pain relievers and crawl underneath the covers. On autopilot, I unplug the room phone.

Since arriving on Saturday, my world has been turned upside down from everything I thought was right-side up. I have met this amazing man, and I've started to live again. I decide to think about it tomorrow after I've gotten some sleep. My pain medicine starts to take effect, and I fall into a deep dreamless sleep.

CHAPTER
5

My body aches, and I feel a little discombobulated as I stretch. It's like everything is on a delay and out of focus. I feel the soreness from when I hit the curb after fainting. *Gah, that was humiliating.*

The clock says it's 4:18 in the afternoon. *Wow, I really slept the day away.* I need a bath, and I stiffly get out of bed to head to the bathroom.

Soaking in the tub, I think about how much I'm going to tell Damien about what happened. He brings me alive in a way that I didn't know was possible, and it scares me on so many levels.

My mom always said, *In the end, it's not going to matter how many breaths you take but how many moments take your breath away.*

Damien takes my breath away. My mind is having all sorts of crazy thoughts. I want him in ways I've never desired anyone. It just seems too good to be true.

I hear a knock at the front door. After I hurry out of the tub, I grab the robe from the back of the bathroom door. I yell, "Just a second," before I head out to answer it.

Looking out the peephole, I see Damien staring straight ahead with his hands on each side of the door frame. He has a dark expression on his face. *What's going on?* Whatever it is, all I can think about is that he's here, and I want to do a little happy dance.

Opening the door, I cheerily greet him, "Hey, stranger."

Damien strides past me into the room. He's obviously been working today. The way he looks in his custom-tailored gray suit with a dark purple dress shirt is breathtaking. The top two buttons of his shirt are open. He's rubbing his forehead furiously, and his black hair is tousled. *Geez, I crave his touch.*

"It looks like you're okay, so I hope to hell you have a good explanation as to why I could not reach you on your cell phone or room phone. It is after six, and I asked you multiple times to call me as soon as you got up."

"Seriously? You're irritated?"

I cinch my robe's belt around my waist as if it is a shield. I look into his concerned eyes, trying to figure out what my best approach would be. The beast inside Damien is rattling his bars, waiting to be unleashed.

"I took the pain medication the doctor had prescribed last night. I woke up around four and started a bath because I was a little sore. I'm fine. I don't understand what the big deal is."

His hand comes down from his head. "Damn it, Alli. You cannot pull disappearing acts like that. I need to know that you're safe."

I raise my hands in peace and walk toward him slowly. When I reach him, I lay them on his chest and look into his mesmerizing blue eyes. "Listen, I wasn't disappearing, and I appreciate your concern, but my cell phone has been off all week. It didn't even cross my mind when I gave you my number. I wasn't trying to worry you."

He lets out a breath and stares at me intently. "I missed you."

And on that declaration, he leans down to give me a kiss with his delectable lips. Like all of the times before, my body instantly zings to life, and I tilt into him, completely surrendering myself. He hauls me against him and deepens the kiss, causing my hands to go to his sides. His hands are beginning to roam from my waist up to my breasts. My nipples tighten into hard little pebbles in anticipation of his hands reaching their goal.

After this short amount of time of knowing each other, it's crazy how much my body longs for his touch. My body needs something. I don't know what it is, but it's craving it. He pulls away from my mouth and begins to kiss down my neck. A soft moan emits from me as his mouth reaches the top of my right shoulder.

His tongue tastes me, and one of his hands comes up and yanks my robe, exposing me from my shoulder to the top of my breasts. When he pulls me even closer to him, I feel his hardness against me. Moving my hands to the front of his shirt, I try to unbutton it, but I am pressed too close against him that I can't even get one button undone. He continues to bite, nibble, suck, and kiss me everywhere on my bared neck and shoulder. His lips and hands leave a trail of fire in their wake.

Breaking the connection, he moves his hands to each side of my face to hold my gaze. His smoldering eyes look at me while I try to bring my breathing under control.

He states firmly, "I was halfway out of my mind, thinking something had happened to you. I need to know you are okay. Do you understand?" The warmth in his voice is laced with steel and concern.

His tone confuses me, and I stare back at him, trying to read him like he seems to be able to read me at times. I tell him exactly what's on my mind. "This type of intensity makes me nervous with how fast everything is going. We just met, and I don't…I just don't know where this is even going. I'm trying to process it all."

He eyes me, still worried and agitated. "Go get dressed, so we can talk. If not, you and I are going to end up fucking this evening, and that's not a good idea yet. We need to talk first. I'll order some food."

I scurry to my suitcase and grab yoga pants and a T-shirt from the drawer. I head into the bathroom and hastily get dressed. I look at myself in the mirror. My lips are swollen from the amorous onslaught, and I feel the space between my legs throbbing again as I relive the moment over in my head. Part of me, a big part of me, wants to end up in bed with him tonight. *How long should I wait? I need to talk to Sam.*

When I come out of the bathroom, I find that Damien has made himself at home on the couch. His jacket has been removed and is lying on the neighboring chair. Especially in my small hotel room, his presence is commanding. He is looking me up and down as he motions for me to take a seat next to him. My damn body is such a traitor. I am already heading to him before I make the conscious decision to do so.

With a chuckle, he says, "Well, at least there's no question about the sexual tension disappearing."

I mash my lips together to repress a smile.

He continues, "Do you want to clue me in on what happened last night?"

The air is humming with residual lascivious intensity. If it gets any higher, I am going to crack.

After taking a deep breath, I lay it all out there. "I came to Miami to get some perspective. My parents died a year ago today. I was so caught up in this," I say, gesturing between the two of us, "that it took me aback when you asked why I was here. The memory of their death came crashing down around me, and I couldn't believe that I hadn't even remembered it."

"Oh, baby. Both parents?"

He pulls me onto his lap and situates me with my back against the sofa's arm. I am angled to where I can still see his face. One of his arms is along the arm of the sofa behind me, and the other has a hold of my hand with his thumb rubbing soothing circular motions. He makes me feel comforted and protected.

Looking down, I continue as the images of Sam's parents telling me about my mom and dad's death flash through my mind. "Yes, they were heading home, and a semi didn't observe the stop sign. The semi crashed into them as they were pulling through the intersection. They died on impact. Since then, I kind of lost myself. That was why I came here…to find myself again." My lower lip begins to tremble, but I keep it together.

He strokes my face. "I'm glad I didn't push you to come back with me last night. I was scared shitless. I didn't know if I had made the right decision."

"I just needed to sleep. It had nothing to do with you. You've been perfect."

I cannot help the smile that emerges on my face, and he matches it.

"Oh, baby, you have no idea how glad I am to hear that."

His fingers brush over my lips, and I close my eyes at the sensation.

"Alli, I want you badly and not just sexually. I want us to be exclusive. I will not share you. I have never wanted someone this intensely before. Do you feel the same way?"

My mind is reeling as I take in what he just said. My insides are humming from all the excitement. This is a huge risk, but I know I'll regret it forever if I don't take the chance. "I do, but I...it's just...this is all so fast."

"We'll take it slow if that's what it takes. I need you to be honest with me if I am pushing too hard. Please give me a shot. I'm not going to hurt you."

I want to jump up and down and scream with elation at his words, but I remain calm. "I want to see where this goes."

He lets out a breath he was holding. "I assume you do not currently have another guy in your life?"

His eyes are watching my reaction, and I smirk.

"No, no guy. I assume you're single?"

He nods. "There's no one else, Alli. What's the most serious relationship you've been in?"

Oh no. I was not ready to discuss my limited to nonexistent sexual history. He's probably going to think something is seriously wrong with me and run away. I am so out of my depth here.

I wonder if someone like Damien wants a girl with a lot of experience. There's no way this guy has been celibate like me. Maybe I should develop a sudden case of narcolepsy. That would end this discussion really fast. Then, I would be the inexperienced crazy lady who gets hit by a moped and falls asleep randomly. Hmm, that defines the word attractive. *Who wouldn't want a girl like that? What a catch!*

He zooms in on my reluctance. "Alli, what are you hiding from me?"

"What?"

Thinking about how we met and my incessant request to repeat his questions, I almost laugh, and he actually does.

"Alli, we both have pasts. It's not going to scare me away. I just need to know."

Is that what he thinks I'm hiding—an excessive amount of guys? Geez, I'm not sure which one is worse.

"Um, well…um, let's see. I guess you could say that my most serious relationship was with a guy I went on, like, probably four dates with during a month at the beginning of college." I send a silent prayer, hoping we can drop the subject at that and move on. *No such luck.*

"So, you are more into one-night stands?"

I cannot believe how calmly he is discussing this with me. My face feels warm from the blush creeping in on my cheeks. "What? No! Oh my gosh! No! Oh wow, I did not mean to give that impression."

I try to get off his lap to hide my embarrassment, but his arms come around me, holding me in place like a cage. *How humiliating! Oh geez, have I been acting like a total slut?* He looks at me intently with his black hair flopping in a sexy way. His chiseled jaw is set, and his eyes search mine as his muscular arms keep me from moving.

"Please explain," he says.

"Are you really going to make me spell this out for you?"

I spill my hair forward, trying to hide behind it like a curtain. A finger comes up and lifts my chin, causing me to meet his eyes as they tell me to continue.

"Oh geez, I guess you could say I have limited experience. Now, can we move on to a different topic?" Maybe if I close my eyes, I'll be magically invisible, like I used to think I was when I was a kid. *I would love to have that delusion right now, but nope, I have to keep moving on into an ever-growing depth of humiliation.*

"How limited?" he asks.

"Very limited."

"Alli, give it to me straight."

Some hair is still covering my face from my earlier stunt. I blow it out of the way, close my eyes like a two-year-old, and quickly admit what I have been avoiding as if I am being chased by hellhounds. "Limited to the point of…I am a virgin."

When I open my eyes, his eyes are wide as saucers. He looks shocked. The pressure of his grip on me has increased. It's not to the point that he is hurting me, but it seems to be in a more possessive manner.

I hurriedly ramble on. "I know you are probably used to being with more experienced women, but—"

I am cut off mid-sentence when there's a knock at the door. I try to disengage myself, but I am still imprisoned in Damien's iron grasp. He still hasn't regained his ability to speak.

"I need to get the door for the food."

"They'll go away. I'll settle with the front desk. We are finishing this discussion without interruption."

After another minute passes, I nervously prattle on while he's still staring at me as if I were a mythical creature. "There's nothing wrong with me if that's what you are thinking." I am not enjoying this discussion.

He ignores my statement. Almost in awe, he states, "How has someone as gorgeous as you not been hounded by every guy within a hundred-mile radius? I'm just taken aback. I was hoping what you were saying about all this being new to you meant that your experiences had been limited, but I never thought that you had never been claimed before. I'm very fucking lucky that our little beach escapade at the cottage didn't get out of control."

"I don't know how to respond to that. I've just never met a guy I felt that type of need for. I figured, why give myself to someone I only have mediocre feelings for when I could save it for someone special?" I shrug. *It doesn't seem like rocket science.*

"Alli, am I someone you want to do this with, not right now, but when you're ready?"

There's no mistaking the hope and desire I hear in his voice.

I nod. From the moment I met him, deep down, I knew he was going to be the one I would give myself to for the first time. After saving myself all these years, I never would have believed I would be willing to have sex with someone so quickly after meeting him. *When you know, you know.*

Before I have a chance to answer, Damien moves me, so I am lying on the couch underneath him. "If you want me to stop at any time, you tell me, okay? We are not going to have sex today, but I do want to give you something."

"Okay." Silently, I plea that he gives my body relief from the crazy feeling that's been building inside me.

His knee slowly moves between my legs. My body is escalating again, and my breathing has picked up drastically. My hands are pinned above my head, and I am helpless to his assault, which further drives that feeling. He languorously kisses my neck, leaving a trail of tingles in his wake. His subtle spice aftershave penetrates my sense of smell.

"Baby, I need you to tell me if this is too much. I am going to show you the beginning of just how special we will be together. When we do have sex, it is going to be the most phenomenal experience of our lives."

Looking into his deep blue eyes, I moan my assent. There is no way I can formulate a sentence with all my senses standing on end. He removes one of his hands from my wrists, and he moves it down to the bottom of my T-shirt. Gently, his hand migrates up my stomach, bringing my T-shirt up with it, and he unfastens the front snap of my bra to free my breasts.

As he stares down at them, his mouth finds his way to one nipple, and he sucks. Need explodes through my body, and my hips start to move against his leg. His other hand moves to my breasts and begins rolling the end of my other nipple between his fingers. This is the most extraordinary feeling I have ever felt in my life. It's building, building, building. Finally reaching the top, I shatter into a million pieces. *Oh, the sweet euphoria.*

Before I know it, my bra is back in place, and my T-shirt is covering the top of my body again. Damien sits me up in the same position I was in before. My senses are gradually coming back to me as my mind tries to clear the fog in my head. His need is evident as I sit on his lap. He pulls my lips to his in an almost reverent kiss.

He whispers, "You're perfect for me. I hope like hell that you just had your first orgasm."

I nod in response. "Shouldn't I do something for you?"

"Not tonight. We'll get there. You are mine, and I will make it special for you. Just trust me, okay?"

"Okay."

Damien seems to know what I need, and he provides it in spades. I just hope my heart can handle it if he walks away.

"We need to discuss something else this evening. I know you said you leave tomorrow night, but I made a decision, and you're probably not going to like it."

I nod. *Where is he going with this?*

"I used some resources and changed your flight to a midday departure, and I have a car picking you up at the Atlanta Airport to drop you off at your residence. If your car is at the airport, I'll have it delivered to you. Your original flight home is scheduled to land so late, and quite frankly, you seem a little accident-prone. I needed to know you would be safe since I'll be here in Miami through the weekend on business. You always have the option of staying here with me though."

Changing flights, car pickups, extending my stay...what the hell? On one extreme, it's sweet of him to be worried about me getting home late, but on the other extreme, it irritates me that he made those types of decisions without talking to me. My head is still somewhat fuzzy from the orgasm I just had. I wonder if this was part of his plan—fill me with sex-crazed emotions and then drop his erratic actions on me.

"Why are you so concerned with my safety? You should have consulted me prior to making those kinds of decisions for me. I'm not yours to control, Damien."

"Alli, you are incredibly special to me. I don't think you realize just how much yet. Your safety comes first. Would you consider staying here a little longer with me?"

I love the hopeful tone in his voice, but there's just no way. "I wish I could, but I do need to get back home. Sam would go apeshit and fly down here on the next available flight, thinking I have lost my mind. I need to explain this in person."

His warm blue eyes turn cold and furious. I have no idea what I just said that could turn his mood so quickly. It takes me off guard but draws me to him at the same time.

"And is this Sam going to be a problem for me? Because I can assure you that I do not share what is mine. This Sam person better fucking realize his place in all of this."

I laugh to myself. *He thinks Sam is a guy.* He's being a tad bit possessive, but I find this funny for some reason.

In a sassy tone, I reply, "Well, I really don't think you have anything to worry about. You see, my friend, Sam, is what you would classify as a girl. You know, the kind with two breasts and no penis? And both Sam and I are heterosexual. She's been my best friend since we were in diapers. So, chill out."

He immediately calms.

I continue, "Honestly, guys are not interested in me. That makes me sound like a total loser, but it's true."

His eyes dance with humor at my words. "We'll see about the guy thing. I really would like to see you before you leave tomorrow."

I want more than just tomorrow morning. Without even thinking, I blurt out, "Stay tonight."

His eyes snap to mine. "I'm not making love with you tonight, Alli. This place will not do."

The promise laced behind those words has my mind going in a million different directions, mostly wondering what he plans on doing.

I lay my head on his chest. "Just stay with me, so we can spend more time together. I'm not trying to be one of those clingy girls. It's just—"

"I feel it, too, baby." He pulls out his phone and calls someone as he hugs me to him. "Ben, please have clothes for tonight and tomorrow delivered to the Miami Beach Resort. Meet me thirty minutes prior to the meeting at the hotel restaurant tomorrow." After hanging up, he puts his phone down on the table beside us. "Let's order more food."

I yawn and then smile as he picks up the room phone to order room service again. The warmth of his body and his deep heavy breaths cause me to drift off before I know it.

CHAPTER
6

When an alarm starts going off, I stir. A finger starts trailing up and down my arm.

"Wake up, baby. I want to take you somewhere for breakfast."

"Hmm…" My mind is starting to come to, and I'm relishing how it feels to be in Damien's arms. The roughness of his voice has my body automatically moving closer to him.

"It's time to wake up. Come on."

My eyes start to flutter open as I mumble, "Just a few more minutes."

"I'm not a saint, Alli. I've had you in my arms all night." His words are almost pained.

Our legs are intertwined, and it dawns on me that something hard is pressing against my thigh. Without even thinking, I sit up straight, trying to make the situation better, but I end up pushing my thigh into him, which causes him to get harder.

"Oh geez, sorry." Finally, I free myself from him.

He looks like he's struggling with his control over his desire.

"I'm so sorry. I don't even remember coming to bed. I hope I wasn't a total bed hog." I scoot to my side of the bed and try to think about what happened last night. "I don't remember dinner either." My hand goes to my mouth. "Oh my gosh. I fell asleep before room service got here. I am the worst date ever."

He's sitting up by this point, and I notice he's in a T-shirt and silk pajama pants.

"You did, but it was perfect—the best night of my life so far."

My cheeks are flaming as he looks at the clock.

He continues, "We need to leave in about forty-five minutes."

"Okay." I scramble off the bed in a fluster. *I spent the night with a guy for the first time, and I don't even remember it. I will never wish for narcolepsy again.*

Like my mom always said, *Be careful what you wish for.*

I grab my clothes, and when I turn around, I run smack into Damien.

"You didn't have to leave the bed like it was on fire. Good morning by the way."

As he leans down and gives me a kiss, part of me wishes he wasn't making us wait for the perfect time. He pulls away, and I shyly smile, thinking about how crazy I must have just looked.

"Morning to you, too."

I skip a little to the shower, feeling alive and excited. I'll do anything to keep my embarrassment at bay. The shower is hot and helps me calm down.

When I emerge from the bathroom, I'm fully dressed and ready. He gives me a smile as he heads into the bathroom, and I just want to melt after he closes the door behind him. I sigh, wanting to go in there with him.

Shortly after, he comes out, completely dressed, and he looks as delicious as ever. Today, he has gone with a charcoal blue-gray suit with an ecru-colored shirt and no tie. His towel-dried black hair frames his deep blue eyes. *I may end up tackling him before this day is over.*

We just stand there, staring at each other. *This has to be a dream.* He walks up to me and leans down. He puts his lips against mine, and immediately, the kiss deepens. His hand goes to the nape of my neck to hold me in place as he kisses me vigorously. His mouth tastes of wintergreen. My hand starts to go to the inside of his jacket when he disengages from the kiss. He pulls my lip into his mouth and gently bites down.

"Let's go eat before I do something stupid," he says.

Our breathing clearly indicates how worked up we are.

"Stupid?"

"Stupid, like I want you so badly that it's taking every ounce of willpower not to have you and claim you right here on the spot. I am dying to be inside you. It's going to happen when you're ready to take that step and not a moment before."

"Um, okay. Avoiding stupid it is." Although it doesn't sound that stupid to me, I grab my purse and bags, not wanting to argue his point. He's right, but my body doesn't care right now.

Damien immediately takes my suitcase from me, and we begin making our way to the elevator. After we descend to the hotel lobby, his phone rings, and I decide I need coffee. As he's debating on whether to answer the call, I make the decision for him.

"I'll be right back. Caffeine is calling my name."

He nods and takes the phone call. In public, he changes. He's more businesslike or maybe distant. I'm not sure.

On my way back to him, I stop as I see Damien arguing with some guy. I know I haven't known him very long, but he is clearly different with me versus whoever this person is. They're having a quiet, heated discussion. Damien's body language alone keeps me from walking up to interrupt them.

I feel like one of those neighbors who hides behind the curtains of their home to watch what's going on. From what I can see, this guy has on a tailored suit. It's similar but not as nice as Damien's. The guy has sandy blond hair reaching the top of his shoulders, and he's almost as tall as Damien. To most people, I'm sure he's attractive, but next to Damien, he doesn't even compare.

All of a sudden, Damien leans into this guy, and his face is full of absolute fury. I have no idea what he's saying, but whatever it is effectively silences the other guy because he takes off in the other direction. Damien is tensely staring in the direction where the mysterious man went.

When he turns and catches my eye, his whole demeanor changes. He swiftly walks my way, looking back only once. When he gets to me, he puts his arm around my waist and briskly moves me toward the exit.

Curiosity, of course, gets the best of me. "Is everything okay? Who was that?"

"It's fine. That was just business."

His tone tells me I don't want to push him here in the hotel lobby. *Plus, who doesn't have intense discussions at times?*

We are almost to the door of the lobby when I remember something. "Oh wait, I need to check out."

"It's already been handled." He's still pulling me through the door.

When we are outside, I yank free of his hold. "Do not tell me you paid for my hotel stay. Damien, damn it, I am not going to be some kept woman. I can pay for my hotel."

He doesn't say a word as he secures his arm around my waist and continues moving us toward his vehicle. He loads my luggage and puts me—*yes, puts me!*—in the front seat. I am fuming. Part of me wants to throw a bitch fit, but my self-respect ends up winning out in the end. This man totally knows no bounds at times. After he's settled in the car, he pulls out from the front of the hotel, drives into the adjoining parking lot, and stops the car again.

His voice is rough and agitated. "First off, you are not some kept woman. To imply it fucking pisses me off. After the conversations and time we've spent together, I would think you would realize you are much, much more to me than that. I am going to take care of you, Alli. Why the fuck should it matter?"

"Hey, you need to calm down and take a step back from this. I was brought up to be a self-reliant woman, and all these gestures limiting my independence are just as infuriating to me as my unwillingness to accept them are to you. We are going to have to find a middle ground. Let's table this discussion for later unless you really want to have it out during our last couple of hours together." I take the tone my mom always used when she was effectively ending the conversation. My dad always knew when it was time to walk away. I laugh inwardly because it seems to work on Damien, too, as I can tell he's about to concede.

He's still a little riled, but so am I. Whatever he and that guy talked about has put a spur in his saddle.

"Fine, we'll talk about it later." As he begins to drive again, he adds more softly, "Have you let Sam know that you have an alternate ride home?"

"Not yet. I know I am going to be barraged with text messages from her responding to the email I sent to her prior to turning off my phone. Answering her questions will give me something to do at the airport." I pull out my lip gloss from my purse and add some to my lips, trying to dissipate the intensity of the situation.

"What did you send her?"

Oh gosh, we are just jumping from one hot topic to another this morning. Why can't I keep my mouth shut? "Listen to the full story before you go all He-Man on me, okay?" I wait for his assent.

"Alli…"

"No, you're a little jumpy, and I'm not sure why." I look pointedly at him.

"I just want you to be safe."

"I am safe."

He doesn't look convinced, and honestly, it's too early for me to delve into that with barely half a cup of coffee in me.

Hoping to placate the conversation, not him, I continue, "So, Sam, being Sam, left me departing words to find a guy on my trip. Of course, she was just playing around because she knows how I am. I sent her an email when I got to my room, saying I was obeying her departing orders. I had not met a guy at the time, and really, I just sent it to provoke her." *I cannot believe I got all that out in one breath.*

He looks over at me curiously. "But now, you have met a guy."

I smile coyly at him. "Yes, I have."

"And are you going to tell her today?" One of his hands comes out and grabs my hand.

"I planned on it." I smirk at him, and then I suddenly realize we may not be to that point yet. "But I don't have to. I shouldn't have assumed."

He looks at me as if I just grew a third head, and I cannot help but giggle at his expression.

"Yes, Alli, I want everyone to know as soon as you're comfortable with it. Is there any way I can meet Sam next week when I get back?"

"Sure. I'm not sure what we have planned though. What were you thinking?"

"Whatever works best. Just talk to her and let me know."

It makes me feel good that he wants to meet my friend and actually engage himself in my life. "Sounds good."

We pull into a quaint little diner off the beaten path. As we walk in, it reminds me of a place two elderly ladies would run. Everything is done in mismatched antiques. The pieces all fit together in that odd sort of way. It's set up in little coves, so each seating area is semiprivate. They have homemade pastries and an assortment of quiches to choose from.

"This place is fantastic," I say.

"I'm glad you think so. It was where I had planned to take you yesterday morning."

My cheeks blush a little, thinking about how I fainted on our first date. *Classy. Definitely need a subject change.* "So, what do you do for a living?"

"I'm in real estate and dabble in other investments."

For some reason, I get a picture of the Monopoly man playing with all his money after he passes Go.

⌒⌒⌒⌒⌒⌒⌒⌒⌒⌒⌒⌒⌒⌒●

It's quickly approaching nine, and the car will be here any minute. Damien pays the bill, and we walk outside just as my ride arrives to take me to the airport.

Damien pulls me to him. "I wish you were staying, but I'll be back on Tuesday. Please be safe. Keep me posted when you land. I'll be in meetings for most of the day, so I'll need to text. But if you need me, call me, and I will pick up. Okay?"

"Okay. Hope you enjoy your meetings. It sounds like so much fun." I cannot suppress the sarcasm in my voice.

He smiles. "I'll talk to you this evening."

He leans down and kisses me. Just as I start to lean in and forget the rest of the world, he pulls away, and it's over.

He puts his forehead against mine and groans. "Soon. It is going to be soon. I may try to get home earlier."

This *soon* he speaks of needs to hurry up and get here. I know I'm going to lose my virginity to Damien, and I am ready.

"That would be wonderful."

After I'm settled in the car, he closes the door and watches as the car pulls away. Being separated from him is going to be hard. When I can no longer see him, I turn on my phone and prepare for the onslaught from Sam. She doesn't disappoint as one text after another appears.

> *Sam: Guy? What guy? Are you serious?*
>
> *Sam: Allison, radio silence is so not cool.*
>
> *Sam: You better be having screaming hot sex.*
>
> *Sam: Please tell me he has a hot ass.*
>
> *Sam: Can't wait to see you tomorrow. Miss you!*

Originally, there was no guy, but now, there really is a guy. I'm actually putting myself out there again. I just pray Damien handles my heart with care. This is probably the most irrational and illogical thing I have ever done. Biting the initial bullet, I text Sam back and break the news to her.

> *Me: Headed to the airport. Yes, I really met a guy. Long story. Want you to meet him next week.*

I hear back from her almost immediately.

> *Sam: Are you shitting me? Don't screw with me, not on this.*

> *Me: Yes, I swear. I'll tell you about it this evening. Pizza? My place?*
>
> *Sam: You're on. If you are screwing with me, just remember payback is a bitch.*
>
> *Me: I'm not. On earlier flight. No need to pick me up. I have a car bringing me home. Long story.*
>
> *Sam: What time do you get back? What is his name? What does he do?*
>
> *Me: I'll be home at five, and I will give you all the deets then.*
>
> *Sam: Okay. Can't wait.*
>
> *Me: Me, too.*

As the car pulls into the airport, I'm pleased at how well that went with Sam. The driver hands me my luggage, and I head inside to check in. The airport lines are short, and I make it to the gate in plenty of time.

While waiting to board the plane, I sit and reflect about all that has happened. I already miss Damien, and I haven't even been away from him for more than an hour. *Oh, that's right. He asked me to let him know when I made it.* I pull out my phone and send him a text.

> *Me: Hey, I made it to the airport. Hope meetings are going well.*
>
> *Damien: Very glad to hear it. The meeting could be going better. I wish I were with you instead.*
>
> *Me: Me, too. Just imagine I'm there.*
>
> *Damien: Not the same.*
>
> *Me: Good answer. About to board the plane.*

Damien: Be safe.

Me: Will do.

I make my way onto the plane. It's hard to believe that just a few days ago, I was coming to Miami with the weight of the world on my shoulders. Now, I am heading home with a whole new perspective and a boyfriend. My parents' death still saddens me, of course, but I am starting to feel free to live my life again.

⋙⋙⋙⋙⋙⋙⋙⋙⋙⋙⋙⋙●

The flight to Atlanta is smooth, and my luggage arrives just as I make it to the baggage carousel. A tall, skinny man in a black driver's suit is standing at the exit, and he's holding a sign that says *Miss Allison Scott*.

As I walk up to him, I extend my hand. "I'm Allison."

He shakes my hand in return. "This way, ma'am. Mr. Wales has been informed that your plane arrived safely."

Of course, he was.

The driver takes my suitcase and leads the way to the car. We get into a black town car with black leather interior. It's nice not having to deal with traffic myself, so I can just enjoy the ride. I text Damien, wondering how his day is going.

Me: I made it to Atlanta, and I'm safely in the car.

Damien: Glad to hear it.

Me: Are you still in meetings?

Damien: Unfortunately. I wish you could have stayed.

Me: Me, too, but it's only a few days. By the way, how old are you?

Damien: There's no way I can be apart from you for that long. I'm definitely going to make arrangements to come home early. Does it matter?

Me: Yay! Honestly, no, but I'll sound like a moron if I don't know your age.

Damien: Twenty-eight.

Me: Oh…wow. Did I mention I have an age rule? I must have forgotten that.

Damien: What?

Me: No one over twenty-five. If I rely on my sound math skills, I think twenty-eight is older than twenty-five.

Damien: Not fucking funny, Alli.

Me: Hmm, I might make an exception for you. That meeting is making you a grump.

Damien: Grump? I'm not a grump. Making an exception would be a lot better than the other option.

Me: Yes. Grump. Other option?

Damien: If I had you in my arms, I wouldn't be a grump. The other option would be to persuade you in a way you cannot imagine that makes twenty-eight an acceptable age.

Me: Hmm, I might choose this option instead. Will your lips be involved?

Damien: Among other things.

Me: Definitely going with this other option. Pulling up. Wish me luck. I'll call later. If I forget, give me a call. Sam and I can talk for hours and lose track of time.

Damien: Will do. Stay safe.

What is his deal with safety? We are going to have to discuss that soon because it's almost all-consuming to him, and I think it causes him to act a tad extreme at times.

The driver opens the door for me, and with my suitcase in hand, he escorts me to my apartment door. *It's good to be home.* I barely make it through the front door when I hear Sam bouncing up the stairs.

Engulfing me in a big hug, she squeezes me tight. "Hey, stranger. I hope you found what you were looking for." She pushes me back at an arm's length, and she eyes me speculatively.

"I did, Sam. I really, really did. It's a little surreal how I did, but I can't remember the last time I felt like this." The genuine happiness in my voice rings true, and I'm smiling that cheesy smile.

"You seem like you again." She brings me back in for another hug.

I know my withdrawal from the world had her stressed out with worry. She is the reason I made it through the last year.

Pulling back from the hug, I notice Sam's pink sorority shirt. "Did you get approved?"

"Yes, we did. We are an official sorority. We've been cleaning out an old place that they are going to let us use as the official house." She gives me a fist bump, then twirls, and does some jumping thing.

"Woohoo! I knew you would get approved." I cannot help but join in on the dance as we prance about laughing.

Suddenly, she stops and grabs me by the shoulders. She takes me to the chocolate leather couch. "All right, enough about me and the sorority. Spill, Allison." She has that no-nonsense look, and she is ready for all the details.

I start slowly, mainly just to annoy her, and I draw out the words. "I met a guy."

She slaps my leg playfully. "Allison, do not pretend you don't know exactly what I want to know. Details. Now. Pronto."

"Yes, mother." Her arched eyebrow spurs me to continue. "His name is Damien. He's twenty-eight, works in real estate, and actually lives in Atlanta. He's gorgeous. I mean, gor-ge-ous. He makes me feel…I don't know…special and wanted and cherished. I actually ran into him while I was taking pictures on the beach. It feels like one of those movies where fate brings two people together, and it just clicks."

"Do you think he's the one? Are you ready for that step?"

My heart falters at her statement. "Geez, Sam, we've only been together for less than a week. Marriage is a little soon, don't you think?"

She picks up one of the pillows from the couch and throws it at me. "Not marriage, crazy. Your V-card. You know, where the P goes into the V and pops the C?"

She hasn't been a virgin since high school, and the hand gestures are completely unnecessary. I throw a pillow back at her as I burst into a fit of giggles.

"I do. The moment I see him, it's like the entire world disappears."

"Yep, it'll be gone next week."

I give a dreamy sigh, and she smacks me with the pillow again.

"What's his last name?"

"Wales."

"What did you just say?"

"Wales. Why?"

"Holy shit, Allison. Where's your phone? I left mine in the car." She starts snapping her fingers at me, signaling for me to give the phone to her immediately.

Clutching it to my chest, I question, "Why?"

"Because I think you are dating the North Carolina football team owner I'm always bitching about because he's taking the talent away from my teams. He inherited the team from his grandfather two years ago, and he has built them into an unstoppable force. They're expected to win the Super Bowl this year. I want to pull up his picture and see if it's him. Sweetie, if it is, you're dating a billionaire."

Shit. The color drains from my face. "He said he does real estate and other investments. Sam, I'm so out of my league." My blood simmers as I feel like he played with words versus just being straightforward about it. My phone beeps. "It's him. Hold on. I'll find out."

> *Damien: How did it go with Sam?*
>
> *Me: Enlightening.*
>
> *Damien: Okay, I'll bite. Enlightening how?*
>
> *Me: I now know what the "other investments" are. You own a football team?*
>
> *Damien: Let's talk this evening.*
>
> *Me: Why did you not tell me?*
>
> *Damien: Let's talk.*
>
> *Me: This is not a game, Damien. I am not a game.*

I throw my phone on the table and lean back, putting my arms over my face. Under my arm, I mumble to Sam, "I guess you've figured out that you were right."

"Yes, but why are you upset?"

"Because, Sam, he intentionally kept something a secret…or he evaded…or I don't know. He didn't share when he was asked. I've been spilling my guts to him on everything he asks me. I mean, I've been really forthcoming. I just have to think."

My phone starts ringing, and I just stare at it.

"Allison, are you not going to answer that?"

I let it go to voice mail, and then it starts ringing again.

"I just need a second to process."

It goes to voice mail again.

"Just pick up your damn phone and ask him. You process too much."

When it rings again, I look at it as I wonder what I'm even going to say.

"Fine, I'll answer it," Sam says, grabbing the phone.

She connects the call before I can get it back from her. "Hey, this is Sam, Allison's friend. Yes, she's right here. I'm not sure if that is a good idea. I think you know why. Before I help you, I want to know something first. Is this a game to you, Damien? Because Allison is like a sister to me, and if you hurt her, I swear I'll hunt you down and cut off all protruding parts you hold dear, *capisce*? Okay, give me five minutes, and one of us will call you back. Okay…chill out. This is your doing." She disconnects the call.

Curiosity gets the best of me as Sam just sits there and stares at me. She knows me way too well, and I fold like a cheap suit.

"What did he say?"

"Allison, you need to call him back. I think he really likes you, honey. I can hear it in his voice."

"I was going to call. I just needed a minute to think about how to handle it. This has all happened so fast."

"It has, but when it's right, it's right. Do you know how funny it is that you're dating a sports guy?" She's smiling and trying to suppress a laugh, but it causes her to snort slightly. She thrusts the phone into my hand. "Call him. I have a feeling you guys are going to be on the phone for a while." She winks. "Call me tomorrow."

"Okay. Thanks, Sam. You're the best. I missed you."

She gives me a hug. "You'd do the same for me. I missed you, too. Next time, you're taking me with you." With that, she leaves.

I make my way back to my room, put on my most comfortable pajamas, and crawl under the blankets. *There is no reason why I can't do this under my covers.* I pick up my phone and call Damien.

He answers on the first ring. "Alli?" He sounds a tad panicked.

"Yes, it's me."

He lets out a long breath. "I should have been more transparent when I answered you. Why did you ignore my phone calls?" His voice is soothing.

"I just needed to think. I've been honest with you about everything, and I don't like the evasiveness or double standards. Why did you not tell me?"

I hear a sound of what I assume is his chair moving.

He responds, "I fucked up. I didn't tell you because I didn't want to overwhelm you. You were about to get on a plane, and it just didn't seem like the right time. I am not playing any games, I swear. I just found you. I'm not letting go of you. No way in hell am I going to let that happen. I will finish up early tomorrow morning and then fly home to see you tomorrow night. Does that work? Tuesday is too far. I can't be away from you for that long."

"Yes, I would like that very much. Tomorrow is a huge improvement. Sports of all things? Ugh, really?" The disgust in my voice is clear.

He chuckles. "A good majority of people pay decent money to watch sports."

"If you say so. Were you an athlete?"

"Nothing major. My grandfather owned the team, and I inherited it upon his death. Per his will, I wasn't eligible to take over fully until I turned twenty-six, so I've only had it for a couple of years now. As I was growing up, he groomed me to take it over one day." He takes a deep breath. "Are we okay now?"

"Yes. Just please be straight with me. I need to believe that what you say and what you do are true. We have to trust each other."

"I can do that, baby." He sighs. "Fuck, I miss you. It's going to be hard to sleep without you in my arms."

I miss him, too—more than I care to admit out loud. I giggle. "Just hug a pillow and pretend. It's not like we did anything else. Next time we see each other, do you think you'll be able to keep me up?" I bite my lip at my overly flirtatious line, and then I smile to myself.

All of a sudden, his voice becomes deep and rough. "Is that a challenge?"

"I hope so." My voice is barely above a whisper.

Something shifts in the background on his end as if he's standing. His voice becomes serious. "Are you saying what I think you're saying? I can't see your face, and I don't want to misunderstand this."

I'm nervous because I have no idea what to do, but my body seems to take over as it knows exactly what it wants. My answer is certain as I softly say, "Yes."

He inhales a deep breath. "Alli, it's taking every bit of restraint for me not to fly up to you tonight. I swear, we are going to be good, baby."

"I know."

"I'll see you tomorrow. I'll let you know what time I'll be there, and I'll meet you wherever. Do you have any plans yet?"

"No, I was going to catch up with Sam. Other than that, I'm free."

"Okay, we'll talk tomorrow. Sleep well and stay safe until I can get to you."

"I'll try. Good night."

"Good night."

CHAPTER
7

Looking in my closet, I have no idea what to wear to the bar we are going to with Sam's new sorority this evening. My nerves are on edge because Damien will be meeting Sam. Plus, I can't forget that tonight could be the night I lose my virginity. I keep staring into my closet, hoping something pops out and says, *I'm the outfit to wear on your big night.*

Thankfully, my phone rings, allowing me to stall this task. "Hello?"

"Hey, it's Sam. I was wondering if you would mind if Brad drove us tonight. His Tahoe will hold nine of us. Then, we can all ride together to the Hitchin' Post."

All the girls at the sorority must be getting ready because it's absolute chaos in the background.

"Sounds good." Deep down, it disappoints me that Sam and I won't be able to talk on the way there, but I know we'll have plenty of time later.

"We'll swing by to pick you up on the way out of town in about two hours," Sam says.

"Great. Oh hey, Sam?"

"Yeah."

"Please don't make a big deal about Damien. I kind of want him to take the lead with where this is going, okay?"

"My lips are sealed. Ooh la la, do I need to tell you how the P fits in the V?" She starts making kissing noises into the phone.

"Ha-ha, funny, and no, biotch! I had sex education back in junior high. I think I'm covered, but thanks."

"Just making sure. I wouldn't want to fail you as your best friend." She lets out a little laugh before continuing on a more serious note. "Are you still planning on going home this weekend to talk to my parents and to go on the interview on Monday morning?"

"Yes, I haven't told Damien yet, but I am continuing forward with my plans. The magazine wants to interview me in Homerville for whatever reason, so I'm going to stay with your parents until Tuesday morning. Originally, he wasn't going to be home until Tuesday, so it just didn't occur to me to share."

"I'm glad. Gotta go. There's a crisis downstairs. Bye, girl."

"Okay, see you soon." I hang up the phone.

She probably has to stop some girl from pulling another girl's hair because of some trivial thing.

My little reprieve from finding an outfit for tonight is over. *Ugh, I need something fun and flirty.* Still not finding what I want, I decide to text Damien to again postpone this horrific task at hand. I haven't heard from him since this morning, and I've got a reason now to text him without seeming clingy.

> *Me: Hey, I hope I'm not interrupting you. A group of us are going out tonight if you still want to meet up. We'll be at a place called the Hitchin' Post, just outside of Atlanta.*
>
> *Damien: You are never a bother. When will you be there?*
>
> *Me: In about three hours.*
>
> *Damien: I'll see you there. How are you getting there?*
>
> *Me: In one of Sam's friend's SUV.*
>
> *Damien: Which friend?*
>
> *Me: Brad. And a bunch of girls will be with us.*
>
> *Damien: Do you know this guy?*
>
> *Me: Yes. You have nothing to worry about.*
>
> *Damien: Stay safe.*

Me: Yes, sir!

My insides warm from thinking about Damien being jealous of another man even though I have no interest in anyone else. *I probably need to tell him about Sam's out-of-town friend, who will be staying with me while he's visiting next month since he can't stay at the sorority house.*

After looking through my closet a million times, I finally decide on a sleeveless, knee-length turquoise dress that sets off my blue-green eyes. I add a dark chocolate belt, matching brown cowboy boots, and thick silver jewelry to set it off. My hair is done up into a French twist with a few strands hanging down, strategically framing my face. *There. Not bad.* At least Damien will know that I own something besides yoga pants and swimsuits.

A car honks, signaling their arrival, and I grab my dark brown clutch and head for the door. After locking up, I descend the stairs of my apartment building and exit the doors. *Shit.* As I walk toward the silver SUV, I notice the only seat available is the front passenger seat. I hope we beat Damien there because I have a feeling if I'm in the front seat of another guy's car, the possessive side of Damien will come out and play. I'll look like an idiot though if I try to get someone else to sit up there. When Brad starts to disembark from his vehicle, I rush to the passenger's side and hop in.

"Hey, Allison. You look different…I mean, you look fantastic." He is sitting behind the wheel of the car, smiling from ear to ear, as he tries to pull off a sexy look.

Brad is not bad-looking. He's tall and lean in a muscular way, and his blond hair is cut short. He just doesn't cause any type of sexual stirring in me. In fact, no other man but Damien has made that feeling arise.

Brad's green eyes continue to stare at me.

Feeling uncomfortable, I turn away as I respond, "Thanks, Brad."

I can feel him still watching me, and I fidget with the hem of my dress. He has asked me out a couple of times, but it felt more like he was doing a favor for Sam. He seems different tonight though. *That's not good, not good at all.*

I look to the backseat, avoiding eye contact with the driver, and I give a wave and a smile to the rest of the group. "Hey, girls. Thanks for letting me tag along."

They all say something at the same time, and I just smile, not being able to decipher anything more than, "Hey," said in return. Sam gives me the look that wordlessly tells me she tried to get me back there with her, but she couldn't swing it without making a scene. That's the nice thing about being friends since we could barely walk. We have developed a way of silently communicating.

∞∞∞∞∞∞∞∞∞∞∞∞∞

About an hour later, we finally arrive at the Hitchin' Post.

As I reach for the door, Brad's voice penetrates the constant chatter. "Wait there, and I'll get your door, Allison."

Oh, hell no. There's no way I am going there. That screams date, and it would give the impression that I want more. "It's all right. I've got it."

Not wanting to argue, I quickly get out of the car and hang back with the girls as they disembark from the vehicle. I can feel Brad right behind me, and I give Sam that look, telling her that he's driving me crazy. She immediately links arms with me, and we make our way to the door. Of course, Brad comes up and is right there on my other side, his arm brushing against mine as we walk.

During the past six months, he has only seen me in either jeans or yoga pants paired with T-shirts, but it is hard to believe that me wearing a dress is causing his testosterone to go into overdrive. Give a girl a new outfit and an aura that she's seeing someone, and I guess that makes her attractive to anyone.

"Do you two-step?" Brad asks, his arm brushing against mine, harder this time.

A shiver goes up my arm, and it's not the good kind.

Sam, being my best friend in the entire world, takes over the conversation. "Of course she two-steps. She's a country girl at heart. How are you and Serena?"

I love Sam so much. Serena must be Brad's current flavor of the week. He doesn't answer Sam's question as we pay our entrance fee.

As I look around to see if Damien is here yet, I notice the bar has that country feel. The walls are covered in rusted tin with various old-fashioned beer signs, vintage farming tools, and pictures of famous country singers who have darkened these doorsteps at one time or another. The tables and floor are all old varnished wood that looks well-used and worn. The stage at the end of the room has a large American flag hanging behind it. The place smells of greasy food and alcohol.

When Brad puts his hand on the small of my back, I go stiff.

"What do you want to drink? I'll go get it." He's looking down at me with a semi-hooded expression.

I freeze, giving him a mystified look, but it doesn't seem to even faze him. I'm about to say something when a voice sounds from behind me.

"I've got her from here."

My body automatically responds even though it is filled with ice. I turn around to see Damien standing there, wearing artfully ripped blue jeans with an untucked white button-up shirt and brown boots. Every time I see him, my heart skips a beat. Without thinking, I walk straight into him, and my hand goes to his chest. Although we just saw each other yesterday, it feels like it's been forever.

He stares at me as he says, "You are breathtaking."

A blush creeps on my cheeks. "Thank you. I'm glad you came back early."

"Me, too. I don't know what I was thinking. The moment you drove away, I started making plans to return home."

He wraps his arm around my waist and guides me as we follow the rest of the group to the table. We sit toward the end, next to Sam. Brad and two of his friends are seated across from us. I've seen them before, but I can't remember their names. When Sam gives me a look, I remember I haven't even introduced her to him yet. His presence completely disarms me.

"Damien, this is Sam. Sam, Damien."

Sam leans behind me to shake Damien's hand. Keeping her voice low enough so only Damien and I can hear her, she says, "Wales, it's nice to meet you, but I've gotta say you are on my shit list, regardless of how taken Allison is with you. Stay away from my players."

Her teasing voice causes me to smile.

Damien responds, matching her tone, "If I keep stealing all your players, then I might have to watch you more closely to see which ones you are rooting for. Seems like you might have a good eye for talent. I think the only way to settle this is to make a wager."

Sam says, "So, if I win, you stay away from my favorite players on any of my teams, and if you win, you have carte blanche access to them. What are the terms?"

"You name them."

She pops her knuckles, like she's a serious gambler. "If you make Allison a sports fan, you win. If you don't, I win. And by fan, I mean, she goes to the games willingly, and she knows what's going on by the end of the upcoming season."

He doesn't even hesitate. "Deal."

She erupts into laughter.

I turn to Damien. "It's not gonna happen. You just lost."

Sam is almost in tears as she barely gets out, "Good luck, Wales. Good. Luck. I'll start preparing a list of people to stay away from."

"We'll see." His voice has an inflection of confidence as if he's already won. He gives me a devilish grin, like he knows something.

When I glance across the table, Brad is looking at us. He asks, "So, Allison, who is your friend?" He says the word *friend* with a sarcastic tone.

Damien tenses beside me. He does not give me time to respond. "I'm Damien, Alli's boyfriend. And you are?" His aggressive voice more than implies he's ready to have a pissing contest if need be, and he knows he'll walk away the winner.

Boyfriend! He said he's my boyfriend. It's the first time he's used that word, and I'm internally screaming with excitement.

Brad looks at me for confirmation, and I smile before he looks back at Damien.

"I'm Brad." Brad turns to me and asks, "When did you start going by Alli?"

Oh man, I hope I can head this off at the pass. "I still go by Allison."

Some of the sorority girls choose that moment to ask the three guys sitting across from us, including Brad, to dance. *Thank heavens.* As they're leaving, the waitress delivers our beers.

Sam moves to sit across the table from Damien, and she kicks up one leg on the empty chair in front of me. She fans herself. "Whew, the angst in here was getting a little high. I would think Damien had just killed Brad's puppy from the look on his face when he found out Allison was off the market."

"I don't think he's gotten the point yet, but he will. So, Sam, Alli says your sorority became an official charter at your university?"

I appreciate Damien's efforts for trying to keep the evening light even though I know he feels challenged by Brad.

She smirks at his question. "Yes. We've been working on it for about six months. Red tape and paperwork can be a bitch." She takes a sip of her beer.

Lifting my bottle, I chime in, "Hear, hear to that! Many congrats!"

"Thanks." She taps my bottle with the neck of hers. "Oh hey, the ribbon-cutting ceremony is next week. Can you make it?"

"Of course. I wouldn't miss it for the world. Let me know the details."

Damien puts his hand on my leg and adds, "We'll be there."

"Sounds great. I'll get you guys all the info." Sam gives me a wink as a striking guy approaches her. He's been sucked into her orbit. *Poor guy.*

"Care to dance?" He tips his cowboy hat our way and smiles back at Sam.

Without answering him, she puts her hand in his. As Sam walks by, she leans down, and keeping her voice loud enough to where I can hear, she whispers to Damien, "Please take care of her. She's my most special friend in the world."

I know I turn ten shades of crimson as my skin temperature rises twenty degrees.

"Sam, I promise."

She gives him a little pat and continues walking. The guy she's dancing with will probably want to propose by the time this evening ends. I give him a mental I-feel-sorry-for-you pat on the back. He'll probably pine after her, and she'll walk away without a second thought.

Most of the table has vacated to the dance floor, leaving me alone with Damien. I turn to him, and he's giving me that smoldering look.

I immediately push my thighs together to provide some type of relief. "How'd your meetings go?"

"We finally came to terms. You are absolutely stunning." He takes his right hand and runs it along my jaw.

I lean my head into his touch. *Ahhh.* That throb is back with a vengeance. I can feel moisture building around my sex. My thighs are not doing a good job at holding the ache at bay.

"You like this?" he asks.

"Mmhmm," I barely get out.

His finger stops its slow, sensual movements, and I look up into his eyes.

"I would like for you to come home with me tonight. No rush on when we leave, but I want to spend some time together. Whatever happens is up to you, baby."

I am captured by this man's deep blue eyes. Putting my hand on top of his, I respond, "I would like that very much. I have to dance with Sam once, and then we can go. Does that sound good?"

"Yes. You and Sam have a dance?"

We are moving closer and closer together. The magnetic force between us is stronger than ever because of our brief time apart.

"Kind of. You'll see. We've been doing it since high school. This is the first time in over a year we've had a chance to do it."

Damien's face softens because he knows why I haven't been out. One of his hands comes to rest on my hip as we scoot a little closer to each other.

"Did you choose to sit in the front seat of Brad's car?" he asks.

Oh, he was watching. Part of me wants to get defensive, but I try to put myself in his shoes, and I would have the same question he does. He's attempting to put all of this together. He doesn't know my friends—really, they're Sam's friends—or my history with them.

"No, they picked me up last. It was the only seat available. If I had known he was going to act like this tonight, then I would have insisted on driving myself. I'm sorry."

His nose is against mine now, and I can smell his wintergreen breath.

"You did nothing wrong. Does he normally act differently?"

"Yes, at least, I think he does. I have been really antisocial for the last year. I've been out with them as a group only a few times in the last six months or so, and it was under duress from Sam. Brad asked me out a couple of times, but it seemed more on the friend level or as a favor to Sam to get me out of my apartment. I said no every time."

My knees are now between his legs. His one hand remains on my hip as the other moves to the side of my neck.

Immediately, electricity zooms between our points of contact, engulfing us in our own private bubble.

He only has to move an inch to give me a kiss, and he finally closes the distance. It starts off gentle and easy, and then he escalates it into a more domineering kiss. It's right on the brink of being inappropriate in front of company. I missed these lips, and I know he is announcing his territory. He is marking me, and I absolutely love it. He is showing everyone here that I am his.

When a cough sounds from beside us, Damien breaks the kiss, but he doesn't look away from me or remove his hands. Immediately, I want the intruder to go away. I glance over to see Sam, and I blush at being caught kissing like I'm a teenager. She knows Damien wants to spend time with me, but it's tradition to do our thing anytime we are in a country bar. Since I haven't been in one for a while, there is no way she is going to let me leave before we dance.

"Geez, we've got to get you guys out of here stat, so you can get a room," she jokes.

I blush again.

"I put in the request for our song. Woot, woot. Are you ready to get your dance on?" Sam asks.

"Lead the way, girl. Lead the way," I respond.

I smile at Damien as I get out of my seat. He is giving me that sexy mischievous grin. He turns and faces the dance floor as I put a little extra oomph in my walk for him.

As Sam pulls me forward, I nervously tell her, "Oh, I hope I can still do this dance, Sam."

"With the thousands of times we have done it, it's like riding a horse. You never forget." She laughs at her choice of words as we make it to the dance floor and line up beside each other. "I'm glad I got to meet him. He's good for you, Allison. It's like he is your missing half."

"Thanks. It feels right."

Big & Rich's "Save a Horse (Ride a Cowboy)" starts playing, and we smile at each other. We start moving and shaking as we do our thing. I am glowing inside from having reclaimed this piece that was missing. We sashay, twirl, ride our cowboys, and crack our imaginary whips. When the song ends, we giggle and embrace as only best friends can.

Before we break away, she quickly whispers in my ear, "I've missed you, Allison. Don't go away on me again. I thought I would never have the old you back."

As we let go, we both have tears in our eyes.

"Yes, ma'am. I'm here for good, girl. Missed you, too."

We smile and wipe our eyes as we begin to leave the dance floor. Sam is called over to the bar by one of her sorority sisters, and I continue to make my way back to Damien.

The dance floor is crowded with sweaty patrons. I'm just about to break free from the crowd when someone grabs my arm. Turning around, I see it's Brad who is pulling me back farther into the throng of people.

"Allison, come dance with me. Now that I know you can move like that, you definitely owe me a dance for holding out on me all this time."

I can tell he's been drinking a bit, maybe a lot. He continues to drag me, causing me to nearly stumble, as I try to stand my ground.

"Brad, I need to get back to Damien. I'm danced out for the evening, and I'm about to leave."

I try to disengage myself, but he strengthens his hold and keeps pulling me out onto the floor. It's not a full-out struggle yet, but he's being way too persistent and inappropriate.

"Take your fucking hands off of her, asshole."

At Damien's tone, Brad whips around and automatically lets go of me. With the sudden release, I stumble back into Damien's front. He steadies me, moves me behind him, and angles his body in a protective stance. He is absolutely furious. *Shit, Brad has awakened a sleeping giant.*

"You've crossed the line. Stay away from her, or you and I are going to have major problems. I don't want you even looking in her direction. It would be in your best interest if you fully comprehend that Alli and I are a very serious couple."

Not even waiting for a response, Damien turns to me and puts his hands on my bare shoulders. I think I hear Brad mumbling something, but I can't be sure.

"Are you okay?" Damien asks me.

"Yes." I cannot break away from his blue eyes as I continue nodding. I want this man so badly.

Seemingly satisfied that I am telling the truth, he asks, "Are you ready to leave?"

"Let me say bye to Sam first."

The gawking entourage of people starts to break apart as Damien escorts me to my friend. The cowboy from earlier is hanging on Sam's every word as she flirts shamelessly with him.

"Hey, girl, we are going to leave. Let me know when the ceremony is, so we can come." I give her a hug good-bye.

"I will. You kids have fun." She looks at me teasingly, and then she turns to Damien. "Great to meet the guy who finally got Allison to go all weak in the knees. Don't worry about tonight. Brad was just being an asshole. He's normally not like that. I have no idea what got into him."

At the mention of Brad, Damien's grip tightens on me. "Thanks, Sam. It was great meeting you, too. You are as wonderful a friend as Alli described. I'm going to take Alli for the evening and spend some time with her. Congrats again on your sorority."

Sam gives me a knowing look.

I cross my fingers, hoping tonight will actually be the night I am truly with Damien.

CHAPTER
8

As we head to the car, Damien is still radiating with tension. He opens the door to a dark pickup truck, and after I get seated, I notice the interior is a warm caramel color. He shuts my door with a little more force than necessary, and then he makes his way to the driver's side.

Once we are safely enclosed in our space, I look over. "I had no idea Brad would be that way."

He glances my way before he starts driving to our unknown destination.

"How long have you known him?" He sounds pissed.

"Maybe six months or so. I'm not sure. There's nothing between Brad and me. Never has been, never will be." I'm trying to remain calm.

"I know you're not interested, but he is definitely going to be a problem. He wants you badly."

Damien is wound up so tight from this incident with Brad. I just don't get it.

Trying to placate the situation, I respond, "His ego was doing the talking. He's with a different girl every week. He was just trying to irritate you."

He glances over at me while he's driving. "I disagree. I don't want you near him if I'm not around."

"Damien, don't be unreasonable. He's at a lot of events that Sam goes to. You can trust me, you know." *Brad isn't even worth arguing about.*

His grip on the steering wheel tightens. "This is not a matter of trust, Alli. This is a matter of me protecting you. If he's around and I'm not, I want you to call me. I don't think you understand what I saw tonight. Every guy in that joint was watching your every move, and that was before you started dancing with Sam. After that...fuck, I don't want to think about it, or I'll turn around, and it won't end pleasantly." His voice is so cold.

I don't understand. Is he mad about the dancing? My head is starting to hurt from all this drama. "I'm not sure what you are talking about, but I really don't get why you are being so distant right now. I don't know what I did. I was there with you, and I only danced with Sam."

He pulls off onto a dirt road and heads down a little way before parking the truck on the side of the road. I have no idea where we are.

He turns my way. The glow from the dashboard casts just enough light for me to see his face framed with his tousled black hair. *Holy hell, he is sexy.* I sure hope we can redeem what is left of this night. If it continues at this rate, it's going to end with me still being a virgin. His jaw is set, and he's pinning me in place with his gaze. My heart flutters with the tension.

"You did absolutely nothing wrong. You have no clue what you do to guys around you. I can see their faces, and I know what they are thinking. It drives me fucking mad, knowing some prick is waiting on the sidelines for me to get benched. I'm staying in the game, Alli. You are not getting rid of me."

Wow, he thinks I am going to leave him for another guy. I need to show him how bad I want him, so I take him completely by surprise. I cannot hide my anticipation as I hastily unbuckle my seatbelt, crawl over the truck's middle console, and straddle Damien's lap. Instinctively, his hands come to rest on my hips as he holds me in place.

Looking at him, I say, "I only want you, no one else."

Immediately, Damien moves his hands to my back and pulls me to him, smashing our lips together, and it is a hungry, insatiable kiss. We are mad for each other. His hands undo my French twist, and my hair cascades around my shoulders. I try to unbutton his shirt, but I keep fumbling, which is causing me to get irritated. I yank hard, and his shirt rips open. Buttons fly around inside the truck, making little pinging noises as they hit the hard surfaces. He groans at my boldness as my fingers begin to caress his chest. It's not even a *want* at this point but a *need*.

While we are kissing furiously, his hands begin to make their way down my neck until they reach the top of my sleeveless dress. He lowers it down, leaving my breasts exposed. I continue to explore the hard muscles of his chest as I grind myself against him.

One hand begins tweaking my nipple, and I arch back and break the kiss. Our breaths are hard and labored as we stare into each other's eyes. His other hand moves down my waist and onto my leg, finding the bottom hem of my dress that has ridden up mid-thigh. His hand dips under it and starts making its way up the inside of my leg. Closing my eyes, I groan at the sensation and lean back onto the steering wheel, letting my body go.

Nuzzling into my breasts, he says, "Alli, I am going to make you come hard and fast, and then I'm taking you home and claiming you as mine."

"Please, Damien, it's throbbing."

The need in my voice is evident as his hand reaches my sex, and by his murmur of approval, I know he likes what he's found. He moves my panties to the side and slips one finger into my slick heat.

"Oh, baby, you are so wet."

The feeling is incredible. I start to buck my hips into him, desperate for the friction. His thumb begins stroking my clit. Whatever he is doing causes a pressure to build inside me, like it did in my hotel room in Miami.

"Let go, baby."

The purr in his voice induces my body to release and skyrocket to euphoria. At this moment, I am completely exposed, and I don't care. I savor the feeling. Damien is lightly sucking and kissing my breasts as I come back down from my high.

"Was that good for you?"

"Mmhmm." I slowly start to open my eyes and lazily smile at Damien. "I hope you live close by here."

Pulling back, he severs the connection between us, allowing my thoughts to clear.

"We are at the back edge of my estate. Are you sure you are ready for this? Because we can take this slower."

"Please."

Damien has a satisfied grin as he hastily tugs the top of my dress back up. Whatever he did has me wanting more, and I lean up to suck and kiss on his neck. I need to feel him right now. I start roaming my hands down his chest in case he's thinking about making me get into the passenger seat.

"Alli, you need...fuck."

My hand makes it to his bulge, and I begin to stroke him through the fabric of his pants. I smile as I hear gravel being shot out from under the tires as he starts to drive, letting me stay where I am. The truck revs faster as I continue my assault.

My mouth moves up his neck to his ear as my top starts to slip down, and we are skin on skin, only intensifying my need.

He moans, "Oh fuck, you feel fantastic."

My sex is starting to pulse again, worse than before, as I mash my body into his. I love the contact. In my urgent need, any reserved behavior I had has left me. His hands band together behind my back as the truck comes screeching to a halt. I look into his eyes, and they are on fire with desire as he rights my dress. This man is mine, and he wants me to be his. I need for him to take me. Anything less will not satiate my hunger.

He slides us out of the truck with my legs wrapped around his waist. My mouth finds his again as his hands hold on to my ass, and he begins to walk. Our tongues battle each other frantically as if we only have seconds left with one another. He consumes me entirely. The sound of the front door opening and closing causes my anticipation to grow. *This is the night I will give myself to Damien.* He holds me tighter as he sprints up some stairs to a second floor. We enter another room as the door closes behind us. The kiss slows as he unwinds my legs and slides me down his body.

Putting a finger underneath my chin, he raises my head until our eyes lock. "We are going to enjoy each other and take it slow tonight. If it gets to be too much, we can stop this at any time. All you have to do is tell me to stop. I have condoms. I'll be safe with you always, regardless of how worked up we are."

I am teetering on a cliff, unaware of what I should do. I go with my gut. "Are you clean?"

His brows bunch in confusion. "What?"

"I assume you have been sexually active, and I am asking if you're clean." My face floods with embarrassment as I play with the hem of my dress.

Taking my shoulders, he responds, "Yes. I would never make love to you if I wasn't. I have always used protection, no exception."

I can tell he has no idea where I'm going with this. I take a deep breath. *Here we go.* "I'm on the pill, and if you're clean, you don't have to wear a condom."

As he just stares at me, I begin to panic.

Have I committed a sex faux pas? I probably sound naive and stupid. I need to get this back on track. "I mean, you can still wear one. I didn't mean to assume. I understand. It's not a big deal," I say, speaking faster and faster.

He is still staring at me, almost openmouthed. "Are you sure?"

My face flushes. "Yes, of course. I would never force you to go without a condom. I don't want you to do something that would make you feel uncomfortable." *Geez, I would never do that to anyone.*

When he starts chuckling, mortification consumes me. *Oh, I should have gotten some pointers from Sam. Why didn't I think to ask about some of this stuff?*

"Alli, I'd like to be inside you without a condom more than you know. I swear that I am clean, and I have never had unprotected sex with a woman. Are you sure?"

"Yes."

My one-word answer causes his eyes to darken into sexual heat. He slowly turns me to face the room. I gasp and bring my hand to my mouth. Damien has had someone put candles on every surface. They are glowing and giving off the most subtle flower smell. The fairy-tale romantic appearance is absolutely breathtaking.

A massive black platform bed is the focal point of the room. It is larger than any king bed I've ever seen. Openly inviting us to make use of it, the heavy black bedspread has been turned down to reveal cream sheets underneath.

Matching furniture—a TV stand, chests, and bedside tables—accent the room, and large pieces of artwork are displayed on the neutral-colored walls. There is a sitting area on the far end of the room in front of a fireplace where a fire is slowly crackling. The air has been turned down to accommodate for the excessive heat.

This room screams masculinity. I am in the beast's lair, and I cannot contain the excited shiver running down my back.

"Baby, do you like it?"

"Oh, Damien…" Turning to him, I grab his face and bring it to mine for a kiss. "This is unbelievably perfect."

"Alli, I…" He stops mid-sentence and starts kissing me again.

The hunger is still there, but the kiss has turned sensual as our tongues entwine while we taste each other. Slowly, my hands feel his hard chest as he backs us up to the bed. When my legs gently come into contact with the side of the mattress, Damien steps back to look at me. I feel self-conscious as he continues to devour me with his eyes.

Unhurriedly, he brings his hands up to my waist and undoes my belt. From our earlier escapade, my hair, I'm sure, looks unruly and wild, like Damien's. His deep blue depths have me riveted in place as I hear a thud from my belt dropping to the floor.

Stepping close to me again, his hand goes to my back. The sound of the zipper coming down one tooth at a time causes the anticipation to build. Damien has woven a web, and I am caught, unable to resist. When he releases my dress, I am standing there in nothing but my lacy boy shorts and brown cowboy boots.

"One day, we are going to fuck with you wearing just your cowboy boots."

I go to say something, but he quickly continues, "Tonight, I'm only making love to you." He takes in a stuttering breath as his eyes roll down my body. "Alli, I am the luckiest man alive to have you here in my room."

Holy hell. With how wet I feel myself getting, if he doesn't start this show soon, I am going to start dripping on the floor. *Can that happen?* He gently lifts me onto the bed and then slides one boot off at a time. He runs his hands up each leg in a slow pace as if he's memorizing the feel of my body. My heart is hammering in my chest. He reaches the top of my boy shorts, and slips them off my legs.

Crawling back up the length of my body, he starts kissing my breast. He licks and sucks each one until they are both throbbing tight points. His assault continues down to my navel.

Is he going where I think he is going? What if I'm not what he's used to? What if I'm lacking in some way? I have never been this exposed to anyone in my life. My body goes stiff as my thoughts spin out of control.

Damien stops and looks at me. "What's wrong? Do you want me to stop?"

"No, no. I just…I, um…well, I…"

"Alli, you are perfect, absolutely perfect. You are more than perfect. Baby, I need you to orgasm for me one more time in order to make it as painless as possible when I enter you. Okay?"

I nod. When he starts tonguing my navel again, all my self-consciousness begins to drain from me. I focus on the pleasure he's giving to my body. As he slowly moves farther south, he continues to watch me for signs of distress.

Blue eyes look into mine as he takes his tongue and slowly licks up my swollen sex. Watching him is so intimate, but the moment he begins to suck, I close my eyes to the feeling. He inserts one finger into my heat and begins moving it inside me—working, stretching, and building me. As I bow off the bed, his other hand comes up to my hip to hold me in place.

He murmurs, "Nothing can even compare to you."

And just like that, I go into the abyss that I'm starting to crave. I'm just not sure that life could get any better than this moment. Damien continues to wring out every bit of pleasure he can get from my orgasm.

As I lie boneless on the bed, he stands to take off what is left of his poor shirt. He sheds his boots and removes his jeans in seconds flat. His graceful quick motions leave me breathless. Damien's black boxer briefs begin right under that V-shaped muscle below his six-pack and end where they hug his muscular thighs. They are removed in one fluid movement, and his erection springs free.

For all that is holy, I have no idea how that is going to fit inside me. There's no way it'll fit.

Watching me closely, Damien notices my subtle tenseness. "We'll fit together perfectly. Do you trust me?"

Instantly, I nod because I honestly do. He brings his body on top of me, and the feeling of his skin on mine is even more pleasurable than it was in the truck. When his mouth comes down on me once more, I notice a salty taste added to the normal Damien flavor. His erection is pressing against my stomach as he uses his muscles to bring me to the center of his bed.

This is it. This is the moment when I give Damien this gift that I will never be able to give to anyone else. He moves his body down to where the tip of his erection is poised at the entrance of my sex. His body weight is resting on his elbows as his hands go to each side of my face. He is cherishing me, making this moment like I have always dreamed.

"You are so gorgeous. Are you ready, baby?"

I nod. I have never been more ready for anything in my entire life.

"This is going to hurt. I am going to go as slow as I can. Tell me if you need me to stop."

Confident and nervous at the same time, I respond, "I promise."

He eases an inch into me and pauses. He feels big, and it's uncomfortable. I stiffen again from the pressure I'm feeling. I'm not sure what to do.

"You've got to relax, baby, and stop fighting me. Breathe, Alli. Trust me."

I follow his instructions and try to relax one muscle at a time. He moves farther in again, and it starts to sting a little, causing me to wince. When he leans down and kisses me, my muscles begin to loosen up. He moves out and then goes in a little deeper. My body feels full with him inside me. As his lips move to my neck, he continues the in-and-out motions several more times, getting my body used to him.

"I'm all the way in, baby. Nothing has ever felt this perfect."

My body is finally acclimating to him. It's just an incredibly full feeling. He pulls all the way out and pushes back in. As he continues this movement several more times, my pain starts to ebb, and a different feeling replaces it. The friction is causing my body to climb again. He repeats the motions a little faster.

"Alli, you're mine. No one else is ever going to have you."

We continue to climb as the pace increases.

"Yes, I'm yours. I'm all yours, Damien. Please. Please. Faster."

We are at a near frantic pace, and I am so close to the edge. He thrusts once more, and I finally fall over. Damien follows suit, and I can feel his warmness spilling into me. I am truly his now as he becomes a part of me.

He collapses on top of me, but he immediately raises himself as he slowly and tenderly pulls out of me before he moves to lie at my side. Right away, I feel empty, and I want him back inside me.

Facing each other with our legs entwined, he is rubbing soothing circles on my hips. I reach out and start tracing the tattoo symbol on his chest, and I absently wonder what it means. His chest is covered in a light sheen of sweat, and I shiver. Instead of recognizing my body's natural response to him, he mistakes my shiver for being cold. He grabs the sheet and pulls it on top of us.

"Alli, did I hurt you?"

"In the beginning, it did hurt, but now, I can't even describe the feeling. It was perfect." Snuggling closer to him, I wrap my arms around his waist and rub my foot up and down his leg. "Thank you for making it so special. Was it okay for you? Did I hurt you? It must have felt like a vise gripping you." Laying my head on his chest, I listen to his strong heartbeat.

His chest rises and falls as he chuckles. "I don't think I have ever laughed as much as I do with you."

I look at him, confused.

"Baby, that was the best experience of my life, hands down. You were perfect. You felt perfect. You fit me perfectly."

"Nice recovery. You were about to be in big trouble if you were making fun of me for asking if I hurt you. How would I know since you're my first?" I lightly hit his chest as I nuzzle deeper into his body.

He pulls me tighter against him. "And I'm going to be your last, Alli."

My body stiffens at his words, trying to think if I heard that insinuation correctly. For now, I just ignore it.

"Baby, I'm going to draw you a bath before your soreness sets in. Now that I've had you, there's no way I'll be able to go a full day without you."

I smile as he gets up and makes his way through a door near the sitting area.

Listening to the fire crackle, I lie there and think about what we just did. My V-card is gone, and he made it more incredible than I ever imagined. Damien Wales has possessed me in a way I never even knew was possible.

I'm in love…whoa. I need to slow that train down. It's too soon. If I start confessing those types of sentiments right away, he will go running into no man's land for sure. We know a lot about each other, but at the same time, we have only known one another for less than a week. *It has to be too soon to feel this, right?*

Damien emerges in all his naked glory, and I just stare. We smile at each other as he continues striding toward me. Seeing his muscles naturally flex as he walks has me wanting him...again. He leans down and gives my forehead a kiss prior to picking up the phone and dialing three numbers.

"Please have the bed linens changed within the next twenty minutes. We will be in the bathroom, and we are not to be disturbed. That will be fine. Thank you."

He hangs up the phone, pulls back the covers, and reaches for me. Now, I see why he has made that odd request about the bed linens. The evidence of my lost virginity is very apparent on the cream sheets. I blush and look away. There's not a lot of blood, but it's enough to know what happened.

"Don't be embarrassed. That was one of the most incredible things we just shared."

Hearing his earnest tone induces me to look into his eyes, and I shyly smile. He picks me up and carries me to the bathroom.

It is, of course, as decadent as his bedroom. When he sets me down in front of the tub, I realize the marble white floors are heated. The warm tiles are soothing as I flex my toes. The tub is large and could easily fit three to four people in it. Three faucets are running simultaneously to fill the tub quickly. Across from the tub is a large walk-in glass shower. Two beautiful and luxurious sinks with a vanity sit in between the shower and tub.

I hold on to his offered hand as I use the steps to walk down into the tub. When I take a seat, the warm water and scent of chamomile envelop me. Damien follows me in and pulls me to him, settling me onto his lap with my back to his front.

He reaches over for a glass of water and two pills and hands them to me. "Take this aspirin. It will help with the soreness."

"Damien, I'm fine. I promise."

"Please take them. If you don't, I won't be able to have you tomorrow, and that is like asking a man to breathe without oxygen."

I immediately take the pills and water. "I wouldn't want to do that."

He chuckles at my eagerness. One of his hands comes around to rest on my stomach. "Thanks, baby. Glad to know you want to keep me around."

I turn around to straddle him. "What makes you think I'm going to leave?"

Pain flashes across his eyes.

"I'm not going anywhere, Damien. You're stuck with me."

"Let's just say I'm trying to learn from my past mistakes."

The look on his face absolutely crushes me.

Leaning into his chest, I try to comfort him. "I have no idea what that means."

He takes a deep breath. "Tonight, let's focus on us. We'll talk about it later. I promise."

Before I have a chance to respond, he dips his head down and starts kissing me. I can feel him getting hard again, and I become consumed with desire. I move against him, making him groan.

He barely pulls his mouth from me. "Alli, we need to stop and let your body rest. There is going to be plenty of time."

"Damien, please. We can take it slow. I want you. I need you. Please. I promise we can still do this tomorrow even if I'm sore. Please." Sex has reduced me to a needy mess.

Forcing some space between us, he grabs me by my shoulders to get my attention. "Alli, I would never hurt you. If we do this, it has to be slow and easy, baby, even when your body tells you to go harder. After this, we've got to let you rest."

Reaching for his shoulders, I lift my hips and then ease onto him. He fills me completely again. The soreness is definitely present, but it's not going to stop me from reaching that high. His hands are on each side of my waist, requiring me to keep a steady pace, as I ride him.

The water is sloshing around us as Damien starts thrusting his hips into me, causing the build to come faster. Releasing one hand from my hip, he pinches one of my nipples and squeezes it.

The heavenly high assails me. "Oh, Damien!"

My words cause him to follow suit, and he pours himself into me again. The thought of him being a part of me stirs a deep emotion within me. He lifts me off of him. My body is languid as we both stand. In a haze, I get out and throw a towel around me, barely drying off the water. Damien follows me out of the tub and wraps a towel around his waist.

"Alli, wait. You're still soaking wet, baby."

Taking the towel from me, he dries me off more completely, and then I follow him to the freshly made bed. This time, satin sheets are on the bed, and I love the feeling of the material on my bare skin. He pulls me to the middle of the bed until I'm against his body. We are two puzzle pieces that fit together perfectly. I feel safe and complete with Damien, and I haven't felt like this since my parents were alive.

He flips off the lamp, and I wrap around him.

Softly, I murmur, "Thank you, Damien, for the most magnificent night of my life."

"Baby, I will cherish this night forever. Thank you for giving me that special part of you."

I close my eyes, draped in my Damien blanket, and drift off, feeling content.

CHAPTER
9

The world starts to fade in, and I'm momentarily startled when I don't remember where I am. Then, the floodgates lift, and the memories come pouring back. Damien was incredible. My face is buried into his chest, and I breathe in his scent. It's manly, indescribably manly. When I start to shift, he automatically tightens around me.

"Good morning. Where do you think you're going?" His voice is deep and rough with a sexy, irresistible tone.

"Nowhere. Why? Did you have something in mind?" My body moves against him.

His eyes slowly lift open, and he meets my gaze. *How can he still look like God's gift to women after sleeping?* I, on the other hand, am a different story. I probably look like I've gone three rounds with some beast, and I was the loser.

"Are you sore, Alli?"

I take stock of my body prior to responding. It feels like a rarely used muscle got an excellent workout. In fact, that muscle would like another workout right now. "A little, but a good kind of sore if that makes sense."

"Good. I'll still have to restrain myself from you for the next few days." His hand drags lazily up and down my arm.

Shooting up, I totally shock even myself as I screech, "You mean, no sex? That's a little over the top, I think!"

He pulls me back down and kisses me.

He drags his nose across my jawline. A need to have him inside me arises again.

"We just have to space it out, baby. We need to keep you from getting too sore. Otherwise, we will have to stop altogether."

His words make me blush slightly as I think about how brazen I was.

"There's no reason to be embarrassed, Alli. We will continue to get to know each other in every way possible." The dominant tone in his voice is undeniable.

His need for a deep emotional connection is as palpable as mine. I know what caused mine, but I wonder what happened to him to create that need. Then, I remember that he completely sidestepped my question about me leaving him last night. Just as I am about to delve into that, Damien changes my train of thought.

"Let's get dressed and have some breakfast on the terrace. If we stay in bed too much longer, we won't leave for a while."

There is no way I am going to survive the morning without some relief. "I'm not hungry." My finger starts drawing on his chest, slowly making its way down his stomach.

"Alli, we have to eat. We didn't have dinner last night."

He begins to push the covers aside. He is slightly turned away to get out of bed when I reach around and grab his already semi-stiff erection. My touch makes him hard immediately. I have no idea what I'm doing, but a smile creeps up on my face. I squeeze him slightly and move my hand up and down. He emits a groan from deep within his chest.

When he twists back to me, he practically tackles me, and I laugh. *Mission completed.* I'm about to get exactly what I want. The moment his lips touch mine, the world falls away.

Lowering one hand, he pushes a finger inside me. He moans, "Fuck, you're so wet." Seemingly satisfied with my state of arousal, he positions himself between my legs, and he leisurely starts to push inside me.

Breathlessly, I whisper, "I need you all the way in."

He complies as he just stares at me, and I revel in how perfect he feels just like this.

"You are going to be the death of me," he murmurs.

Then, we are both lost in the sensations of each other as our bodies become one once again.

The terrace looks like something from an old movie. This is what I imagine it would feel like to live on Tara, the antebellum house, from *Gone with the Wind*. When the light breeze shifts the air slightly, I get a brief whiff of a nearby honeysuckle patch. I close my eyes and just listen to the sounds of the birds.

This moment is perfect. Being here with Damien feels more right than it should at this point. It's a lot for me to process.

A hand grazes my shoulder before setting a coffee cup in front of me. "Breakfast should be out in a few minutes. Penny for your thoughts?"

Wearing only his black silk pajama pants hanging low on his waist, Damien takes a seat beside me, and his abs naturally flex with the movement. I'm wearing a matching black silk robe and nightgown that he'd bought for me before I came over last night.

I pick up the cup, savor the aroma, and then take a heavenly sip of the dark and strong coffee. "Just thinking about how fast this is all going or at least how fast I think it's going."

To get my mind off of what I want to do right now, which is to beg him to make love to me again, I look out onto the perfectly manicured lawn. I see a stable off in the distance, and it reminds me of home.

He's watching me intently. "Did we rush this? Alli, I won't…I can't let you go. Last night…well, it was incredible. We can slow down if that's what you need."

The serious note in his voice causes my head to snap in his direction as two breakfast plates are put in front of us.

Shit, that did not come out right. I can tell exactly how he took it. "No, it's just fast, not wrong but fast, especially since I've spent the last year emotionally secluded. I don't regret last night at all. Please don't ever think that. I like where we are."

As I reach for his hand, he moves it quickly to the back of my neck. Pulling me toward him, he starts kissing me. Just as I'm about to climb into his lap, his lips move away from mine.

"Let's eat. Regardless of how fast this might seem to you, remember what it's like when we're together. It feels right, and that's all that matters."

Words evade me, and all I can do is nod. With all the nodding I do when I'm around him sometimes, I feel like a bobblehead. Trying to restart my brain, I turn my focus to my plate and take a bite of the omelet. The burst of flavors from the fresh vegetables, cheese, and ham is delicious. "Mmm…oh my gosh, this is fantastic."

"I'm glad you like it. What is your schedule like this week?"

I've just taken another bite, and my eyes go wide as I recall the plans I completely forgot about. When I try to sputter a response, I start choking. Damien gets up and pats my back. *Will I ever stop embarrassing myself around him?* When I'm through the worst of it, he sits back down, still eyeing me as I take a sip of orange juice. I have no words to describe how flustered I feel from my unladylike behavior.

"Shit, Alli. Are you okay?"

I wave my hand, signaling that I need just one more minute, as I take another drink. "I'm fine. I just…I totally forgot about my plans this weekend."

He looks at me, waiting for me to continue.

"Oh, right. I'm heading to Homerville tonight, and I'll be back Tuesday morning. It totally slipped my mind since you weren't supposed to be back until Tuesday also."

"When do you have to leave today?" The domineering voice is back.

"Sometime this evening. Why?"

I can tell he's taken aback because I'm leaving so quickly. Knowing he wants me around would make me smile if his jaw wasn't set tightly and his eyes weren't pinning me to my seat.

He rubs his forehead, and his brows crinkle in thought. "When will you get back? I wanted you to accompany me to a benefit this next week. When Sam texted you this morning, did she say when her sorority thing is?"

"I'll get back Tuesday morning. Um, Sam's thing is Tuesday night. What's the benefit?"

He picks up his phone and starts typing a message as he talks to me. "With some adjustments, I can leave for Vegas tomorrow to handle some meetings earlier than planned and come back Tuesday in time for Sam's event. Afterward, we could fly out later that evening for Vegas. That way, we could attend the sports benefit on Wednesday evening together that I am sponsoring."

I'm working through all the logistics in my head. With today being Friday, it's going to be difficult to be apart from each other until Tuesday.

He continues, "Please say yes, Alli, because I don't know how I'm going to survive not having you for four fucking nights."

Wow, this is hard. Right now, it's difficult for me to go a couple of hours without him. However, I cannot lose that part of myself I have started to find since meeting Damien. He is a powerful force, and I need to find my strength to withstand him.

"That should work. I just want you to know that if this wasn't really important to me, I would cancel."

He rubs his hand down his face. Being apart from me seems to stress him out, which causes my heart to do a happy dance.

"Knowing this will make you happy is the only reason I'm able to let you go. What are you going to be doing there? Where are you staying?"

"With Sam's parents. I'll tell you what it's all about when it's over. If it doesn't work out, it will be easier to tell you afterward."

"Alli…"

The inflection in his voice incites my irritation.

"Don't take that tone with me, Damien. You've been evasive with me, too, because you aren't ready to share. If we want to bare all to each other right now, that's fine." It shocks me how much I sound like my mother.

The muscles in his arms go taut, and his jaw looks like it might snap in half. "It's not the same fucking thing. If I don't know what you're doing, then how will I know you're safe?"

"Why are you so concerned with my safety? I've managed all these years without you just fine."

He doesn't respond as he continues to stare at me. His knuckles are white from grabbing the wrought iron arms of the chair.

"See, there's another question you won't answer. You're creating double standards here. This is a two-way street, Damien."

He releases his hands, opening and shutting them, probably to get the blood flowing again. "How long is the drive?"

"A few hours." I am starting to shift impatiently in my seat. With the tension building between us, this arguing has worked me up both emotionally and sexually.

Substantially softening his tone, he asks, "So, to avoid wasting time in a car today, if you need something from your apartment, can Sam gather it for you? I'll have my second-in-command, Ben, pick up your belongings and your car and bring them here. I'd rather you get on the road this afternoon, so you aren't driving late."

It seems like a reasonable request, and I want to compromise. There's always a middle ground. "I'm sure Sam won't mind. I'll ask her what time she can get my things together for me."

He sits there with his phone in hand, appearing to think things through. He's like a caged tiger, waiting to escape.

I text Sam, hoping she can help me out.

> *Me: Hey, could you do me a favor?*

> *Sam: First, has the deed been done?*

> *Me: Yes.*

> *Sam: And?*

Me: A girl doesn't kiss and tell.

Sam: Oh, you will tell me. What do you need?

Me: Can you get my bag ready to take home?

Sam: I'm glad you're still going.

Me: Me, too. I need to do this. I owe it to myself and my parents.

Sam: Good. I like Wales, but I agree. Of course I will.

Me: What time? A guy named Ben will pick up my bag and take my car.

Sam: Ten? Ben?

Me: Ten works. Damien's guy.

Sam: Okay. Must be nice. Just kidding. I'll call you later. xoxo

Me: Okay. Thank you. xoxo

Sam's been worried that I wouldn't go through with the interview because of Damien, but this is an opportunity I can't pass up.

I look up and realize Damien has been watching me exchange texts with Sam. "She said she could be there at ten if that works."

"Perfect. Anytime will work if it means I don't have to waste my last few hours with you in a car." He picks up his phone and hits a speed-dial number. "Ben, Damien. I need you to go to Allison's apartment and meet a Sam Matthews there to retrieve a packed bag and Allison's car. She has a key to Allison's car. You can meet her out front. I'll send the address. Please bring them to my house by one. Plan on staying for a few hours to go over some things. Yes, bring both the real estate and sports contracts. Very good. Thanks." He disconnects the phone.

It's a little after nine, so that gives us less than four hours together. He stands and offers his hand, and I take it.

"You want to take a tour of the pool house?"

"Sure."

He's thrown me off with this sudden change of mood. As we walk barefoot through the soft, wet grass, my black silk robe and nightgown begin to get damp around the bottom. We enter the dim pool house. I can see that it is done in masculine colors, black and taupe, like the rest of the house. Black leather furniture surrounds a massive big screen television on one end. Off to another side is an assortment of exercise equipment. Damien continues to pull me toward the opposite side of where we just entered. He stops by a panel and pushes some buttons.

"Where are the lights?" I ask.

"We don't need them."

He opens a door that would be hidden to the casual observer as it blends in with the black wood. The room we walk into is barely lit. As my eyes adjust, Damien's features are faintly visible. Benches surround the perimeter of the entire room, and a stove of some sort sits in the center. It dawns on me that we are in a sauna. He leaves me for a second and goes to the corner. He brings a cup of water over to the stove and pours it on the warm stones. As the room begins to fill with steam, my gown starts to stick to me.

The air between us changes, charging like it has the three times we've been together so far. He stalks toward me, grabs my waist, and pulls me to him. Immediately, I am his, his clay to mold. The silk allows me to feel every detail of him, and my sex automatically responds when he hardens against me. The throbbing pulse is back, causing me to moan, as I entwine my fingers through his hair.

This man makes me insatiable. Around Damien, my body reacts and knows exactly what to do under his touch. His hands move from my hips to my belt tie. He releases the tie and pushes my robe off my shoulders, letting it drop to the floor. The temperature in here is rising, and I can feel sweat forming on both of us. It causes my need for him to surge.

Damien leans down and sucks on my breast through the silky nightgown. *Heaven help me.* I am about to explode on the spot from the sensations of the heat and his mouth. Excitement pulls deep within my belly, knowing what is about to come. He pulls the fabric up over my head and drops it to the side. Reaching for the top of his silk pants, I untie them and push them to the floor to join my gown. His erection springs free, and we both move to close the gap between us. Immediately, he starts to back us up to one of the wide benches on the side of the room.

After our disagreement, I need him inside me even though we haven't necessarily settled anything. His finger dips to the folds of my sex, and he groans, knowing I am ready for him.

"Baby, we are going to try a different position. Let me know if it's uncomfortable."

I nod. *How many positions can there be?* I make a mental note to talk to Sam about this.

He lies down on the bench, and I go to straddle him. His hands come to my hips to stop my progress.

"I think you'll like this position. It's called reverse cowgirl. Face the other way and settle yourself on top of me. Then, just move according to how it feels best for you, baby."

What? I'm in charge of the pace? I start to panic, not knowing what to do.

"Your body will take over, baby, just like it did in the truck and in our bed."

The images of those moments flood my mind. *Damn it, I am a wanton creature.* Grabbing hold of my courage, I saddle up on my lover, making sure to give him a good eyeful of my sex and ass. I can tell he likes it because his dick jumps to attention underneath me.

"You're beautiful, Alli."

Feeling him slide into my slick heat is the best feeling ever. We enter our bubble, and I know everything is going to be okay. The smell of desire fills the air. Teasing him, I slide him in a little and then out. His hands are fisted to his sides. When I think I have pushed him to his limit, I impale myself onto him in one swift motion.

"Fuck, Alli. Don't hurt yourself, baby."

His hands have immediately gone to my hips to stop my movement. It does hurt a little, but his satisfied voice laced with concern makes it worth the pain.

"I'm fine. I promise."

His hands release slightly, and he allows me to start moving again. Our bodies are dripping and slick with sweat from the heat in the sauna. I start to move up and down, increasing the pace. My body takes over and begins moving in wild abandonment, raising our sexual need for each other.

In one fluid motion, Damien leans up and starts rubbing my clit vigorously, causing me to plummet into the depths of pleasure. He says my name like a prayer, and after a few powerful thrusts, he releases himself into me. I try to fall forward, but his hands are there, strong and steady. Keeping me upright, he wrings every last bit of pleasure out of me.

He gently pulls me off and brings me to his side, and we entangle our sweaty bodies together.

Rubbing soothing circles on my arm, he says, "How the hell am I going to make it without you for four nights?"

Laying my head on his chest, I try to reassure him. "I just don't want to lose myself again, Damien. I need to do this. You wouldn't like the person I was."

"Oh, baby…" He squeezes me. "I don't want that either. You're just more precious to me than I think you realize. We'll figure it out."

Those words warm my body. "Thank you."

"Alli, pretty soon, there's no way I'll be able to be away from you for that long."

"I feel the same way." I smile into his chest.

A few minutes pass while we relish the feel of each other.

"Why don't you see if Sam wants to come with us to the benefit in Vegas? It's a black-tie sports gala."

I start tracing his tattoo, thinking about how deliriously happy I am with this man. "Oh, Sam will come even if she has to cancel plans. She'll move heaven and earth to go. I'll stop by some dress shops on the way home."

"I'll take care of both of your attire. I'll have a designer bring a wide range of dresses for you two to choose from."

Does he think that I'm not capable of finding a dress? "Damien, I can pick out something for the event that will not embarrass you. I've been dressing myself since I was three." My voice has a little more bite than I intend as my irritation flares unreasonably.

He raises us both into a seated position. Matching my tone, he says, "Alli, don't start this right now. I understand you have a need to show your independence to me. I'm trying to do something for the girl I am very crazy about. It's nothing more. Don't make this into something it's not."

He's right. I'm just on edge with everything. "I know. Thank you, and I'm sorry."

He lets out a breath at what I assume is relief from my quick agreement. We are still learning each other's ways. I know he was only being nice, and I overreacted. Sometimes, it's easier to react than think it through.

He gives me a kiss and moves to stand up. "We need to get ready before Ben gets here."

Realization dawns on me that our time together is quickly coming to an end.

He lifts my chin with his finger, so he can see my face. "Why are you frowning?"

"I just realized we have less than two hours together. It seems like we never have enough time."

He sits back down and looks at me earnestly. "If going keeps you from losing yourself and gets you something you want, then you need to go. Every part of me wants to try to get you to stay, but you said you needed to do this. We'll have plenty of time together. In the future, we'll coordinate our schedules to minimize our time apart."

I blow out a long breath to keep my tears at bay. I think of how my mom always said, *Absence makes the heart grow fonder.* I'll just hold on to that for the next few days. "Thank you. It's harder than what I thought it would be."

He gives me a gentle kiss. "I feel the same way, baby."

He gets up and goes to a closet on the far side of the room. He returns with two white cotton robes. I am grateful for his thoughtfulness because my silk robe and nightgown would have been like wearing a wet T-shirt, leaving nothing to the imagination.

∞∞∞∞∞∞∞∞∞∞∞∞∞∞●

After getting ready, I walk into the kitchen and take a seat. Damien puts a plate with an elaborate sandwich in front of me as he sits beside me with a sandwich for himself.

"Thanks for lunch. I'll have to make you dinner sometime when we stay at my place."

"I would like that. Do you like to cook?"

It's still amazing to me at how deep our feelings run, yet we still have so much we have to learn from each other.

Smiling at a memory, I respond, "I love it. My mom and I used to cook breakfast together every morning while my dad was out doing chores. It was our alone time every day. It's probably why breakfast is my favorite meal."

"That sounds like a great memory."

I smile at him. Since meeting Damien, I have welcomed these memories instead of feeling pain from them.

"I know you're staying with Sam's parents. Promise me that you'll let me know if something changes."

The doorbell rings, and I know that it is probably Ben who has arrived. My heart plummets as I realize my time with Damien is coming to an abrupt end.

"I promise. Where I'm going is like Mayberry. Everyone knows me."

Damien grabs my hand and leads me toward the kitchen entrance. Before we get there though, he pulls me off to the side and kisses me like I am his only way to breathe. My body starts to respond, and I lean into him. I'm sorer than I was earlier, but I don't care. All too soon, the kiss ends, and he puts his forehead to mine.

He murmurs, "I'm not going to survive these next four days."

I just hold him tight. I'm afraid if I speak I will change my mind and end up staying.

Outside, a man of average height with brown hair and brown eyes is standing beside my car. He's dressed in a classy but average suit. He's just normal-looking, like me. It's a relief to feel like I fit in here.

Damien pulls me to him as he makes introductions. "Ben, this is Miss Allison Scott, my girlfriend. She goes by Allison. Alli, this is Ben Powers."

It's endearing how Damien ensures that everyone knows only he calls me Alli.

I smile and extend my hand to Ben, and he shakes it professionally and returns my smile.

"It's nice to meet you, Ben. Thank you for bringing my car."

"It's not a problem, Miss Scott."

Part of me wants to tell him to call me Allison, but I decide against it. I am sure Damien does not want me to become semi-friends with his employees. I wouldn't want my boyfriend doing that if the roles were reversed.

"Ben, please wait inside in the office, and we will start going over the contracts after I say good-bye to Alli."

I give Ben a thank-you smile, and he immediately excuses himself and makes his way into Damien's home.

Last night, in the midst of our passion, I didn't get to see what the front of his house looks like. I glance back at the house, and it is just as I expected. The antebellum-style continues in the front with large white columns and black shutters. It is massively impressive.

Grabbing my hand, Damien slowly takes me to my driver's side door. "Text me the moment you arrive safely. At any time, if you need anything, you let me know. I have to know you are safe, Alli. If you feel otherwise, you have to promise me that you will communicate with me. It's the only way I am going to be able to be apart from you."

My safety seems to be a true concern for him. It doesn't feel right asking about that again after my unwillingness to share what I will be doing in Homerville. At some point soon, I'm going to need more information though, but I have to be just as willing to share.

"I promise, Damien."

He leans in and kisses me good-bye. It's more reverent and reserved but filled with all the emotions we are both too scared to voice aloud right now. At least, that's how I feel.

I get into the car, and he softly closes the door behind me. He puts his hand to the window, and I smile and mirror his action as I put the car into drive. Even with a window separating us, the connection between us zings to life.

When Damien steps back from the window, my heart feels heavy. As I drive off and see him in the rearview mirror, standing there and watching me, I realize my life will never be the same.

My mom always said, *Where there is a high, there is a low.* I hope she's wrong. If she happens to be right, I hope the low has nothing to do with Damien and me.

CHAPTER 10

It's Tuesday morning, and I am headed back to Waleska from Homerville. Finally, the day has arrived. Damien and I get to see each other this evening. It's felt like an eternity has passed. With all that has happened, my mind is a chaotic mess. Thoughts regarding this weekend's events and my relationship with Damien are swirling around. I'm working on cataloging and processing all the decisions I've made. I think I appear calm on the outside, but my inside feels like I have consumed twelve cups of coffee in less than two hours. Yeah, mind jitters don't even begin to describe it. Having nervous energy to expel, I pick up the phone and call Sam.

"Hey, girl. How's it going?" I ask.

"It's like a circus around here." She pulls the phone away. "Those go over by the podium." She comes back on the line. "Hey, sorry. What's up?"

"Do you need any help?"

"Girl, if I had any more help, I'd go nuts. Thanks though. I appreciate it. Go get ready for your man. We're bound for Vegas tonight." Something crashes in the background. "Gotta go. See ya later."

"See ya."

She hangs up the phone, and I smile because I know she's in her element right now.

The miles tick away as I think about the last couple of days. When two people are forced to interact solely over the phone without sex getting in the way, it's amazing how much they learn about one another. I grin, thinking about my phone conversation with Damien last night.

"Hey, baby. How was your day?"

The soft purr in his voice has me instantly missing him, just like every night when we have talked.

I jump a little on the bed as I energetically tell him, "It was good. I have some exciting news to tell you tomorrow."

He chuckles at my enthusiasm. "I can't wait to hear about it. I'll be in early, so we can spend some time together before Sam's event. Did you see the announcement today about us?"

He sounds so pleased, but my stomach immediately bottoms out, like it always does before a presentation in front of one of my college classes.

Damien's publicist put out the word that Damien is off the market and is in an "extremely serious" relationship. It made national news.

"Yeah, it's a little overwhelming to see my name in the paper and to hear it mentioned on TV."

The worry in my voice must have been discernible.

"Fuck, I knew I should have waited until we were together. Has anyone bothered you?"

"No, no. I didn't mean it like that. You were right with how it was handled. I'm still trying to wrap my head around the fact that the media finds our dating status newsworthy. As a simple country girl, I'm acclimating to your lifestyle. I'm fine."

"Alli, I need you to promise to tell me if my lifestyle gets to be too much. Don't leave."

"I promise." We need a subject change. "So last night, we talked all about my parents. I want to hear about your childhood tonight."

"I'd rather talk about you."

He's trying to sound seductive to sway me, but it's not happening tonight. I'm a girl on a mission.

"We talked about me the last three nights. Your turn to spill, buddy."

I hear a small sigh of frustration on the other end of the phone. It's obvious he doesn't want to talk about his family.

"Let's see. My parents live in North Carolina. My father is a lawyer, and my mom stays home. They traveled a lot to climb their little social circles. They weren't present for most of my childhood unless I was deemed useful in getting them to a higher social status. I see them occasionally, but we're not close."

Geez, that must have been rough. *My parents were the exact opposite. Having no idea what to say, I respond in the lamest way, "I'm so sorry."*

"It's fine. I had my grandparents while I was growing up. Besides the football team in North Carolina, they also had a ranch in Texas. I spent my summers there as a kid. My grandfather got his money from being an oil tycoon. They taught me everything important in life. When I was a junior in college, my grandmother died of a heart attack, and my grandfather followed within a month. The doctors couldn't determine his cause of death. I personally think it was due to a broken heart. He loved her with everything he had. He fell in love with her when she was fourteen, and on her sixteenth birthday, he took her to this ridge on his property and proposed. The night they got engaged, they carved their initials on this tree, and it's still there to this day."

Sniffing from the heartfelt story, I respond, "That's a beautiful love story. My grandparents died before I knew them." To have a true love like that is every person's dream.

"Don't cry, baby. They had a lifetime of love. I'll take you to the ranch in Texas sometime."

"I'd love that."

I hear a beeping noise in the background.

"Baby, I've got another conference call, but I cannot wait to have you in my arms tomorrow."

"Me either."

There's an awkward silence, like the last few nights, as neither one of us knows how to end the call.

He sighs. "Bye, baby. Sleep tight. Text me when you make it home."

"I will. Bye."

After I hang up my phone, it beeps with a text message flashing across the screen.

He's not good enough for you.

Ugh. I knew there would be some jealous person out there after everyone learned about my relationship with Damien. How the hell did someone get my number?

Pulling into my apartment, I stop thinking about the text from last night. After sleeping on it, I think the person was probably trying to get me riled up for some reason or another.

I'm just going to ignore it for now since Damien tends to overreact about things.

It feels good to be home. I walk through the apartment door, and before I do anything else, I text Damien.

> *Me: Home safe. Are you about to take off?*
>
> *Damien: It's been a fucking nightmare of a day. I'm running behind. I swear that I'll be there before the event.*
>
> *Me: It's okay. If you can't make it, Sam and I can catch a flight to Vegas on our own and just meet you there.*
>
> *Damien: I'll be there.*
>
> *Me: Okay. Muah. Miss you.*
>
> *Damien: You have no idea. Heading into a meeting. Wait for me.*
>
> *Me: Yes, sir.*

It's silly for Damien to fly all the way here just to fly back out to Vegas. As my mom always said, *Allison, you live and learn. Choose all your battles wisely. Not everything is worth fighting for.*

Listening to my mom's wise words, I choose not to say anything more about it to Damien. *If he wants to fly back and forth across the U.S., that's up to him.*

Nothing but unpacking, washing, cleaning, and repacking are in my near future.

Since Sam's sorority ribbon-cutting ceremony is a semi-dressy event tonight, I decide on an emerald green baby doll dress with spaghetti straps. The fabric is a soft silk-like flowing material that wisps as I walk. I pair it with some ridiculously tall black high heels and add classically styled gold jewelry. I leave my hair down, but I add a few curls for volume. It's fun dressing up for Damien, knowing how he reacts to me even if it is over the top.

Looking in the mirror, I straighten my necklace. *I hope Damien likes what he sees.* To keep from getting too nervous, I turn my attention back to the task of packing. The last thing I have to pack is my makeup. After getting my cosmetic bag from the bathroom, I place it in my suitcase and zip it up. It's almost time to leave, so I send Damien a text.

> *Me: Hey, are you close? I can meet you there if you need me to. I need to be there on time for Sam.*

> *Damien: I'll be there. We will make it on time. I'm less than five minutes away.*

> *Me: Okay, I'll meet you outside.*

> *Damien: No, I'll come get you at your door.*

Good grief. I don't respond. We are barely going to make it on time as it is. Grabbing my bags, I lock up and head downstairs as a black town car pulls up to the curb. When Damien jumps out of the backseat, he looks a little agitated, but he continues his stride forward to give me a kiss barely suitable for the public.

"It feels like it took a lifetime to get to you today. I wanted to come to the door and greet you like a gentleman."

My heart beats faster at having him here in front of me. I missed him so much. The driver quickly takes my bags as Damien ushers me into the car. Once we're in the backseat, he pulls me in next to him.

"You look beautiful tonight. I'm sorry that I'm so late. Inexplicable fucking delays kept occurring for various reasons, and then we ran into more at the airport."

Poor guy looks stressed beyond belief.

He appears to be still dressed from his business day, wearing his dark-colored suit and light blue shirt. I'm itching to strip his clothes from him and run my fingers through his hair.

It's been too long. The energy pulsing through the car is almost intolerable.

"Thank you." I lean into him, needing as much contact as possible. "I've missed you. You're here, and that's what's important. Are you okay? You look really tense."

He kisses the top of my head and starts rubbing those soothing circles on my hand. I think he likes the constant contact, and the motion calms him as much as it does me.

He drops his voice as he starts talking. "I don't like running behind schedule, and I was hoping to have some alone time with you before the event. I'm aching for you. Today has been an endless day of problematic delays."

"Hey, at least now, we can do those pesky delays together."

He gives my head another kiss. "We better be through with them. I should have been here at least two hours ago. When do I get to hear your news from the weekend?"

Looking to the front of the car, I respond in a low voice, "I would prefer to wait for when we have complete privacy."

He nods in agreement after his eyes shift for a millisecond to Ben and the driver.

He lowers his voice. "Did it go as expected?"

I beam back at him because, try as I might, I cannot contain my excitement. "It went even better than I had expected. I'm really ecstatic about it."

He brings my hand up to his mouth to kiss it. "Good. I'm relieved to hear that." He leans in closer and drops his voice to a whisper. "If I had known you were going to wear those fuck-me heels, I would have had a limo pick us up, so we could make better use of our time."

My eyes snap up to his. "That was an option? Regardless of my shoe choice, you should have definitely gone with the limo."

What was he thinking? After almost five days without him, my body is a crazy, craving mess. His very words cause my libido to jump into hyperdrive. *Who would have thought that I'd abstained for over twenty-one years?*

Chuckling, he replies, "Well, I didn't think you'd want the extra attention from arriving to the sorority that way. I won't make that mistake again." He leans down and kisses my neck. "It's good to know that you want me just as badly. I'm dying to get inside you."

My panties just caught on fire with that statement. Needing a deeper connection, I lean up to give him another kiss. The moment our lips unite, our kiss instantly intensifies. I have missed this, and I am so sexually frustrated right now.

Ben's voice, coming from the front of the car, makes me jump, effectively breaking the kiss.

"We have arrived, sir."

Damn it. I keep forgetting we have a constant audience. I blush with how I was about to practically mount Damien. Damien's impatient breathing tells me he's right there with me.

∞∞∞∞∞∞∞∞∞∞∞∞∞∞∞∞∞∞

The sorority event ends, and a massive sea of people are all trying to get to Sam. Everything is pink, pink, pink. From a distance, I smile and give her a wave as she fields an endless amount of questions. Her knee-length pink silk dress is stunning. Her curvy figure would make any guy go crazy for her.

Damien's popularity among the sports fans keeps halting our progress to Sam. We're trying to make our way closer when a heavy balding guy comes and slaps Damien on the back and leaves his hand there.

"So, Wales, who are you gunning for now?"

Politely extricating himself from the man's semi-embrace, Damien responds, "There are a lot of great players out there. It's looking to be a fantastic season this year."

Nodding his head, the balding man acts as if Damien has just solved the mystery of how the pyramids had been built. "I know, man. I don't know how you pick them. I'm a huge fan."

Damien gives the man a polite smile and shakes his hand. "Thanks for your support."

We continue moving through the crowd, but after several failed attempts to get to Sam, we finally make our way to a corner in order to get away from all of Damien's fans.

Damien gives my cheek a light kiss. He whispers, "You are absolutely mesmerizing. If you weren't already mine and I saw you here tonight, I would not stop until you said yes to a date." He leans in closer to my ear and nibbles on my lobe.

I am going to strip down in front of everybody here if he's not careful. I need him. Pronto.

"I can't wait to have my cock buried deep inside you."

Turning to face him, I pleadingly look at him. "Please. I can't wait."

He shakes his head and mouths, *Later.*

Damn it. Not fair. I want to stomp my foot and demand a different answer.

He chuckles, and in that roughened sex voice, he says, "Soon, baby. Be patient. There are too many people here, and I plan on making you scream in pleasure." He's so pleased that I am in a wanton state of mind.

I need a breather, and I take the opportunity as another fan approaches Damien. "I'll be right back. Nature calls."

He's about to respond when the tall, skinny man hits him on the back.

What is it with the back-hitting thing?

"Wales, I didn't know you sponsored this university."

"I'm attending the event with my girlfriend," Damien says.

As I'm walking off, I smile at Damien's response.

An idea strikes me while I'm in the restroom. I remove my panties, and I giggle at the brazen side Damien seems to bring out in me. There's no way I could verbally say what I've just done without blushing ten shades of red, so I decide to send a text and let him make the next move. *Maybe this will spur him into action.*

> *Me: By the way, I thought you might want to know that I am now without my panties. Maybe I should*

*soothe this ache myself? Hmm, what to do? What to
do?*

Walking out of the restroom, my nerves go up another
notch as I think about what I've just done. I hope it forces
Damien to take me off somewhere, so he can have his wicked
way with me.

Stowing my phone, I look up, and my heart misses a beat.
Brad is standing right in front of me. Last time Damien and
Brad were in the same room, it didn't go so well. Brad moves
to the middle of the hallway, blocking my path, as he crosses
his arms over his chest.

"Hey, Brad. It's good to see you. Would you mind moving,
so I could pass?" *Kill him with kindness.* I do not want a scene
here.

"So, you're dating Damien Wales?" he asks in an almost
accusatory tone.

"Yes, I'm heading back to him right now. Have a nice
time."

All of a sudden, I remember my panties are gone, and a
blush creeps up my face. *This is not good. Oh geez.* I do not want
to have a conversation with Brad of all people while I'm like
this. *This will teach me to play with the big boys.* The one time I go a
little crazy, of course, it bites me in the ass. *Karma can be such a
bitch sometimes.*

"Are you free this weekend to get a drink and catch up? I
want to apologize for how I acted last time we were together."

"I don't think that's a good idea. I'm exclusively with
Damien. Please excuse me."

When he refuses to move, my temper rises. *Why is he
suddenly being an asshole? I just don't get it.* His behavior is either
off, or this is just how he really is. "Brad, I am not going to ask
again. Please step aside."

This time, he complies. As I walk by, his hand comes up
and grazes my shoulder. *Ugh.* My body feels repulsed from his
touch.

As I make my hasty departure, Brad calls after me, "Allison, we'll catch up later when you have more time. You look beautiful tonight."

I pick up my pace and don't look back. When I round the corner, Damien catches me before I smack right into him.

"Whoa."

I stumble, and he grabs me, steadying me.

"I've got you." He looks me over and immediately knows that something is up. "Alli, what's wrong?"

I don't want to have a confrontation at Sam's event this evening. "I'll tell you when we get into the car. I don't want a scene."

"That fucker is here, isn't he? He approached you, didn't he?"

He goes to step around me, and I grab his arm. He has that same demeanor as when he confronted Brad at the bar. He is seething, and his body is rigid. He's ready to rumble, and he will not lose.

"Damien, please. Not here. It's Sam's event. Please. I'm begging you."

He's torn between pummeling Brad's ass and staying here.

"Please," I say again.

Finally, his body relents, and the rigidity under my touch relaxes. I know he is going to stay with me. *Whew, crisis averted for now.*

"Tell me what happened." I go to object, but Damien won't have it. "Alli, you've asked me not to go confront the fucker, and I'm asking you to tell me. It's meeting in the middle."

His hands go around my waist, and I lay my hands on his arms.

"Okay, you're right. I was coming out of the restroom. He blocked my way and asked me out for drinks. I said no and left. He said we'd catch up later when I had more time."

By the time I finish, his hands have dropped away from me. They are now fisted at his sides with ghost-white knuckles.

My fingers cinch tighter on his sleeves, hoping to anchor him to this spot.

Through gritted teeth, he tells me, "Alli, if he comes around you again, I want to know immediately. I'm not going to put up with his shit. He's up to something." The rage on his face is undeniable.

"He's just trying to piss you off." He goes to speak, but I hold up my hand. "I promise though. I'll tell you. Let's just enjoy tonight, and we will worry about it later. Okay?"

He nods. As I look around, the crowd is starting to thin. Brad is nowhere to be seen. *Thank goodness.* Damien is hanging on by a thread at this point. There's only so much self-control I can expect him to exert in one night.

From across the room, Sam starts making her way toward us. She looks exhausted but excited at the same time. When she walks up, I embrace her in a hug.

"Many congrats, girl! Fantastic job. It was a great ceremony. We tried to make our way over to you, but you were so busy."

A smile emerges on her face, and her green eyes are twinkling. "Oh, I know. No worries. You think it went well?"

I nod enthusiastically. "Yeah, very well."

"It was exhausting but fun. I can tell you one thing. I am ready to get on a plane and head to Vegas, baby." She does a tired shimmy.

Damien leans in to give Sam a friendly congratulatory hug.

Over his shoulder, she gives me the are-you-okay look. I nod and mouth, *Later,* to her.

"Congrats, Sam. We're ready whenever you are. No rush." He has reined in a lot of his irritation. It's gone but not forgotten.

"Oh, I'm ready. Let me go grab my bags, and I'll be right out." She immediately turns and heads up the stairs to the left of the kitchen area.

Damien pulls out his phone to send a text. "I'll have Ben pull up the car to the front of the house."

I keep forgetting Ben is here with the driver. I wonder what he does with all that free time. *Ugh, it would have to be boring to just be at someone's beck and call.*

Damien and I walk outside. The air is warm, but the slight breeze makes it a perfect evening.

He leans into me. "So, was the text you sent earlier a statement of fact? Or were you toying with me?"

"Well, I would tell you, but...I guess you'll just have to find out on your own."

He moves closer to me, dropping his voice. "Is that a challenge?"

"It is if you want to know." I flutter my lashes a little, baiting him.

He has that full-on predatory look in his eyes. I have unlocked the cage to the beast, and he is going to find a way to devour me soon. *Yes! Oh, yes!*

"Challenge accepted, baby."

He starts looking around, taking in all of our surroundings. My sex clenches, thinking that he might haul me off to a dark place outside to give me some much needed satisfaction. Of course, at this particular moment, the car pulls up. *Ahh!* I want to scream. *Ben needs to stop being so efficient.*

Damien begins rubbing my shoulders. "Don't worry. We won't have to wait much longer. I have a surprise for you."

"A surprise? I love surprises." My insides are all giddy.

"Yes, and it will get you what you want."

We smile at each other before we get into the car.

Just as we get situated, Sam comes out, still wearing her dress. She heads down the walkway, rolling her bags behind her. The driver stows her suitcases as she gets into the car. Settling into the seat, she lays her head back with a smile. Her face looks tired as she starts to let her guard down.

"Finally. It's been a bitch of a day, and I am ready for this vacay," she says.

Damien's hand naturally gravitates toward mine, and his fingers start with the soothing circles. *I love it.* I wonder if he realizes how often he does this small little act.

He leans forward slightly. "Sam, you know you could have brought someone with you this evening. If you would still like to invite somebody, I can make the necessary arrangements to get him there."

Sweetly, she responds with a tad bit of sass, "Thanks, but I'll pass, Wales. You are about to put me in a room full of hot, testosterone-filled athletes, and there is no way in hell I'm going to be chained to someone for the evening. No way. This girl is going to have some fun." She gives a nod as if she's solidifying her statement to herself.

I roll my eyes and let out a laugh.

Leaning back against the seat, Damien says, "I feel sorry for all of those players. Just don't cause any of mine to start playing shitty because they are off pining for you. Target the other team's players if you don't mind."

She slants her upper body forward and gives him a big wink. "No promises."

I mash my lips together. Damien should be worried, especially if he loses their bet.

Soon, we are pulling into a secluded entrance on the airport grounds. Suddenly, I realize he probably has a private plane. *How in the world did that not even cross my mind?* My suspicions are quickly confirmed when we pull alongside a white jet. On the side, *Wales Enterprises* is displayed in black lettering with blue trim. I know he's wealthy, but I don't think I really understand the magnitude of it all.

I can sense Damien is irritated as we pull to a stop.

His tone confirms my suspicion as he asks, "Ben, why is the wrong plane here?"

"Sir, the Dassault Falcon was not available on short notice. Therefore, I had to schedule the Learjet at the last minute." Ben's voice is even and calm.

"Ben, I should have been informed of this immediately, so I could have made other plans."

His cold business tone still takes me off guard.

"Yes, sir," Ben says.

"I suggest you remember to run those important details by me prior to the fact. After today's events, this is unacceptable," Damien says.

"My apologies, sir."

Wow, I feel bad for Ben. He seems like he has so much on his plate, and to get in trouble in front of Damien's girlfriend and her best friend seems a little harsh. I tell myself that he's not my employee, and it is Damien's business to handle. Obviously, Damien and Ben have a good professional relationship because they have been working together for around three or four years. *I'll leave it to the boys to figure out how to play nice together.*

Sam and I just look at each other silently. *Dassault Falcon and Learjet?* As far as I am concerned, a plane is a plane, and I'm just excited we don't have to go through the usual throng of people in the airport.

We head to the plane. It's a fairly windy night, and I have to keep my hand on my dress to stop it from flying up and exposing my bare self.

Stepping across the threshold of the aircraft, the extravagance is overwhelming, and of course, it's what I would have expected. Obviously, this plane has been remodeled. Six plush cream leather chairs fill the front of the cabin. Each seat has its own side table. The back has a cream leather love seat with a table in front of it. Apparently, it is where Damien does most of his work, and this is where we settle in for the flight. It's endearing that he doesn't even want a chair separating us.

Sam takes a middle seat and starts going through her carry-on bag before facing Damien. "Do I have time to change before we take off? I plan on sleeping most of the way, and this dress is not that comfortable."

"Sure. We are set to depart in about ten minutes. There is a bathroom right through that door pass the galley."

Changing clothes sounds really good. I start to go through my carry-on when Damien's hand moves to mine to stop my rummaging.

Quietly, he asks, "What do you think you are doing?"

From my crouched position, I look up at him, confused. "I was going to change after Sam was finished."

"You issued a challenge, and I am not about to concede a loss." His blue eyes are raking me over from head to toe.

I snap back to sit straight up. I continue to stare at him as I involuntarily lick my lips. Our trance is interrupted by someone speaking, and it takes me a second to realize it's Ben.

"Sir, the pilot will be ready to take off in about five minutes. He has a couple of questions for you. If you don't want to get up, he can come back here once he's done with the preflight check. The stewardess will begin her service in just a moment. If you do not require anything else, I will take my seat."

"I'll go talk to him." Damien turns to me. "I'll be right back. I want to expedite our departure. Considering how late we'll be getting in, you're going to be exhausted."

I nod and smile. As long as I'm with Damien, I don't care how late we get in. He leans in and gives me a kiss on the cheek before he strides to the front of the plane.

I hear my phone chirp from my clutch. I grab it and see I have another text message from a blocked number.

He's not good enough for you. Trust me on this.

I turn the phone off immediately. *How did this person get my phone number?* I'm instantly irritated, and I work on controlling my emotions. I know I should tell Damien about the two weird texts because he would want to know, but at the same time, he's been pushed to his limits this evening with the whole Brad thing.

Why do people have to be such assholes to get attention? I'm sure the texts are harmless, and someone is just trying to get a rise out of Damien or me. The messages are strange, but they're not worth ruining our evening. *If it happens again, I'll mention it to him.*

Damien returns as I'm stowing my phone.

"Is everything all right?" he asks.

I look up at him and smile. "I'm just tired. I needed to turn off my phone before we took off." *There. That should work. I haven't lied. It's all true.*

He takes his seat next to me when the door in the back opens.

"Damn, Wales, you have some pretty fancy digs here. Thanks for bringing me along for the ride." Sam slaps Damien on the shoulder and winks as she strides by him.

I envy how she can adapt to any situation and seem perfectly at home in it. She takes her seat and gets comfortable as the stewardess begins the preflight service of distributing beverages, blankets, and pillows.

Just then, I remember the question I wanted to ask Damien about the jet crisis. "Why were you upset that the other jet wasn't available?"

When he looks over at me, some of his earlier irritation returns into the corners of his eyes. *Do I really want to know?*

He lowers his voice to where no one can hear but me. "It's a bigger plane, and it has a bedroom. I use it for my overseas flights. I thought you would rest better if you had a bed to lie on, and I wanted to make love to you at ten thousand feet. I had visions of you wrapped around me with those fuck-me heels."

Oh wow. I'm pissed at Ben now, too. He cost me the chance to join the Mile High Club tonight. Turning my head slightly, I give the best death glares I can manage to the back of Ben's head.

Damien chuckles. "That's a scary face. Glad it's not pointed at me."

I let out an exasperated breath and keep my voice just as low, ensuring our privacy. "Ugh, I could have been a Mile High Club member tonight, and I blame him."

"Shh, don't worry, baby. It'll happen. We'll have the plane for the ride home."

My irritation fades slightly, and exhaustion from today's events starts to set in as we begin our ascent into the skies.

"Why don't you lie down and rest? I'll finish up some work, and we can talk when everyone goes to sleep."

"Sounds good. I'm tired." Finishing my sentence on a yawn, I take off my shoes and lay my head down on one end of the couch with my legs spread across his lap. "Is this okay?"

"Absolutely." He puts the caramel-colored blanket on me, so I am covered from my neck to my feet.

The blanket is so soft, like rose petals caressing my skin. One of his hands is on my knee, rubbing it ever so lightly. The constant hum of the plane lulls me to sleep, and I am gone.

My leg twitches as something tickles my inner thigh. I try to move away from it to stay in my slumber. Seconds later, it resumes and then travels up my leg slowly and persistently. Moving my legs, I try to stop it. I just want to sleep. That ticklish thing is now about three inches from the top of my leg when realization dawns. *Oh, holy hell.* It's Damien's hand. My eyes shoot open to meet his gaze in the darkened cabin.

He takes his other hand and puts his finger to his mouth in a shushing motion, letting me know that I have to be quiet. I nod in understanding, hoping he continues quickly to his destination. I desperately want him to win this challenge. When he reaches the apex of my thighs, his eyes widen because he now knows that I was telling the truth in my last text. *Good. In the future, he'll know that I'm not just all talk.*

He reaches my sex and closes his eyes when he feels how wet I am. After not having me for a few days, I know this has to be killing him. It's killing me. His thumb begins tracing circles around my clit, and he dips a finger into my heat. I want to bow into his touch, but I remember where we are, and I keep my eyes locked on him. The intimacy of this moment is unreal despite the fact that two people are seated less than seven feet away. It only makes the moment more erotic, knowing we could be caught.

He picks up the pace, and I am frantic inside with need. I bite down on my lip to keep any noise from escaping. This is getting to be too much. I want to writhe and scream his name. The restraint I'm using heightens my need to feel him inside me. It is taking everything in my body to keep myself grounded and immobile. He presses his thumb hard against my clit, and I shatter, never breaking eye contact. The relief has only taken an edge off my need. It's like throwing a little water on a fire. If it doesn't completely extinguish it, then the fire comes back with a vengeance.

Damien slowly lets out a deep breath. I can feel his throbbing erection beneath my legs as I shift. An idea strikes me. As I get up, Damien gives me a questioning look. Biting my lip, I grab my bag.

Leaning over, I whisper in his ear, "Come join me."

Well, I didn't have to ask him twice. He quietly gets out of his seat and practically pushes me into the bathroom. It's a little larger than what it would be on a commercial flight. Damien locks the door behind me before he descends on me. The feeling of his tongue is exquisite as his wintergreen flavor penetrates me.

When he picks me up, I automatically wrap my legs around him. My back goes against the far wall as he leans into me and undoes his zipper. I can feel him at my sex, eagerly seeking entrance. He wants to be rough with me, and I want him to be.

"This is going to have to be fast and quiet, baby. I need you now. It's been too long. Tell me if it hurts."

"Yes, please take me."

In one movement, he plunges into me. *Ah, the relief.* He starts to move at a quick pace. My inner muscles begin to shudder, and he knows I'm close. I put my head on his shoulder and bite down to keep from screaming out loud as he continues his deep penetrating thrusts. *It feels so good. I wish we could take our time.* We are both getting what we've needed all night long—some satisfaction.

After thrusting a few more times to massage out our climaxes, he puts his forehead to mine as we try to slow our breathing. "Welcome to the Mile High Club, Miss Scott. I hope you enjoyed your flight."

I start to giggle, and he puts his hand on my mouth, muffling the sound. *Oh yeah, we aren't alone.* He pulls out of me, and immediately, I feel bereft, and I whimper at the loss.

"We are so perfect together. You need me inside you as much as I need to be there. We'll have all night long when we get to the hotel. Go ahead and change. Then, meet me back in the cabin, so you can rest comfortably for the rest of the flight."

Damien helps me clean myself up, and then he tends to his still semi-stiff dick. After giving me a kiss, he leaves. When I look in the mirror, it's as if I have totally changed from the person I was before Miami. My body glows from being around Damien. My eyes shine brighter than before. I am so in over my head and in love with this guy. *Yes, love. I am in love with Damien.* It's fast and chaotic, but deep down, I know that it's real. *I wonder how strong his feelings are for me.* There is no way I am saying the L-word first. I need to stay grounded in all of this, so my heart doesn't get broken if he doesn't feel the same way.

I finish changing and walk back out into the cabin. Ben is awake now, reading something on his tablet. I curl into Damien's side, and I smile at the comfort his arms provide with his protective embrace.

Before I start to drift off to sleep again, I ask, "How much longer until we land?"

"We should touch down within two hours. Is there anything specific you want to do while we are in Vegas?"

After a yawn, I respond, "What about a show?"

"Any particular one?"

Our conversation feels as if we have been together for a long time. It's easy and comfortable. We are more than just sex.

"No, you pick. I have no idea what's good."

"I'll make the arrangements."

I kiss the side of his neck while he resumes reading. *Does this guy ever stop thinking of me?* There is so much Damien and I need to talk about, but it needs to happen in private. *I'll think about it tomorrow.*

Soon, I doze off again, feeling content in his warm embrace.

CHAPTER
11

Stretching across the bed, I reach to locate Damien, but I come up empty. It feels cold and abandoned on that side. Opening my eyes, I realize I'm alone in a king-size bed. *What in the world?* When I catch sight of a note on his pillow, I immediately feel my anxiety diminish. I can't help from being terrified that he's all of a sudden going to be tired of me and move on to greener pastures.

My Beautiful Alli,

I had to take care of some business prior to tonight's gala, and I didn't want to disturb your peaceful slumber, considering how little sleep you got last night.

You are as beautiful asleep as you are awake.

The hairdressers and makeup artist team will show up later this afternoon. I should be back sometime before they arrive. Until then, stay safe.

Damien

Smiling from ear to ear, I put on some lounge clothes and head out of our bedroom. We're staying in the penthouse. The furniture is ultra-modern and is done in the most monochromatic colors. Colorful contemporary artwork hangs from the walls. *I don't understand the hype behind splashing various colors on a canvas. I say, go to a kindergarten classroom and end up with the same result. It would be a whole hell of a lot cheaper.*

The scents of food permeate the suite as I hear someone moving around in what I assume to be the kitchen area down the hall. *It's probably Sam.* After arriving late last night, we all quickly retired to our rooms. Damien had his revenge on me in the bedroom through his sexcapades after the joke I played on him. Thinking back, I laugh.

We are all standing at the top of the stairs.
I lean in to give Damien a kiss. "Good night."
He looks at me quizzically.
Answering his silent query, I say, "I'm going to stay with Sam and catch up. You know, girl time." I give a shrug as if it is to be expected, and I start walking to my friend, giving her a wink in the process.
Before I make it three steps, he swiftly picks me up and slings me over his shoulder. "I don't fucking think so. Night, Sam."
She laughs at his barbarian manners as he strides toward our bedroom. She calls after us, "Night, guys. Keep it down."
My face flames as Damien slaps my ass. My best friend knows I'm about to get down and nasty with my boyfriend.
She yells even louder, "You're in for it now, Allison."
Traitor.
"You're mine tonight, Alli."
The dark sensuality of his tone has me excited for what he has in store for me.

He finally let me go to sleep sometime after four in the morning, not that I am complaining by any means. If that's the punishment he dishes out, he can guarantee himself more hard times in the future.

As I enter the kitchen, Sam is fixing a plate from an array of foods at the breakfast bar. Her pink sorority shirt and green sweatpants are adorable.

Hoping to avoid any innuendos, I cheerily greet her, "Good morning, sunshine. Did you sleep well?"

Sam turns to face me, smiling coyly. I know then that my plan has failed.

"I sure did. I would wager, being in Vegas and all, that I got a lot more sleep than you," she says.

I blush. *Geez, I hope she didn't hear us.*

"Thought so. I must say, if the state of your hair this morning is any reflection on the sex you had last night, then I would bet you must be feeling mighty fine. Dreadful sex hair is the best."

Automatically, my hand moves up to fix the craziness resting on top of my head. Deciding the best way to end the innuendos is to go along with it, I quip back, "Well, all I can say is that the P fits into the V very well."

I smile playfully at her, and we both bust out into a fit of giggles. It's silly to be juvenile about penises and vaginas, but being around my best friend brings out the adolescent in both of us.

"Damn, I'm so jealous. My V needs some P."

We start laughing again as we finish filling our plates before we head over to the glass breakfast table.

She continues, "In all seriousness, how are you doing with all of this?" She waves her fork around the room, emphasizing her point.

"Honestly, I go from one extreme to another. On one side, I am so overwhelmed with how fast our relationship is going and with everything that accompanies Damien's life. I wonder, why me? And then, on the other extreme, I don't want it to slow down at all. I am ready to jump headfirst into anything that comes my way. That only sends me back to the other side, and the cycle repeats itself over and over again. Oh, I am such a mess about this whole thing." I sit down with a humph and try to calm myself down. A freak-out on the day of the big gala is not a good idea, considering all the mingling we will be doing.

"Oh my gosh, you're in love with him."

My head snaps up at Sam. She's holding her hand up to her mouth, just staring at me. *Good grief, I must stay calm.* At her spoken words, regardless if I have admitted them to myself or not, the freak-out is on the verge of breaking free.

"What...no...why...no...how...what makes you say that?" Sputtering like a buffoon, my voice is all squeaky and dry as I try to form something coherent.

What if Damien sees how deep my feelings are, and he isn't ready for them? My crazy emotions might just ruin this yet. I've been trying to block out the L-word from my mind, but it's right there, front and center, demanding to be dealt with now.

Sensing my impending meltdown, Sam leans over and grabs me by the shoulders. She gives me a little shake to bring me back into the here and now. "Allison, I have known you practically my whole life. If I were in your shoes, you would sense if I were in love. You might not push the issue like I do, but you would still know how I felt. I doubt he has a clue at this point."

What she says has merit because I would know the exact moment something changed within Sam. When she and Greg broke up, I knew that something major had happened. She's right that I don't push. We complement each other in that way, which is one of the many reasons we are so close. It's been over three years, and she still hasn't shared what happened with Greg, but I am convinced that she will tell me when she's ready.

"Allison, it's going to be okay. From what I can tell when I see you two together, Damien is as head over heels about you as you are about him."

"It terrifies me." My voice is just above a whisper.

She reassuringly pats me on the shoulder. "Just continue being yourself. If it's meant to be, it will happen. Have you told him about your plans yet?"

"No, not yet. I intend to tell him soon. He knows we need to talk, but I told him I wanted complete privacy. Alone time with him has been hard to come by unless it's in the wee hours of the morning. At that point, I'm too tired to have the conversation."

She's giving me that mom look, like my mom used to give me when I stalled on things. "Well, just make sure you guys keep communicating. If you love him, he needs to be a part of this journey, too. So, what's on the schedule today?"

"The hairdressers should be here late this afternoon, but until then, there are no plans. It's just you and me, babe." Taking a sip of my drink, I try to calm my nerves.

"Good. I have some tips on sex positions you can try out with Damien."

When I spit out my juice, she laughs hysterically.

❮❮❮❮❮❮❮❮❮❮❮❮❮❮❮❮❮

Girl time is interrupted by none other than Mr. Wonderful himself with Ben in tow. Ben looks professional as always. He's wearing a plain gray suit and white shirt. Damien is wearing dressy khaki slacks with a black button-up shirt. He's simply irresistible, and I'm so glad he's mine. I cannot hide the smile that spreads across my face as he strides over to take a seat next to me on the couch.

"Hey, ladies. How has your morning been?" Leaning over, he gives me a light kiss.

After I give him another quick kiss, I respond, "Great. Sam and I have been catching up." The way he always gives me his full attention makes my heart skip a beat.

Sam starts to rise. "I'm going to go take a shower before the hair and makeup team arrive, and then I'm going to respond to some emails about the sorority event last night. That'll give you guys some time to talk." Sam looks at me meaningfully.

Well, if that doesn't send a strange signal to Damien, I don't know what will. I'm watching Damien's response as he looks at Sam's retreating body.

A voice sounds from the other side of the room. "Sir, we need to get going to our next appointment."

Why do I always forget that Ben is around? Damien has now turned my way again, and he is eyeing me up and down. Ben also looks my way. I feel a little self-conscious with all eyes on me.

Damien doesn't take his eyes off me when he gives the next order. "Ben, cancel my meeting. I'll be spending the rest of the afternoon with Alli until it's time to get ready for the gala."

I don't want to be a distraction from his work. "Damien, that's not necessary—"

"Alli, I'm canceling them. Ben, make it happen."

His tone has that finality to it, and I know that it is not worth arguing over. Part of me is excited to get more time with him. When I smile at him, he, of course, returns his affection by stroking those small circles on my hand.

"But, sir, the—"

"Excuse us, Alli." Damien gets up, and Ben follows him out of the room.

I only hear murmurs, and I can't necessarily make out what they are saying. From his tone, I discern that Damien is laying down the law.

Striding back into the room by himself, Damien comes to me, grabs my hand, and leads us out onto the balcony before shutting the door behind us.

As the door clicks, I try to reiterate my earlier point. "Damien, you don't need to cancel your meetings for me. We have plenty of time."

He completely ignores me as he pulls me to a two-person chaise lounge off to the side of the balcony. This is a more private area that has a screened-in shade with some kind of reflective surface on the outside. It keeps the sun at bay and outside eyes from looking in. I immediately relax into his side. I feel both excited to be with him and guilty because he probably has a bajillion things to accomplish, and we can talk when he has a free moment.

"No, it's fine. We need to talk about a few things before tonight anyway."

Oh gosh, if that doesn't ratchet up a girl's anxiety, I don't know what does. Is there something he needs to talk about?

"There's nothing to be nervous about, baby. We just need to make sure we take time to talk about the important stuff. All this other shit doesn't matter if we aren't okay."

How does he know I'm nervous?

He answers my silent query, "You slip on this perfectly neutral face, and it seems like nothing is bothering you. I'm sure it's something you've practiced in the last year with people being so concerned about how you were doing. When we first met in Miami, I thought your indifferent attitude was because you weren't interested. We've both brought each other back to life, baby. There's no reason to hide your feelings from me ever, regardless of what they are."

"You thought I wasn't interested in you?" *I'll focus on this for the time being.* His first observation hits a little too deep to delve into at this point.

He grabs my hand with both of his before unleashing those deep blue eyes on me. "Yes, but I still pursued you. From the moment I saw you at the pool, I knew we had to meet."

Pulling away slightly, I sit straight up and look at him. *Has he confused me with another girl? That would be beyond uncool.* "We didn't meet at the pool. We met on the beach."

He shakes his head.

"What are you talking about? You were on the beach, unwinding, and I ran into you when I was taking pictures."

He stares pensively at me for a minute. He's calculating his response, just like he did that first night at dinner. Both his hands start rubbing those soothing circles on my hand. At this point, they are only semi-soothing because my nerves are at Defcon 1.

"Well, actually, I saw you before then. I had a meeting in your hotel that morning, and I saw you down at the pool. I wanted to approach you then, but you were giving some guy, who was trying to strike up a conversation with you, a clear fuck-off vibe. So, I waited until I had a moment to arrange a more mutual introduction between us."

It's as if he's speaking Greek. "Whoa. What? You mean all that at the beach—the evening stroll to unwind from a busy day and not knowing where I was staying—was a lie? What the hell? I know I was evasive with my first and last name, but I was honest with you." My blood is boiling at the deceit, and my heart hurts from the lie. I wrench my hands free, stand abruptly, and start pacing the length of the balcony. I don't even know how to process this. *He played me. Damn it! How could I have been so naive?*

As I continue walking back and forth, tears are burning my eyes, trying to break free. Damien is watching me closely but not advancing on me. *That's probably a good idea, buddy. This hurts. Bad.*

When I pass by the doors, they open suddenly, and I jump. I must look distraught because Ben's face softens for the smallest instant before I turn to the balcony rail and look out toward the Vegas skyline.

I can hear Ben behind me as he clears his throat, and then I listen to Damien's footsteps approach Ben's location. The blood starts pounding in my ears, and their conversation becomes a garbled sound as I focus on my situation. *He played me, he used me, he…I just don't know what to make of it all.* The rushing in my ears stops, and I hear Ben reply to whatever Damien has just said.

"Yes, sir."

Then, the doors close behind me. My brief moment of reprieve has past. *I'm in love with a lie. Our whole relationship…is a lie. What else has he not been truthful about?* In the middle of taking a deep cleansing breath, two arms come around on both sides of me, effectively halting any movement as I continue looking into the Vegas skyline. I try to move away, but the cage is trapping me in. When I feel his embrace, tears start to fall freely from my face. *My heart hurts so much. How can a man who has been so in tune to my needs do this? Has this been a game the whole time?*

"Alli, listen to me."

I try to break free again, but his arms move in closer, completely limiting my mobility. In no way is he hurting me, but I feel trapped. I refuse to speak or look at him right now. *It may be a little childish, but what the hell? So is a fake beach run-in.*

He talks directly into my ear, "Listen to me. I don't regret what I did. I was right in my assessment that you completely ignored any male who even breathed your way. I had to change the way I ran into you. If you even thought I was coming on to you, you would have brushed me off, like that other fucker who wouldn't leave you alone. Do you know how hard it was not to go and talk to you right then and there? I spent the afternoon trying to plan how to accidentally run into you in the lobby of your hotel. I was praying that you would come down to see the sunset.

"I had to have you, Alli. I had to have the *us* that I knew we could be. I had never reacted to someone the way I did with you. Just looking at you had me crazy for you. You also felt that energy between us that first time, and you know it. Did I deceive you by knowing more than I let on? Yes, I did. I didn't know your last name, but yes, I could have found it out if my hand had been pushed. Alli, I'm a man who knows what he wants and goes after it. Part of that is why you are attracted to me. Can't you see that?"

He pauses to see if I am going to respond, but I stay silent. Tears are still running down my face in endless streaks.

When I say nothing, he continues, "Classifying this as moving fast is the biggest understatement of the year, but I don't think either one of us could slow this down if we tried. We were meant to find each other, Alli. What if I had gone about us meeting in the normal way, and you shut me down like the others? Would you prefer that we hadn't met and then missed out on everything that's happened between us over the past couple of weeks? Because, baby, that's where it would have gone if I had done it the other way. And even though you're pissed right now, deep down, you know it's true. I would have never gotten the chance to fall in love with you. I can't regret something that brought you to me."

Holy hell, did he just say he's fallen in love with me? Has he fallen this hard, this fast, too? He's right on so many different levels. He still had no right though even if we probably wouldn't be together right now. What a freaking circle my mind has become. Wasn't it just a few hours ago when Sam brought me to face this realization out loud? This is so fast and overwhelming on one hand and so beautiful and perfect on the other. He has fallen in love with me!

I start sobbing because all these emotions are just too much. My emotions are normally much more in check, but the extremes I feel with Damien are causing me to have stronger outbursts. He makes it impossible for me to suppress myself around him, like I was able to do for the last year before I met him.

Leaning his head on my shoulder, he soothingly says, "Please don't cry. Talk to me."

I turn from the skyline in his embrace and cry into his chest. Letting go of everything I have been holding in is therapeutic on so many levels. By no means do I want to become that crazy, emotional girlfriend, but that was a hell of a lot to take in.

In between unladylike sobs, I manage to say, "Can we sit down?" *Maybe if we sit, I can pull myself together.*

"Of course, baby."

He leads me back over to the chaise lounge, and we sit down on the edge. *This is a good position.* We are close but not intimately close. I still need a little distance and perspective.

"Talk to me, Alli. I know I fucked up."

I sit there for a few minutes, trying to get my thoughts straight. "This is a lot to take in. I won't have our relationship based on omissions, Damien. That's not healthy. That doesn't build trust."

He leans over and uses his thumb to gently wipe away my tears. My body automatically moves toward him at his touch. He knows that I can't help but respond to him.

"I should have come clean about it sooner, but I didn't want to do that on the phone. You were so skittish about putting yourself out there, and I couldn't take the chance you'd leave. I wouldn't give you a reason to walk away. I'm sorry you're hurt and feel betrayed. Honestly though, I'm not sorry for what I did to meet you because I have you in my arms right now. What I did gave me the best night of my life, the night I made love to you for the first time. I won't apologize for my actions because it led me to falling in love with you."

I inhale a shaky breath and look him in the eyes. "What?"

He meets my gaze, and in a strong, unwavering voice, he answers, "Baby, I'm in love with you. I've been in love with you since the night you slept in my arms in your hotel room in Miami."

I can't hold back any longer. This man just confessed his love for me. I tackle him onto the lounge and start kissing him with everything I have. It's a little unladylike, but he loves me! We're both trying to find our way through this relationship, but at least I now know that he feels the same as I do.

Before I know it, he has flipped me onto my back, his body hovering on top of mine. Interlocking our hands, he intimately brings them above my head and stares at me. "I'm in love with you, Alli. You're it for me."

Staring back at him, I say, "I'm in love with you, too."

He groans as he unites our mouths together. It's cathartic after the emotional roller coaster that just transpired. We both need to feel that connection that says everything is okay between us.

Slowly, he peels my clothes off of me, then his.

As he slips inside me, he says, "There's nothing more perfect than when I am inside you."

In that moment, everything is right in the world. We take our time and appreciate each other's bodies as we come to a slow, loving climax.

Returning to reality, I'm thankful for the privacy provided by the screen since we are outside, lying naked with our bodies entwined. While I'm lying against him with my leg across his, his hands are leisurely worshiping me, moving from my hip up to my shoulder.

"Say it again." His eyes are beckoning me.

Resolutely, I respond, "I really love you. Please don't mislead me like that again."

"I love you, too, Alli, and I won't."

We lie there and stare at each other, taking in the gigantic step we have just made in our relationship.

After a while of just basking in our love, Damien takes me from my thoughts. "So, when are you going to tell me about what happened while we were apart? I should have canceled my morning meetings today to talk about it, but I figured you needed some sleep and time with Sam."

"Your late-night antics wore me out." I smile sweetly at him, so he knows I'm kidding.

He kisses the top of my head. "If memory serves me correctly, I was provoked."

I just giggle, and he pulls me closer to him. I place my hand on his tattoo and start tracing it. It seems to bring us both comfort.

"Last week, I went home for a job interview. Only Sam and her parents knew about it. The only reason I didn't tell you was because I was afraid I would jinx myself. Everything in my life has been going so well, and I just didn't want it to stop."

"And how did the interview go?" His voice is consoling and inviting. Most importantly though, he sounds supportive.

I take a deep breath. I'm nervous about what he is going to think because I'm sure he finished college. "Good…actually, I've decided, for the time being, not to continue my college education."

He lifts his head to see my face. "Why would you do that?" It's not a judgmental tone but a perplexed one.

"Well, I've just been going through the motions to get a degree in something I have no interest in. Right before my parents died, a magazine was interested in giving me an internship. They reached out to me before I left for Miami. They said they had an opening and wanted to interview me. They offered me a position. I'll be given first right of refusal to provide certain images they need, and I'll be in charge of photo shoots. So, basically, if I don't want to shoot it, I don't have to. Any shoots I turn down will go to a backup photographer. It's what I've always wanted to do, but I was too scared to go after it."

"Congratulations. Which magazine is it?"

I'm so excited that he seems happy for me. "It's *Do-It-Yourself Home Interiors*. I'm really thrilled about it. I know I should get my degree to be safe, but I just can't pass up this opportunity. My parents always wanted me to be happy. They encouraged me to pursue my photography dream, but I was terrified of failure. My choice regarding my career was the last thing we argued about prior to the accident." I continue focusing hard on the intricate design on his chest in order to avoid getting bogged down by those memories.

"What happened?" Damien is lightly stroking my hair with one hand while the other is resting on my upper thigh.

Maybe it will feel good to get this off my chest. "Well, a few days before they died, my mom was worried that I wasn't doing something I loved with my life. We argued about it, and my mom said, 'We have to take risks with our hearts and not follow our minds.' I disagreed. They just wanted me to be happy and not necessarily do what I thought was safe.

"The first day of summer break, Sam and I went to a college art show where I had an exhibit, and by the end of the show, I was offered an internship at this magazine. I couldn't wait to tell my parents the good news. Before I headed home, I took Sam to her parents' house, and that was when I found out about the accident. I never got to tell my mom and dad that I was going to follow my heart instead of my mind. After they died, I decided to follow my mind because my heart felt like it was gone." A tear slides down my cheek as I hug Damien.

Soothingly, he responds, "I didn't know them, but there's no way they wouldn't be proud of the woman you've become."

"That's what Sam and her parents said after we discussed my plan. My parents just wanted me to be happy above anything else. Sam's mom and dad said my parents wouldn't have cared what I did as long as I was happy." Nervously, I add, "I'd like to show you my work sometime."

"I'd like that very much. So, when do you start your new job?"

"In a few weeks. Their current photographer is retiring in five months or so. He's been there forever. I'm going to apprentice under him and accompany him on a few shoots to get the feel of the magazine before he leaves."

Damien lovingly looks at me as I speak passionately about what I will be doing.

"I'm so happy for you, baby. Don't take this the wrong way, but if you need anything, it's yours. Don't stress about things. I can help."

What? Is he implying that I need his money? "That is not why I told you. I'm fine. I don't need or want your money, Damien, if that's what you're insinuating." My voice has more ice in it than I intend.

"Calm down, Alli. I wasn't trying to insult you. You won't be in school, and you'll just be starting out professionally. I don't want you to go without anything you might need."

When he puts his hands up in mock surrender, I smile. It's hard to stay irritated at him when I know he's only concerned. However, he still needs to understand where I stand on this.

"I appreciate your offer, but I can take care of myself. I am not some gold digger, Damien. I would have never made the decision to quit school if I couldn't support myself. I don't expect anything but your love from you."

Now, he's getting agitated.

"I was just trying to help the girl I love. Like I said, I don't want you going without, baby. I work hard for what I have, and I want you to have the best."

I can tell he's using a lot of control to keep a calm tone.

Geez, we both need to calm down. Maybe if I tell him about my circumstances, he'll stop trying to overcompensate for a situation that doesn't exist. I take a deep breath. "My parents left me a small fortune, and I still have money from when I had to sell the farm, which had drastically increased in value since they bought it years ago. They saved every penny to try and give me a good inheritance one day. You don't have to worry about me."

His finger comes to my chin, bringing my face up to meet his, and he looks into my eyes. "Alli, I'm still going to take care of you, like a boyfriend should, but I'll respect your need for independence."

Well, good. At least we have that cleared up. "Did we actually compromise on something? I can't believe it."

My mouth drops open in feigned shock, and he squeezes my ass. We are smiling at each other.

"I believe we did, baby."

I'm surprised he hasn't asked me a million questions about my schedule. "Are you worried about how me not being in school will affect us?"

Confidently, he responds, "It won't affect us. We'll adjust where we need to in order to make this work. If you think I would let something like that come between us, baby, you have seriously underestimated my commitment to you. If this is something you want, that's all I need to know."

Just when I think he can't get any more magnificent, he takes his depth of feelings for me to a whole new level.

Nonchalantly, I continue, "Well, there are some additional benefits, but if you're not worried about it at all, there's no need to discuss." It's so much fun to play with him when it's just us.

"And those would be?" His eyes flash with mischief.

"I thought you didn't care?"

At that, Damien starts his own kind of torture as he slowly moves his hand to my sex. *He is going to drive me mad.* If I let this go much further without giving in, I know he will torment me even more.

"Okay. I call uncle. I give," I say through breathy heated laughter. *Oh man. Mental note—no goading unless at a safe distance away.*

As he continues his torturous onslaught, I hurriedly say, "Well, no school means a lot more free time with you because there will be no studying, homework, and papers. Also, I get to make my own schedule as long as I meet the magazine's deadlines, and I can pass shoots on to a freelancer. Whatever the magazine has to pay the freelancer is just deducted from my pay. So, bottom line, my schedule will be more flexible, and with your crazy work schedule, we need all the flexibility we can get." *Shit, that was wordy, but his hands are making me lose focus.*

His soft lips lean down and kiss me. Before I can deepen the kiss, he pulls back, "Now, those are great benefits."

I wink at him. "I thought you might like them."

For the second time that morning, Damien and I make love outside in our screened-in area.

I know it's not going to be as easy as I think. We still have a lot of hurdles to overcome. For now though, I am going to enjoy this moment. The rest will come in time.

CHAPTER
12

Sam and I have been buffed and shined within an inch of our lives. With the amount of makeup that has been caked and sculpted on my face, I could probably open up a beauty supply store. I look completely transformed from just an average Joe to someone who is actually worthy to be on Damien's arm.

My dress is beautiful. I chose a pale pink halter dress that is fitted through the bust and flows from the waist down. Paired with silver translucent heels, I feel like a princess waiting to meet her Prince Charming. Sam has gone with a sexy updo, showing off her bare shoulders and nearly bare back in her emerald long dress. Simply put, she is stunning.

"Girl, we're gonna drop it like it's hot." She gives little snaps and hits her booty to mine.

As she continues to do her little dance moves, I joke back, "Sam, behave. Pace yourself. You're about to be surrounded by a lot of athletes."

"Hmm, I'd love to get sacked tonight."

I hit her on the shoulder and laugh.

She asks, "Do you even get the double meaning in that?"

Double meaning? My brow bunches. "Doesn't it just mean you're getting laid tonight?"

She gives me one of those adoring little pats. "Just checking. Seems I'm going to win this bet with your boy toy."

I roll my eyes at her as I figure the term *sack* has something to do with sports.

∞∞∞∞∞∞∞∞∞∞∞∞∞∞∞∞

As we are walking down the stairs, I look up and freeze midway. At the bottom landing, Mr. Prince Charming himself is waiting for me in his sleek custom black tux that fits his toned body like a glove. His tousled black hair and blue eyes top off the delicious sight perfectly. I wish we didn't have to go, so I could take him back to our room and slowly peel his clothes off his body. When he holds out his hand, my body immediately begins to move toward him.

Belatedly, I realize Sam has made herself scarce to give us some privacy. As I reach the bottom step, Damien closes the gap to where we are almost touching but not quite. My body is alive, zinging with want from being near him. *I can never get enough of this man.*

"You are so beautiful. Part of me wants to keep you hidden from the world, and the other cannot wait to show you off this evening." His reverent tone melts my insides.

"Thank you, but I'm afraid that I'll turn back into a pumpkin after midnight. Then, you'll be stuck with plain ole me again."

"You could never be plain. You are exquisite in every way, regardless of the situation."

I cannot help the blush that creeps up through my several layers of makeup. *I still don't get what he sees in me, but I'm not going to complain about why he loves me.* "Thank you. You are quite dashing yourself. Shall we?" I hold up my arm.

"We shall." He links his arm with mine, and we are off.

The gala is the most formal event I have ever attended. Damien was right about the photographers. They are more focused on the sports legends who really bring in the money shots. A few flashes go off as we walk up the red carpet, but then they quickly move on to other guests. As we step into the ballroom, the room is flowing with champagne and hors d'oeuvres.

Beside me, Sam grabs my arm. "For all that is holy, there is some hot ass in here." The way she says it with admiration in her voice makes Damien and me chuckle. "I'll catch you guys later." After giving us a big wink, she's off to work the room.

Damien keeps me by his side as we continue to make our way deeper into the crowd.

"Wales, glad you could make it. Who's this lovely lady?" The man is an older gentleman with graying hair, and he's slightly heavy around the middle section.

"Harry. This is Allison Scott, my girlfriend. Allison, this is Harry Walters. He's the sports physical therapist for the team."

I extend my hand, and Harry gives it a kiss. Damien's grip tightens infinitesimally on me.

"Nice to meet you, Harry."

"Likewise, Allison. Wales is one lucky man."

Blushing, I retrieve my hand as he gives me a warm smile.

Looking at me adoringly, Damien steps in and responds, "That I am. It was good seeing you."

"Likewise," Harry says.

As the night progresses, it's amusing to see how Damien introduces me to people. With any unattached guys, his hand is possessively around my waist, giving me barely enough room to shake their hand. The unattached women look at me with almost hate in their eyes as if I have stolen their favorite toy. *I must admit that he is a very fun toy to have in my toy box.*

In a lull of conversation, I spot Sam over on the other side of the room. She can definitely be the socialite of the party, and she has several guys eating out of her hand.

Catching sight of where I'm looking, Damien states his observation to me, "Seems Sam can hold her own with these jocks."

I laugh. "Yes, you should bring her on as an undercover secret weapon to get your deals cheaper. They'd never know what hit them."

Damien chuckles beside me, and he continues to watch her interact with the athletes. His wheels are turning, but I don't know what he's thinking about. *I bet that poor man's brain never gets to sleep.* My thoughts are interrupted by Ben's approach.

"Sir, there's an urgent matter that needs your attention."

The way Ben says the word *urgent* flares my curiosity a little.

Before he even has a moment to ignore his responsibility, I say, "Damien, please go. I'll hang out with Sam for a bit and give those poor unsuspecting guys a break. It'll be fine. I'll be fine."

He's about to object, and I decide to give him my no-nonsense look.

"Don't be difficult. The sooner you deal with whatever it is, the sooner you'll be back."

He leans down and gives me a kiss on my neck. "I'll be back soon," he whispers.

"Sounds good."

Damien makes his departure and disappears behind a door across the room. I turn and work my way over to Sam. Without Damien by my side, it is substantially easier to move about. Sam is talking to an incredibly toned blond guy. He's lean and not bad-looking, and he has green eyes that are all for Sam.

When I walk up, I give Sam a little bump on the shoulder.

She makes introductions. "Hey, girl. Allison, this is Mark. He's the quarterback for Damien's team. Mark, this is my best friend and Damien Wales's girlfriend, Allison. "

Subtle, Sam, very subtle.

Mark extends his hand and shakes mine briefly. "Nice to meet you, Allison."

He's being pleasant to me, but his eyes are all for Sam. *She should come with a warning label.*

"Nice to meet you, too."

He turns toward me again. "Hopefully, Sam will get to come with you to some of the games."

Ha! I know that look, and that look tells me he wants my friend in a major way.

Sam puts her finger up to her chin as if she's thinking. "Which team was it that sacked you four times in the same game last year? Maybe that's the game I should attend."

He just looks at her, smiling, like she can do no wrong.

She gives him a little pat on the arm, like a teacher would give a student. "It's okay. We can't win them all."

The way Sam is goading Mark is funny, and I have to work really hard not to laugh. I'm sure he's used to fans falling all over him, so Sam's attitude must be all that more endearing to him.

Feeling like a third wheel in this flirtatious game they are playing, I take the opportunity to leave and find a secluded area where I can get some space. "Hey, Sam, I'm going to go freshen up a bit. Can I bring anything back for you guys?"

"We're good. See you after a while." She gives me a wink.

I know she's about to sink her teeth into her next victim. *Yes, victim…because he'll never be the same.*

"Okay. Nice meeting you, Mark."

"Likewise, Allison."

Trying to repress my laugh, I smile at his excitement over having Sam all to himself again. I like him.

I grab a glass of champagne from a passing waiter as I make my way across the room. I take a seat at a nearly vacated table in the corner.

"Excuse me, miss. Is this seat taken?"

Gah, I cannot seem to find any place to just be alone to think for a few minutes. I smile politely and shake my head. Maybe if I don't start speaking, he will let me be.

"You're here with Damien Wales, correct?"

No such luck. Oh no, buddy, you will not get any brownie points with Damien through me. I smile and nod cordially. Please, please take the hint.

This guy is somewhat attractive, and there seems to be something familiar about him. I could swear I've seen him somewhere. Fairly tall, he's lean and toned with brown eyes and sandy blond hair that is pulled back.

"You don't say much, do you? How long have you and Damien been together?"

"Just a few weeks." It's actually been just right at two weeks, but I'm not getting too specific with this ass-kisser. Then, realization dawns. *Oh shit, this is the guy Damien was arguing with in the hotel in Miami.* I knew I had seen him before. My guard immediately goes up.

"Damien and I used to be business associates. I'm Martin Mills."

My eyes scan the crowd, searching for Damien, because I'm not sure how to proceed with this guy. In Miami, Damien seemed absolutely livid with Martin, but it's not like Damien and Ben have the closest relationship either.

I decide to be pleasant for now. "Allison Scott. Nice to meet you. How long have you known Damien?"

I extend my hand, and he takes it with both of his hands. He holds on just a little too long. *Okay, that's a little weird and too friendly.* I firmly retract my hand and grab my glass of champagne.

He puts his hand to his chin. "Oh, let's see, we were good friends back in school, and we worked together for a few years, so I've known him for a while."

"That's nice."

"Yes, people used to mistake us for brothers all the time. We started off as the best of friends as children, and as time passed, our friendship evolved into a business partnership."

He leans his glass in to toast mine. I clink my glass to his, prior to taking a small sip.

"I haven't seen Damien so captivated with someone in a long time. I can't believe he left you alone, considering how possessive he's been all evening."

I really don't know how to respond to that. It's creepy that he's been observing us at all.

"I'm really glad he's finally trying to move on after the last four years."

Just remain neutral, Allison. You can talk to Damien about this later.

"I probably shouldn't have said anything. I'm just relieved that Damien has finally found someone to take his mind off his ex."

Taking a minute to respond, I look him over as he's watching me. He gives me the feeling that he's trying to stir the pot, so to say. This is something Damien and I should discuss. I should not be listening to his ex-business partner.

"I don't think it's appropriate for you to discuss Damien's past with me.

He smirks in appreciation of my candidness. "You seem like a nice girl, and I just want you to be on the level. Cassandra Williams is Damien's ex, and he hasn't been able to get over her for the last four years. They were engaged, and she left him because of his unfaithfulness and his past. Basically, she got tired of constantly running into his recent bed conquests at events like this, and his past didn't help out at all. Since then, he's been pining after her, hoping for a second chance. Rumor has it that she's here tonight to give that to him."

Refusing to sit here and discuss Damien's past, I get up. Martin follows suit. "Please excuse me. It was nice meeting you, Mr. Mills."

"Martin, please. Do you not believe what I've told you?"

The asshole is continuing to size me up.

"Mr. Mills, I find it inappropriate that you would obviously try to start something behind Damien's back. If you'll excuse me, I'm going to find my date." I start to step away when his hand comes out toward me, and I stop.

He moves slightly in front of me in order to maintain eye contact. "Here's my card." He's trying to give me his debonair smile.

Repulsion is the only thing I feel toward this guy after what he's tried. "Thank you, but I'll have to pass."

He withdraws the card. "Don't say I didn't tell you so when he betrays you one day. He does it to everyone he cares about."

I don't respond as I walk past him, making my way toward the door where I last saw Damien. Part of me wants to throw my champagne all over Martin for his audacity, like the way actors do so dramatically in the movies. *Martin is probably the one behind those texts. Asshole.*

Finally reaching the door, I open it and walk into the room, remembering a moment too late that Damien left me to deal with a crisis of his own.

Holy fuck! The blood drains from my face, and my heart rate triples its pace as I see some woman's mouth mashed to Damien's. At the noise of my entry, he instantly pushes her away with evidence of their kiss smeared on his lips.

Everything goes into super slow motion. An indescribably gorgeous blonde is standing beside Damien. She is tall. I mean, she's as tall as Damien, and her legs seem to go on for miles. Her dress has a very high slit that showcases every one of her assets. *Big boobs...check. Phenomenal body...check. Itty-bitty waist....check. Yep, I think that about covers it.*

Damien looks shocked and petrified. His expression probably mirrors what my own face looks like. When his hand goes up to wipe away her lipstick, I immediately feel sick. I look to my left, and there is an older couple sitting together, holding hands with smiles on their faces. *I need to get out of here...but I have to verify if this is who I think it is.*

In a monotone voice, I ask, "Cassandra?"

She nods and gives me a cat-ate-the-canary smile.

Bitch. It's time for me to leave.

Damien starts walking toward me, and I immediately take steps back.

"Alli, wait."

I shake my head. If I speak, I'm going to end up losing it. There is no way I'll let them see me in a full meltdown. When I turn around, I almost run into Sam. She looks around me. With my back to the room, I take in a shuddering, brokenhearted breath, and she moves out of my way instantly, having figured out what I'd walked in on.

After making my way out of the room, I hear Damien's voice call after me.

"Alli, wait! This is not what it looks like. Sam, move the fuck out of my way." His panicked voice sounds behind me.

Pressing forward, I move quicker and quicker, needing to distance myself from this situation. I know we'll have to talk at some point, but my heart is breaking right now.

As soon as I clear the ballroom, I take off running to the nearest exit. I need to get somewhere fast before I fall apart on Vegas Boulevard.

I run across the street and walk into some random hotel. I use the cash I have in my clutch and get the cheapest room. The only thing I even remember about the hotel is that giant purple fluorescent birds are everywhere.

Since I didn't hear any voices calling after me on the way here, I assume Sam played blocker to let me escape, or Damien just doesn't care what happens to me now that he has Cassandra. *Why'd she have to be so beautiful? I feel so inadequate next to her.* It hurts too much to think about it right now.

Finally, I make it to the room. I flop onto the hard mattress, not bothering to turn on the light. Sobbing in the dark is easier with my broken heart.

Once the tears start, they don't stop. Wracked with sadness, my body shakes, and my chest hurts. A crushing weight won't let up, and I want to let it swallow me. I have no idea how much time has passed before I am cried out. I can't even focus on any one specific thought because I'm so upset. It's a fuzzy, foggy, jumbled cloud in my head.

He said he loved me. We confessed our love, and then I caught him in the arms of another woman. I want to cry more, but I have nothing left to give.

Sam is probably worried. I grab my cell phone, and the screen shows that I have at least fifty missed calls along with numerous text messages and voice mails between Damien and Sam. *I can't deal with all that now. One thing at a time.* First, I text Sam.

> *Me: Thanks for your help. I'm alive.*

> *Sam: Where the hell are you?*

Me: The hotel across the street from the gala. No idea what the name is. Big purple birds. I'm in room 213. I'm sorry if I worried you. I had to get away.

Sam: I understand. I'll be right there. You need anything?

Me: Clothes would be nice. I'm a mess. Thanks.

Sam: No prob. Give me ten.

Me: Okay.

Sam: xoxo

Ugh, I need to talk this out with Sam. She'll help me keep all this in perspective, considering Damien and I have only known each other for, like, two weeks. *How could it be true love just after two weeks? Whatever it was, it hurts like a son of a bitch now that it's over.*

I collapse back onto the bed and throw my hands on my face. *What a mess! What a gigantic screwed-up mess.* I can't even begin to make heads or tails about what went down tonight.

Maybe now that Damien has Cassandra, I can just disappear quietly into the night to lick my wounds. I can't stop myself from thinking about how she is one of the most beautiful women I have ever seen. I don't blame him for pining after her, but I am furious at the fact that he declared his love for me. *Maybe he never thought she would give him a second chance. Well, I should have at least been informed. Face it, Allison, it's not the first time he's omitted something.*

A knock on the door startles me out of my thoughts.

CHAPTER 13

When I open the door, I freeze when I see who's standing there. How can my night get any worse? Well, I have the answer. I was just betrayed by my best friend because she sent my ex-boyfriend to my hotel room even though he had hooked up with his ex-girlfriend while he was dating me. Yep, that will do it.

I try to shut the door, but Damien's foot wedges between the doorjambs, effectively halting the door from closing.

"Alli, listen, we need to talk." His hair is a mess. He's still in his tux pants and shirt, but his jacket has been removed.

Is he serious? "Not tonight, Damien. Please go." I try to push the door closed again. I'm not even causing him to budge. *Ugh, he's as strong as an ox.* If he were at least wincing just a little bit, I'd feel better about my attempts to keep him from entering.

"Alli, let me in, so we can talk, or so help me, we will have this conversation out here in the hall for everyone to hear. It's your choice."

Really, he's agitated with me?

My voice begins to rise as I respond, "You have some nerve coming here and giving me ultimatums after what I just witnessed. Just go."

He's vibrating with irritation. "No! Let me in the fucking room, Alli. We need to talk. If I have to break down this damn door to get to you, I will. You are not running away from this."

Fuming, I stare at him while he pierces me with his eyes. I have two options here—continue to piss off Damien in the hallway in which a scene, a big scene, will be caused...or let him in. *Haven't I suffered enough humiliation tonight? There has to be a reason Sam gave him my location.*

"You can come in on one condition. When I'm done with the conversation, you leave immediately and let me be." He doesn't answer me, and I push the door against his foot to emphasize my words.

Through gritted teeth, he replies, "Fine."

This conversation is probably going to be over before we are even seated if this is how he's going to act.

Moving swiftly toward the only chair in the room, I take my seat with Damien hot on my heels. I need the space the chair provides. It hurts just being in the same room with him. He takes a seat on the couch closest to the chair. Petulantly, I stare at the outdated purple Parisian flowers on the carpet, focusing on the lines in the petals.

"Alli, I need to ask you a question first."

I press my lips into a hard line, trying to keep my temper in check.

"How did you know her name was Cassandra?"

Closing my eyes, I start massaging my temples. *Gah, he's so frustrating and exhausting!* "Damien, it doesn't matter if it really was or wasn't Cassandra. You were kissing another woman."

"Please answer the question, Alli, even if it doesn't seem relevant to you." From his demeanor and tone, he seems to be beyond frustrated, too.

Slowly letting out a deep breath, I try to gather my thoughts and not fall apart in front of him. With all the crying I did earlier, I'm sure my face looks like something from a horror show. At least, it wasn't in front of him.

"Your friend slash ex-partner, Martin, came up to me and tried to stir up stuff. It was obvious what he was doing, and I remembered him from the hotel lobby in Miami. So, I left to find you to let you know. He told me about your past with Cassandra. When I saw you kissing another woman, I assumed it was her. Is it true that you guys were or are serious?"

"Motherfucker. Son of a bitch. Fucking asshole." He starts rubbing his head, and then he stops and looks at me. "You're wrong about Cassandra, baby. You came in at the worst possible moment. She took me off guard, and she did it just as you were walking in. I want no part of her. I only want you."

I drop my head in my hands. "That's what every cheater says when he's been caught." Raising my head, I pleadingly say, "Can we not do this and just end things on an amicable note? If you want Cassandra, you can have her."

Calmly, he responds, "I'm in love with you, Alli. *Us* ending things is not an option. Cassandra means nothing to me. You are mine and only mine. Please tell me what Martin said exactly, baby." His tone and eyes seem serious. He's looking at me like he did earlier this afternoon on the balcony.

Was it really one of those moments when I walked in at the worst possible time, and she had just kissed him? Does he really love me? My heart starts to beat again for the first time since the incident.

Treading carefully, I explain the situation, not letting too much hope take hold. "Basically, he said you were his friend and ex-partner. He's never seen you so taken with someone since your breakup with your ex-fiancée, Cassandra, four years ago. He was surprised you left me with how possessive you seemed toward me all evening. He was glad you were finally trying to move on from Cassandra. She'd left you for being unfaithful and for something in your past. I immediately went to find you because I wasn't about to discuss your past relationship with a man you obviously don't get along with. You know the rest." I lay my head back on the chair and close my eyes. *This is so tiring.*

His velvet words penetrate the black haven I am trying to create. "Think about our time together. Think about the first night I made love to you, and the connection it formed. Think about all our conversations these last few days. Think about this afternoon on the balcony. Think about how it feels when I'm inside you."

Memories, loving memories, flood my mind.

"Now, do you really believe that I would betray that? I'm in love with you and no one else."

Tears start to prick my eyes. "Damien…"

His hand comes out to touch mine, and I open my eyes. The look of grief flashing over his face makes my heart come to life.

I trust him. "I believe you. I still need a more detailed explanation of what I walked in on this evening though because it looks pretty damning."

He leans forward, barely sitting on the edge of the couch, as he holds on to my hand like it's a lifeline. "Can we talk about this with you over here with me? This distance, not having you in my arms, is killing me."

I want to give in to him, but there's too many unanswered questions. "Honestly, I'm barely hanging on here. I need some answers." I stop to try and collect myself as my bottom lip quivers again. I put my sole focus on one of the small pink flowers printed on the carpet.

In two seconds, he's on his knees in front of me. His hands are on my face, forcing me to look him in the eyes. "Oh, baby, I'm yours. Once we get done talking, we are going to leave this rathole and go back to our room. There is no Cassandra and me. There's only you and me. I'm in love with you. Please sit with me. I'm calmer when I can feel you. I'm not sure of everything that went on tonight, but I am going to figure it out, that's for damn sure."

I look into his deep blue eyes, and his sincerity is clear. I nod, not trusting my voice right this second. Before I even blink, he has picked me up, and we are on the couch. In the back of my mind, I think about how Damien looks out of place in this room. It's almost comical to see him on such an ugly piece of furniture.

As soon as he has me safely in his arms, he asks, "What do you need to know?"

A million questions flash through my mind, but I pick one of the more pertinent ones at the moment. "Who's Martin?"

Looking straight into my eyes, he says in a serious tone, "He's my childhood best friend and now ex-partner. I liquidated my part of our hotel business when I caught him sleeping with Cassandra about four years ago."

My head is starting to hurt again with how confusing all this is. "Damien, I am so confused at this point. So, you and Cassandra were a thing?"

"Yes...no...yes, technically. She was a passing interest. I never had any intention of proposing to her. She spun her lies to everyone, saying we were serious and about to walk down the aisle. I knew it wasn't going to happen, but honestly, I didn't care what she said. I knew the moment we called it quits, all of those rumors would be gone. At the time, I didn't see the point in stopping them."

His thumb starts stroking those circles on my arm, and it causes me to relax minutely. Moving my neck from side to side, I try to relieve the tension. I sigh deeply as I try to put the pieces of the puzzle together.

I continue, "That doesn't explain what I walked in on. Actually, it still doesn't explain a whole lot."

One hand drags down his face. "The situation that Ben informed me about was Cassandra being on the premises. I had no idea she was even coming. Through the years, she's been trying to get back together with me, but I have no feelings for her. I swear to you that you're all that I want and will ever want."

I'm twirling some of my hair through my fingers as I look down at my lap. I feel a finger at my chin, and he lifts my gaze to his. He wants absolutely no distance between us.

"Alli, there is no way I am getting back with her. I told her that I'd found someone I am deeply in love with. She started pleading with me to give it another try. I said no, and then the moment you walked in, she grabbed my face and kissed me. Her lips were on mine for no more than a few seconds. I pushed her off, and then all hell broke loose."

The image of him kissing her causes me to focus on the purple shade of the lamp sitting on the end table for a second in order to clear my mind. I let out a deep breath before I can continue. "So, Martin and Cassandra orchestrated this?"

His eyes become tight. "Probably. I haven't seen Cassandra in over six months, and prior to Miami, I hadn't seen Martin in over a year." He takes his thumb and rubs my cheek, and I lean into him. "They've taken it too far by trying to fuck with the most important part of my life. We'll get to the bottom of this, Alli. I'm assuming she's getting desperate because of our relationship and has asked Martin to help sabotage us."

"How long ago did they break up? Why would he help her?"

"They stopped seeing each other shortly after I ended things. I never cheated on her. Our relationship was a little different, but everything we did up until Martin was mutually agreed on." The cold business tone causes a shiver to run up my back, and Damien starts rubbing my arm as he brings me even closer to him. "I assume Martin's motivation comes from when I liquidated my half of the business. It nearly ruined him, and his father had to bail him out."

Geez, these people are nuts. I wish they would leave some kind of instruction manual on how to deal with these people. Quite frankly, I don't speak nut job. I close my eyes, trying to organize my thoughts. My next question bubbles up. "Martin said something about your past was also a problem. Is that true? Or are those just more lies?"

"Yes."

One word? That's all I'm getting? I don't think so. "Damien, I don't need all the details, but you are going to have to give me something to go on here."

He looks at me, torn and thoughtful.

"This isn't an ultimatum. I don't have to know everything, but between this and your incessant worrying over my safety, I need something."

He lets go of me and begins massaging his temples. "Fuck, fuck, fuck." He leans back and closes his eyes. "When I was in college, my sister was kidnapped and taken from the safety of our home. A few weeks later, she was found dead."

The pain in his voice causes a few tears to stream down my face.

"They never found the guy."

My hand instinctively goes to his chest. "Your tattoo?"

"It's Hebrew for Becky, my nickname for her. Her real name was Rebecca. I've had the letters intertwined together to look like a symbol."

The hurt in his voice is palpable with how deeply rooted it is. It makes sense now. I lean in to hug him. We both need this close contact.

"I love you, Alli. I'm sorry you had to deal with that part of my life."

I love being in Damien's arms. It's one of the safest places in the world, and it makes me feel like I can handle anything. "I was heartbroken, thinking you had cheated on me. Cassandra's very pretty."

He stiffens a little at my drastic change in subject. "I used to think so, but she doesn't compare to you."

"Please, Damien. Be serious."

At my comment, he grabs me by the shoulders, so he can look at me. "Oh, I am. You really don't understand how you have possessed me. From the moment I saw you, everything else in my life paled in comparison."

He has such a way with words. I give him a smile, and he gives me one in return, making my insides warm. We lapse into silence for a few minutes while his hand strokes those little soothing circles on my back.

He kisses the top of my head. In a lowered voice, he says, "What would you say to us getting you cleaned up and back to our hotel room? I brought you clothes to change into, and Sam sent some makeup remover. I can't bear to see your tear-stained face any longer."

He is such a beautiful man, and he's mine, all mine. Clutching him to me, I murmur into his chest, "I'm sorry I overreacted and ran off. It all took me by surprise. I'm not used to dealing with this level of deceit. It's overwhelming that people really act this way."

"It's me who should be sorry. I will do my best to protect you from this. We'll work through it, baby. Just trust me. Alli, don't be scared to keep putting yourself out there for me."

Oh, it's good to be back on level ground with him.

He insists on helping me change my clothes and clean the makeup off my face. I know he wants to help me, so we don't have to break contact with each other. When we touch, it's a soothing balm for both of us. Afterward, I feel much better.

"Are you ready to head back now?" he asks.

"Yes."

He starts to pull me toward the door, but he abruptly stops and spins around to face me. He grabs both sides of my face to ensure I look straight into his eyes. "Please don't ever disappear or run from me like that again, Alli. I nearly died, thinking of everything that could have happened to you. You need to promise me that you'll talk to me first. Never run. If you need your space, fine, but don't disappear. I love you."

Thinking about Damien having to relive losing his sister breaks my heart. Without hesitation, I say, "I promise. I won't run, and if I need space, I'll tell you where I'm going."

He nods, seemingly satisfied with my response, and he starts to turn around.

I add, "By the way, Damien, I'm in love with you, too."

Looking to me, he smiles endearingly. "You're my world."

Before leaving, I go to grab my discarded dress off the bathroom threshold.

Damien stops me. "Leave it. The dress is beautiful on you, but after seeing you so upset in it, I would rather not have it in our closet."

Turning away from the dress gives him my answer.

As we head back to the hotel room, Damien's grasp on me is even more possessive than it was at the gala.

"By the way, I got some show tickets today. Do you still want to go tomorrow?"

I take in a deep breath, trying to relieve all the tension that set up shop in my muscles. "Honestly, I don't think I'll be up for it. Can we just spend time together instead? I can reimburse you for the tickets. We've been so up and down today that I would like a day with you, me, no drama, and just room service."

I don't want to sound ungrateful, but I've had too much public interference today. I need time to relax and regroup even if most of that time will be spent with Damien between my legs. My sex clenches instantly at the thought of having him to myself for an entire day.

He softly smiles at me. "I much prefer your plan to mine. The tickets will go to good use. I'll donate them."

∞∞∞∞∞∞∞∞∞∞∞∞∞

I lean my head on him as we make our final ascent to the penthouse in the elevator.

"By the way, Sam is staying in a different hotel room."

I look at him questioningly, feeling like a bad friend. In my plans for never-ending lovemaking tomorrow, I completely forgot about Sam being here.

He senses my worry. "She's fine. I got her a room just in case, but I believe she has a date. She wants you to text her when we get back to the room, so she knows that you're okay."

Hmm, Sam has probably decided to have some fun with one of her athlete friends from tonight. My money is on the quarterback.

I grab my phone out of my purse as we approach the suite door. "I'll go ahead and let her know."

He nods as we walk into the hotel room.

> *Me: I'm back at the hotel with Damien. Thanks for everything. Sorry for the drama.*

> *Sam: Drama is my middle name. You know that. No worries. That was some messed-up shit. She's a total bitch. I would have done the same thing. xoxo*

> *Me: Are you sure you're okay with staying in another room? xoxo*

Sam: Um, if you saw this fine piece of ass I'm with, then you wouldn't have to ask. Thank your super horny boyfriend for me.

Me: Oh geez. Be safe. See you tomorrow.

Sam: Ha-ha.

The living room's fireplace is crackling.

"What do you want to do? I don't want to push you on anything, but I want and need to be inside you. It's how I know we're truly okay," Damien says.

Without a word, I slip my shirt over my head. Damien's watching me closely, not wanting to assume where this is going. Next, my pants slide down my legs, and I kick them off to the side. I'm still wearing the same undergarments that I had on underneath my ball gown. The bra and matching panties are white sheer lace adorned with a pale pink imprint that leaves nothing to the imagination. He's savagely staring at me, and my nipples immediately perk up as the wetness between my thighs increases.

"I need you, too, Damien."

Those magical words are all it takes for Damien to seize control. Graceful and determined, he moves on me like a predator stalking his prey. His hands cup my breasts, and he begins to knead them. "You are so beautiful. You're the most exquisite thing I have ever laid my eyes on."

Moaning, I throw my head back and arch into him. In one swift movement, he grabs my bra and tears it in two. I am barely aware of it being discarded somewhere behind me. His mouth descends on my erect nipple, priming me, working me, building me. He gives each one equal attention as his hands move to my waist where he instantly rips my thong away from my body. *Holy hell, this animalistic approach is such a turn-on.*

He's sucking and kissing his way to my mouth. With the amount of force he's using, I'm sure I'll have some marks on my body after tonight, and that realization only causes my need for him to reach an all-time high.

I go for his shirt to start undressing him, but apparently, I am too slow because he takes a step back and tears his clothes off his body. In two seconds flat, he's on me again, backing me up. I know we are getting closer to the fire because I can feel the heat licking my legs as my bare feet step onto a rug made of some kind of soft animal skin. It seems so surreal. As we lower to the floor, our limbs are wild, moving without our control. Starved for one another, we touch each other to the brink of madness.

Damien breaks the kiss to grab a pillow from nearby before he lays it next to me. Before I have a chance to register what it's for, he has flipped me onto my stomach on top of the pillow. It tilts my ass up into the air at an angle, leaving my sex exposed to his perusing. I might come from just thinking about what will happen next.

"One day, baby, I want to claim your ass but not tonight. For now, I'm going to take you from behind. Eventually though, I will claim and mark every part of your body. Let me know if it's too much."

Turning my head, I look into his blue eyes, which are burning like an inferno. The beast has definitely broken free tonight, and I love it.

"Yes, I need you inside me."

He takes his length and teases my swollen sex with the tip. It's like tickling a scratch. The itch still exists, and it's getting worse with each stroke. I start moving my hips to get some friction. Damien grasps my hip with one hand while the other is resting on the upper part of my back, effectively rendering me immobile.

"Please, Damien. Please."

"Shh." He continues his torture by barely putting the tip of his cock into my sex before withdrawing. "Alli, you're so hungry for me. I can feel you trying to suck me in."

"Please…"

He buries himself inside me to the hilt, and he is so deep in this position. He has rammed so hard into me that the pleasure I feel mixes with just an edge of pain. It is absolutely heavenly. He stretches me in a new way, and I love it.

His hands are still in the same spot, submitting me to his will. He begins moving with a slow withdrawal followed by a quick, jarring thrust in. It's absolute torture. Every time I get to the point of no return, Damien decreases his speed, and I ease away from my climax. Our bodies are sweaty from all the exertion.

"Please, Damien…please!"

"You're mine, Alli. We belong together."

"Yes, yours…only yours."

His dominance has reduced me to a whimpering need. He must be at his brink also. This time, he doesn't stop moving inside me, which results in the most intense orgasm I have had yet. As Damien explodes inside me, he bends down and kisses my shoulder just below my neck.

Damien pulls a blanket from the couch, and we lie satiated in front of the fire, cocooned together and basking in our love. We are lost in the comfort we find in each other.

As I lie in his arms, without thinking, I say, "I can't imagine a more comfortable place in this world."

Damien squeezes me tighter. "I couldn't agree with you more, baby."

"Can I ask you a question about tonight?"

"Sure," he says, looking at me warily.

Considering all that has been revealed, I am sure this is not the most palatable topic of conversation, but I want to reassure him because we have to continue talking. "As long as we communicate, I can handle it. I might need to think or talk it out, but as long as you are honest with me and loyal to me, we can work through it."

"Alli, I will never cheat on you, and I will endeavor to be level with you all the time. What are you curious about?"

He's a little less leery, but I know he would rather focus on enjoying each other instead.

Thinking back to the couple who were sitting at the table in the room, I ask, "Who was the older couple in there with you and Cassandra?"

When Damien's eyes tighten infinitesimally, I can tell he does not want to answer that question.

His lips thin as he responds, "My parents, Meredith and Jon Wales."

Surprised by his answer, I cannot help my quick intake of breath before my jaw drops open.

Stating the obvious but needing confirmation, I press the subject. "Don't they live in North Carolina?"

"Yes. They came with Cassandra. Before you ask, the reason why they were here was because they want me to be with Cassandra."

"Why do your parents want you to get back with Cassandra after what she did?"

"They believe our relationship benefits the family."

I am struggling with the fact that those were his parents in the room with his ex-girlfriend who cheated on him, and they want him to get back together with her.

"What could your relationship with Cassandra do for the family?" I ask.

His tone turns mildly angry. "Our dads are both powerful lawyers in the Northeast, and if we were to marry, they would join their firms and create a conglomerate. That was never my agenda though, and it never will be. They don't believe the truth. They believe the lie she sold them."

His parents sound like horrible people for not trusting their own child. I could not imagine having parents who didn't show unconditional love.

If I were him, I would feel so betrayed. I'm going to need therapy just to wrap my head around all this. "That sounds archaic. Why can't they just join the firms if they want to?"

He's looking at me with such sincerity. "It's an old-fashioned idea the two of our fathers have. They want a tie between families prior to uniting the law firms."

"What lie did she sell them?"

"None of what I am about to tell you is the truth, okay? Please listen to everything first before you jump to conclusions."

I can tell this problem with his parents affects him more than he is letting on. After having such loving parents myself, my heart hurts for Damien. *No wonder he's been withdrawn.*

"Okay, all lies," I say.

He continues to study me, making sure I have registered his request.

This must be one doozy of a lie. I try to reassure him one more time. "I understand that what you are about to tell me didn't actually happen."

He nods this time. "She told everyone that I cheated on her all the time. She said the reason we broke up was because she had gotten pregnant, and the stress from my infidelity had caused her to miscarry. She told my parents I couldn't handle the sadness that accompanied the miscarriage and that I continued to sow my wild oats to work through the hurt. Apparently, she's convinced everyone that she's willing to work with me through my problems because she's so in love with me. My parents find it incredibly romantic that she's sticking by my side through all these troubles."

Oh, what a conniving, manipulative bitch! "Wow…I mean, oh my…I mean…oh, I don't know what I mean." I am so flustered that someone would actually lie about such a topic. I take a deep breath to calm my frustration. "That is seriously screwed-up on so many levels. And you tried to tell your parents the truth?" I look straight into his beautiful eyes. *How could anyone not see this loving man before me? How could his parents believe such toxic garbage?*

"Yes, I did. They've chosen to believe her, so there you go."

He shrugs like it doesn't matter, but I know he must feel different.

"I'm so sorry." Absentmindedly, I start tracing his tattoo. "I bet Cassandra is behind the texts I've been getting."

He tenses immediately.

Oh shit. Oh shit. Oh shit. Why did I pick this time to let my filter slip and disclose this little tidbit of information?

He shoots straight up with me in his arms. "What texts? What the hell are you talking about, Alli?"

"Um, it's not a big deal. I've just received a couple of texts about you since you made our relationship public." I add a little shrug to downplay the situation, but my ploy doesn't work.

"Damn it, Alli. Tell me what you are talking about. Now."

I know I should have told him earlier. "I've gotten two texts. The first one was sent while I was in Homerville. It said, 'He's not good enough for you.' And then, I got a second one on the plane while you were talking to the pilot before takeoff. It said the same thing, but 'Trust me on this,' was added to the message. I just figured someone was trying to scare me because he or she wanted to get to you or something. It's not a big deal."

"Not a fucking big deal? Why the fuck did you not tell me?"

His loud tone causes me to flinch. Still sitting in front of the fireplace, naked, I draw the soft blanket up under my arms like a shield. Damien, on the other hand, has no problem displaying his nudity while arguing.

I must remain calm. "I didn't tell you because when I was in Homerville, I knew you would drop everything to be with me. Before I knew about what happened to your sister, I thought you just overreacted to some things. When we saw each other afterward, I forgot about it because I missed you.

"Then, there was the Brad incident that happened right before I received the one on the plane, so I didn't want to upset you again. I was fine and safe both times. Now, I'm pretty sure it was your ex sending the texts. She's just trying to come between us."

He's so irritated with me. "If you get any more texts, you need to tell me. It is something I could see Cassandra doing. The messages might seem harmless, but you have to tell me immediately if you get another one."

"I didn't mean to upset you. I promise I will tell you if it happens again. Please calm down, and let's just enjoy each other."

I let the blanket drop, and his eyes immediately zero in on my breasts.

"I'm safe, and we're good." I move to straddle Damien, and then I lean in to kiss his jaw as I stroke my sex against his hardening length. Against his lips, I say, "Why don't we try to break a few records tonight? Let's just forget about the rest of the world."

He moans as he captures my mouth, and we become consumed in each other. The heat between us is a fire that can never be extinguished.

CHAPTER
14

Twelve Weeks Later

While packing for a weekend away with Damien, I'm giddy with excitement to have some alone time with him. I can't wait for us to be away from the responsibilities of our worlds.

My life has turned into a whirlwind as of late. It's rare for me to be at my apartment in Waleska. Mostly, I stay with Damien since the magazine's office is much closer to his place than mine.

For the last couple of days, he's been working in North Carolina, and I have had a few photo shoots in Atlanta, so I wasn't able to go with him on his trip. Whenever he's away from me, he still gets nervous about my safety and whereabouts, but knowing about his sister has caused me to be as compliant as possible.

As I finish placing the last few things in my suitcase, the jittery feeling I've had starts to abate. I've missed him, and while we've been apart, I made a gift for him—a photo album of our time together. It's a conglomeration of pictures, some from events we've attended and others I've taken, along with special notes from me to him.

Taking one last look at it before I pack it away, I run my fingers over the cover of the album. It's a picture of the two of us staring at each other as candles glow in front of us at my birthday party.

For my birthday, Damien set up a full day of pampering at the spa for Sam and me. At the end of our last treatment, Sam has to leave unexpectedly for a sorority crisis. As she's waving good-bye, the spa staff bring in a rack of dresses for me to choose from for my dinner date with Damien, and I pick a peach silk baby doll dress with spaghetti straps.

After getting ready at the spa, I head down the staircase to meet my love in the lobby. The air is instantly sucked from me when I see Damien wearing a titanium-colored suit, black shirt, and dress shoes. He is mouthwatering.

He immediately walks up to me and places his hands on my hips. The smell of his spice cologne consumes me.

"You look beautiful. Did you have a good time?"

I lean up and give him a brief kiss. "It was the best. Thank you."

"You are most welcome. Happy birthday, baby. Shall we?"

Smiling from ear to ear, I link my arm with his, and we make our way out to the car. When he opens the passenger door for me, I see a black velvet box with a single red rose on top. I look up at Damien inquisitively.

After handing the box and rose to me, he says, "It's for you."

I flip open the lid, and my heart stops when I see a note written in elegant script.

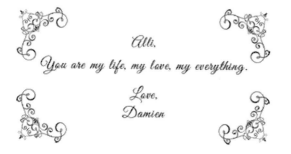

Alli,

You are my life, my love, my everything.

Love,
Damien

Behind the note is a simple silver bracelet with one charm. The diamond-encrusted charm has the letters D and A intertwined in the most delicate, intimate way.

I caress the connected letters. "I love this. Thank you. You've already done too much for me today."

He takes the bracelet out of the box and gently puts it on my wrist. "You are most welcome, and I could never do enough for you. I also booked us a room in the city, so we can have some uninterrupted time after dinner."

Wrapping my hands around his neck, I kiss him with everything I have, feeling my need and desire stir. After he slightly pulls away, we both restrain ourselves as we steady our increased breathing.

Against my lips, he says, "We better go, or we'll never make it to dinner."

I give him a pout, and he nips my lip before assisting me into the car.

Half an hour later, we pull into an upscale restaurant in downtown Atlanta. Walking through the doors on Damien's arm feels magnificent. The maître d' escorts us to a private room.

Right before we enter the room, Damien looks down at me. Anyone within earshot can hear him as he declares, "I love you, Alli."

The mega-grin on my face cannot be tamed even if I tried. "I love you, too."

When he walks me through the door, I am greeted by loud voices yelling, "Surprise! Happy birthday!"

Sam and her parents, Dean and Chandra, are waiting for me. No wonder Sam had to leave the spa an hour early for a supposed sorority crisis. *The moment is perfect as I have everyone I love, everyone I hold near and dear, with me.*

The room is decorated with mostly white roses, my favorite color for flowers. For a dramatic statement, each flower arrangement has one red rose in it.

Leaning down, Damien whispers in my ear. "Happy birthday, baby."

I'm in awe as I take it all in. "It's beautiful. Thank you."

"Each red rose, standing out above anything else, symbolizes my love for you."

Looking up into his crystal blue eyes, I feel the love I never thought I'd have again. A tear slips out as he leans down to give me a sweet kiss.

Smiling, I look down at the bracelet that I rarely take off. I flip through a few pages and stop at a picture of Damien and me in New York City. We're riding on a ferry to see the Statue of Liberty. It was a lovely trip that had resulted from one of our biggest fights to date.

After attending a fundraiser for Sam's sorority, Damien and I head back to my apartment for the night.

We decide to watch a movie, and we get settled on the couch, cuddling together underneath a blanket. As I drape my legs over his lap, I remember Sam's reminder about her friend coming into town this weekend.

"Oh, hey." I give Damien a little nudge to get his attention away from his tablet.

He's handling some kind of problem with a real estate deal he's been trying to close for the last few days.

"I keep meaning to tell you that Sam's friend is staying here for a few days. She had asked a few weeks before we met, and I'd forgotten about it until she said something to me tonight."

That got his attention.

He lays down the tablet and looks at me. "Who is this person?"

"Sam's friend. I don't know him." I give a little shrug.

"Him? What's his name?"

His voice changes, and in that instant, I know he's not going to let this slide.

I playfully nudge him with my foot. "His name is Daniel. I figured I would stay at your place. I'll just need to drop by a couple of times to make sure he's settled."

Damien fishes out his phone and makes a call. "Hey, Sam. I'm taking Alli out of town this weekend. I know your friend Daniel was supposed to stay here. I'll put him up in a hotel instead. It's my treat. Thanks. You, too."

My blood is boiling by the time he hangs up. I pull my legs off of him as I unleash my icy glare on him. "You had no right to do that."

He meets my gaze head-on with a determined look on his face. "Alli, I had every right."

"Um, no, you didn't. I'm not going anywhere with you this weekend, and Daniel is staying here. Don't be ridiculous." I'm so mad at him that my insides are shaking.

I stand up to get some space. I walk into the kitchen and pour myself a glass of water. What the hell? Putting both hands on the counter, I lean my head down and close my eyes, trying to calm my heart rate.

I hear footsteps behind me, and then two arms come around me.

"Alli, don't be like this. Would you want a girl coming to stay at my place?"

I turn around and push him back lightly to get some space.

"Probably not, but I would talk to you about it. I wouldn't become a bitch and just start doing things without us discussing them first." He is about to say something, but I hold up my hand since I'm on a roll. "I get why you wouldn't want me to stay in my apartment with a guy you don't know, but don't order me around. I told you that I would be staying at your place. We are in a relationship, and that takes two of us working together. It is not about you telling me what to do."

He starts pacing the floor, rubbing his forehead as if he's deep in thought. I hate fighting with him. He stops, turns, and then comes up to me. He presses his lips to mine. At first, I refuse him passage, but the harder he tries, the more my will crumbles. When my mouth gives in to his, he kisses me within an inch of my life.

After he pulls back, he says, "I get it. Just the thought of you coming over here by yourself to, I'm sure, one of Sam's fuck buddies had me scrambling to keep you away."

"You can trust me, Damien. I would never cheat on you."

He lays his forehead to mine. "Baby, I trust you completely. It's all those other fucking assholes out there I don't trust."

I put my hands on his hips. "Then, talk to me. Don't just react. We can work it out together until we come to a compromise. I wouldn't want you to feel uncomfortable with something I was doing. Since I figured I would be with you the whole time, it didn't seem like a big deal."

"Even though I fucked up, come with me to New York City this weekend. I want some alone time with you before I have to go out of town next week. We'll have a good time."

Leaning up, I kiss him, giving him his answer, before he hauls me back to the bedroom.

New York was wonderful. Everything was amazing—the shows, the food, and the way he made love to me in the back of a limo.

I turn a few more pages and stop at a picture that appeared in the society pages. Damien and I are at a children's charity event. Sitting together at the dinner table, our heads are close, and we are smiling intimately at each other. It is a picture of pure love.

The unfortunate thing about this event was the reappearance of Martin. It's hard for me to imagine Damien and Martin ever being close friends. People don't change that drastically without having a lobotomy. My mom always said, *A tiger cannot change his stripes, Allison.*

Tonight, Damien's business is sponsoring a charity event for a children's shelter. The room is overflowing with colorful balloons and flowers, matching the shelter's rainbow logo.

As we are seated for dinner, Martin makes his entrance and finagles a seat at a nearby table, sitting directly in our line of sight. He has a beautiful woman with him. She is rail thin with brown eyes and dark brown hair. She obsessively keeps looking our way.

Leaning into my side, Damien whispers, "Her name is Trina. I dated her. I wanted you to be aware in case someone mentions it. She meant nothing to me."

I nod and look back toward Martin and Trina. Disgustingly gross and dirty doesn't even come close to describing how nasty it must be for Martin to keep dating Damien's exes. It would be like eating someone else's leftovers. Yuck. Yuck. Yuck.

In a soft voice, I murmur, "It looks like she'd rather be in my seat than the one she's in now."

The loathing look I am receiving from Trina evidently shows where her thoughts are.

Underneath the table, Damien's hand grabs my mine, and he starts rubbing soothing circles. "I have only loved you. Just keep that in mind, regardless of what they try."

My reassuring smile placates him, but it is obvious he is still tense.

Dinner progresses, and then his phone vibrates.

After looking at the screen, he says, "I need to take this. I'll be right back."

"Okay. I'll be right here."

He gives me a kiss on the cheek before he leaves the table.

As soon as Damien exits through the doors, a waiter drops a note on my plate. Curious, I open it.

> YOU'RE STILL MISSING A BIG PIECE
> OF THE PIE, DARLING.
> ARE YOU SURE THAT YOU'RE SAFE WITH HIM?

Immediately, I put the note in my clutch. I roll my eyes as I mutter, "Juvenile," under my breath. Martin and Cassandra need a new trick.

Just as I close my clutch, the devil himself, Martin, sits in Damien's chair. "You look beautifully stunning tonight. Did you know Damien and Trina had quite a wild thing together?" He looks over at the girl he brought. "Apparently, he couldn't keep his hands off her."

My stomach roils at the thought. Politely, I respond, "Trina, I'm sure, would prefer the company of her date."

He chuckles and then his finger touches my shoulder, causing me to stand instantly.

Damien is beside me, and he moves to secure me behind him. Low and deadly, he says to Martin, "You ever lay one fucking finger on her again, and I swear, motherfucker, you will regret it for the rest of your life. You keep whatever shit we have between us."

Martin smiles, obviously satisfied with the response he received from his actions.

Without saying another word, we leave for the limo.

Damien pulls out his phone the moment the car door closes. "Ben, for events I sponsor, it is your responsibility to ensure the people on the fucking no-entry list don't get a fucking ticket. I don't give a shit. Do your fucking job."

He hangs up the phone, seething.

I wrap my arms around his waist and hug him. "It's okay. We're okay. He's just a prick."

"Alli, the fact that my past keeps trying to taint our future is not acceptable. That fucker crossed the line tonight."

Although the night ended in drama, the look of love in the picture is undeniable. Regardless of what Cassandra and Martin do, the problems they try to create only cause our love for each other to grow stronger.

Looking across the page, I bite my lip at the next memory. We were in Damien's bed at his house. My camera was on the table next to us, and we ended up taking a few candid shots together. While we smiled at each other with tousled hair from making love, I took a picture to freeze the moment of us gazing into each other's eyes.

I trace his tattoo as Damien is drawing lines up my back.

"Alli, do you have any questions about my past relationships?"

He's obviously thinking about the incident with Trina and Martin at the charity event the other night.

I appreciate his willingness to communicate more and more with me. "Are they all beautiful, like Cassandra and Trina?"

He shifts in order to make sure we have solid eye contact. "They pale in comparison to you."

"Smart answer, Romeo."

He chuckles at my laid-back response.

But I have my answer. They were. I have him though, and that's what matters.

"I don't think I want to know unless I need to know…if that makes sense."

Just hearing Martin talk about Trina and Damien pretty much made the decision for me. Unless I need to know, I don't want to. As my mom would say, Alli, you have to find the fine line between knowing when knowledge is power and when ignorance is bliss.

"Whatever you want, baby. Just know that you can ask me anything."

As I sit here and look at the pictures, I'm amazed at how much Damien and I have actually been through together. My heart is completely open to Damien. My mom always said, *Love means giving someone the chance to hurt you but trusting them not to.* Trust is the key to any relationship.

After going through a few more pages in the album, I stop and smile at a picture Damien took of me. He dared me to dance in the rain in front of his house. A week prior to that moment had been a very different scene out there.

After having lunch in the city, we pull into the driveway at Damien's house. He stops the car abruptly. I'm staring down at my phone. I've been texting back and forth with Sam, bantering about Ps and Vs.

Bringing me out of my little rivalry with Sam, Damien says, "Alli, listen, I want you to stay in the car while I deal with this."

"Deal with what?" I look up, trying to figure out what he's talking about.

Then, I spot a car with two people in it. They look oddly familiar. My eyes grow big as I quickly realize it's his dad, Jon, and Cassandra. I wonder what they are doing here. It must be important since they made the trip from North Carolina.

The one time I went with Damien to his hometown, his parents were unavailable to meet me. When Damien said he wasn't close with his parents, he had put it mildly. His parents have crazy ideas of Cassandra and Damien being meant for each other. Considering they think I'm the object standing in the way of their son achieving true happiness, I'm not sure I really want to meet his dad right now.

Before Damien has a chance to respond to my question, I say, "Oh."

"Yes. Oh." He scrubs his hand down his face. "I don't know why they're here. I'll deal with it."

He starts to get out of the car when I grab his hand. "We'll deal with it. Together."

He looks torn.

"They can't say anything that will change how I feel about you. Plus, it might help for them to see that we're a united front."

Since Vegas, Cassandra has continued to try and get in touch with Damien. So many times, I have wanted to send her a dictionary with the words stalker, liar, infidelity, loyalty, bitch, *and* irritant *highlighted.*

Damien nods before extricating himself from the car. He comes to the passenger side and helps me out. Jon and Cassandra exit their car, and we meet them near the front door. Damien and his father look alike with their similar builds and same hair color. The most notable exception is the color of his dad's eyes. They are a pale green versus Damien's enigmatic blue. His mother must be the one with the blue eyes.

Damien is holding me possessively by his side. "Father, Cassandra, this is Allison."

Jon looks at me. "Allison."

I smile at him. I'm about to say something when he glares at Damien with obvious dislike for me in his eyes.

"We'd like to talk to you alone," Jon says.

Talk about an awkward encounter with the parent and the ex-girlfriend.

"Allison and I are together, Father. I suggest everyone understands that."

Damien's tone shocks me. Speaking to my father that way would have never happened. Then again, my parents wouldn't have ever dreamed of doing something like this.

At that, Cassandra musters up some excellent tears as she leans into Jon for support. I want to yell the word traitor *to his dad, but I refrain. The more pressing need is to slap some sense into both of them.*

Jon responds, "Damien, it's time to get out of this phase you're in. We just want what's best for you. You can't keep running from all the pain. At some point, you are going to have to face all your mistakes."

Cassandra pats his dad's shoulder as she looks at Damien sadly. "I forgive you. Come home to me. She's trying to trap you."

The situation is getting out of control, and I can feel Damien tense, preparing for a strike. Oh shit.

Damien steps in front of me. "I will not tolerate either one of you disrespecting Alli or my relationship with her. She is the most important thing in my life. I suggest you both back the fuck off." He turns abruptly and wraps an arm around me before he starts walking us to the door.

Cassandra calls after Damien, "How can you say that about a gold-digging whore who is probably trying to get pregnant and trap you? She wants your money, sweetie."

That's it! *That's the straw that broke the camel's back.*

Before Damien even has a chance to respond, I spin around. In a scary tone I didn't even know I had, I say, "You might have everyone fooled with this little charade, but you're not fooling me. I'm not the one who screwed up by sleeping with his best friend." Turning to his dad, I keep going. "I cannot believe you buy into these lies. You should be ashamed of yourself."

With that, I turn and walk inside the house without looking back.

The thought of Cassandra and her lies just makes my blood boil. I have yet to meet Damien's mom, Meredith, and honestly, I'm not looking forward to when that time comes.

Flipping through the last few pages, I smile at the photos of Damien and me at his house. I used the timer function on my camera to capture these moments of us together. In one, he's spinning me around in front of the stables in his backyard. The next one was taken after a picnic. We're lying on the grass beside each other, looking up at the sky. Finally, I stop at the last picture of us. We're kissing while snuggled up for movie night in the den.

I close the album and store it at the bottom of my bag, so Damien doesn't accidentally see it. *I hope he likes my present.* I head back to my closet to look for my teal button-up cowgirl shirt. *Ugh.* I've come to realize that the thing I hate the most about living in two spots is that my stuff goes missing in the transition. There's no telling where I put it or misplaced it.

After zipping up my suitcase, I check the thermostat and turn it down a few more degrees. In the last days of August, the heat in Georgia has been brutal. Last week, Sam started back to school, and she has been thriving on all the social events that come with a sorority. I don't miss school at all though. It's actually a relief that I have started my career. Being a photographer is what I am meant to do.

When my phone pings, I see a text from Sam.

> *Sam: Hey, girl. Are you still going to Texas this weekend?*

> *Me: Yes, I can't wait. What's up?*

> *Sam: Having a party next weekend and want you to come. '80s theme. Please say yes! You haven't come to one yet.*

> *Me: I'll be there. I promise.*

Sam: Great. Tell Mr. Worrywart that it'll be fine. Have fun. xoxo

Me: You, too. xoxo

Oh, Damien is not going to be pleased. His party-thwarting days are coming to an end. Sam has been patient with him since he's always sweeping me away every time something comes up, but I know she's about to put her foot down, and Sam's way is much more abrupt than mine. Sometimes, she and Damien are so alike that it's scary.

When I hear keys jingling at the door, I cannot help but run through my small apartment to wait for who will greet me from the other side.

Damien and I exchanged keys right when he began persistently pushing me to move in with him. It seemed to placate him since it further tied us together. Although I wouldn't need his keys to get into his place since he has staff at his house at all times, he seems to like the thought that I could get in if the Wales compound were ever in complete lockdown. He's adorable on so many levels.

As soon as he clears the doorway, I throw myself into his arms.

He kisses my neck sweetly. "Hey, baby. Sorry I'm late. Guess you're glad to see me?" He spins me around while giving me a good and proper kiss hello.

As he sets me down, I breathlessly say, "Of course I am. I'm even more excited about where you are taking me this weekend. And you're forgiven for being late."

He smells divine, and with his denim-clad thighs and button-down shirt, he looks like he just walked off a magazine shoot. *How can someone always be this incredibly sexy?* He brings his mouth down again for another kiss. I feel so loved and cherished by him.

"Are you almost ready? I have your favorite plane fueled and ready whenever you are."

Yes. Oh yes. I jump up and down like a little schoolgirl. This trip just keeps getting better. Since Vegas, we have taken the plane with the bed every time we fly somewhere for a getaway. It really is a classy way to travel. Being wrapped in my lover's arms makes the time fly by, no pun intended.

"Let me grab a few more things, and then I'll be ready to go. Texas, here we come."

"Hurry, and we'll be on our way."

I cannot help the bounce in my step as I make my way back to the bedroom. I can hear Damien chuckling from the other room.

He's taking me to the ranch he inherited from his grandparents when they died.

As I return with my suitcase, I tell him, "I can't believe I get a whole two days with you to myself out in the country. What's not to be ecstatic about? Plus, think of the trouble we can get into."

I give him a big kiss on the cheek as he smacks my ass, and we make our way out the door.

CHAPTER
15

It's the middle of the day when Damien and I emerge from his bedroom. Like everything else Damien owns, this home is absolutely stunning.

While Damien is taking a quick phone call in the office, I grab his gift from the bedroom and then decide to look around the house. It's fashioned after a log cabin. Both the inside and outside décor are done in a manly rustic theme. The backside of the house has floor-to-ceiling windows looking out to the large wooden deck and prairie. It reminds me of those log towns I used to build as a child.

Walking outside, I lay his present on the chair seat and then make my way to the deck railing, gazing out to the prairie. The stables and barn are done in complementary woods to match the main house. As the wind sways the dry grass in the distance, the scent of wildflowers permeates my nose. *I could live here forever and be completely content.* I decide that I'll take some photographs for my collection before we leave.

While I'm standing on the back porch, lost in my thoughts, I feel two arms come around my waist.

"Do you like it here?" Damien nuzzles my neck with his nose.

Absorbed in the ambiance, I lay my head back against his chest. "Of course I do. You have such a lovely home. It's like a dream."

"I was hoping you would like it. I came here a lot as a child when my parents didn't need me to climb the social ladder. It's always felt like home to me."

My heart melts a little as I listen to him. He misses his grandparents like I miss my parents.

He continues, "It could be your home, too, if you would move in with me."

He makes it sound so romantic, but I must stay the course on my decision.

"Oh, Damien, we've talked about this. It's just too soon."

Momentarily, he pauses at my words. I try to make my voice soft and understanding, so he doesn't get offended, but my voice goes up a few notches when he runs his nose along my jaw. *Gah, he's going straight to playing dirty to try and persuade me to move in with him.* He resumes his assault as he begins sucking on my neck. Goose bumps form in his wake.

"Yes, but I don't like the answer I've been getting. I've been asking for two months, and you have yet to say yes. I want you to move in with me, Alli. It's time."

"We've been through this. I want to keep my place for now. I will continue to think about it. As my dad would say, I'm taking it under advisement. Plus, I already stay with you every night you're in town." My thoughts are starting to become less coherent as he keeps touching me.

He makes it to my earlobe and gently bites down. He whispers, "That's not an answer, and you know it." He continues kissing my neck. "I love you, Alli. What's causing your reservation? Do you think I am not serious about us?"

He raises his head and turns me to face him. His blue eyes are drilling into me, trying to penetrate my thoughts.

How am I going to answer this? Geez, now would be a good time for some type of interruption. Why is it when I want privacy, we are constantly interrupted? And now, no one is around. Good grief!

We maintain our connection as we look into each other's eyes.

He asks, "Do you need more of a commitment from me?"

"Damien, I know you're committed. I just need to be ready." Honestly though, I do feel like it's putting the cart before the horse. I don't want to officially live with anyone until I am married, but telling him that seems like I am pushing for a proposal.

"What are your thoughts on marriage?"

Oh shit, he's narrowing in. He's like a bloodhound, searching for why I keep saying no to moving in with him. Why has he decided today of all days to be so intuitive?

A general response—that's what I need. Think…think…think. Okay, I'll go with what I know. "My parents had a wonderful marriage. I think it's a beautiful thing between the right people."

Our eyes are still locked in a trance. *This conversation took a huge left into very serious territory.*

"Would you like to see more of the grounds?" he asks.

Whoa! Now, we've just taken a severe right. It reminds me of riding in the car with my dad when I was a kid. He would be driving along, and all of a sudden, he would start moving the steering wheel back and forth as he said, *Captain, captain, she's out of control.* I could not stop giggling at the jarring motion. But this type of swerving right now is causing me to be carsick.

I take a deep breath to calm my nerves. "That sounds great, but I have a gift for you first." I go to the table, grab the box off the chair, and hand it over to him. A wave of excitement rushes through me.

He gives me a curious glance before he tears open the box like a kid on Christmas morning. Immediately, he sits down and starts looking through the album, staring at the photos and reading the notes. He doesn't say a word, but the happiness on his face tells me I have made, using his world's terminology, a touchdown.

He stands, swiftly walks to me, and brings me into him. "I love it. I love you. Thank you. It's the best gift I've ever received."

"You're welcome. I love you, too. Each time you flip through that, you can see how much I'm head over heels for you."

He slowly leans down, and our lips meet. His tongue swipes for entry, which is immediately granted.

I'm about to try and deepen the kiss when he pulls away.

"Do you want to go horseback riding with me and see more of the ranch?"

I cannot hide the excitement in my voice. "Yes."

"How well do you ride?" Although he's very pleased with himself for planning this next adventure, he's still concerned for my safety.

I give him my best no-nonsense look. "I did grow up on a farm. I might be able to show you a thing or two, cowboy."

He gives me that damn smirk before he makes a phone call. "Please have two horses saddled and waiting at the north side of the barn in fifteen minutes." After putting the phone back in his pocket, he grabs his gift and then my hand. "Come on, let's get changed, cowgirl."

∞∞∞∞∞∞∞∞∞∞∞∞∞∞∞∞∞

We are both dressed in jeans, button-up shirts, and cowboy boots as we head out to the barn. When I glance inside, I see a perfectly clean floor and sparkling rails on the stalls. I'm not sure if this can even be called a barn with how grand and clean it is.

At the end of the barn are two beautiful quarter horses. I can tell that they are purebred. One is a blue roan, and the other is a brown buckskin. They're dazzling. The buckskin whinnies at our approach. I walk up to her and let her get used to the smell of me while Damien sits back and observes.

Turning my head to him, I ask, "Which one is yours?"

"I don't have a specific one I ride. I take it you want to ride Amanthia?"

I look back at the buckskin. "Amanthia, you are such a pretty girl." I smile at Damien. "Yes, yes, yes, I would like that very much."

He gives me one of those endearing smiles as he stands and approaches me. "Would you like some help mounting Amanthia?"

In return, he gets one of my playful as-if looks when I mount her by myself. Sweetly, I reply, "I think I've got it."

I head out into the field, forcing Damien to hurry and catch up with me. When he does, he sets the pace abnormally slow, and I roll my eyes at his obvious actions. He's probably scared I'm going to get bucked off, but I can feel that Amanthia wants to stretch her legs.

From in front of me, Damien calls out, "I helped my grandfather build that pump house one summer. I hit myself so many times with that damn hammer. I'm lucky I still have my fingers."

"Ah, poor baby." I make a clicking noise, and Amanthia trots us up next to Damien.

Here's my chance. I squeeze Amanthia lightly with my legs and heels, giving her the signal to go faster. When I start to pass him, I yell, "First one to the pump house..." I leave it open-ended as I take off toward the goal.

"Yah! Yah!"

Amanthia takes off like lightning.

From behind me, I hear Damien shout, "Alli, stop! Wait! Fucking hell, woman. You're going to kill me."

He'll lighten up when he realizes I can actually ride really well. When I look back, I can see that Damien is catching up to me, so I kick Amanthia into another gear. She is absolutely amazing.

When I make it to the pump house first, I start to gloat. "Hmm, looks like I won. I'm going to have to make you pay up, big mister."

He ignores my bragging as he looks at me with pride and awe. "Alli, where did you learn to ride like that? I knew you could ride, but you're really good, exceptionally good."

Memories of my mom teaching me how to ride flood my mind, and I smile. "Mom was a riding teacher before she had me. She taught me how to ride on a pony when I was three. I grew up with that pony, and Mom and I would spend hours riding together."

We continue moving forward to what I think is a lake in the distance. As we make it to the water's edge, we dismount and let the horses rest and drink.

Damien leads me to a large tree by the shoreline. After we sit, he pulls me onto his lap, so I'm straddling him.

I like where this position is going. "Thank you for bringing me here."

"Anything for you, baby. What happened to your horse?"

I knot my fingers in my lap and look down at them. He knows I had to sell the farm when my parents died, but I haven't shared what all that truly meant. *Maybe talking about it will make it less painful.* "I had to sell her when I sold the farm. There's not a place at Sam's parents' house to keep a horse properly. It was the right thing to do for her. I miss her, and I've kept in contact with the new owners. They are really good to her, and that's what counts."

In an instant, Damien starts to console me. "I'm so sorry, baby, for everything you've had to endure. If I had known you existed, I would have kept you from having to go through that pain."

Times like this, feeling his unconditional love, are when I miss my parents and home. I lay my head on Damien's chest and listen to his breathing. Being wrapped up in him is a soothing balm to me. I am so glad to have Damien in my life. He fills a void I thought would never be filled again.

We stay there for who knows how long, just listening to the birds singing to each other, as the horses graze on the prairie grass. *It's so peaceful.*

Damien soothingly asks, "Are you ready to head back? I wanted to make love to you out in the open prairie, but now, I really want you back in our bed."

I've noticed how he has started using the word *our* to describe things he technically owns all the time. It used to be sporadic but not anymore. *If it gives him peace of mind, so be it. We both know the truth.* I think part of him wants me to argue about it, so I'm the one bringing up the subject of moving in with him.

"Yes…although the prairie does sound like fun."

"Not tonight, baby, but we will soon. It's going to be our bed tonight. I want to make love to you slowly."

I like the commanding tone he uses when it comes to matters of our love life. It makes me shiver in anticipation. Casually, we make our way back to the horses, hand in hand.

As I am about to mount Amanthia, Damien asks, "Will you ride back with me? I want to have you close."

"I'd like that."

The ride back is set at a leisurely pace with my head laid against his shoulder. Amanthia's reins are tied to Damien's saddle as she follows. *This is my new favorite way to ride for sure.*

As we near the barn, in a voice made for sin but soft as velvet, he tells me, "I love you so much, Alli. You are my complete world now."

"I love you, too…so much. You've brought me back to life, Damien."

After leaving the horses where we met them at the barn, we walk up to the back porch and head inside the house. Damien leads me straight to his room and makes sweet passionate love to me.

CHAPTER 16

The week following our return from Texas has gone by in a blur.

Just arriving home from my biggest photo shoot yet with the magazine, my phone rings. When I hear Damien's ringtone, I automatically smile. He had to leave on an emergency business trip to North Carolina, and with my planned shoot, there was no way I could accompany him.

Sweetly, I answer, "Hey there, stranger."

"It's good to hear your voice. How was your shoot?"

He sounds tired. I know he's been working a crazy amount of hours.

"Great. Chris is a fantastic mentor. I love it so much."

Forty years my senior, Chris was the retiring photographer I'm stepping in for. Now, he's decided to stay on as a freelancer. He'll help out when I'm not available to do shoots, giving me more flexibility with my schedule. It's the best of both worlds for us.

"I'm glad. Everything should be finished today, or I'm shipping both the manager and the player's asses off." He lets out a sigh of agitation. "Fucking sports drama. I hate it. I need someone to handle this shit."

From what I've gathered, the manager and the running back, whatever that person does, were having issues with each other regarding contract obligations. Lawsuits were threatened, things were said…*blah…blah…blah.*

Trying to ease his annoyance, I respond in a flirty tone, "Aww, well, I'll soothe away your irritation tonight when you get here. I can guarantee you that there will be no sports talk from me with what we'll be doing."

His voice turns seductive as he says, "That's right. I still have that bet to win against Sam. How about we stay at your place tonight and head to our place tomorrow?"

Just the insinuation in his tone causes shivers to run up my back.

Then, I hear a door opening and closing in the background. "I gotta run, baby. Love you."

"Sounds good. Love you, too."

After we hang up, I remember that I need to talk to Damien about the note I accidentally found on his desk after he'd left. It's not something I want to discuss while we are apart. Situations like this should be talked about in person to avoid any miscommunication. I now understand why he waited to disclose information to me in the past. I've tried to make sense of it, but I can't get anything to add up.

We are in his bedroom. Damien is getting his clothes together for the impromptu meeting in North Carolina. Damien's been in a state of chaos with all the sports drama that ensued this morning. I can't travel with him because I'm in charge of a big shoot in Atlanta today. Since I started working at the magazine, this will be the first time I'm taking the lead as head photographer.

As he finishes packing his bag, he says, "Alli, I'm sorry I have to go out of town all of a sudden. I hate that I won't be here this evening to celebrate your first day of being the lead for the shoot."

Before I can respond, there's a knock at the door. Damien answers it, and someone hands him a large envelope. He checks his watch, and then he takes off toward the direction of his office.

When he returns five minutes later, he seems agitated as he gives me a kiss. "I'll miss you. Have fun today and congratulations. Love you, baby."

"Travel safely. Hurry back as soon as you can. Love you, too."
Poor guy. He looks as if the weight of the world is on his shoulders.

He kisses me thoroughly before grabbing his suitcase and sprinting out the bedroom door.

As I'm getting ready to leave for the day, I remember I left my camera in his office. I'd used his computer yesterday to download pictures from our picnic. After heading that way, I walk over to his desk and reach for my camera. I catch sight of the envelope that was delivered to Damien. A part of a torn note is hanging out of it, and I wonder if he might need it for his business trip. Thinking he accidentally forgot it, I pull it out and read it.

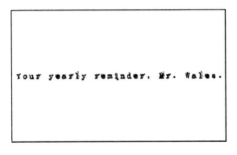

Your yearly reminder, Mr. Wales.

I have no idea what it means, but I make a mental note to ask Damien as soon as he gets done dealing with his current crisis at hand. As my mom always said, Being nosy never pays off. How right she was.

I start packing a few things for a weekend away in Atlanta with Damien. Deciding on what to wear for our dinner date, I try to find my damn red scarf that I want to pair with my black dress, which is at Damien's house. *Gah, this living in between places is getting more and more annoying.* My search is interrupted by a phone call. I grab my phone and see that Sam is calling.

"Hey, Sam."

With music blaring in the background, she says, "Hey, girl. What's going on?"

"Oh, the usual. Damien's coming home this evening, and then we're headed to his place tomorrow. Finally finished the big photo shoot today, so I'm about to lie on the couch and take it easy."

"Oh no, you don't," she says, using her no-nonsense tone.

Confusion laces my response. "No, I don't, what?"

"You are not getting out of this party tonight, Allison Scott. If I have to drag your ass over here, I will. You have to come to my party tonight."

Shit, shit, shit! I have to go, and I completely forgot to tell Damien about it. *Hell, I completely forgot about it.* "Of course, I'll be there. It's just been a long week, and it slipped my mind. I cannot wait to pull out your dad's famous sprinkler move. You know, the one he's constantly showing us from his archives?"

She starts laughing. "Oh gosh. Please don't. I'll have to disown you if you do."

I can tell Sam is very pleased that I am coming, which makes Damien's potential wrath worth it.

Teasingly, I add, "Wasn't it called the dean special?"

"Allison, not funny."

I hear all sorts of commotion on her end, and I can tell she's on the move.

"You want me to swing by and pick you up? Then, Damien can get you from the party later. I got us both some stuff to wear tonight. I can be over in twenty. I'll honk when I get there."

Oh, that's right. It's an eighties theme party. I want to slap myself for forgetting. "Sounds good. You're the best. See you in a bit."

"Bye, girl."

I am going to be in so much trouble. The party doesn't start for another few hours. He's going to worry because he is not fond of the idea of me attending a college party. I throw my head back against the couch, dreading the impending argument.

My doorbell rings, momentarily taking my mind off the nuclear bomb I have on my hands. Peering through the peephole, I see a flower guy holding a massive bouquet.

As I open the door, he greets me, "Flowers for Allison Scott."

I can barely see the head of the delivery guy behind all the flowers. "That's me." *They're beautiful.* There must be at least two-dozen white roses with crimson tips. *Absolutely stunning.*

I sign for them quickly, and he hands them off to me.

"Have a good day, ma'am."

Damien's beautiful gestures know no bounds. Rushing to the kitchen counter, I eagerly open the card and read the elegant script.

Thinking of you...

It makes the guilt of what I'm about to do a hundred times worse. I know how he'll be concerned about me going to Sam's function this evening. It's not like he keeps me in a locked cage, but the death of his sister has caused him to worry excessively, and I try to be understanding. They were incredibly close, and I get it, but Sam's done so much for me, so I need to be there for her. I feel like I'm being pulled in both directions.

Should I call him or text him? Since he's in a meeting, I decide to text him. When I grab my phone from the kitchen island, I notice I need to charge it. *I'll do it once we get to Sam's.* As I start to type my message, a car honks. It must be Sam. Focusing on anything that allows me to procrastinate a little longer, I decide to text Damien from the sorority.

I rush out the door and into Sam's car. She is bouncing with excitement behind the wheel.

As she starts driving, Sam says in a hurry, "We are going to have a blast tonight. I think it's going to be our biggest party yet. You won't believe the outfits I found for us."

"Geez, Sam, what are you on? I'm only getting about half of what you're saying because you're talking so fast."

She's practically jumping in her seat, and her black hair is a crazy mess as she moves. "Girl, we're gonna drop it like it's hot."

"I'm excited. When we get there, I need to text Damien to let him know."

As we are pulling up to the sorority, I know it's about time to break the news to Damien. My stomach starts to knot, thinking about how irritated he's going to be.

Sam looks at me, noticing my discomfort. In a sassy tone, she says, "Oh, he needs to lighten up. It's a college function."

Sam doesn't know about his sister. It's not my place to tell her, and Damien tends to be secretive about his life.

I shrug my shoulders. "He just worries." *Ugh, I'd rather be subjected to watching sports for twenty-four hours than deal with this.*

I get out of the car and head over to the side of the front porch. "Let me text him, and then we'll get our party on." I smile and give a little shake, which she returns.

> *Me: Hey, I'm at Sam's. Will you pick me up from here when you get back?*

> *Damien: Absolutely. What are you girls doing? Should be there around ten p.m.*

Okay, that's not so bad. I'll be at the party by myself for only two to three hours max. He should be able to deal with that.

> *Me: Oh, girl stuff, a little party. Have the adolescent jocks worked out their problems?*

> *Damien: What kind of party?*

Oh shit, here we go. Of course, he's honed in on that one teeny-tiny word in my text. *I wish I could have just omitted it altogether.*

> *Me: It's an '80s party.*

> *Damien: Is it one of Sam's house parties?*

> *Me: Yes. You have nothing to be worried about.*

When my phone starts ringing, it startles me, and I realize I have been holding my breath. It's Damien.

In a sweet voice, I answer, "Hey, there."

"You're not going to the party, Alli, and that's final." His tone is not as sweet as my greeting, and it makes me cringe.

Keeping everyone's feelings in mind, I try the reasonable approach. "Damien, I promised Sam, and I forgot to tell you about it. I'm sorry, but I have to go. I haven't been to one yet because each time she's had one, we magically have out-of-state plans. I'll be here for only two to three hours max."

"Alli, you need to get in your car and get your ass back over to your place."

His commanding tone has my temper slightly flaring.

"I didn't drive, and there's no harm in me staying. Stop being irrational. It's a college party. I'll be fine." My irritation is coming through my voice, regardless of how calm I am trying to stay.

"I'm not fucking around here. Do as I ask. Now!" he yells.

I don't think so. I'm all for reasonable discussions, but yelling is unacceptable.

As I'm about to respond, Sam plucks my phone out of my hand. She has that no-nonsense look on her face. *Shit, the bomb I'm holding just went active, and it's about to explode.*

With her hip cocked, she says in a sassy tone, "Wales, this is girl time. I'm invoking a no-phone rule. You get her all the time, and now, it's time to share."

I can hear Damien's voice on the other end, and he's not happy.

"She'll get her phone back after the party starts. See you soon. Muah." She gives me a wink as she hits the End button.

Balancing my relationship with Damien and my friendship with Sam has been more difficult than I expected.

Instantly, I have a headache from how wrong this has all gone. It happened so fast. He knows I hate it when he orders me around without talking it through. My phone has been ringing incessantly. I go to grab it from Sam, and she moves it out of my reach.

"No, no, no. This is girl time. He can chill." The phone continues to ring as she laughs. "Boy, he is a tad bit possessive and controlling. He must really like his P in your V."

That does it. We both burst into a fit of giggles. It's immature, but that just seems to come out of us when we are together.

The party will be fine, and then maybe he'll lighten up some. Sam stows our phones in the coat closet as mine continues to ring.

Forcing the stress from the drama to the back of my mind, I look around. "You guys are getting this place into pretty good shape. All the pink makes me feel bubbly."

"Yeah, we have to add some more green. We might have gone a little overboard. It looks like Pepto threw up in here."

I nod and press my lips together. *Better it come from her than me.*

She grabs my hand and pulls me along. "Come on, it's time to get spiffed-up."

As we climb the stairs to Sam's second-floor room, I notice the liberal application of pink continues upstairs. Since she's the president of the house, she gets one of the few rooms with its own bathroom. Her room is painted in a neutral color with pink and green accents.

When I see our outfits laid out on the bed, I know I made the right decision in coming. I can tell she has put so much effort into them. The outfits are identical in style. The only difference is that one is pink, and the other is purple. She's even chosen lots of accessories to go with each outfit.

"Oh, I likey, Sam."

"Good. I get the pink one."

"Perfect. Please tell me we have a hair crimper."

She scoffs. "Do not insult me. We are going to rock this joint with our eighties getup."

She plops me down in a chair in front of a vanity. As she starts brushing my hair, I look around at the mess before me. There are eye shadow cases with colors that should be banned, cans upon cans of hairspray, a crimper, a teaser comb, and a massive amount of scrunchies. *Getting ready like this every day seems like it would be painful.*

Laughing, I look at Sam in the mirror. "We are going to look like clowns."

Sam parts my hair and starts crimping away. "Hey, don't knock what my mom says was the greatest decade ever."

"If you say so." I pick up the teasing comb, eyeing it with fear, as I put a mock look of horror on my face.

"I do say so. Keep still. This thing seems like it could be deadly." She begins snapping the crimper, like it's a mouth coming to eat my hair.

I move my body away from her, giggling. Our chortle boxes have been turned on. "Shit, Sam. Tell me you have used one of those things before."

"Oh, ye of little faith. It'll grow back if I singe it."

This time, I give her a real look of horror.

"Oh, stop being a baby. Why do you think I wanted you to go first?" She continues snapping the damn thing with an evil little look on her face.

I cover my eyes as she goes to town. I say a silent prayer that my hair stays intact as Bon Jovi's "Livin' on a Prayer" plays. *Yep, that seems about right.*

∞∞∞∞∞∞∞∞∞∞∞∞∞

Once we're ready, we look like quite the dynamic duo. Eighties music has been playing the entire time we've been primping. At this particular moment, Cyndi Lauper's "Time After Time" is playing. With our pretend mikes up to our mouths, we are singing to each other as we dance and shake it across the room. We are belting it out as if we were rock stars in the making.

We look ridiculous dressed as eighties pop-star divas. I am wearing a black camisole and pettiskirt with artfully ripped black hose and purple leg warmers. To accessorize, my middle section has a black-and-purple splattered corset, and my hands are tucked into fingerless see-through gloves. Complementary beaded necklaces and bangles have been liberally added. Large purple hoop earrings add the perfect touch to my rocker-crimped hairstyle that is singe-free.

"Girl, we're gonna drop it like it's hot." She gives her best Roger Rabbit dance impression.

Mimicking her dad's sprinkler move, I add, "Girl, we were born in the wrong decade. The B-52s have nothing on us."

"Bet your ass they don't." We continue dancing around, and then Sam suddenly stops. "Allison, on a serious note, thanks for coming. I know Wales didn't want you to stay, but I appreciate you hanging with me tonight."

"No problem. He just gets nervous about things like this, especially after Vegas. I know he's a tad overprotective, but we're trying to find a middle ground with each other. I'm still your best friend, and I'm always here for you."

She comes and gives me a hug. "I know. I just miss you so much. I miss us hanging out all the time. Don't get me wrong. I'm happy for you. You guys are good together. You keep his temper at bay, and he brings you out of that shell. It's a good mix."

"Thanks, Sam. I'll always be your bestie."

"And I'll always be yours." She pulls away with a smile. "I think we should head downstairs."

"Let's go, girl."

Interlocking our arms, we leave the room. When we get downstairs, the party is in full swing. We must have lost track of time when we were dancing around in her room.

Sam retrieves both of our phones, and she hands me mine. *Damn, I forgot to charge it, and it's almost dead.* As suspected, I have several missed calls and texts from Damien. I'm following Sam, but I fall back a little as I open only the last text since I need to save my battery.

> *Damien: I'm on my way. I will be there as soon as possible. Please stay near Sam and be safe. I love you. Keep your phone on you. Stay away from Brad.*

Besides one apology text after Sam's inaugural sorority function, Brad has completely left me alone. He's the least of my worries, and I don't understand why Damien is so bothered by him. I text back, hoping to ease his concern.

Me: I have my phone again. Battery dying. I love you, too. Will stay near Sam. No worries about Brad.

I feel better knowing Damien will be here sooner rather than later. *He'll see that everything is fine, and hopefully, he won't worry so much.*

Catching up to Sam at the bar area, she asks, "Is everything okay?"

"Yep, Damien's on his way. Shall we go show this party how to really dance eighties-style?"

She grabs my hand. "Let's get this party started!"

Cheers erupt around us as we make our way out to the floor. We shimmy and shake and laugh while we attempt dance moves, like the elevator and the lawn mower. The fact that these are actual dance moves has me laughing the hardest as we try to replicate them.

The party is getting crazier and crazier by the minute. *Only two more hours at most until Damien gets here.* I'm anxious and excited to have him back.

Heading to the bar area in the kitchen, Sam and I snag two seats and grab some beers. Our pop-star diva outfits have been getting a lot of attention.

Another guy comes up to us. Leaning on the countertop, he drunkenly slurs, "You ladies are the hottest ones here."

Sam responds, "Thanks, but I think there are some hotter ones on the dance floor."

The idiot pushes off the counter and starts stumbling that way as we roll our eyes at each other. A bunch of girls from the sorority join us. While they're talking to Sam about where she got our clothes, I notice Brad and a girl walking in through the back kitchen door.

He gives a slight nod toward me and then goes back to chatting up his newest conquest. It reinforces my feelings that he was just being a prick since I had turned him down a few times when I first started dating Damien. However, per my promise to Damien on the night we left the Hitchin' Post, I send him a text.

> Me: *Hey, no need to worry. I'm with Sam, but I wanted to let you know that Brad just arrived. He's with a date. Can't wait to see you. xoxo*

Of course, after my phone sends the message, it decides it is out of juice and dies. *Great, just great.*

One of the guys who was with us that night we went to the Hitchin' Post comes wobbling up to the counter. He flops his elbows down in front of me, and he reeks of alcohol. He slurs, "So, Allison, where's that hotshot boyfriend of yours?"

"He'll be here shortly."

This guy is completely inebriated. He just nods and strolls off. *Weirdo.* He probably wanted to get some insider info from Damien, like everyone does when Damien attends events.

I turn back to the conversation at hand.

One girl says, "He actually thought by saying 'Are you religious? Because you're the answer to all my prayers,' would get him a boob shot. Um, I don't show these girls just for fun. You gotta work to get a show."

We all start laughing as she shakes her boobs. *I'm glad I came.* I needed some group girl time. I can see why Sam puts up with all of this. The sorority is not my deal, but I see the reason behind loving it so much. The sorority gives a sense of sisterhood, and I'm so glad Sam has found this while I have Damien.

All of a sudden, two guys start pushing and shoving each other, and we all rush away from the kitchen bar.

One of the girls mutters, "Fucking Neanderthals."

It's a short-lived quarrel. When they clear the area, we all resume our seats and conversation. The girls are repeating the cheesiest pickup lines they have heard tonight. I'm trying to concentrate on the conversation, but my ability to focus is getting worse.

I look down at my cup, and I'm only halfway through my beer. Suddenly, my body starts to feel really hot and flushed. *Maybe if I splash some cold water on my face, I'll feel better.* I don't have a high tolerance for alcohol, but almost one beer shouldn't affect me like this.

Leaning over, I tell Sam, "Hey, I'll be right back."

She shoots up an eyebrow in question. "You want me to come with you?"

"No, just going to the bathroom."

She gives me a wink and resumes her conversation.

The music is blaring as I make my way up the stairs. *Man, I feel really off.* My body is becoming more flushed, and now, some dizziness has set in. *Maybe I'll lie down for a minute.* Finally making it to the bathroom in Sam's room, I lean on the sink, turn on the water, and wet my face. The cool water feels good, but it's not helping.

Oh man, it's just getting worse. The room is actually starting to sway a little. I feel tired, and my vision is becoming blurry. *I'll lie down for a minute, just a minute, and all will be okay.*

Just then, I hear the bedroom door shut. *Oh, thank goodness, Sam didn't listen to me.* I stumble out into the room and stop dead in my tracks. *Oh fuck!*

"Hey there, princess. How are you feeling?" His voice has a vicious sneer. "I'm glad to see that your boyfriend decided to let you out of his sight, so you can play. I've been waiting all summer for this chance."

Oh no, this is not good, not good at all. I stumble to the side, and he mirrors my direction. It is taking every ounce of energy to focus on staying coherent and upright.

I have to get out of here. "It's good to see you, Brad. Gotta go. See you around." At least, that's what I hope I said in my slurred state.

Brad takes off his red leather jacket and places it on the bed. Next, his black T-shirt is whipped over his head, and then he undoes the top button of his red leather pants.

Oh shit. I need to get out of here now. My brain is on a delayed reaction. I make a move for the door, but he catches me by the waist, pulling my back to his front. He buries his nose into my neck and takes a deep whiff. *How disgusting.* I shiver at the contact and not in a good way.

"Oh, you smell so good. You're trembling with want. Princess, I'm about to deliver exactly what you're asking for."

I can smell cigarettes and beer on him, and my stomach turns. I start to struggle and scream as best as I can in my state. "Let me go!"

The noise from the party is so loud. Brad spins me around, and slaps me hard across the face. I instantly see stars. If he wasn't holding me up, I would have fallen to the floor.

"Not yet. I've waited so long for this, princess. We are going to enjoy this, and you will be quiet. Next time you scream, I'll knock you unconscious."

When I try to fight him again, he harshly throws me onto the bed, knocking the breath out of me. *What is wrong with me?*

"You've been teasing me with your cunt since I met you. I was just giving you time, but then you started dating that bastard. He's so possessive about you that you must be great in the sack. I'll be the judge of that here in a minute."

I whimper and try to move, but my limbs are so heavy. I am fading fast. I need to hold off until I can get out of here.

Brad is towering over me. "You won't remember this in the morning. It will all be a hazy dream. The drugs should be running through your system by now. In a few minutes, you won't even struggle, and you'll welcome my dick in you. Better yet, you'll like it, even more than that pussy you have as a boyfriend."

I say a silent prayer to get me out of this situation. This is one of my worst fears coming to life. *Please, please, please stay coherent just a little longer.* I need to figure out how to get to the hallway.

Brad bends over me and rips my corset from my body. When I try to get away, I receive another hard slap across my face. The pain radiates from the same place as before. *This cannot be happening.*

He starts to go for my skirt, and I muster up everything I have and kick ferociously. I land one solid kick to his groin with my stiletto boot, giving me the chance I need to escape. I fumble off the bed and land on my knees. Instead of wasting the energy to stand, I crawl on all fours across the room.

Brad is moaning in the background. *I hope I impaired that asshole for life.* I finally reach the door. My world is definitely closing in. Using my hands, I pull myself up and fumble to unlock the door as a fog starts setting in. Forcing the knob to turn is almost too hard.

Brad yells, "You bitch! Get back here!"

His voice spurs me into action. Using my adrenaline, I wrench the door open and stumble clumsily into the hallway. Brad continues to curse louder and louder in the background. Just as I am about to reach the stair landing, I consider throwing myself down the steps. Suddenly, I see Damien bounding up the stairs at an unprecedented pace. His eyes and face look worried, and his motions become frantic when he sees me.

"Damien," I slur.

He's at me in two strides, and I collapse into his arms. Finally, I can let the oblivion take me under. I know I'm safe with him.

"Alli! Alli, what's wrong, baby? What happened?" He's searching me over with his hands and eyes, desperate to see if I'm okay.

I can see the panic on his face, and I feel the tension in his body.

"Brad...drugged...me." It's all I can get out as my eyes close. The darkness is calling for me.

"Fuck! Alli, baby, stay with me. You have to stay with me. You are going to be fine."

I want to respond, but I can't as I go farther into the abyss.

CHAPTER
17

Beep...
Beep...
Beep...

I vaguely hear a sporadic beeping noise in the background. *What is that?* I see vague images, but they're like a fuzzy black hole. I can't see past the darkness.

The last thing I remember is being at Sam's party. Everything after that is just blank, regardless of how hard I try to hold on to it. I try to open my eyes, but it causes me more anxiety because it feels as if two-ton weights are on each lid. I hear another beeping noise that's slightly faster. Lethargically, I will my eyes to open. It's semidark in the room, and it takes me a moment to adjust my vision. Then, realization dawns. I'm in a hospital room.

The monitors surrounding me cast an ominous glow. My head hurts so badly. I have an oxygen mask on. *What happened to me?* When I turn my head slightly to my right, I see Damien resting in a chair next to me. His eyes are closed, and his hand is holding my hand on the bed. He looks exhausted. Sam is sleeping on a couch behind him. *I wish I could make sense of this.* My mind feels so choppy. I use my other hand to slowly push the oxygen mask off my face.

"Damien..." It barely comes out in a croak. My throat is so dry.

Damien hears me and immediately leans forward. "Baby, you're awake. Oh, thank God. Do you need anything? How are you feeling?" His blues eyes are bloodshot as he looks at me with worry and so much love.

When he leans down to give me a kiss on the forehead, I realize he is in one of the most disheveled states I have ever seen him in. His clothing is severely wrinkled, and he looks like he hasn't shaved for at least a day. I want to reach out and comfort him, but I can't with how heavy my body feels.

By this point, Sam has heard the commotion, and she is at my other side with tears streaming down her face. Still in her costume with ratted crimped hair, she looks just as atrocious as Damien does. From the looks on their faces, I guess that this is really serious. Other than the drowsiness, nausea, and headache, I feel like I'm all intact.

Damien is staring at me, waiting, and I realize belatedly that he asked me a question.

"Water. What happened?" My voice still sounds all hoarse and crackly. It honestly feels as if sandpaper has been rubbed up and down my throat.

Damien punches the button above my hospital bed. "Please send in the doctor. Alli is awake." Grabbing my hand, he starts rubbing those circles. "Hold on, baby. I'll get you some water as soon as the doctor looks you over, okay?" I nod. "We'll explain everything in just a moment. I just need to know you're okay."

In less than a minute, a doctor and two nurses arrive. The doctor is a middle-aged man with graying brown hair. He's physically fit and has kind eyes.

"Good evening, Allison. I am Dr. Ferguson, your personal physician. Do you remember what occurred last night?"

Sam grabs my hand.

Again, I try to reach into that black hole and grab anything. "I was at a party with Sam, and then it all goes blank."

Sam starts to sob beside me. I squeeze her hand with what little strength I have. When I glance over at Damien, I can see his neck muscles are twitching with tension.

As the doctor reads the papers coming out of the machine beside me, he asks, "How do you feel?"

Automatically, I respond with what comes to mind. "My head hurts…my body feels really heavy…my stomach hurts…I think that's all, but I'm really confused. What happened?"

"That's to be expected. I want you to keep your eyes open and follow my finger."

I do as I am told.

"Now, look into the light."

I do as I am told.

"I am going to test some of your reflexes."

I sit there, and my body seems to react appropriately when different spots are hit with that mallet thing.

No one is telling me anything, and not knowing why I'm in the hospital is making me more and more anxious by the second. "Please...someone tell me what happened."

Damien goes to speak, but the doctor beats him to the punch. I have no doubt that his years of training are kicking in. He knows to give the patient an explanation in a straight and factual manner without attaching any emotions. It's probably what I need at this point.

"You were given a drug called Rohypnol, which causes memory loss, confusion, and abnormal sight. That is why you do not remember what happened. There were no signs of sexual assault. All of your head scans have come back normal. It appears you sustained one or more heavy blows to the face. You have been out for approximately twenty-four hours, which is to be expected. Withdrawal from Rohypnol is the most critical during the first twenty-four hours. So far, you have not experienced any adverse effects from it. With that being said, we will still need to keep you under observation for the next two to three days to ensure there are no lingering side effects."

I am stunned into silence. *I was drugged? How did I let something like that happen?* I need some answers. "Do we know who drugged me?"

Damien is the next to speak. "She would like some water. If she is allowed to eat any food, please order her some. I would prefer non-hospital food for Alli. You should have the number to call to make such requests from my staff."

Dr. Ferguson nods and turns to the nurses. "Keep it simple. Broth for now."

They respond in unison, "Yes, sir," and leave the room.

There are so many words swimming in my head with no explanation. *Drugged…sexual assault…withdrawals…blows to the face.*

Who did this to me?

CHAPTER 18

One of the nurses arrives with a drinking container and straw. *Thank goodness.* My throat is so scratchy that it hurts to talk.

"Miss Scott, I'm Nurse Tina. Here's some water for you. Please take slow sips to begin with, so your stomach can get used to having something in it. I'll be stationed right outside your door if you need me. Your soup has been ordered from the restaurant, and it is on the way. It should be here within thirty minutes."

I take a small sip. The liquid relief is heaven. "Thank you."

She smiles and makes her departure.

Now, I need answers. I turn to look at Damien first and then Sam. "You guys, please tell me what happened. I know what the doctor said, but I'm starting to freak out." When my voice wavers at the end, that beeping noise starts to increase. It must be my heart rate monitor.

Sam bursts into more tears. It's unnerving to see Sam like this. She is normally so controlled. Barely able to speak through her sobs, she says, "I'm so sorry, Allison. I'm so sorry."

"Sam, don't cry. I don't know what happened, but I know you didn't hurt me." I put my hand back on hers and squeeze.

When I look over at Damien, I can tell he hates how Sam is feeling this way, but he hasn't tried to ease her guilt at all. *He must blame her for something.*

With one hand still holding mine, Damien's other hand runs over the stubble on his face. "Sam, let's just walk Alli through everything. You can't blame yourself for what that fucked-up, sick bastard did."

The way they're acting toward each other tells me something happened between them, too. He stands, pulls up a chair for Sam, and resumes his position in his chair right next to me. He starts rubbing soothing circles again on my hand. I need this contact with him, and he knows it.

He looks at me, giving me his full attention. "Baby, what is the absolute last memory you have of last night? That way, I know where to begin."

I think about it, but all I have are fuzzy memories. Something starts to take shape, and I grab it and focus. "There was a fight in the kitchen between two guys, I think."

Sam nods her head. The tears have stopped, but her body is still recovering from all her crying.

Damien dips his head slightly in acknowledgment and takes a deep breath. I've never seen him this shaken.

"The two who fought in the kitchen have confessed to their part in this after they realized the wrath of hell they were about to receive. They still will to some extent. Fucking assholes." His face is absolutely menacing. "That fight is when they switched your drink out for a drugged beer. After some guy figured out I wasn't there, the fight was staged just so that could happen."

Another memory comes to the forefront. "There was a drunk guy who asked me about you, I think."

Sam nods, confirming my statement.

Damien's jaw clenches. "After the fight, you went up to the bedroom to use the bathroom. We aren't sure what happened while you were in there because Brad refuses to speak. He has lawyered up."

My mind feels jumbled. "Brad did this?" I cannot believe he did this. He hasn't said a word to me in months.

Damien looks at me. "Yes, he came out of the room while I was with you in the hallway. From the bruises that have appeared since the attack, we assume he hit you pretty hard on the head."

My hand automatically goes to my face, and Damien's fingers gently brush one of the bruises. His touch is tender, but his eyes are filled with pure fury.

"Where is he?" I ask.

"Police custody at the moment. I nearly fucking killed him when he came out of the room. He was shirtless with his pants unbuttoned. We found one piece of ripped clothing in the room, but other than that, it doesn't appear he touched you anywhere except your face. Thank God." He closes his eyes and takes a deep breath.

This is taking a toll on him. His imagination has probably been running wild, thinking about what went down in that room.

"Did you get to the party earlier than expected?"

He continues, "I started to come home as soon as I knew you were going to be at the party. I was landing when you sent the last text. I tried to call you immediately, but your phone was dead. When I called the house phone, no one was coherent enough to get me through to you. I made it to the house in record time. After Sam told me where you were, I tore through the house to make sure you were safe, and I found you coming out of her room, barely able to walk and talk. You told me Brad had drugged you, and then you passed out."

I shudder as I think about what could have happened. Damien's free hand is gripped so tightly that his knuckles are white against his tanned skin. While grinding his teeth together, his jaw is drawn to the point that it's about to snap. His blue eyes are on fire with irritation.

Part of me is glad that I don't remember the encounter, and the other part of me feels so violated to have something like that taken from me. I never thought something like this could happen to me, but it did.

Sam goes to stand up from her seat beside me, and I give her a questioning look. I still feel so disconnected from everything right now. It's almost as if I'm in a dream.

"I'm going to give you guys some alone time. You need it. I hope you know how much I love you, Allison."

I lift my arms for a hug, and she obliges. *My poor best friend is unnecessarily blaming herself for this.* "Sam, it's not your fault. Go get some sleep. I love you, too. Will you come by tomorrow, so we can talk when I'm not so out of it?"

She nods and gives me another squeeze before she starts to leave the room.

As she's heading for the door, Damien says, "There's a car waiting for you to take you back."

With her head hanging down, she responds, "Thank you," and then she disappears into the hallway.

I need some alone time with her soon to make sure she's not punishing herself for all of this.

"Damien—"

He cuts me off with a kiss on my lips. It's gentle but possessive at the same time. My face must look horrendous because he's not grabbing it like he usually would when he needs to show me that I'm his.

Pulling away, he whispers against my lips, "Baby, over these last twenty-four hours, I have said so many prayers, asking God for you to be okay. You could have died. I can barely keep it together when I think about what that fucking idiot did to you. I love you, Alli."

A tear slides down my cheek from the pain I hear in his voice. "I love you, too. I'm sorry I didn't listen."

"Baby, all that matters is that you're okay."

The severity of the situation is going to hit me eventually. I think my brain has just distanced itself from my emotions to keep me going while I recover. It's just hard to reconcile my mind with something I have no memory of.

The nurse enters, carrying a tray. "Miss Scott, your dinner has arrived. It's chicken broth with tiny bread dumplings. Eat slowly." She lays the tray in front of me, and it smells heavenly. "Let me know if you need anything else."

"Thank you."

She leaves, and I take my first bite. It's the best thing I have ever had in my life. I'm so hungry. Damien watches in appreciation as I finish it off.

After my last bite, Ben comes into the room, and he looks at me with sympathy. "Good evening, Miss Scott. I am glad you are doing better. Is there anything else you need?"

It's odd seeing Ben in jeans and a T-shirt. He always wears suits.

"No, Ben, thank you for your help." I say as I give him the best smile I can manage at this point.

"No problem, and you're welcome." He turns to Damien. "Sir, the requested items from your home have been packed in this bag. If there is nothing further, I am going to retire for the evening, but I will be on standby if anything else should arise."

As Ben lays the bag down at the foot of the bed, Damien says, "That's all, Ben. Thanks for your help."

Damien removes the tray and pushes the button to start reclining the bed. *It's nice that we're alone finally.*

"Why don't you get some sleep? I'm sure your body is exhausted," he says.

"Will you lie down with me?"

"Alli, I don't think that's a good idea. You need the rest."

Pleadingly, I respond, "I sleep better with you beside me. Please."

He's so torn, but the moment he pulls off his shoes, I know I have my answer. He needs to be close to me as much I do him.

Lying beside me, he gently envelops me in an embrace. I snuggle into him as best as I can, and then I begin to drift off to sleep.

Right before I go under, listening to the sound of his breathing, Damien says, "I love you, Alli. I'll thank God every day for the rest of my life for not taking you."

∞∞∞∞∞∞∞∞∞∞∞∞∞∞∞∞

A squeezing sensation around my arm causes me to stir and open my eyes. Nurse Tina is taking my blood pressure. I look around the room and notice that Damien is gone.

"Where's Damien?" My voice is dry.

"Oh, good. You're awake." She automatically hands me my cup with straw. She moves to the monitors and pushes some buttons. "Mr. Wales needed to make a phone call, so he stepped outside. As soon as we get you situated, we'll let him know you're awake. How are you feeling this morning, Miss Scott?"

"Better, I think."

I start to sit up, but the nurse is right there, pressing buttons to bring my bed into an upright position. She has an excellent bedside manner. Her bright red hair is done up into a neat bun. *I don't think I've ever seen hair that red in my life.* Behind her calm nurse demeanor, she seems like she would be an absolute no-nonsense firecracker. It suits her perfectly with her short, pudgy stature. I immediately like her.

"Lunch should be here in half an hour. Is there anything I can get you?"

I notice my pressing need. "I need to go to the restroom."

"Absolutely. Let me assist you." Nurse Tina goes about lowering the rail on the side of the bed.

When I try to get up on my own, she steps in, halting my progress. Using her stern tone, she says, "Miss Scott, let me get your robe, and then I'll assist you. Please lie there for just a moment longer."

Yep, definitely a firecracker.

She brings me a purple silk robe, and then she aids me out of bed. When I'm standing, she helps me put the robe on.

"This way, Miss Scott. Please lean into me as much as you need to." Nurse Tina puts her arm around my waist as she helps hold me up. "If you start to feel light-headed, please let me know immediately."

"Okay, thanks." My body feels a little out of sorts, and my head hurts, feeling like a freight train ran into it. Other than that, I feel kind of okay.

Our progress is an easy pace, mainly due to Nurse Tina setting the speed, but we finally make it.

After doing my business and washing my hands, I close my eyes and prepare myself to take a first look in the mirror. I refused to look at it when we first walked in. Raising my head and taking my first peek, my mouth falls open. There's a girl staring back at me, but it's an ugly image. I think I see me somewhere in all the bruises. One side of my face is a solid purplish-black bruise. My reality crashes as I reconcile the fact that Brad did this to me.

This is serious on so many more levels than I even thought. Seeing my battered reflection and having a clear head to think about it all is sobering. I look away, not wanting to see that haunting face staring back at me again. That face has endured something horrendous.

"Alli, where are you?" Damien's voice sounds from outside the restroom.

Before I have a chance to say anything, the efficient Nurse Tina replies, "Mr. Wales, we will be right out."

As I step away from the mirror, the nurse stays by my side as we make our way back to a waiting Damien. He comes up to me and Nurse Tina takes one step back, giving a little space.

He looks me over from head to toe as he addresses the nurse. "Thank you, Tina. We'll let you know if we need anything else."

Being effectively dismissed, she makes her way out of the room without a word.

Gently pulling me to him, he kisses my forehead as I wrap my arms around him. I need for him to hold me. The emotions inside of me are starting to spew out as the damn bursts. Now that I've seen the damage to my face, it brings the gravity of the situation to light.

As I sob into his chest, Damien must have known this was coming. That's why he ensured we were alone. "Shh, you're safe now, baby. You're safe. Everything is going to be okay."

"I'm so sorry. I should have listened. I could have been...he could have..." I cannot continue through the sobs.

"Shh, he didn't. Don't think about that. It didn't get that far, baby. Let's get you back in bed."

He picks me up and gently lays me on the bed while I'm crying hysterically.

After my body purges itself, Damien gently says, "What do you need, Alli? Anything is yours. Just name it."

"I just need you to hold me for a while. I know I don't remember what happened, but the severity of the whole situation just came crashing down on me. When I saw my face, it all became reality." My voice is choppy from the crying.

Pulling me to him, he says, "That I can do. Come here. I wanted to be with you when you first saw your face."

He sits on the bed beside me, and I cuddle up into him.

"Sam came by again this morning while you were still sleeping. She is going to stop by again later. Also, the officer needs to come and talk to you today. Is that okay?"

"Yes, that's fine. You'll be here though, right?" The thought of Damien leaving my side while the officer asks me questions terrifies me because I don't know what I'm going to say since I don't remember anything.

"Baby, they couldn't drag me away at this point." His tone is affectionate as he strokes his hand up and down my arm.

Thinking about all his worry and what he had to endure with his sister causes me to get emotional again. "I'm so sorry, Damien. I should have listened. How did you know Brad would be such a threat to me?"

He's rubbing my back now, and some of the tension starts to ease from my body.

"I had no idea he would go to that extreme. If I did, you would have never been there in the first place. I just knew he wanted you. My misjudgment nearly got you raped."

My body shivers, thinking about what could have happened. "There's no way we could have known. Please don't blame yourself. Have they said when I can go home?"

He lets out a cleansing breath. "Dr. Ferguson is working on that now. He's been appointed as your private physician along with the two nurses. I told him that I would prefer to have you looked after at the house. Once the results come back from this morning's blood work, we'll know when you can be released and moved home."

Do hospitals have private physicians? That doesn't make sense.
"What do you mean by private physician and nurses?"

"I made a sizeable donation in exchange for the stipulation. I needed to know you were receiving the doctor's full attention in case anything happened." He pulls me to him, and I feel a slight shudder in his body.

"Damien...there's—"

"Don't argue, Alli. Not on this. We've both been through a lot. I thought I lost you, just like I did my sister."

At that, my heart breaks for Damien and for what he must have suffered through over these last twenty-four hours.

The nurse comes in with a tray of food. "Here's your lunch, Miss Scott. Mr. Wales, more flowers have arrived. What would you like for me to do with them?"

"Make arrangements for them to be delivered to the house. We are hoping to leave this afternoon."

Before she leaves, I say, "Thank you."

It's another fabulous meal with a different kind of broth soup and the same little dumplings.

Remembering the tension I sensed between him and Sam, I ask, "Are you upset with Sam?"

"Yes."

I stop my spoon midair as I just stare at him. *That is so unreasonable.* "Why? Are you upset with me, too?"

"No, I'm not mad at you, baby. My anger toward Sam, I know, is completely unfounded, and I'm working on it. But that fucking policy about no phones, so you can disappear during girl time is done. No more. I almost lost you. I know she's your best friend, and I would never make you choose, but she's not going to interfere in our discussions and relationship again. Those are things for you and me to decide, Alli. If there's something you want to do, we decide, not Sam."

I feel like he's not telling me everything about him and Sam, but right now, I'm just going to let them work it out. The panic he probably felt from this experience comes to the forefront of my mind.

"Going forward, we'll work things out together, you and me. But you need to *talk* to me without demanding me to follow your orders. This whole relationship thing is so new to me. Our relationship is my first priority, Damien, as it should be." I can feel him smiling into my hair before he kisses it.

Sam arrives moments later. She looks worlds better than she did last night, but a deep worry is still emitting from within her.

Leaning into me, Damien whispers, "I'll be right outside. I think you two need some time together, too."

So, he doesn't mind me being with Sam. He just wants to be more involved in the terms when I'm not with him. I can live with that.

Cautiously, she approaches. "Hey, how are you feeling?"

I motion for her to sit on the bed, and she gives me a smile as she walks toward me. Her green eyes are sparkling with so much emotion. Her long dark hair is thrown up into a haphazard ponytail. She still looks exhausted.

"I'm okay. I just had the first of many meltdowns, but I'm coping. It all seems surreal since I can't remember anything."

"I think that's to be expected. Are we okay?"

She bites her lip, and I reach out and grab her hand.

"Of course we are okay. I want to talk to you about something."

She looks worried. "What's that?"

"Stop blaming yourself. You and Damien had nothing to do with the sicko's plan. It's none of our faults."

I can't believe the relief I see in her face.

"Love you, girl."

"Love you, too, bestie."

She gets on the bed and hugs me, causing us both to burst into tears. *My emotions are out of control today.*

As we start to settle down, Sam leans her head against mine. "So, I'm starting an awareness program to help educate students on how to avoid situations like the one you were in last night. I'm meeting with the university board this afternoon to discuss. We are going to put a huge emphasis on girls speaking up against sexual assault and knowing it's not their fault."

More tears start falling down my face. "You're pretty damn special, Sam. If there's anything I can do to help, let me know." She gives my hand a squeeze. "What happened after I passed out?" I ask, knowing she'll give it to me straight.

She takes a stuttering breath as we sit there together. "Damien came into the house in a panic, looking for you. He tore off up the stairs, and I followed. When I came up, you were out cold in his lap. He was trying to wake you up as I kneeled down beside you. You were lifeless. All color had drained from your face, and your breath was shallow. Brad came out of my room, calling you a whore and a bitch. Damien handed you off to me, and then he pummeled Brad's ass. It took four guys to peel Damien off of Brad."

For a second, she stops to take in a deep breath. "From there, Damien came rushing back to your side. When someone announced the paramedics had arrived, he carried you downstairs and left in the ambulance with you. He didn't leave your side the entire time."

Hearing about the aftermath through Sam's unfiltered mouth makes my stomach drop. "Is Damien in trouble for hurting Brad?"

"Charges might be pressed, but he has a huge team of lawyers on it, so I highly doubt anything will happen."

More tears start to fall down my face. The thought of Damien getting into trouble for that just feels wrong.

"He'll be fine, sweetie. I'm going to apologize to Damien for taking your phone away from you and for not letting the two of you handle the disagreement about the party." She gives me a reassuring look.

"Sam, you don't need to do that. I was just as much a part of that as you were. For now though, I need Damien to know that I'm safe, so I'm going to be a little more understanding of his overprotective actions. I know he'll be on edge for a while, so just be patient. I don't want you to think I'm choosing him over you, but I can't let him worry, especially after what just happened."

Sam's eyes glass over as she tries to hold back her tears. She lays her head down beside mine, and we begin whispering back and forth, like we used to as kids.

"I get it, and I understand. I won't get involved in your relationship with him again. You're strong enough to handle him yourself." She gives me a wink. "I just miss seeing you all the time, but I know that our lives are evolving. We will always be best friends. As long as he treats you right, that's what matters. It's just hard sharing you." She looks at her watch. "I need to get back to the sorority for a meeting. Love you, girl."

"Love you, too."

With that, Sam leaves with some pep back in her step.

⸎⸎⸎⸎⸎⸎⸎⸎⸎⸎⸎⸎⸎⸎

Damien strides in shortly after and sits down next to me. "How did things go with Sam, baby?"

"Good…great. She's my best friend in the whole world. I hope you know that I let her take my phone. It wasn't under duress. I wanted to show you that I'd be okay, and I'm so sorry for that." I start to choke up. "Sam never meant to disrespect our relationship. This has been an adjustment for her…and me, too. It's not a bad change. It's just different from what we are used to. Unless you try to take me out of her life forever, Sam will respect our boundaries."

He kisses me on my head. At this point, he's avoided touching my face because of the terrible bruises. "Baby, I'd never do that, and I know her actions weren't meant to lead to what happened. I just need to know you're safe."

"I don't want to worry you."

He kisses my forehead as all that sinks in. "On a happier note, the doctor said we can go home."

I cannot help my answering smile. "What about the officer?"

"He'll just have to come to where you are."
Thank goodness. A real bed sounds so good right now.

CHAPTER 19

"You are cleared to resume all normal activities, Miss Scott. Your bruises are healing nicely, and they should be gone within the next week or so. Please call the office if any new symptoms should arise." The doctor lays a business card on the kitchen table, and then he starts packing up his things into his bag.

"Thank you, Dr. Ferguson, for everything." I pick up his card and put it into my pocket. I like him as a doctor. He has a calm bedside manner that doesn't ratchet up my anxiety.

He snaps his bag shut and picks it up. "You are most welcome, Miss Scott."

He walks out of the house.

It's been three days since I was released from the hospital. Since then, this is the first time I can remember being alone. Between Damien, Sam, Dr. Ferguson, and the nurses, I've been in someone's sight the entire time.

Damien hasn't made love to me since before the incident, and it's starting to wear on me. At least, he is sleeping with me in the same bed, but he refuses to take it further than a gentle kiss, like I'm only a dear friend. He's even been wearing pajamas to bed. After he had to listen to the answers I gave the officer, part of me wonders if Damien is repulsed by me because another man tried to touch me, even though I have no memory of it.

Aimlessly, I start walking through the house as I think about one of the interrogations.

"Miss Scott, I'm Officer Daily, and this is Officer Huron. We'd like to ask you a few follow-up questions regarding the alleged drugging and assault."

This is the second time the police have come to the house since I was released from the hospital. Although it's a different set of officers, they have all used the word alleged. I hate that word.

We are all seated in the formal living room. Damien wraps his arm possessively around my shoulders as we sit on the couch.

"Hello, officers. I'm not sure what more I can do to help. I have no memory of the event. I told the previous officers everything I remember from the party, which wasn't much."

When Officer Daily shifts in his tight uniform, I notice residual doughnut flakes on his collar.

"We've spoken to Mr. Wales and Miss Matthews extensively about the event, but we have a few other follow-up questions for you, Miss Scott. Officer Huron is here to observe the questioning," Officer Daily says.

I give a polite smile as he pulls out his little notepad.

"Were you and Mr. Brad Paxton ever sexually active?"

My face flames with embarrassment. Damien looks like he's going to shoot through the roof. Before he has a chance to respond, I lay my hand on his knee and squeeze gently, hoping to keep him at bay.

I look Officer Daily straight in the eye. "No, Brad was only an acquaintance I saw at events I attended with my friend, Sam Matthews."

As he jots down a few things in his notepad, I notice his comb-over from this angle.

"Did you dance with Mr. Paxton at an establishment named the Hitchin' Post?"

Oh geez. By his tone, it seems like I'm being accused of doing something wrong.

Trying to keep my voice level because my stress is increasing, I say, "No, I danced with Sam. As I was leaving the dance floor, Brad dragged me back and tried to dance with me."

"So, you did dance with him?" The officer is just sitting there, looking at me.

It's as if he's trying to catch me in a lie. The way he's treating me is becoming borderline hostile. I give Damien's knee another squeeze.

"No, there was no dancing. He tried. I refused."

Officer Daily notes a few more things. "Earlier that same evening, did you elect to sit in the front seat with Mr. Paxton as he drove to the Hitchin' Post?"

*I feel Damien's posture get more erect beside me. This officer has
about reached the end of his rope. It's as if he's jumbling the order of events
that evening to throw me off.*

*"Yes, I sat in the front seat. Seven other girls were also in the car,
and when they picked me up, the only seat available was the front seat."*

*He continues making notes in that damn notepad. I want to go grab
it and beat him with it. I'm the victim here.*

"So, you two went together to the Hitchin' Post?"

*Damien stands up. "I think that's enough for today. I do not
appreciate you coming here and harassing my girlfriend with false
accusations in that condescending tone. That asshole drugged her, and he
was going to rape her. Point the fucking finger in the right direction."*

Both officers rise from their seats.

*Officer Huron speaks for the first time. "Sir, we meant no disrespect.
Thank you for your time. We'll be in touch."*

They leave.

Going up to Damien, I give him a hug from behind.

*"Alli, I'm ordering extra security detail for the house until this is
behind us."*

*My anxiety starts creeping into the red zone, and I tighten my hold
on Damien. "Am I still in danger?"*

*"No, baby. You're safe. I'm just taking more precautions to make
me feel better about your safety." He turns around and gives me a kiss to
soothe me.*

Every once in a while, an image from that night flashes
through my mind, but I can't keep it long enough to form
anything concrete. Brad has robbed something from me that
I'll never get back, and it's annoying and scary at the same
time.

As I round the corner on the way to Damien's office, I
nearly run into Ben.

"Excuse me, Miss Scott. I didn't see you there."

He instinctively reaches to steady me, but then he
immediately withdraws his hands.

"No worries. I was just going to see Damien."

Since my accident, Ben has been very nice, and he has tried to help in any way he can. I'm glad that he's accepting me as Damien's serious girlfriend.

"Just so you know, he's been on a conference call for quite some time. How are you feeling?" He adjusts the bag he's carrying on his shoulders.

"Better. Thanks for all you did for Damien and me while I was in the hospital. I appreciate it."

He smiles as he shifts from one foot to the other, obviously embarrassed from receiving the compliment. He has a nice warm smile that matches his eyes. *He should smile more often.* I cannot help but return his expression.

"No problem, Miss Scott. Have a good day, and let me know if there is anything you need."

I smile and nod, and then he continues his way down the hall.

As I approach Damien's office door, I can hear his aggravated voice rising in that no-nonsense tone. I pause outside the door, waiting for a better moment to enter.

"Listen, I am not coming there to sort through some squabble that you should be able to handle with the amount of money you get paid. If you can't sort out your department's shit, I'll hire someone who can. No, consider that a statement of fact. In three hours, I want an update on the progress that has been made, or make no mistake, I will follow through."

Good grief. It's rare for me to see him in true business form. I get such a tender side of him that this part of him surprises me.

After hearing him slam the phone down, I knock on the door.

"What?" he yells.

Oh, he doesn't want to be bothered. I should have known. I don't know why, but I've been feeling so timid and unsure around him lately.

Through the door, I mutter, "Um, never mind. I'll come back later." I start walking down the hall as fast as I can.

I just feel so out of sorts with Damien right now. *Maybe I just need to go home for a few days to think everything through.*

I hear Damien calling my name from behind me, and I stop and slowly turn to face him. He's striding toward me with a look of concern on his face. Even when working from home, he wears a button-down shirt and business slacks. If it were me, I wouldn't get out of my pajamas.

"Alli, I didn't know it was you. Is something wrong? Are you feeling okay? What did the doctor say?" He touches my arm as he looks me over.

I love his touch. I shake my head. "Um, I'm fine. Dr. Ferguson says I'm good to go. I was just coming to say hi. You're obviously really busy, so I'm thinking about going back to my place."

He stands more erect. "No."

Geez, he's not going to order me around like this. I'm immediately riled up. *I cannot believe he's actually pulling this again instead of discussing things with me.* "No?" I ask, my voice reflecting my shock.

"No. If you need something from there, I will get it for you. Other than that, you need to remain here."

His sternness takes me off guard. Everything is just out of sync with us.

I smile, trying to keep the peace. "There's nothing in particular I need. I just thought I should check on my place. You can finish up your business, and then we will see each other later. I'll have Sam pick me up since my car is not here. She's in Atlanta today, so it's not a big deal for her to drive me back to Waleska."

He begins rubbing his forehead. "Alli, I'm not going to argue with you about this."

"Good. Give me a call later after you're done working."

I turn on my heel and make it about three steps before he scoops me up and carries me down the hall.

He's not the only one who can be irritated. "Put me down, Damien."

"No, we've discussed this."

"No, we've discussed that I would not vanish completely off the face of the Earth with no way to communicate with me. I never agreed to being held a prisoner. We also discussed that you wouldn't just command me around like a dog." My voice is escalating in volume.

He doesn't say a word as he carries me down the corridor. I just want to scream with all these emotions I have bubbling around inside me.

He stops in front of a wall and pushes open a door hidden within the paneling. *How clever.* He brings us into a room I haven't been in before, which is odd. The room is exquisite with its rich, warm inviting colors. The deepest chairs and couches I have ever seen are arranged in the middle of the room. I look around in awe at the floor-to-ceiling bookshelves lining three walls. The fourth wall in the back of the room is made of glass with water running behind it. I can hear the sound of the water flowing, and it's very soothing.

Almost in wonder, I say, "How did I not know about this room? It's wonderful."

"It's a surprise I had done for you. It's a place for you to come and relax. They just finished it." He strides toward one of the couches and gently deposits me on the edge.

I honestly have no words as I continue to take in the room.

He kneels in front of me. "I'm not keeping you prisoner, Alli. I just had to deal with you being drugged and nearly raped. Brad has been released on bail, and there's no way in hell I'm letting you out of my sight until he's back behind bars. He's probably pissed beyond belief and looking to finish what he started."

The blood completely drains from my face. I had no idea. *Brad's out there, potentially looking for me.* No wonder Damien has been so agitated. However, it still doesn't explain the nonexistent sex part of our relationship.

"I had no idea. How did it happen? Can they rearrest him?"

Sensing my unease, he sits beside me and brings me to him. "You're safe, Alli. Just please listen to me on this. I'm a little on edge, and I'm sorry I just didn't talk to you. I panicked. He was supposed to be refused bail. My lawyers are working with the prosecutor to file a motion to have the bond revoked. They should have him within the next twenty-four hours."

After taking a deep breath, I put it all out there. "Is that why you won't touch me? Because you're afraid he's going to get to me again and taint me more than I already am? I can't remember what happened exactly, and I understand if you don't want me anymore. I just need to know. You've been so different with me these last few days."

He looks at me incredulously, like I just grew two heads. "What are you talking about?"

I fiddle with my T-shirt. "We haven't *been together* since before the incident. I just want you to know that I understand. You don't have to keep up pretenses any longer." I'm trying to keep my emotions under control in case Damien tells me that he doesn't want me anymore.

"You think I haven't touched you because of what you've been through?"

I nod my head as tears start to pool in my eyes. *Damn betraying tears.*

"That's the most absurd thing I've ever heard. It's taken everything I've had in me not to take you and make love to you until we both can't walk for days. I have this urge to let the world know you're mine, and nobody fucks with what's mine."

My head snaps up. "What? Then, why?" *I'm so confused.*

"Because you've been through a terrible ordeal, and I don't want to hurt you with how possessive I've been feeling. I never want you to think that I don't want to be with you. I just wanted to make sure you were okay, and I was waiting until I knew you wanted it. If I even tried to kiss you deeper than what I've been so far, I wouldn't be able to stop.

"I'm so desperate for you, but keeping you safe in every aspect possible will always be my first priority. I want you to move in with me, Alli. I've been trying to get you to move in for months. I'm in love with you, and like I've said a thousand times, I'm never giving you up."

The thought of losing Damien has been terrifying. I start to cry at his eloquent and beautiful words. "I'm sorry. It's been painful, thinking you don't want me anymore because I didn't listen to you. I'm so sorry. I just…I don't know. It's all so overwhelming."

He grabs me and pulls me to him, and he starts soothingly stroking me. "Baby, nothing has changed between us. I just wouldn't be able to handle it if you thought I was *him*. I didn't want you to panic while I was making love to you. I would stop anytime you wanted me to, but having images of the attack come back to you and then associating me with him would absolutely kill me."

Oh, wow. He was afraid I would have some sort of flashback and struggle against his touch. There's no way in this world that could happen with him. "I could never think you were him."

I lean in to kiss him, and he immediately responds to my touch like before. My anxiety about us slowly begins to fade.

His thumb tenderly touches my face. "We need to take this slow because you are still healing. Let me know if anything is too much, okay? I need you right now, Alli. I can't stand to go without you for another second."

I nod, and his hands cup my face, gently bringing me to him. The bruise is still tender, but Damien only brings a healing touch to it. He stands me up, and we begin to undress. We take our time, enjoying each other to the fullest extent.

He slowly takes off my shirt and then his. My yoga pants are the next to go, and then his pants follow before we remove all remaining undergarments. His abs are taut as I trace his V-lined muscles, and he quivers underneath my touch. I'm bare before him as he begins worshiping my body with his hands.

He lowers to his knees, and then his face reaches the apex of my thighs. I throw my head back and moan as he continues sucking my clit vigorously. It's been so long that I come in no time at all. My legs go weak at the sensation, but Damien is right there, scooping me up as he stands.

He lays me down on my back, and he drops down on top of me. *Is this leather couch heated? I think it is. Good grief, that's awesome.*

With his mouth on my breasts, he starts priming me again. His fingers work in and out of my sex in a crisscross pattern. It's divine, and I arch off the couch. He's ensuring that I am ready to accept his large, thick length. Once I shatter for a second time, Damien poises himself at my entrance. I lift my hips as an invitation, and he pushes in. *Ah, it's so incredibly perfect and right.* He's like the yin to my yang.

"Ah, Alli. You're so fucking perfect every time. Never doubt my love for you."

He picks up the pace until our breaths are out of control. Finally, sweet ecstasy claims us. I can feel Damien filling me with his come, and I love the completeness it gives me.

We are entwined and wrapped under a blanket Damien found nearby.

As we come down from our high, I murmur, "I missed this."

"Me, too, baby. Never be afraid to tell me what you want. If it's in my power to give it to you, I will."

Tracing his tattoo, I respond, "I don't deserve you, but I'm not giving you up either, so you're stuck with me."

"There's no place I'd rather be than stuck between your legs."

I slap his chest at his crassness, and he chuckles.

He shrugs his shoulders. "What? It's true."

"You're just horny."

He gives my ass a squeeze, and I squeal.

"On a serious note, thank you for this room," I say sincerely.

Pulling me to him tightly while being mindful of my face, he responds, "Over the last couple of months, I've had it redone for you with the colors you seem to like. The builders were only able to work on it when we were out of town."

"Oh, Damien. It's too much, but I love it." I know I should be overwhelmed, but this room is too soothing to cause my anxiety to rear its head.

Minutes go by as he trails his finger up and down my arm. He seems to be lost in thought. "I was terrified when I saw you come out of that room, unable to function. I thought you were dying, and I'd never have you again in my life. I know you're not ready yet, but I need you to start mentally preparing yourself for marriage."

I stiffen in his arms for a moment. *Marriage? Oh geez. Have we been together long enough? Is he really ready to settle down? Am I enough for him?*

"Baby, I'm not asking you tonight, but I know how you need to process and think everything through, especially when it comes to big decisions. I just want you to start processing it before I ask you to be my wife. I'm not living without you, Alli, and it solves both of my problems at the same time. Trust me, baby. This is the right step for us."

The word *wife* sends an uncontrollable want and desire through my body. *He wants me to be Mrs. Damien Wales. It has a nice ring to it.* But, like he said, it's not time yet. Something is still missing, and I don't know what it is. *Marriage? Me? Married at the age of twenty-two?* It is a lot to think about.

"What two problems are you trying to solve?" I ask.

"Well, the living together problem would be solved because you would move in with me as my wife. And my other problem of guys waiting for you to be done with me would be solved because the world would know you were mine."

My heart melts as I look into his eyes. They are filled with so much passion that I don't think I can respond in words and do the moment justice. Instead, I nuzzle into him, trying to convey my feelings through touch.

"Get some rest. I love you, Alli."

"Love you, too."

CHAPTER
20

Stirring in Damien's arms, I start to wake up.

"Morning, baby. Did you sleep well?"

While stretching my limbs, I relish the fact that I'm lying naked next to my lover. "I slept very well with you by my side. I love my room."

When his hands start to move languorously down my stomach, I smile on his chest.

"Good. The contractor has a few things to finish up in here today, but I couldn't wait to show you."

One finger dips inside me and then two, causing my need to rise. He's still taking it easy with me. Reaching down, I pull his hand away from me, and he immediately looks at me, confused.

Moving quickly, I straddle him, positioning him at my entrance. "I'm ready. I can't wait. I'm not made of glass. Please."

The devilish smile that emerges as he pushes into me in one solid movement nearly stops my heart. It makes me feel whole. In an instant, he flips me onto my back, and he continues to drive into me. He brings our interlocked hands above my head as his lips come down to tease my hard nipples. He doesn't stop until he pushes us to that euphoric edge.

When he shifts his hips slightly, I scream out, "Damien," in complete and utter pleasure.

Rolling us back to where I'm on top, we lie there, connected. His fingertips trace lines from my ass all the way up to my shoulders as he continues to twitch inside me.

"Baby, I don't need you to respond or say anything right now, but I need you to know I'm serious about you thinking about becoming my wife."

Last night's conversation shoots to the forefront of my mind. I don't know what to say, so I kiss his chest to give him something.

"That's all I'm asking for, Alli. Just start thinking about it. When the time is right, I'll make it as special as our first night together."

"I love you, Damien."

"Love you, too, baby. We need to go get ready. I have a few things to take care of this morning. Ben is dropping off some contracts for me to look over, and then we'll spend the rest of the day together."

I hold him tightly, dreading the moment he has to pull out. "I'll edit some photos from the shoot while you're working."

"Sounds good, baby. Be prepared to spend the afternoon together like this. I love being inside you."

∞∞∞∞∞∞∞∞∞∞∞∞∞∞∞∞∞∞

Trading my black silk robe for some lounge pants and a T-shirt, I look one last time for my purple silk robe that I had at the hospital. *The housecleaner, Dolores, must have sent it out to be laundered.* After arriving home from the hospital, Damien handed off our bags to her. *It's hard getting used to people doing all that stuff for me.*

I make my way to a small den off the kitchen. Until he gave me the library, the den had been my favorite place in the house. It's a little room, and the simple furniture is cozy. It's more Damien, more like home. The rest of his house looks like an interior designer got a hold of it without getting to know Damien first. It's beautiful but cold at the same time. I especially like this room because we've made this space ours by replacing the original artwork with photographs of us together.

I prepare to work for a while. I take a seat on the comfortable black leather couch and get lost in the world of my photos. I had to miss one photo shoot at the beginning of the week because I wasn't medically cleared to work, but my mentor, Chris, handled it.

I'm in the middle of adjusting the lighting on one of the fall-themed décor door shots when I hear some commotion at the front door. I get up and head that way. I can hear the security guard speaking to someone.

"You are not authorized on the premises. We ask that you leave now, or we will have to escort you off the property."

When I round the corner, I see a couple in a heated argument with the security guard. I probably should go back to my room, but curiosity gets the best of me. All of a sudden, Damien pulls me behind him, effectively blocking my view of the front door. He's in his no-nonsense stance.

"Alli, go back to the den. I'll be there in a minute. Security will watch you." He's tense and radiating fury.

There's no way I can leave him. I'd be a nervous wreck while waiting for him. I grab the back of his shirt in a pleading manner. "I can't. If you're this tense with what is going on, I can't leave. I feel safe when I'm with you."

When he looks back at me, he sees how nervous I am, and he capitulates to my request. He knows I am safest when I am around him, too. It's a low blow, but I'm not leaving.

His eyes search mine. "Okay, but you stay behind me, Alli. If I tell you to go, then you run to our bedroom and lock the door. No arguments on this, okay?"

"Okay." I try to keep my voice even, but my anxiety spikes to a whole new level because he thinks the situation could escalate to something like that.

Running one hand through his hair, he walks confidently to the door with me behind him. When the couple sees his approach, they start to speak in a rush, trying to get everything out before security escorts them off the premises.

"Mr. Wales, my wife and I have come to plead our son's case. He had no intention of hurting that girl. The other boys were the ones who meant to do her harm. We want to see what we can do to get the charges dropped against our son. The police just picked him up for a second time, and we were told no bail will be set. Please…we love our son."

Oh, holy hell. Brad's parents are at the door. His father has the same blond hair and green eyes as Brad. The only differences between them are Brad's father has wrinkles, and he is slightly heavier than Brad.

I shiver at the resemblance, and of course, Damien notices and tenses his stance in front of me.

"You need to get the hell off my property. Your son drugged and attempted to rape my girlfriend. If that's not intent to harm, then the both of you need to get a fucking clue. I will have him prosecuted to the fullest extent of the law. Do not set foot on my property again, and never approach my girlfriend about it, or I will press harassment charges against the both of you. The fact that you would even dare to ask me to do such a thing after what Allison has suffered is more telling than not." Damien's menacing voice is like cold steel.

I put my hand on the small of his back, hoping this keeps him from doing something stupid. My head is protruding from the side of Damien's body as I watch everyone's actions.

His mother, a short petite thing with auburn hair, makes eye contact with me. "Are you Allison?"

"Yes."

She starts to walk toward me, but the security guard stops her progress. Pleading her case, she says, "Please tell them the truth. You're Brad's girlfriend, and he said there was a misunderstanding with the other boys. They ran off, and he was trying to save you. Sweetie, you know Brad could never do this to you. He said he was going to bring you home for Thanksgiving this year, and we have been so excited to meet you. He has been sending us pictures of you because of how shy you are about talking on the phone."

I have no words. I don't know how to respond. *Are they all deranged and delusional? They thought I was going to their home for Thanksgiving? They knew about me? They saw pictures of me? Shit, Brad is scarier than I ever imagined.*

Holding Damien tight against me, I can feel his muscles begin to roll with fury.

"I suggest you get your fucking facts straight. Allison has never been Brad's girlfriend, and we have been seriously involved for months. You showing up here is complete bullshit. I don't care what misguided story you were fed. This conversation is over."

With that, the security guard steps outside and closes the door. I can hear Brad's mom yelling from the other side.

"Allison, please, honey. He's not mad. He just wants you to tell the truth."

I'm still speechless. Brad had fabricated an entire relationship between us.

Unbelievable.

Damien pulls me into his chest and kisses my head. "I'm sorry you had to hear that, baby. I don't know how they got through the gate. Fucking delusional assholes."

"I'm okay." Nuzzling deeper into his chest, I murmur, "He's crazy." My voice cracks on the last note.

Damien rubs my back as he holds me to him. "Shh, you're safe, baby."

I just nod against his chest.

Someone speaks from behind me. "Mr. Wales, we instructed them not to return, and they are off the property."

Damien has an absolute death grip on me. "How the fuck did they get through security, Bane? I want a meeting. Five minutes, my office."

"Yes, sir."

Oh, that's not going to be pleasant. When I turn around to a stoic Bane—who, I think, is the head of security—I see him shake his head slightly as he takes in Damien's words. He begins speaking into an earpiece as he walks toward Damien's office.

Damien looks at me endearingly. "Are you okay? I'll stay with you if you need me to, but I need to set some things straight. These fuck-ups will not be tolerated where you are concerned."

After letting out a breath, I respond, "I'm a little shaken, but I'll be okay. I just need to process. I'll lose myself in my edits for a while. Go take care of what you need to. Just remember to stay calm. I need you in one piece, too."

He gives me a quick kiss on the lips. When he pulls away, he says, "Alli, they have their orders, and they are paid to follow them. They're going to get a wake-up call with how serious I am. You are to be their first priority, and something like this should have never happened. I will be right back. I love you."

"Love you, too."

At my words, he escorts me back to the den. A security guard is now waiting outside the door. Bane might look tough, but I have a feeling that Damien's about to unleash a wrath that no one wants to see.

I head over to my computer, forcing the encounter out of my mind. Instead, I focus on pumpkins, hay bales, and cornstalks.

Later, when I look up at the clock, I see that an hour has passed. Clicking Upload, I send all the edited photos back to the magazine for the initial layout.

A familiar voice sounds outside the den entrance. "Bane needs to talk to you in my office."

When I hear footsteps, I assume the security guard is leaving his station outside the door.

A moment later, Damien comes striding into the den, rubbing his forehead. He seems to be doing that more and more lately. *It's definitely time for us to do something fun together.* When he gracefully sits next to me on the couch, I close my laptop and snuggle into his side. Immediately, he returns my affection.

"Are you done editing your photos, baby?"

"Yes. What a relief. I finished ahead of schedule. Our next shoot is in two weeks. Chris and I talked about it, and we are going to start condensing shoots. The magazine was splitting the shoots over a two-week period. Now, we are going to combine it all into one-week shoots. It's going to save the magazine money in rental and setup fees, and it gives Chris and me more free time."

As I am talking, his manly intoxicating smell permeates the air, and I love the comfort it brings me.

"That makes financial sense for the magazine. So, you're mine to do with as I please for the next two weeks?"

His voice takes on a sexual, teasing tone, and my sex clenches in response. *Will I ever tire of this man? Um, no, I don't think I will.*

Rubbing his stomach, I try to take on a seductive tone as I respond, "Yes. Do you have anything specific in mind?"

He looks at me a little cautiously. His blue eyes are searching mine as a smirk starts to play on his face. Instantly, my body is curious.

"Well, I thought we could go to a football game this coming weekend. The season starts this Sunday. I've been lax on winning my bet with Sam. I need to start turning you into a sports fan."

Whatever sexual moment we were building is officially broken.

I groan as I throw my head back and close my eyes. "Not on your life, buddy. That sounds like the opposite of fun."

He chuckles. "Is that a no? I'll owe you one, and I can guarantee that is a position you want to be in."

Peeking through my lashes, I see his eyes have a hint of wickedness in them now. I love this side of Damien, and I cannot help but soften to the idea of going to North Carolina because he seems so excited about it.

"Fine, I'll go, but you better pay up good, buddy. I mean, multiple pay-ups." I suggestively move my eyebrows up and down. I cannot stop the giggles that start coming out as he lightly tickles my side.

"Oh, I'll start paying up right now."

Before I know it, he's thrown me over his shoulder, and I squeal in excitement. He carries me out the den and makes it to the staircase. He takes them two at a time, careful not to jostle me too much. When we pass Ben in the hallway, Ben gives a slight nod in acknowledgment. My face flames, and I try to get off of Damien's shoulder. Damien doesn't care though.

"I don't think so, baby. You're about to get a lesson in downs."

Oh geez. My face flames once more for good measure.

After closing the door behind us, Damien swiftly walks to the bed and playfully throws me in the middle, causing the down comforter to come around me like a cloud. After quickly removing our clothes, he hovers on top of me, sucking on my neck. When he takes my earlobe between his teeth, I moan and writhe beneath him.

Seductively, he murmurs in my ear, "Alli, I think it's time that I explained the concept of a first down to you, and then if you're a good student, I will progress to a second down."

I lick my lips. *Oh, I hope there are a lot of downs.* "How many downs do I want?"

"You definitely want to aim for a touchdown, baby."

I wriggle my hips in anticipation. *Maybe sports isn't as useless as I've thought all this time.*

CHAPTER
21

Damien, Ben, and I are getting ready to leave for North Carolina to attend the opening football game for Damien's team.

As the car approaches the Atlanta airport, Ben tells Damien, "Sir, the group accompanying us on the flight today have all arrived, and the plane is ready for takeoff as soon as we board."

"Thanks, Ben."

We pull up to the hangar, and the driver hands off our bags to one of the airport crewmen. When we board the plane, I am greeted by a lot of unfamiliar faces. As we make our way to the back, they all greet Damien with extended hands as they make comments on all sorts of sports-related things.

"Wales, it's gonna be a hell of a season."

"Your grandpa sure would be proud of the team you've amassed."

"Our boy, Mark, seems to be in the best shape he's ever been in."

They pay little to no attention to me. It's obvious they are trying to make an impression on Damien. I smile politely as I follow him to our love seat at the back of the plane.

After we take flight and we're in the air, they continue their banter with Damien. Ignoring all the ass-kissing, I look out the window and watch the clouds go by. My mind starts to drift to one of the lessons I received during the past week. The crazy thing is I am actually retaining what Damien has been teaching me. *Sam will be so irritated when she loses this bet.* I laugh internally, thinking about the look of surprise that will surely be on her face when she discovers how much I've learned.

He's teasing me with his dick, barely entering me, and it's driving me into a near frenzy. He lines himself up, pushes into me slightly, pulls out, and then slides his length up my sex.

"Alli, fuck...you like these lessons. You're so wet."

My body is pulsing for a release. "Please...I want the touchdown. I need it."

"What's it called when a player catches the ball and then drops it?" Positioning his cock at my entrance, he hardly penetrates me before moving his dick up my sex again. "I'll give you what you want if you answer correctly."

I scream, "Fumble, fumble, fumble! It's a fucking fumble! Please!"

As he enters into me, he nips at my nipple, and I cry out in pleasure. "Oh, baby, you're going to get your touchdown now."

As I watch the clouds pass by, I hear a low voice in my ear.

"Keep looking like that, baby, and you're going to end up naked below me."

Boy, that comment will snap me out of a daydream any day of the week. "What?"

"I can tell you're thinking about us. You keep squeezing your thighs together while licking your lips. I'm getting hard for you, and if you don't stop, you're going to get sacked. What lesson were you thinking about?"

"The fumble one." I take in my surroundings, and part of me badly wants a penalty. His words ratchet up my desire in no time.

He gives me a predatory grin, looking like he wants to eat me. "Hmm, I liked that lesson a lot. I remember a lot of screaming in that one."

He returns to his task on his tablet as if he didn't just strike a match in my panties. As I recall some of my recent lessons, I think turnabout is fair play. He's been teasing me all week long, nearly taking me to the brink of insanity.

I casually lean into him and drape my blanket over his lap as I go to hug him. *Step one is complete.* Innocently, I lay my head on his chest. "What are you working on?"

Trying to feign genuine interest, I look at his tablet and see some kind of financial sheet. He doesn't seem to mind the small show of affection in front of people. With the way he drapes his arm around me, I think he likes me being possessive of him as much as he likes being possessive of me.

"I'm reviewing and challenging budgets for the team's departments. None have been approved so far."

I tsk-tsk him. "You're a tough cookie to please."

He chuckles as he continues to peruse his numbers. *Time to put step two into action.* I nonchalantly but swiftly place my hand on his cock, and it immediately begins to grow harder from its already semi-stiff state. With the table in front of us, no one can see my movements. If anyone turned around, he or she would think I was just snuggling up to Damien.

His hand descends on top of mine, stopping my massaging motion. In the same low, rough voice he uses when we are intimate together, he whispers, "What the hell are you doing?"

I coyly smile up at him. In my sexy voice, I say, "What? I thought I would give you a lesson on encroachment. Or are you the only one who can give out lessons when it comes to sports?"

At my brazenness, he eyes me incredulously. *Yes, Mr. Teacher, I can look up football terms on the Internet.* I can tell he's turned-on by my spontaneity. Glancing around, I am reassured that no one is paying any attention to little ole me. The other passengers are drinking and carrying on among themselves, not even looking in our direction. I bring my knees up to form a tent-like structure as I further cuddle into him.

He releases my hand, allowing me to continue my assault. "By all means, baby, proceed with the lesson."

I don't even realize someone is asking Damien a question until he responds without hesitation in a louder than normal volume.

"You know I can't disclose those facts, Charlie, but nice try."

The guy laughs and resumes his other conversation from the front of the plane. Damien focuses back on his tablet, selling the facade that he is working. The only way I know I am affecting him is from the small smile playing on his lips.

I unzip his pants slowly. The noise from the zipper coming undone is covered by the hum of the engines. When his length springs free, I start to massage him at a good pace, and it gets him worked up fairly quickly. As he's nearing his release, Damien drops his tablet to adjust the loose blanket around the front of his cock. *Holy shit, he's actually going to let me get him off right now.* With how the blanket is draped over us, no one can see any movement. He resumes looking at his tablet as I infinitesimally increase the speed.

His length hardens even more, telling me he'll be there with a few more strokes. The naughty part of me wants to slow down, bring him to the brink, and then stop, but I'm just not feeling that bold in my current surroundings. Before I know it, his hot liquid spurts onto my hand and the blanket as I stroke out everything he has to give. The only way anyone else would know Damien is having an orgasm is by the small tightening of his eyes and his slightly deep breaths. Otherwise, he's completely himself. *Geez, if that were me, I would have been so much more shaken.*

Putting his hand under the blanket, he uses an edge of it to clean both my hand and himself before he's zipped up and ready to go. I excuse myself to go to the bathroom to clean up.

When I return, I take my seat next to him.

Leaning into me, Damien says, "I'd say encroachment has become one of my favorite lessons. That was so fucking hot. This evening, I have a lesson for you that I think you are going to enjoy."

I beam at him as I give him a wink. "You're a good student. I'll be sure to work on your next lesson."

He laughs as the plane begins to descend.

When we arrive at the stadium, I am amazed at how much work goes into preparing for football Sunday. I figured it was a big deal, but it's really quite the production. It started last night with the team dinner, and today, we are attending back-to-back events.

It's becoming more and more apparent how much Damien has underneath his empire. When he walks into a room, everyone wants a moment with him. Everyone also knows who I am, too, and I find this unnerving, considering I'm just the girlfriend.

"Hey, baby, I need to do a few interviews."

As I take in the surroundings, I see the camera crews are all lined up. Instantly, fear shoots into my heart as I think about all the public attention. Although my makeup conceals the small remnants of the bruises on my face, I do not want to chance being on national television. I'm glad I brought my camera with me to keep me occupied while Damien works.

When Damien follows my glance, I respond, "I may just stay here and take some pictures. I can practice taking candid and action shots since all I currently photograph are inanimate objects." I say a silent prayer, hoping that he doesn't ask me to go over there with him.

He gives me a quick kiss. "Sounds good. Security is all around us. If you need anything, just say the word."

Whew. "Will do. Go. National television awaits you."

After giving me a wink, he takes off toward the cameras. They are all pointing at him as the reporters start to speak. I cannot stop myself from admiring his fine ass as it moves underneath his slacks. He looks back once and smiles at me, making my tummy flip as I think about how incredible he is.

I shake my head as I crouch down, and then I start getting lost behind the lens.

Click.

Click.

Click.

Currently, the kickers are practicing long-distance kicks. The control they have is incredible.

Click.

Click.

Click.

I catch the second string in action as they run through a few last-minute plays.

"Allison, right?"

When I glance up, I see a giant towering over me. His brown hair is slightly windblown. He's dressed in khakis and a blue polo shirt with the team logo on it. He must sense I don't remember his name from the dinner last night.

"I'm Dustin."

"Oh, right. I'm sorry. I'm terrible with names. How are you doing?"

He is one of the many players I met last night at the team dinner. I stand and extend my hand, and he grabs it and holds on a little longer than necessary. He seems a little too friendly, and there's something off about him. I have to jerk my hand away to release his hold. When his eyes move up and down my body, I instinctively take a step back.

"I'm good. Where's Damien?"

"He's off doing interviews." *Short and sweet. Hopefully, he leaves me alone.*

I quickly realize I'll have no such luck as he continues the conversation.

"I've been following the news. You were in college, but you dropped out to be a photographer for a magazine, right?"

This guy is coming across a little too friendly, and he knows way too much about my personal life. He gives me a creep vibe. Taking precautions, I glance around until I find the nearest security guard. Since the Brad incident, my nerves are a little more on edge. *Last night at the team dinner, he seemed normal when we briefly talked.*

I don't want to encourage more conversation, so I give a simple answer. "Yes."

When he takes a step closer, I take a step back.

"Do you want me to show you around while Damien's occupied? I'd like to get to know you better. My family lives in Atlanta. I'm there frequently." His tone implies that he wants to do more than just physically show me around.

My throat tightens. Out of the corner of my eye, I notice that Mark, the team's quarterback who was enamored by Sam at the Vegas gala, has stopped talking to a fellow teammate. With his eyebrows bunched in concern, he is now watching Dustin and me, which makes me feel better.

"Thank you, but I'm going to stay right here on the sidelines. Damien will show me around." Holding on to my camera like a shield, I move further away from Dustin.

Quicker than lightning, Dustin grabs my elbow, and my heart rate escalates. I'm about to yank myself free, set this asshole straight, call for security, or whatever else I need to do when I hear a familiar voice behind me.

"Dustin, I've got my girlfriend from here. I'm sure the reporters are ready to go through your pregame interviews with you. With all this free time you seem to have, I expect that you'll perform on top of your game tomorrow," Damien says, his tone filled with steel and ice.

Oh, he's pissed. I notice that Mark has also started to walk this way, but then he stops. I can tell he's ready to back Damien up if need be, and this endears him to me. *Sam needs to get her head out of her ass and go after this guy.*

Pure distaste goes through Dustin's eyes, and I move back into Damien's embrace.

Sarcastically, this guy replies, "Sure, Mr. Wales. Allison, it was great to see you again. Rain check on the tour? Maybe I'll give you a call for a photography session when I'm in Atlanta." He doesn't wait for me to respond before he winks, turns, and jogs across the field.

Oh boy, he has some balls.

I look over at Damien. He's outwardly unaffected, but I know he's raging internally.

"What did he mean by *again?*"

Damien's in uber-protective mode, and I'm trying to stay calm as this was really my first encounter alone with another man since the Brad incident.

"He came up to me last night at dinner when you went to the restroom. He just introduced himself and left. That was it."

I attempt to make my voice sound as blasé as possible even though my insides are trembling.

Damien's eyes close briefly. When he reopens them, he sounds resigned as he says, "I can't take you anywhere. I'll have to think about adding additional security."

I massage my temples. "More?"

After storing my camera, Damien takes me by the waist and starts to move us off the field. "Don't worry about it now. We'll talk about it later." He gives me a little squeeze as he continues, "I can't catch a break. You're like a siren to all of them."

That does it. That last comment causes my tension to leave my body, and I start to laugh as we near the walkway at the end of the field. "You're a funny, delusional guy. Trust me, every girl in this place is waiting for you to get tired of me and move on. Remember, I was a virgin when I met you. Guys are not after me like you think. Even if they were, it wouldn't matter."

We stop walking, and he gives me a kiss for everyone to see. I taste his signature wintergreen flavor as my hands go to his taut stomach. I love the feel of his tongue inside my mouth.

He pulls back. "First off, I'm incredibly lucky that you were a virgin. I'm sure you had no idea the amount of attention you were probably receiving on a daily basis. It drives me mad, thinking I could have missed you if I wouldn't have looked up as I was leaving that hotel. Second, another girl capturing my heart will never, ever happen. I don't give a shit what they want. I'm yours."

Each and every day, he continues to find ways to melt my heart, ensuring that I am his.

"Same goes for you, Mr. Wales."

We start walking again and enter the connecting walkway to the stadium exit when he asks, "So, have you thought any more about us getting married?"

Oh, wow! I freeze on the spot, halting our progress. He picks the most awkward places to discuss these topics. *I wonder if he does it on purpose.* He knows I won't freak out when we're in public.

Unsure of where he is going with this, I simply say, "Um, some, yes."

"And?"

His blue eyes are staring at me, trying to suck my thoughts out of my head, and his black hair is a little disheveled from the wind. This only adds to his sexiness. *I will never get enough of this man.*

Cautiously and slowly, I respond, "I'm warming to the idea."

He starts smiling at me, which causes me to do the same. We look like love-struck teenagers.

He's still holding something back from me, and I'm not sure what it is, but I need to know before I'm completely ready to say yes.

He puts his nose against mine. "I like that response a lot, baby. You're getting closer. You're not there yet, but you will be soon."

He places his hand on the small of my back, and we head for the exit to get into the awaiting car.

With his free hand, he pulls his phone out of his pocket and sends a text.

"Where are we going?" I ask.

"Back to the hotel. I need to give you a refresher lesson before the game tomorrow."

At his deep, rough tone, my inner muscles start to spasm, ready to have him inside me.

Teasing him, I respond, "What if I'm a naughty student?"

He gives me a devilish grin. "Well then, I'll have to penalize you with a personal foul."

A small shiver runs up my back, and I make a mental note to be very naughty.

"I like what you're thinking, baby. Just hold those thoughts until we get to the hotel, and then I'll give you a play-by-play of the man-to-man play."

CHAPTER
22

It's game day, and Damien's makeshift office in our suite is in absolute pandemonium. We've been up since the crack of dawn, and the game starts this afternoon. From the breakfast alcove where I'm sitting, I can see security escorting people to and from Damien's office area for interviews, press releases, and who knows what else.

Since I had known so many people would be coming in and out of our suite, I got ready for the game as soon as I woke up. After adding large loose curls to give my hair more body, I decided on a wraparound dark blue sheath dress sans hose—*I hate hose*—with black heels and chunky black jewelry that stands out and makes a statement. Blue and black are the team's colors, and I thought I would blend in while showing my support for the team.

After the front door of our suite closes, a woman with a tight updo and spiked heels comes walking through the hallway.

"I was not informed of this increase in security. What is going on?" she asks, clutching her clipboard.

I bet she's all sugary sweet in front of Damien.

In a businesslike tone, the security guard replies, "This way, ma'am."

I smile into my coffee as she scoffs, and her little heels go *click, click, click* on the tile.

As I continue editing my photos from yesterday at the stadium, I let out a huge yawn. *Who would have thought being an A+ student could be so exhausting?* I giggle to myself, thinking about what Sam's face will look like when I unleash my knowledge on her. I'm not quite ready yet, but I will be soon.

My email pings, and I open the message from my boss.

From: Mack Presley
To: Allison Scott
Subject: Re: Idea for Next Photo Shoot

Allison,

As I've mentioned before, I believe your decorating suggestions
have added an upscale look to the magazine while we are still
able to maintain a low price for our readers.

We have decided to move forward with your latest idea of taking
hotel-inspired decorations to show homeowners how to decorate
their vacation rental properties. As you've stated, hotels have to
find things that can take a beating but still look good for an
extended period of time.

We'll work on setting up some dates for the next shoot after the
design team reviews potential sites.

Best regards,
Mack

This makes me smile. I feel like I'm making a difference
while earning the respect of my peers. *I'll reply to him in a little
bit.* After compiling the best shots from yesterday, I email them
to Damien. *Who knows? Maybe he'll find one he can use for something.*

From: Allison Scott
To: Damien Wales
Subject: Photos from the Sidelines

Dear Mr. Defensive,

Here are some of the better pics from yesterday's
home field advantage prior to the play-by-play
I got when we returned to the hotel.

Hopefully, you can use some of these shots.

Love,
Alli

I cannot stop giggling from all the sports lingo I used. My
dad would have pushed me down the aisle if he knew a man

could get me to have anything to do with sports. He might not approve of how I've learned these concepts, but there would be no reason for any type of explanation on that.

One of the security guards comes to the entryway while Bane is escorting Miss Clickety-Clack out the door. Mentally, I like to call him Mr. Badass. He's built like a linebacker, and he's really kind of scary with his bald head and tribal tattoo. I've seen it a couple of different times when his collar shifts.

"Miss Scott, you have a flower delivery. The flowers have been checked. Do you want to accept?"

"Yes. Thank you, Bane."

When he raises his hand, another security guy appears and places the flowers on the kitchen counter. *Damien wasn't kidding yesterday when he said he would increase security.* They both take their leave as I smile at the roses. There must be at least four dozen of them. They are the same exquisite white roses with crimson tips that Damien sent to me at my apartment on the night of Sam's party. With everything that happened that night, I haven't been back home since then, so I didn't have a chance to enjoy them. Until now, I completely forgot about them.

They are by far the most beautiful roses I have ever seen. He's just down the hall, but he still thinks of me when we can't be together. I love him so much.

I open the card and read the elegantly scripted words.

> *Allison,*
> *You remind me of Rebecca*
> *in so many ways.*
> *xoxo*

My blood instantly turns to ice. Rebecca was his sister who was taken from their home and then later killed. These are obviously not from Damien. I head to find him immediately. I burst into the office and quickly shut the door with a loud thud as if someone is actually chasing me. My breaths are coming in and out quickly. When I walk in, Damien's back is facing me.

When he turns around and sees me, he immediately says into the phone, "I'll call you back." Without even waiting for a response, he hangs up. "Alli, what is it?" He comes around the desk and stands by my side.

With shaking hands, I give him the card. "I just got this. I might be overreacting."

One hand comes out and touches my shoulder while the other takes the card. He's watching me with concern. I normally tend to underreact to things, but my recent experience still has me on edge.

He reads the card and then his eyes meet mine. Rapidly, he asks, "Where did you get this?"

"From the flowers that were delivered to me just now."

He pulls out his phone and starts barking orders. "Bane, lock this place down. We're in the office. Figure out who sent the flowers. I need a source ASAP. Tighten down security at the stadium. Only people on the list get into the skybox today. I want you and at least two other people on Alli at all times. I'll give you more details shortly. I need to talk to Alli first. Okay. Thanks."

He ends the call, and I'm now petrified. The look he gives me is sheer terror.

Pulling me to him, he asks, "What type of flowers did you get?"

I grab hold of him tightly, and he rubs my back. "Um, they're white roses with red tips…just like the ones I thought you sent me the day of Sam's party."

"Motherfucker!"

He temporarily releases me and starts pacing the room, running his hand through his black hair several times. He's working his jaw hard. When he looks back at me, he must see how scared I am.

Then, he's right back at my side. "There's nothing to be afraid of, Alli. I promise." His phone beeps, and he picks it up. "Yes. Fuck. Okay. Give us a few minutes."

He hangs up and moves us to the couch where I cuddle into him.

"Am I in danger, Damien?"

He pulls me closer to him, almost squeezing me. "I don't know. Those flowers were Becky's favorites. I'm not taking any chances. The anniversary of her death was last week. We're no longer going to the game. Even though I asked Bane to increase security, we'll stay here. I didn't mean to scare you, baby."

Part of me wants to completely withdraw and hide, but Damien needs to go to this game. It's important for him to be there because it's his team. Plus, I'm not letting some asshole rule my life.

Grabbing my inner strength, I respond, "No, let's go. I'll be safe. We need to do this."

"Alli—"

I hold up a finger to his lips. "I'm not going to lie. I'm a little freaked-out right now, but I'll be by your side the entire time. We have to continue living. When we get back tonight, maybe we'll have some more explanations."

He scrubs his free hand down his face.

I try to reason with him. "It'll be less stressful for me if we go. The media and whoever else won't speculate as to why we aren't there. This can stay between us."

"Fuck. Fuck. Fuck." He lets out a breath. "I'm a complete dick for agreeing to go. We're definitely skipping the after-party." He looks at me, and I nod in agreement. "You're staying by my side, no matter what. I need to feel you next to me to know you're safe."

He watches me, and with the worry emanating from him, I can tell he wants to stay.

"We can still cancel and not go," he says.

It's ironic that I'm the one pleading to go. "No, we need to do this."

He grabs my face and gives me a deep kiss. It's laced with fear, and it does nothing but heighten my anxiety.

As he ends the kiss, something registers on his face. "Wait, you said you received flowers like this before Sam's party? What did the card say?"

My stomach bottoms out. I try to swallow the acid building in my stomach. "Yes, the card said, 'Thinking of you.' I thought you had sent them because of the photo shoot. I forgot to thank you with us arguing about the party and then the incident. They should still be on my kitchen counter." I'm nervous. When I'm nervous, I talk fast to try and purge everything at once.

He gives me a kiss on my head and then takes in a deep breath. "Are you sure you want to go today? I just want to keep you here."

That's exactly why we need to go. Otherwise, we'll both start becoming prisoners to this fear. *I've been a prisoner to my emotions before. I can't go back there.*

"Yes. I'll do whatever you ask of me. We need to go, Damien…for us."

"I love you, Alli. I'll protect you."

"I know, or I wouldn't be going. I love you, too."

He grabs his phone to make another call. "Bane, we're going to the game. Is everything set? Very good. No fuck-ups. Okay."

After he hangs up, he brings me to him, and I instantly feel safe.

We'll make it through this.

CHAPTER
23

It's after the game, and we're getting back into the limo.
Despite both of us feeling tense, a small part of me enjoyed the
game. Damien scoots in behind me and lets out a sigh. There
are two security guys with us, one driving and one in the
passenger seat. More security guards are following us in
another car.

After he pulls me into him, Damien lays his head back.
"I'm so glad that's over."

Cuddling into his side, I say, "I actually understood some
of the game. Sam's going to be pissed."

He gives me a small laugh. It's the first one I have heard
from him all day.

"Yes, she will be. I had very different plans for us today.
I'll bring you back to a game to fulfill those in the future."

My body involuntarily shivers. With all the stress coursing
through me at this moment, it's amazing that my body still
responds to him. It works on a completely different
wavelength than my mind. "Sounds like a date. What's the plan
when we get back?"

He cracks his neck from side to side. "We need to talk
more about what's happened and then give the details to Bane.
We're taking the plane back to Georgia tonight. I need to fill
you and him in on some things."

With his last statement, my mind goes to all sorts of places.
"Will you tell me first? That way, I'm not hearing whatever it is
for the first time in front of Bane."

"Of course. I planned on that. We'll talk as soon as we get
back to the hotel. Our plane doesn't leave for a few hours."

When we get to the hotel, security men surround us as if
we were royalty. As we make our way up to our hotel room, I
hear the guards repeating things like, "Living room, check,"

"Master suite, all clear," and then one of them marks a little piece of paper.

I release a slow breath to try and dissipate my built-up energy. *Nope, that didn't help.*

As we approach the suite, Bane says to Damien, "Sir, all rooms and exterior exits are secure and clear. As discussed, security will remain in place outside. If you need anything, push this button." He hands over a small pen-looking device that appears to be a panic button in disguise.

On one hand, it's cool that something like that exists, but on the other hand, it's so uncool that we are in a position to need something like that. *Oh, I'm a mess.*

"Thanks, Bane. I'll be in contact. Has everything been arranged as I requested?"

Bane nods in his badass manner. "All has been taken care of. Car is on standby. Per your request, I'll be the only other passenger on the plane with you and Miss Scott, so we can talk. Security will be waiting on the ground at the Atlanta Airport."

Damien tips his head to Bane before he turns to leave. The click of the door upon his exit seems like a doomsday call.

As Damien walks me to the couch, he asks, "Alli, do you want anything to drink? Do you want to change before we talk?"

"No, I'll change on the plane. I just want us to talk and then go home." My hands involuntarily start rubbing up and down my legs.

He looks at me endearingly. "We'll be home soon."

As I sit on the white couch, he takes a seat across from me on the matching ottoman, putting my legs between his. He starts off by making sure we have complete eye contact.

"Just know, what I am about to tell you is not who I am anymore. I've changed."

I nod. "Damien, I know who you are. I love you for who you are. Whatever you are about to tell me won't change that. I trust you with my entire being."

He takes a deep breath. "Let me start by explaining what I was like seven to eight years ago. I've told you a little about my grandparents."

I nod as I mentally scroll through what I know about them.

"After my grandfather passed away, my sister and I inherited my grandparents' entire estate. Becky was three years younger than me. I was twenty-one and in college. She was eighteen and in high school at the time. Anyway, my grandparents didn't get along with my parents, and they wanted to make sure that we were taken care of to the best of their ability. They didn't trust my parents to do right by us. Therefore, they left their entire fortune and sports empire to us.

"My parents blamed me, thinking that I had talked my grandparents into changing the will, but I hadn't. My sister and I just loved our grandparents. My grandparents had never even talked about their intentions with me, so it was just as big a surprise to me as it was to my parents. Well, my parents didn't trust what I had to say, regardless of what I told them. It shredded every last bit of the relationship we did have, which hadn't been much to begin with. My grandparents probably never thought of that happening. They knew my parents were selfish, but my grandparents would have never believed my parents would practically disown me because of the inheritance. They already had so much themselves."

I look at him with understanding. I know what it's like to deal with the heartache of losing a loved one. The part I can't comprehend is not having parents that give unconditional love. Automatically, I grab his hands.

Looking down, he continues, "Well, when you give a twenty-one-old boy millions of dollars on top of an already volatile relationship with his parents, it's sure to turn into a disaster, especially when his guiding forces are no longer around. Drinking, sleeping around…you name it, and I tried it. I'll share any and all of it with you if you need to know more details, Alli. I'm not proud of it, and honestly, I hate that you even have to know this part of me."

I picture Damien mourning the loss of his grandparents while his father and mother treated him with disdain. I imagine his father's behavior was similar to how he acted when he was with Cassandra in front of Damien's house a month or so ago. It fills me with sadness that Damien didn't have the same unconditional love I had with my parents.

I slightly dip my head for him to continue.

"My parents have always been all about the social side of things. As I told you before, they only care about appearances and the continuous climb up that imaginary social ladder.

"Seven years ago, I was in college and the dorms were closed for break. I got drunk and high prior to coming home to see my sister and deal with my parents for the weekend. I was staying out in the pool house, away from my parents. I decided to throw a party with all my high school friends who were in town that weekend since my mother and father had gone to their own event in the city. At some point in the evening, my sister came out to say hi because she was lonely. Some guys ended up saying horrible things to her, and I didn't stop them because, honestly, I wasn't all there. I was numb to it all.

"My sister and I had been close until I started throwing my life away. That was the first time I could ever remember hurting her. Even though those guys kept bothering her, I didn't stop it. I just wasn't right in the head. It's not an excuse for how she was treated. In the end, she ran back to the main house, crying from the relentless cruelty of our drunken asses."

He takes a deep breath as he runs his free hand through his hair over and over again. With the hand I'm holding, I give him a reassuring squeeze, letting him know he can continue when he's ready. This next bit must be the most difficult part, considering how he's pausing to gather himself. His life is so much more emotionally complicated than I ever thought.

When he looks at me, his eyes have a slight sheen to them, and my heart breaks into two because I know what's coming.

"When I came to the next morning, she was nowhere to be found. There appeared to be a struggle of some kind in her bedroom. Becky was gone.

"Magazine articles were published, newspaper articles were printed, news broadcasts were done, and flyers were hung. Nothing was found—no sign, no trace, no ransom note, nothing. It was as if she had completely fallen off the face of the Earth. Several articles started calling it foul play, which caused a lack of enthusiasm in the search. Police continued to search for three weeks before she turned up dead on a side road in the woods."

He takes a stuttering breath in, before continuing. "I'll never forgive myself for not protecting her."

Tears are streaming down my face as I take in his story and his broken posture. It's heart-wrenching on so many levels. He had to go through that kind of grief without the support he should have been able to depend on—his family. His parents basically abandoned him.

Because of my parents, I know what unconditional love feels like. I'm so grateful that I had my parents while I did. My childhood was full of love and happiness.

Damien reaches over to my face and gently wipes my tear-stained cheeks. I immediately lean into him, needing the contact.

"I'm so sorry, Damien. I'm so, so sorry. I had no idea."

He pulls me onto his lap, and he holds on to me as if I'm his lifeline.

"You can never run from me, Alli. I mean it. Becky ran from the pool house, and I never saw her again. I can't ever lose you, baby. I wouldn't survive it. You are my world. You have to listen to me, so I can keep you safe."

The tears are flowing again at the raw pain I hear in his voice. No one, I'm sure, has ever seen Damien this vulnerable.

I put my face against his neck and take in his scent. "I promise, Damien. I swear. I could never stand to lose you either. I love you."

He breathes a sigh of relief. I never even thought about how I didn't know the specifics of what had happened that night. He gave me the overall story, just not the parts he blamed himself for. Damien's trust issues and his fear for me all make sense now.

My hand automatically goes to his chest where his tattoo is. His hand comes up to cover mine, pressing my hand there.

"I got this tattoo to represent my biggest mistake. It's a reminder to never repeat it. Since Becky's death, I have kept everyone at a distance. I never thought I would have something like what I have with you…unconditional love."

Oh, Damien. My poor Damien. He's punishing himself by taking the blame for everything. His tattoo shouldn't be a painful reminder of all his mistakes. It should be a memory of someone he loved with his whole heart.

Through my tears, I try to reason with him. "Damien, it wasn't your fault. You were dealing with so much yourself, and you had no support system. She was kidnapped, you didn't cause her death because she ran to the house."

"Alli, please…it was my fault. Don't push that topic tonight, please." He looks down at our hands on his chest.

His parents don't deserve him. He might have been messed up from the death of his grandparents, but his parents contributed to it by turning on him. They should have been there for him. I'm disgusted at the thought of giving up on someone for something as unfulfilling as money.

At the core of it all, Damien and I are more alike than I thought. We've both had to cope with an unfair loss. I just don't know if he has actually dealt with it or just buried it.

When I lean back to grab a tissue from the side table, I see an envelope with a piece of paper partially sticking out of it, and it reminds me of the note I received at the children's charity event and the note I found in his office. It becomes clear to me then that whoever this is has been trying to cause problems for a while now.

He's on high alert from the expression on my face. "Alli, what is it?"

As I try to piece it all together, I absently respond, "The note."

"What? The note with the flowers?"

I shake my head at his assumption. Suddenly, I feel like the world's biggest idiot for not sharing the incident at the charity event when it happened. *Oh shit.*

Damien gives me a slight shake to bring me back to the here and now. With an edge to his voice, he asks, "Alli, what is going on?"

"This summer, when we were at the children's charity event, you left to go to the restroom, and a waiter came by and gave me a note. I thought it was Martin or Cassandra trying to break us up again, so I didn't say anything to you. I thought it was just a part of their juvenile game."

He sits straight up and grabs hold of my shoulders. "What are you talking about? What did the note say?"

"The note said, 'You're still missing a big piece of the pie, darling. Are you sure that you're safe with him?'"

"What the fuck, Alli? Why wouldn't you tell me something like that?"

What the hell? Is he seriously agitated after everything I've had to put up with? "Really, Damien? You're really asking me that after the couple crazy people I have had to deal with this summer? Every time I turned around, someone was trying to come between you and me. By not giving that note more than five seconds of my time, I was demonstrating how much I actually trust and care for you. I would have told you if I thought it mattered. You and I are not enemies in this. It was an honest mistake." I'm proud of how calm my voice remained through my little speech.

Our eyes are locked—my blue-green with his charismatic blue. His eyes start to soften as he takes in my words.

He pulls me back to him. "I know, baby. I'm just a little on edge. Some lunatic knows all about the incident with Becky and is targeting us. I'm sorry."

His words move me. "I'm sorry, too. We're both stressed right now. We just have to remember that we're on the same team." Laying my head on his chest, I continue, "Do you think it's all connected—the flowers, the notes, the texts?"

"I don't know. Do you still have the note from the charity event?"

I respond, "Yes. It's at my apartment."

"We'll need to get it."

"Okay." I focus on listening to his heartbeat through his shirt. It's faster than normal, but it seems to help calm my nerves.

Then, I remember the other part of my revelations. Nervously, I start rambling. "I have something else to tell you. I wasn't intentionally snooping. You left in a hurry to deal with that manager and player crisis. My camera was on your desk in your office, and I went to get it for the photo shoot. I saw a piece of paper sticking out of the envelope you had received. I was checking to see if it was something you needed for your trip. I read it, and it said something like, 'Your yearly reminder.' I decided to ask you about it the next time I saw you, but then things got crazy, and I forgot. I'm guessing it's related to all this, too."

It feels like an eternity before I feel his finger come underneath my chin. He brings my eyes to meet his.

"Baby, I don't care that you went through my things. My house, my shit, everything that is mine—it is all yours, too. I planned on explaining more of my past to you at some point, but then that fucker Brad tried to assault you. I just never thought my past would collide with my future." His thumb comes up and caresses my cheek. "Alli, you know I would stop at nothing to keep you safe, right?"

I nod to answer his question. I have never felt safer than when I'm in Damien's presence. "Was there something else in the envelope besides the note I found?"

"Yes." He pauses for a moment. "There was also a newspaper article from when Becky's body was found. I get a clipping every year around the anniversary of her death. Since I have been caught up in you, it took me by surprise this year. It's kind of like what happened to you at the Pancake House in

Miami. It served as a reminder that there were things you still needed to know."

"I'm glad you told me. I hope you know that I love you, regardless of what's in your past."

Our voices are just above a whisper.

"I love you, too, baby. I never realized how much you trusted me. No one has ever trusted me like that."

My heart breaks a little more with that small admission. His asshole parents deserve to be taken out back to have some sense beat into them for causing him to have so much self-doubt.

"Have you been able to trace the article back to its source?" I ask.

"No, not at all. It comes from a random city every year in a plain manila envelope with no distinct markings or fingerprints. I've asked Bane to look into it. The investigators I've hired through the years found nothing. We'll see if he's able to make more progress."

I am in shock that someone would go to great lengths to send Damien a painful reminder year after year after year. The dedication this crazy person has is unnerving.

"Is it the same article every year?"

"No, it's a different one each time. There were so many papers that covered Becky's abduction and death that this person will have an endless supply to choose from. It's the only time throughout year I get one."

This person sends nothing else all year? It doesn't make sense.
"What was this article about?"

Damien furrows his brows as he thinks about my question.

"This was one of the more detailed articles about her abduction." His face pales as he says the word *abduction*. At the same time, he starts fishing his phone out of his pocket. "Let's get packed, baby. I want to get us home."

I look at him questioningly. "What's going on?"

He doesn't respond. *Something just clicked in his mind.*

"Please, Damien. Don't shut me out."

He grabs my shoulders as absolute terror seeps through his eyes. "This is the first year I've received one about how Becky was abducted."

My hands start to tremble slightly. "Do you think this person is after me now?"

He grabs my hands and starts rubbing those soothing circles. "Baby, I'm not taking any chances. I want to talk this out with Bane. I'll feel better with you safe at our home. We'll look at everything. There may not be any meaning to the articles. We could be overreacting. I will keep you safe though even if I have to give up everything I have. Make no mistake about that. Let's go pack. I want to get you home."

I swallow deep and nod as we start to move toward the bedroom. I'm really trying not to panic. I need to keep my cool, so Damien will continue to share information with me.

Holy shit! There's a serious freako out there, and they are jonesing to hurt Damien in any way he can. I just happen to be the perfect pawn in this game. Whoever this person is seems to be incredibly sick and patient, and I think that's the part that worries me the most.

"We'll need to run by your apartment to get the note and the flowers."

"Okay. It's probably still in my clutch from that night."

We walk into the bedroom and quickly pack the essentials in order to leave immediately.

As we are leaving the hotel, Damien's arm is wrapped tightly around me in the most reassuringly protective way. Before, I hadn't known what was missing, but tonight, he gave me what I needed all along. Now, I know I'm ready to be his wife because he's shown he trusts me as much as I do him.

CHAPTER 24

We are sitting at the dining room table with all seven newspaper articles and their accompanying typed notes and manila envelopes, phone record bills from when the texts were sent to me, the notes I received, the dead flowers from my apartment, and the live ones from the hotel. My stomach is twisting into knots from seeing this sicko's work displayed on the table.

"Miss Scott?"

Bane's words snap me out of my trance, and I stop staring at the objects.

"Have you thought of anything else regarding the guy who delivered the flowers to your apartment or the waiter who gave you the note at the charity event?"

Putting my hands on my head, I try to conjure the images back to see if there is anything else I remember. It's exactly what I've already told Bane. I have nothing new. "No, I'm sorry. I wasn't on guard, so I didn't give either person a second thought."

He looks away from me to write in his notepad. Since we got on the plane and Damien outlined the entire situation to him, he's been writing constantly.

"Miss Scott, since meeting Mr. Wales, can you think of anyone who has made you feel uncomfortable, regardless of how small it was?"

It's amazing that Bane is still in his suit, looking pristine and crisp. I'm exhausted and look like I've been up for a solid forty-eight hours.

Questions, questions, questions are what we've been answering for the last few hours. Most of the questions sound the same to me even though they are asked in different ways. *What did this guy do before becoming Damien's head of security?* I can sense Damien trusts him…at least as much as he seems to trust people in general.

"Um, besides Martin, Cassandra, Brad, Dustin, and Damien's dad, I can't think of anyone else." I look over at Damien. Mentioning his dad just accidentally slipped out. "Sorry."

"It's fine, baby. Don't even worry about it."

Bane picks up the articles and reads them again, one by one, before taking more notes. "Mr. Wales, here is the list of names I've compiled of everyone you said you have had some sort of altercation or disagreement with. I need you to prioritize who you believe are the worst threats. I will look into each person, but your input will give me a basis to start with."

He pushes the notepad to Damien, and after briefly looking it over, Damien starts making notations in the columns. The list is long. It seems that emotions run pretty high in the sports business.

Bane picks up another article and starts writing away in another notebook. He lays his pen down and pours himself a glass of water.

"Mr. Wales, Miss Scott, I believe I have a theory."

That gets our full attention.

"Mr. Wales, after hearing your summary of the last seven years of your life, I believe this person is trying to convey a message to you with each article."

Damien lays his pen on the notepad. "Please continue, Bane."

Sitting across from us, he arranges the newspaper clippings in a row. "For now, I'm going to assume that this is the killer communicating with you. However, we'll need to keep an open mind to other possibilities. I believe this person has been sending you clues and warnings throughout the years. I have gone through all the articles and categorized them as a clue or warning. It appears that this person is letting you know that he or she has been watching you. Without the more aggressive tactics toward Miss Scott, I'm not sure we would have pieced this together. In my opinion, the killer has been laying a trail, waiting for the perfect moment to act."

He picks up the first article and slides it to Damien. In an informative tone, he says, "The first year you received an article, you were twenty-two. It was the one-year anniversary of Rebecca's death. The article was centered on the wealth you and your sister had inherited shortly before her death. It implies that people with this kind of money should watch their backs, especially when they make a lot of enemies.

"I've marked this as a warning article. Earlier that year, it was officially announced you would be taking over the football team when you turned twenty-six as stipulated by your grandparent's will. The announcement created a considerable amount of enemies for you."

Damien's hand automatically reaches for mine, and he gives it a squeeze as if I'm going to disappear. He seems to be keeping a strong facade, but I know this must be killing him. I'm feeling a little panicked. In the article, there is a picture of Damien hugging Rebecca. She was beautiful. She looked like Damien but in a female form.

After Damien is done reading the article, Bane hands him another one. "This is the third article you received."

Before Bane begins, I ask, "What about the second one?"

After shuffling the articles around, he pushes forward the second, fourth, and sixth articles. "From what I have surmised, I believe the even years are clues to what happened to Rebecca. All three of these articles have similar theories—she was taken out of state, the killer was someone your family knew, and your parents withheld information from the authorities. These articles were all more factual, but I will keep looking to see if anything correlates to what was happening in Mr. Wales's life during those years."

Damien is focused on the articles, meticulously reading them. At this point, my eyes are so tired. I just sit there, taking in this huge convoluted mess that seems impossible to decipher. *I can't believe someone would go to these lengths to get revenge.*

Once Damien is finished studying the articles, he sits back. "Carry on, Bane."

As Damien is absorbing it all, I have no idea if he agrees or disagrees with Bane's theory and assumptions.

Bane returns the second, fourth, and sixth articles into the pile. Then, he brings the focus back to the third article. "This one speculated that one of Rebecca's immediate family members killed her. The article insinuates that people can never trust those who are closest to them, including family and friends. I consider this a warning article. This was the same year when you found out Martin Mills had betrayed you by sleeping with Cassandra Williams, effectively dissolving your relationship with them."

I feel sick from looking at the newspaper articles and seeing the pictures of Damien's beautiful sister who had her life robbed from her because of a crazy person. The creepier Bane's theory gets, the more my headache grows.

Damien does the same as he did before. He reads the article without saying a word, and then he pushes it back to Bane.

"Any questions so far, Mr. Wales?" Bane asks as he hands over another article.

"No, carry on."

The fifth article has a picture of Damien's parents on a stage in front of a room full of people. I know my eyes bulge slightly as I stare at his mother, who does not appear to be grief-stricken at all. She's done up to the nines, and it looks like she's giving a speech. Based on the caption, I realize they were at a ball that took place less than two weeks after Rebecca's disappearance but before she was found. *Bleh, bleh, bleh.*

Bane continues, "Sir, this article alludes to how your parents were enjoying all the publicity. The paper claimed that Rebecca's disappearance was a potential stunt to get attention. It referred to how public attention makes a person a target and puts loved ones at risk. I'm marking this as a warning article. It was the year you took over the sports empire your grandfather had left you. That year, you also won Man of the Year along with other awards. Basically, it was the year you were publicized the most. I believe the killer was implying that anyone you loved would be in danger."

Immediately, goose bumps form on my skin. *This is too much crazy shit to digest.*

Damien squeezes my hand again to get my attention. "Alli, I will keep you safe. No one is going to get to you." He lifts my hand and kisses it. "I swear that we will find this fucker."

Leaning into his shoulder, I respond, "I know."

Bane gives us a minute until Damien focuses his attention back to the article.

"Carry on, Bane."

When Bane grabs the seventh and last article, his eyes shift to me for a second. "The article received this year was a detailed account of how the police believed Rebecca had been kidnapped. Similar to the articles received on the even years, it is more factual, and it theorizes that the intruder knew the house well and was waiting for Rebecca's return. Police assumed she had been subdued. The article notes the only thing missing was a white quilt with pink flowers. To date, that quilt has not been found. I presume that this is close to how the killer actually took Rebecca. I consider this a warning because I think this person is letting us know that he plans to try and take Miss Scott like he did Rebecca."

My vision blurs a little, but I focus on taking regular breaths to stay strong. *Plans for me? Shit.* I put my mask in place, so Damien can focus on the task of finding this guy instead of worrying about how I am handling the situation.

Damien reads the last article and sits back in his chair. He hasn't removed his hand from mine. "How the fuck did I not see this?" He's beyond agitated with himself.

"Mr. Wales, is there anything you cared about that could have been taken from you before Miss Scott came into your life?" He's looks at Damien and then glances my way.

Damien keeps his gaze on me as he answers Bane. "There was nothing. I had this all investigated before, but nothing was ever linked because they just appeared to be random articles to fuck with me. Alli's the one thing that I want more than anything in this world, and this asshole knows it."

A tear rolls down my cheek at Damien's words. Until I came into his life, he has just been passing through the motions, distancing himself from everything around him.

Damien and Bane start discussing the articles in more detail as I space out. The scariest part of this craziness is that this nut job apparently thinks I am incredibly special, and he is playing his ultimate card by using me. This sick person has been waiting all this time to have something that was worth threatening Damien. Chills run up my spine from just thinking about it.

As dawn starts to break, I begin to drift off to sleep. *Maybe if I just rest for a second, I'll get my second wind. Don't...want...to...miss...a...thing.*

I'm awakened with a slight jostling as I am being carried in the most lovingly gentle embrace. Sleepily, I nuzzle into his chest. Through a yawn, I say, "Damien, I can walk. Are we done? I don't want to miss anything." My body is beyond tired, and his scent further lulls me as I close my eyes.

A door opens and closes, and then my body hits a soft mattress. He kisses me on the forehead and starts to pull away.

"Damien..."

"Shh, baby, go back to sleep. I promise to fill you in on everything in the morning. We're just going to go over some more details. You need your rest. There will be a security guard outside our door if you need anything."

I can't ignore his request with how exhausted I am. *A little sleep will do me some good.* Laying my head back on the pillow, I fall asleep before Damien even leaves the room.

Feeling warm, I slowly awaken, engulfed in Damien's naked limbs. *I wonder what time he came to bed.* I crane my head to see the clock. It's 4:34 p.m. *Wow, I was really tired.* Damien is fast asleep beside me. He looks peaceful. When he is calm like this, it becomes evident to me how much stress he's been under during the last couple of weeks.

After freeing myself, I decide to get ready before heading to the kitchen for some food. I want so badly to know what Damien and Bane talked about, but Damien must be exhausted. He didn't even stir when I left the bed. Being a light sleeper, he is normally in tune with my every movement.

My mind is still a whirlwind with everything I learned yesterday. In just the last twenty-four hours, it feels like a year has come and gone. *Can someone really be that crazy?*

As I open the bedroom door, I am taken aback when I see a security guard standing right there.

"Good morning," I say to him.

He tips his head to me.

Geez, this is awkward. "It seems like a lovely day," I say.

He tips his head again to me.

I'd have better luck talking to the dead at the rate we're going. As I start walking, he follows. That weird silence surrounds us all the way down the stairs and into the kitchen where he stands along the side of the wall, constantly observing everything around us. The silence is slightly maddening.

As I open the fridge, he mutters into his earpiece, "Scott is in the kitchen. Will advise when we move."

I close my eyes as I think of how I'll dread these next few months. *I can't even go to the refrigerator without someone detailing my every move.* Opening my eyes again, I glance to the counter and notice a note from Dolores, the cook.

Mr. Wales and Miss Scott,

Lobster-filled tortellini is in the warming tray.

Enjoy,

Dolores

I open the tray and find the tortellini. *Be still my heart.* My mouth salivates since I barely ate anything yesterday. Sitting at the bar with my food, I start eating. In my head, I catalog the events that have happened. It's so much to take in and process. When I'm halfway through my meal, I jump when two arms come around my waist. Immediately, I relax at the familiar feel of Damien.

"I didn't mean to scare you. I missed having you next to me this morning, baby." He's nuzzling my neck.

Maybe I should have stayed in bed a little longer. "Mmm, it was nice waking up wrapped in your arms. You were sound asleep, and I didn't want to disturb you. With how Bane was on a roll last night, I figured you came to bed much later than me."

He drags his nose up my chin, but then he gets distracted by my plate. "I'd never consider you a disturbance, baby. Is there more of that tortellini? It looks delicious."

"Over in the warming tray. Do you want me to get it for you?" I take another mouthful in case I need to get up.

He makes his way over to the warming tray. "No, I've got it. I got your email with the pictures last night."

Oh, holy hell. Damien shirtless with loose silk pajama pants has to be one of the most divine sights I have ever seen. His hair is a sexy, floppy black mess. I love how the style can be so clean-cut but rugged at the same time.

He grabs a fork and makes his way back toward me.

"Oh, good. I'm sure you guys get tons of pictures from your photographers, but I had some extra time to edit them while you were in meetings. I just wanted to send them along in case you could find a use for them."

He's staring at me in a way that makes me think he's trying to see through me. It's unnerving when he does that because I feel like he always gets a glimpse into my soul. It's not that I mind, but it's unsettling to have your soul bared that much to anyone. I start to fidget in my seat.

Finally, he says, "Alli, the pictures were phenomenal. I forwarded them to my PR team, and they want to use them provided you'll sign the release for us to be able to do so. You'll be paid for them. They want to know if you are available to do more photo shoots for the team."

"What? Are you serious? Of course I'll sign and you don't have to pay me. I can't imagine that they were that good. I was just having fun that day." My voice sounds shocked and disbelieving.

"You're phenomenal. The pictures are phenomenal. Would you consider it?" There is such pride in his voice.

I am honestly floored at the request. I was not expecting it.

I tap my fingers nervously on the counter as I think about his offer. "Um...well, yes. It would be a great opportunity. Wait, you didn't have anything to do with this, did you? Undue influence and all with you being the boss?"

He smirks at me. *Damn his smirking.*

"No, I promise. I only forwarded the pictures, and the PR Manager, Bridget, got back with me. I didn't tell her you took the pictures. She responded and wanted your contact information. So, no undue influence. I wanted to check with you first to see if you were interested before I let her know your information." He takes another bite. He's almost done with his plate.

I cannot contain my excitement as I practically tackle him while he's trying to eat. "Oh, Damien. Of course I would like to do that. Maybe I can work it into our schedule as we travel together. It'll give me a reason to travel with you more."

After giving me a swift kiss, he responds, "Alli, you never need a reason to come with me."

"I know you feel that way, but I like earning my way, Damien. I like being busy. Now, I just have the best of both worlds." I cannot contain my elation at the thought of officially doing photography as I travel.

He puts his hands up in mock surrender. "Hey, I'm not complaining."

We've argued about this so many times that I'm glad he finally gets it.

As I look down at my empty bowl, I bring up the more unpalatable subject. "So, what else did you and Bane talk about after I went to sleep?"

He's calmer today even though a tenseness remains in his eyes. "Bane got copies of the all the investigations I've had personally done over the years and the official police report. There weren't any additional leads. He's continuing to look at everything."

From the tone in his voice, I can tell he respects Bane. It's rare to hear that tinge of reverence when Damien talks about anyone.

"Not to state the obvious, but could it have been Cassandra or Martin?"

"They're both being looked at. We aren't ruling anyone out, regardless of when I met them or what I think I know."

I thought Damien would try to keep me out of the loop just a little bit, but he doesn't. He's keeping me involved, and I feel like his partner.

A security guard passes by the door, which leads to my next question. "So, how does this impact our lives currently?"

"Well, I was going to send a team to pack up your stuff and move you in here. There's no way you're going home to your apartment in Waleska."

At the word *pack*, I shake my head vehemently. *No way in hell is he getting his way on this.*

"Alli, be reasonable."

Calmly, I respond, "No, please listen to me. I'm not moving in here, Damien. I want to do things in a specific order. I promise to stay here while this threat is out there, but I'm keeping my place."

Pushing his plate away, he stares at me with a pensive look. I know he knew this would be my answer.

"Point taken. Plus, that issue will be fixed soon enough. In regard to how this impacts your life now, you'll have a security guard with you twenty-four/seven. We'll work out the specifics as they arise."

For now, I'm going to ignore the marriage innuendo. "I haven't seen Sam in a while. I need to spend some time with her."

Without his shirt on, I can see his muscles immediately tense and twitch. The sight is distracting and mouthwatering. *I cannot stay focused around this man, and he's mine.*

"I know you're worried, and I won't fight any of your conditions on this. Neither will Sam. I'd feel the same way if the tables were turned. I just want to see my best friend," I say.

He visibly relaxes. *I love being protected by him.*

"I want you two to meet here. This place is big enough that you can have your privacy, and I'll know you're safe the entire time. Sam can stay as long as she wants, but you're in our bed at night."

His dominating tone warrants no argument. Honestly, it's not as bad as I thought it would be. It could have been worse, and it's not unreasonable, considering everything that has happened recently.

"Sounds good. I'll get with Sam, and we'll work on a date."

Now, he's eyeing me curiously. "It's really that easy? What's the catch?"

"No catch, I swear. After what happened at Sam's party and what we're dealing with now, all I want is for you not to worry. I don't want to cause you stress. I just need to see my best friend. If you're satisfied with the arrangements, then you'll relax, and we will all have a better time."

He's absolutely shocked, which causes my smile to widen.

"See? I can be amenable when I want." I lean over and give him a kiss.

His lips are controlling, and pretty soon, I'm lost in Damien, just like always when I am touching him. When his arms snake around my waist, I start to climb onto his lap. *Kitchen counter sex? Yes, please.*

I freeze when a discreet cough comes from just outside the kitchen entryway. I immediately blush and bury my face against Damien's shoulder. *When I get caught up in Damien, why can I not remember people are always around?*

He slightly chuckles at my behavior. He whispers, "We'll continue this later, love. We'll have to be on better behavior with all of the additional personnel. I just can't seem to help myself where you're involved."

Mumbling into his skin, I say, "Oh geez, I'm so humiliated."

"It's only Bane. He didn't see anything, or I would be pissed."

I bury my face deeper into him.

"Bane, are there any updates?" Damien says.

I start to extricate myself from Damien, but he keeps me on his lap. My face feels hot from embarrassment. *I hope I wasn't moaning loudly enough for him to hear me.*

Bane is wearing a suit similar to all his others, looking fresh as a daisy. He states, "Sir, with your permission, I'd like to go investigate a few leads regarding Rebecca's disappearance. At this point, I want to keep my thoughts limited to just us for the time being."

Overall, Damien's demeanor is much more relaxed, even while talking about this with Bane. "That's fine. We were planning on staying here for the day anyway. I'll need you back and ready to go tomorrow evening."

"May I use the plane, sir? I need to go to your hometown, and that's the only way to accomplish my task by tomorrow night."

"Yes, whatever you need. Keep me posted."

Bane nods.

Seriously, all the nodding is starting to drive me nuts. I know I nod, but Bane might just break me of this habit. I can tell he's on a mission with the way he strides out of the kitchen. *I wonder what he's up to and what leads he's following.*

I'm staring pensively out the kitchen entryway when I feel Damien nuzzle my neck.

"How about you and me go find us some privacy?"

I nod. *Damn it! No nodding!* "I'd like that."

He swiftly leads me from the kitchen back to his room.

Hmm, being trapped with Damien for the foreseeable future could have some great benefits.

CHAPTER
25

While stretching my limbs after working and reading all morning in my new library, I look at the time. It's the middle of the afternoon. Yesterday, we didn't leave the room at all. We spent it just enjoying each other in our little bubble. We both needed that uninterrupted time together. Other than my morning wake-up call from none other than my favorite piece of anatomy on Damien, this morning has been all work and no play for him.

When my email pings, I look to see an incoming message from my boss.

From: Mack Presley
To: Allison Scott
Subject: Re: Idea for Next Photo Shoot

Allison,

The design team is coordinating the photo shoot at the Majestic today in Atlanta. It's a middle-class hotel that I think will work perfectly for the vision. Due to the hotel's availability, we will need to shoot the day after tomorrow. It needs to be a condensed shoot. We'd prefer to keep it at two days, three at most.

Hope this works with your schedule. Sorry for the short notice. I won't be able to make it, but I will stay in touch. I know you and Chris have this under control.

Best regards,
Mack

The vote of confidence makes me smile. My biggest debate is whether or not to tell Mack about the security guards who will be accompanying me. Since he's not going to be there, I decide omission is the best course of action for now.

```
From: Allison Scott
To: Mack Presley
Subject: Re: Idea for Next Photo Shoot

Mack,

No problem. I'll coordinate with Chris, and we'll get
it taken care of. We'll try to condense it to two full
days of shooting and one day of last-minute shots
if needed. One of us will keep you posted.

Allison
```

I'm not sure how this is going to go down with Damien, but with the proper precautions, I don't see why a photo shoot at a supervised set at a hotel would be a problem. *Hell, the game I just went to had thousands upon thousands of people there.* The one thing we have to make sure we do is to keep living safely.

Before I pay Damien a little visit to talk about everything, I text Sam first to set up a date.

> *Me: Hey, friend! Are you up for some girl time?*

> *Sam: Um, you have to ask? Hells to the yeah!*

> *Me: I can do today or tomorrow. Then, I have a photo shoot for the next three days, but I'm free after that.*

> *Sam: I'm in Atlanta. I can be at Damien's in thirty minutes.*

> *Me: Perfect! See you in a few. What's in Atlanta? You've been here a lot.*

> *Sam: Girl, I don't kiss and tell. xoxo*

> *Me: xoxo*

Gah, I don't think I want to know about Atlanta. Poor guy—whoever he is. I feel lighter, knowing I'll be laughing uncontrollably with Sam soon.

I skip down to Damien's office. When I'm outside the door, I can hear his voice, and he's discussing financials of some sort. This time, I barely pause before entering. I don't feel the need to, like I did before when there seemed to be something between us after the Brad incident.

The scowl on his face from the conversation immediately changes to a smile when he sees me. His tone though does not mirror the loving look I'm receiving.

"I'll call you back. However, when I call back, make sure you have the corrected financials ready to discuss. You're the last department to submit an approved budget. Ben should be in the office up there. Get with him." He hangs up the phone and leans back in his chair. His tone softens and warms when he speaks to me. "Hey, baby, I was going to come find you after this. What's going on?"

When I stretch, Damien's eyes immediately go to the strip of my stomach that is shown as my arms reach up.

I laugh. "Pervert. I was in the library, and I needed to stretch my legs. I texted Sam, and she's coming over here in about thirty minutes. I don't know if she's staying the night or not."

His eyes are looking me up and down, and he has a smile that brightens his entire face. "I'm always a perv around you. Is there a particular room you want to use for your girl time?"

Without hesitation, I respond, "My library."

He chuckles. "I'm glad you like it. I'll let security know." He stands and starts slowly stalking toward me, causing me to bite my lower lip in anticipation. "Was there anything else? If not, I think it's time the student got a new lesson."

Oh geez. When he talks like that, I lose all sense of control. Maybe I could wait until after my lesson to go to the less palatable conversation.

"I can tell you have something else to tell me." He continues walking to me.

I grin at the thought of how well we know each other.

I rush to get it out because that look on his face has my heart racing with want to have him in me. When he makes it to me, I'll lose all coherency. "I have to work at a hotel photo shoot the day after tomorrow for three days."

He stops mid-stride to look at me. "I don't fucking think so. You're not going." His tone has an obvious finality to it.

I am immediately annoyed by his reaction. *Stay calm.* I have to continue on even though I hate putting him in this situation. "Damien, be reasonable. I have a job."

"No, Alli. You're staying here."

There has to be a safe middle ground. Raising my hands, I slowly walk to him and wrap my arms around his waist. "Damien, please don't take that tone with me. We've talked about that, and we get a lot further when we discuss things together, not when you demand things of me. This is supposed to be a relationship."

As I look up into his face, he leans his head back and blows out a long breath before returning his gaze back to me. "I don't want you to go."

"I know, but I have a job. It's at the Majestic Hotel, which has far less people than we had at the game. You even have more security here than you did there. I won't complain about any of the precautions. We still need to live our lives though. We just need to be smart about it."

I add a sweet grin, which causes a momentary lapse on his controlled face.

One hand leaves my back, and caresses my cheek as he lets out another long breath. "Okay. Give me the specifics, and we'll take care it."

"See? Now, wasn't that a lot more fun than us arguing, getting all agitated, and not accomplishing anything?"

I rock my hips into him, and I can feel he's already in a semi-hard state. Before he has a chance to say anything, I drop to my knees.

He immediately puts his hands on my shoulders as if he's about to pull me back up. "Alli, what the hell are you doing?"

Looking up coquettishly, I start undoing his belt. "Isn't it obvious?" My hands go to the button of his slacks. "I want to taste you again." Slowly, I pull his zipper down. I set him free and stroke him a few times. "I'm starting your second lesson and educating you on a blowout."

I lick my lips in anticipation and then bring him into my mouth. Using my tongue, I suck and lick him like a lollipop. His hips automatically thrust forward, and I continue to take him deeper.

He moans, "Oh fuck, baby! That feels so good."

Seeing him let go as I take him even deeper is my favorite part. His musky taste drives me wild with want. He grabs the back of my head, encouraging me to speed up my pace.

Through gritted teeth, he spits out, "Baby, I'm going to come."

Making an even stronger suction around him causes his hot come to spurt into my mouth, and I swallow every last bit of it.

"Shit, I love it when you do that!"

He grabs me and hauls me to the nearby couch. He collapses with heavy eyes, and I wrap myself around him as I watch him come down from his orgasm.

When his phone vibrates, he pulls it from his pocket and answers the call. "Yes. Show her to the library. I want someone posted outside the door the entire time. Have Bane call me immediately. Thanks." He hangs up and zips up his pants before he confirms my suspicions. "Sam's here."

I start giving those fun little claps, and then I plaster my lips to his in a big noisy kiss.

"Hey, Alli. You can share the story about Becky with Sam. It might help explain why I'm so overprotective. I ask though that you keep all the stuff we've discussed with Bane a secret for now. I know you trust Sam, but until we figure it out—"

I cut him off with another kiss. "I'll only tell her about Rebecca. Thank you for letting me give her some sort of explanation, and I understand."

We get up from the couch. Making our way through the door, I add, "Oh, and thanks for having security stay outside. It's a little weird when they're in the room with me and don't say a word or even move."

He stops and faces me. "Alli, they're there to protect you, but if you prefer, I can have them wait outside the room you're in while you're in the house. Out in public though, I want them with you, no matter what."

Turning, I grab his hand and start to walk again. "I believe we have reached another compromise, partner."

Damien's about to respond when I hear, "Allison!"

Sam comes bolting down the hallway, wearing skinny jeans and a tight red shirt. I see the security guard about to run after her, but he stops when he sees Damien's small hand gesture. My money would be on Sam if some stranger tried to tackle her.

Giving me a hug, she says, "Oh, you look so much better. It's so good to see you." She lets go and gives Damien a slap on the shoulder. "It's my turn."

He gives a wink. "Have fun, ladies." As we start to walk off, Damien calls after us, "Sam, I only share until bedtime, so don't get any ideas."

She turns to me. "Allison, what's a safety?"

That came out of nowhere. In true confusion, I respond, "What?"

She turns around to face Damien. Laughing, she rubs her hands together. "Hmm, I think I know what my winnings are going to be for our next bet. Are you ready to concede a loss, so we can move on to something a little more challenging for me?"

Putting his hands up in almost defeat, he retorts back, "Hey, I have until the end of this season. I'm not giving up until the last game."

She turns away, and he gives me a wink. *Oh, he's good.* I smile back, thinking about him trying not to laugh. *Sam's going to be so pissed when she loses this little bet.*

∞∞∞∞∞∞∞∞∞∞∞∞∞∞∞∞∞∞∞

"Girl, I'm definitely staying here tonight. I cannot believe he had this room done for you," Sam says.

Covered in a soft blanket, we are seated on the heated sofa with our knees drawn up.

"So, what gives with all the extra security?" she asks.

After taking a sip of the hot tea that was delivered to our room, I respond, "Damien, as you know, is overprotective at times."

"Girl, if he were any more protective, you'd be put in a glass case."

I roll my eyes. "He actually has a reason. He said I could tell you, so you'd understand all the extra security after what happened with Brad. Damien had a sister. She was kidnapped from their home and found dead three weeks later."

Sam sits more erect. "Shit, I'm so sorry, Allison."

"Hey, you didn't know. I'd think the same thing if I were you."

Sam looks almost ashen. "When did this happen?"

"Seven years ago. There was a party at his parents' pool house, and she was taken at some point during the night. They never found who took her."

She moves to a cross-legged position with worry etching her face. "Are you okay, Allison? You're not in any danger, are you?"

This is the part where I want to tell Sam how freaked-out I am because a nut job is potentially trying to use me to further hurt Damien. However, I understand why Damien is keeping all this in such a tight circle.

"The whole Brad incident scared Damien, so he just wants to make sure I'm okay. That's the reason for the security."

She lets out a sigh of relief. "Okay, that's good. Man, I had no idea. I feel like a total bitch now with what I pulled."

"Sam. Don't. You didn't know." We need a subject change. I hate lying to her. "I saw Mark at my recent photo shoot. I like him."

She kicks my leg. "Don't you start playing matchmaker with me. Not happening. On a fun note, I got you a gift." Leaning over, she rummages through her bag and pulls out a book. "I thought you'd put this to good use."

As she hands it to me, she flips it over. The front of the book says, *101 Ways to Make Your Guy Scream in Pleasure.*

After I open and flip through it, my eyes shoot to hers. "Oh my gosh, Damien is going to love you."

"I know."

And with that, we bust out into a fit of giggles.

CHAPTER 26

As I put jelly on my toast, I ask Sam, "So, how did you sleep last night?"

"Magnifique." She gathers her fingers together and kisses them, like actors do in the movies. "I spent most of the night trying to figure out how to steal that damn water wall. I'm in love."

After I put the jelly back on the table, Sam grabs it.

"Um, no. That water wall is mine. So, how is your sexual assault awareness program going?"

She stretches to each side to pop her back. "It's going. It's getting more and more attention, which is good. Hopefully, it makes an impact. Even if we help only one person, it means the program is worth it."

"I think you're pretty wonderful."

She's about to respond when Damien comes wandering in, wearing a T-shirt and his black silk pajama pants. He's smiling and looks relieved.

Coming to sit beside me, he grabs my hand and gives it a kiss. "Baby, Brad is going away for a long time. They've decided to prosecute him to the fullest extent of the law."

Some of my accumulating stress dissipates.

I don't have a chance to respond before Damien continues, "He can now be linked in the drugging and raping of five other girls over the last few years. When they took his DNA after the attempt on you, they matched it to those five girls who had had the rape kit done when they filed a report. Apparently, he didn't use condoms with any of them. One girl became pregnant after he'd raped her, and the child is his."

My stomach drops, and Sam grabs my free hand. *That could have been me. Just a few more minutes, and I would have been one of his victims.* It's hard reconciling the fact that not too long ago, he seemed harmless.

I know it's difficult for Sam to hear this, considering the guilt she feels from that evening, but I'm glad she was here to hear it firsthand. Hopefully, this news helps us all heal from that horrific experience, and we can be the wiser for it in the future.

She starts her rant, "I still can't believe his parents pulled what they did. What a couple of sorry pieces of shit. They're all sorry assholes. I hope they fry his ass." Taking a breath, she adds softly, "Those poor girls."

I shiver, thinking about someone getting pregnant from a night she'll never even remember. I just have no words.

"Baby, I've already made arrangements to get those girls help if they haven't received it already."

Rubbing my arms to chase away the goose bumps, I respond, "Thank you. I love you."

I think even Sam is touched by his gesture. At a loss for words, she simply squeezes my leg lovingly.

Since I have to leave at the crack of dawn for tomorrow's photo shoot, I'm laying out my clothes now. At that time of morning, every minute of extra sleep is precious. I choose a pair of jeans and a dressy green semi-fall sweater that swoops barely off my shoulders. I still haven't found my black chunky necklace that I wore to the football game. I'm going to have to learn where the staff is putting my things or ask them to leave it for me.

Just as I finish getting dressed, there's a knock at the door. "Come in."

The door slightly cracks open. The security detail states, "Miss Scott, Mr. Wales has requested your presence in his office."

"Okay, thanks. I'll be right there." *Why didn't he come get me himself? He must be in the middle of something.*

The way these guys are so formal wears on my nerves. I make my way toward the office with security in tow. I've given up on attempting to have a conversation with any of them as I only receive one-word answers or nods. *Stupid nodding.*

As I walk into the office, Damien and Bane are in a heated discussion. It's not toward each other, but something is going down. Their heads snap up at my presence.

Damien is the first to speak. "Alli, Bane has found some new evidence regarding Becky and the person he believes is sending the notes. I would prefer that you not listen to everything, but I promised you equal footing in this, so I wanted to give you the choice."

Uh, that's a no-brainer. I go to take my seat next to him on the couch, silently conveying my decision. He gives me a loving smile as I grab his hand. I need the connection while I hear the new developments.

Damien instructs Bane, "Continue on."

"Miss Scott." He nods in greeting, and I return the nod.

In my mind, I've nicknamed us the *nodders* because of how much our heads bobble all the time.

"As I was telling Mr. Wales, I believe someone from the party he threw at his parent's house that evening was involved with the kidnapping and murder of Rebecca. I've been up to Mr. Wales's parents' home under the premise that I was investigating their daughter's disappearance. They were very accommodating and asked if reporters would be by later to take additional statements."

I'm seeing red when I hear all his parents can think about is getting more publicity for an already horrifically tragic event. Damien tenses beside me.

Bane continues, "What I found and they confirmed is that there is one door in the pool house that appears to be monitored, but it really isn't. They have never had the camera hooked up to the monitoring system, so there are technically seven cameras but only six feeds. Therefore, someone could have left the party at any time and come back, essentially moving about unnoticed with the inebriated state everyone seemed to be in. The cops notated the observation regarding the camera feeds, but they never put two and two together."

I hear Damien swear under his breath as Bane continues, "From there, I went to the site where Rebecca's body was found. I knew nothing would be there after all this time, but I needed the lay of the land. After looking at records and nearby places, I found a connection. On this piece of property," he says, pointing to a section on a map that means absolutely nothing to me, "was an abandoned shed. It was probably built some fifty plus years ago. When I searched it, I found this." He grabs a photo from a folder. "It has been properly tagged and secured for the time being."

The moment Damien sees it, he sucks in a harsh breath, and his muscles go taut. The veins in his arms are pulsing. It's a picture of a yellowed quilt that was probably white at some time, and it has some faded flowers on it. I remember Bane's words from our last discussion. *The only thing missing was a white quilt with pink flowers.*

Oh shit! Bane found it. After all this time, badass Bane found it.

Without having to be asked, Bane continues, "This was found on Mr. Mills's property, Mr. Wales. Technically, one of the subsidiaries he has formed to protect his assets owns the property, but it's been in his possession or his family's for the last fifteen years.

"From there, I cross-referenced other properties that Mr. Mills owns with the cities noted on the postage of the articles you've received. Mr. Mills has hotels in all of those towns. I am working to see if we can put him in each city around the time the articles were sent, but that's going to take a little longer to correlate.

"I know that Mr. Mills was present at the party where Miss Scott received the note. Also, in both instances of flower deliveries to Miss Scott, the orders were made over the phone, and they were paid for with cash. I am working on tracking down the delivery boys, but I have no verification at this time. I can also put Mr. Mills in North Carolina at the time of the game. He was attending an event of his own."

My head is swimming with all this information. *Martin kidnapped and killed Rebecca, and now, he's after me.* He's obsessed with Damien. He wants everything that Damien has. His infatuation with all Damien's exes is proof of that. *Ugh, I feel like I am going to be sick.* I look over at Damien and give him a squeeze. This has got to be one of the hardest things to hear. His best friend killed his sister and potentially wants his girlfriend now. I can't even imagine Sam and I doing that to each other. *What kind of person does this?* The betrayal is unfathomable.

Bane continues on, "Sir, we have tracked Mr. Mills, and he left earlier tonight to go out of the country with his family. We did not get a visual verification. We received this information after they had already departed, but all records show him boarding the plane. Airport footage confirms this. They are due back by the end of the week. I will continue to monitor him.

"I need further instruction on how you want to handle everything. The suite where Miss Scott will be working in tomorrow has been secured. Her security detail will consist of four people. Three will maintain a perimeter, and one will remain with her. Security has been given detailed instructions on how to handle the situation."

"Thank you, Bane. Let me reassess, and I'll get back with you. Don't let Martin out of your fucking sight. Have someone on the ground to keep track of his every movement when he lands." Bane goes to stand, and Damien continues, "Bane, thank you for your work. Excellent job. Hopefully, by the end of this week, this sick bastard will be behind bars."

Bane nods and leaves the room. I immediately embrace Damien in a hug, not knowing what to say. He pulls me with him as he lies back on the leather couch. Remaining silent, we just hold each other. The only sound in the room is his elevated and steady heartbeat in my ear.

Finally, I whisper, "It's almost over. I'm glad you'll finally have closure for your sister."

"Me, too, baby. Me, too. Please don't talk to anyone about this, including Sam, for right now. We need to be able to surprise him before he's able to slip away. Bane's going to use this extra time to further build our case against Martin." The hurt in his voice is evident.

"I promise."

He nods, and we continue to just hold each other. I'm sure Damien is feeling all sorts of betrayal right now. It's one thing to sleep with his girlfriend. It's a totally different story to pretend to be his best friend and then abduct and kill his sister. Then, Martin continued to pretend to be Damien's friend after all those years.

Damien is so incredibly strong to have endured what he has and to have come out a better person on the other side versus wallowing in his sorrow. I'm so incredibly proud of him, and I can't wait to spend the rest of my life showing that to him.

CHAPTER
27

As I walk through the hotel suite with my coffee in hand, my head is in a fog from waking up so early this morning for the photo shoot. Damien has a few business things he has to take care of, and then he is going to join me over lunch. Even though he seems to be doing okay, I think he needs some time to process things by himself.

Chris is in the kitchen of the suite, making some adjustments on his camera.

"Morning, Chris."

He's one of those older men who I just want to pinch on the cheek because he's so adorable. He's slightly frumpy around the middle, and his short white hair is always a chaotic mess.

"Morning, Allison. You got some extra friends with you today." He tips his head to the men in suits following me.

Smiling, I respond, "Protective boyfriend."

He just laughs and continues messing with his camera.

"Looks like the interior design team made a lot of headway. We should be shooting within the hour with some minor adjustments. I was thinking we could shoot the kitchen and table shots in the morning light to give it a fresh feel," I say.

Looking out the window toward the dark sky, he responds, "That should work. Then, were you thinking about shooting the bedroom at sunset to give it a romantic vibe?"

"Oh, Chris, you read my mind. I must have been trained well." I give him a little wink as he chuckles.

He walks up to me and pats me on the shoulder, like a grandparent would do to a grandkid. "Let me show you where they put the extra props in case you need something. Repairs are being done to that room, so it's been restricted from use."

With security in tow, I follow him to the office that's been designated off-limits for shooting.

⚬⚬⚬⚬⚬⚬⚬⚬⚬⚬⚬⚬⚬⚬⚬⚬⚬⚬⚬

About an hour later, I am almost ready to begin shooting the breakfast nook. I have about five minutes before the sun rises, and I need a higher basket to give the table height and dimension. I remember seeing one in the office where we are storing the extra décor.

Walking into the office, I spot it immediately. Belatedly, I remember I should have told the security guy where I was going. He's posted right outside the breakfast room, and I left through the opposite entryway. I hope he doesn't notice. If Damien finds out, he will be so agitated with both of us.

Right as I grab the basket, I hear the door shut, causing me to spin around.

Oh shit! I drop the basket on the floor. My world stops, and panic consumes me. Martin is standing in front of the door, blocking my way, with a silver object in his belt. His hair is shorter, and he looks tired.

Oh double shit! That silver object is a gun. My body freezes as if I'm stuck to the floor. I can't move even though my brain is shouting, *Run!* The blood pounds in my ears. The fear is trying to consume me, and I fight to keep it at bay. *How in the world did he make it past security? If I scream, they'll come in a heartbeat.*

"I wouldn't think of screaming if I were you." He taps the butt of the revolver as a silent threat.

I gulp, and my throat tightens.

Think. Think. Think. My brain feels as if it's weighed down, making it hard for me to form rational thoughts. *Maybe if I keep him talking, I can buy some time until someone arrives.* My palms are sweaty as my eyes dart around the room, trying to come up with something…anything.

"Okay, Martin, I'm not going to scream."

"I don't have much time. I'm being framed for Rebecca's murder. I don't want to hurt you, Allison. I just need to use you right now to deliver a message and to keep Damien rational when he shows up."

My voice is a little shaky as I respond, "Okay, why not just call Damien and tell him? Why hold me hostage with a gun? That doesn't scream, 'I'm innocent.'" After thinking about my bold statement, I softly add, "Sorry."

He's not even affected by my jab. It doesn't seem to have irritated him.

Thank goodness.

"It's the only way I know I'll get out of here alive. He will not take a chance of hurting you. This was the only way I could get close to talk to either one of you."

He's too calm, and that scares me even more. Either, he's not going to hurt me, or he's going to flip out on me all of a sudden.

After taking a stuttering breath in, I respond, "Damien's not going to let you take me from here."

"I don't plan on taking you, Allison. I just need you to listen to me for a couple of minutes." His stance is casual, but his hand is still on the gun.

It's hard for me to take my eyes off of it. *I just need to keep him talking.* "How did you get past security? You're supposed to be headed overseas."

"Didn't get on the plane. I have connections, and I arranged for this hotel to be offered to your magazine. I was hoping I'd be able to get to you this way. I knew it was a good place to stage a run-in since there's a connecting door to this office. It was locked when security swept this morning, and since it was added after the hotel was built, it's not included on the original blueprints. It's hard to see since the door is just like the paneling in the room, and the tapestry obscures it. By the way, your boyfriend is going to be quite upset at that oversight."

I turn to look at the opposite side of the room, and sure enough, there is a door at the end of the room with the tapestry pulled off to the side. *Why is he telling me all this?*

Turning back, I scoot away just a hair. "Okay, who killed Rebecca then?"

"Don't move any farther back." He taps the gun again, and I immediately stop. "If I give up all my information right now, you guys will go straight to the cops, and you won't be inclined to help me. The real killer arranged it, so I'll still go down as the murderer because of the current evidence against me. He's a smart, sick bastard. We are going to have to build trust first, my dear, for both our sakes."

Just keep the crazy-nut bag talking. "How long have you known the identity of the actual killer?" My eyes continue to dart around the room to see if I can find anything useful to defend myself or make my escape.

Anger flashes over his face as his jaw pops. "Let's just say I've known for a few months, but I had to unwillingly remain silent."

I know I shouldn't argue with him, but I don't know what else to say. Hopefully, as long as I keep my voice calm and non-aggressive, he'll stay as he is. "You slept with Damien's exes. That makes it hard for me to believe that you suddenly want to help me."

"Yes, I did do that. Cassandra came on to me, and I figured, what the hell? If he's not satisfying her, she's more than welcome to play the field with me. The others also approached me. Who am I to deny them a good time? They were great quick fucks. Damien is not as innocent as you think he is. He has a past, too."

Oh, I think I'm going to puke. He's beyond disgusting.

"I understand you think I don't have many endearing qualities, so we are going to start small. I'm going to give you a piece of information that Damien has no clue about. I've known about it for a year. When he figures it out, he'll want to hear more from me, and he'll be willing to work with me. I'll only communicate through you because I know he won't risk your life. Once you figure out the answer, we'll go from there."

"How will you know when he's figured the clue out?" I silently pray that security is going to be here any minute. They're always speaking into their earpieces. By now, someone has to know that I'm missing.

"I'm not worried about that. Damien will know how to get in touch with me, just like he did in college."

There's still so much that doesn't make sense. "Why'd you send me the texts, notes, and flowers?"

He shifts his weight toward me. His T-shirt and jeans look old and ratty. "I only sent you flowers to spring Damien into action to protect you. I saw the article about your incident with that college boy. I'm sure that caused the flowers at your apartment to be forgotten. I needed to get the ball rolling, so I sent them a second time. You and I have a problem much larger than me, my dear. This guy is smart, and he's way ahead of us. At first, when I saw you with Damien in Vegas, I just wanted to fuck with him. Then, I happened upon the information that's gotten me into this mess. We are running out of time, Allison."

My body starts tingling with fear at his words.

Just then, banging starts on the door. Suddenly, he lunges for me and grabs me. He points the gun to my head, and he wrenches me so close in front of him that I'm nearly immobile.

I scream, "Ahhh!" *I wish I knew some self-defense moves.* My heart is thudding so loudly in my chest that I'm not sure it can stay contained there with how hard it's pounding.

This could be the end. This could really be it. I just keep thinking that over and over in my head.

As Martin starts backing us up toward the secret door, I try to remain calm. In a low voice, I say, "This isn't helping your cause." My voice hitches on the last word.

"I just need to keep you in front of me until I get to the door, and then you'll be free. They won't shoot as long as you are blocking me."

Just then, the door bursts open with Bane at the forefront and Damien right behind him. Bane's gun is drawn to the side. He is ready to shoot. Martin angles my body between Bane's gun and him as he continues to walk backward while tsking at Bane. *Jackass.*

Damien steps in front of Bane. "Bane, keeping Alli safe and unharmed is your priority."

I can hear the panic in his voice. He then turns to Martin with his hands up in the air.

"Martin, please let her go. This has nothing to do with her. Take me instead."

I sob, "No." I know Martin might just kill Damien if we were to switch spots.

"Wales, I don't think so. Just stay where you are, and no one will get hurt. Your goon needs to drop his gun and lie down on the floor."

At his last command, he yanks me a little, and I whimper at the pressure of his grip.

Damien blanches at the sound. He extends his hand backward toward Bane as he keeps his eyes on me. "Bane, do as he asks."

Bane hesitates for just a moment.

"Damn it! Drop your fucking gun now and lie down!" Damien yells.

Finally, Bane obeys him as Damien continues his conversation with Martin. "You can have anything you want. I'll give you everything I have. Just don't hurt her."

Damien is outright terrified as Martin and I keep approaching the back door.

Tears are endlessly streaming down my face. *This could be the last time I see him. I have to tell him how I feel one more time.* "I love you, Damien."

My words visibly tear through him. He knows I'm preparing for the worst. His body is ready to strike at a moment's notice as soon as the gun isn't pointed at my temple.

"Alli, baby, I love you, too. You are going to be okay. Martin, please don't hurt her."

He's trying to keep his voice calm, but I can hear the panic and fear loud and clear.

Leaning in, Martin whispers into my ear, "Here's your juicy little tidbit. Cassandra has slept with more than just me in her recent years. I'll be in touch, Allison. I suggest you only tell people you really trust because the real killer is out there, and he wants you. You don't want him to know that you're going to find him."

I stiffen at his words. My mind is a molten mess right now.

Martin pushes me so forcefully that I stumble into Damien. He immediately takes me roughly to the floor and lies on top of me. Instinctively, my eyes squeeze shut as I hear the door slam. The noise causes me to flinch, and Damien presses me tighter to the hard floor, protecting me from anything that might come my way. His body on top of mine is making it hard for me to breathe. I have never been so scared in my life.

He yells, "Bane!"

"On it, sir."

I can hear Bane's footsteps echoing through the room, and then I hear a door opening. Everything is happening so fast that I can barely process it all.

The other security guard arrives. "Mr. Wales, we need to get you both to a secure location."

Damien pulls me off the floor, keeping me in front of him, as we practically run out of the room. My feet falter, and without missing a step, Damien lifts me up into his arms as we continue to make our way to another room. He's got me in a death clutch as I hear the security team talking into the earpieces about getting the magazine personnel to a safer location. My head is so messed up with all that has happened that I'm just about hyperventilating.

Damien sits me down on a bed. Kneeling in front of me, he methodically looks me over. I wince when he touches my head and my elbow.

"Where else do you hurt, baby?"

I can't get my mind to connect with my body. I was nearly shot, and I almost lost Damien for the rest of my life. When he gives me a slight shake, it jolts me into speaking.

"Other than what you saw, he didn't hurt me." My need for Damien takes over as I slide onto his lap.

He sits us on the floor, and I hold him tightly, realizing how close I came to losing him. A sob erupts from me as I grasp on to the man I love more than anything in this world.

"Shh, I've got you. Baby, you've got a bump on your head, when I pushed you to the ground. I'm so sorry."

All I can manage to say through the tears is, "We're together. That's all that matters." I am going to turn into a hysterical mess. Taking deep, calming breaths, I try to bring my emotions under control. I whisper into his side, "I thought he was out of the country."

"We did, too, baby. As soon as I found out he wasn't on the plane, we came straight to you. We couldn't get through to security. Lines have been down. You're safe now."

Two guys are standing near the entrance of the room. They are poised and ready for anything.

Mumbling against Damien's chest, I say, "He set this all up. He said all sorts of…" I cannot finish. I start to have a breakdown as I sob into his neck again. It's just too much for me to handle right now, and I cannot keep my emotions at bay.

"Shh, baby. We will talk about this later. Let's wait for Bane, and then we'll make a plan. I swear that you're safe now, Alli."

I shiver. Things could have turned out so differently.

He's clutching me so tightly against him. His shirt is bunched up in my grip as I clutch myself to him.

"I love you."

He gives me a gentle, reverent kiss on my head, and I can feel his love. It is that forever kind of love. I just need his touch right now. It's something concrete to focus on.

"I love you, too, baby."

Bane enters the room, and I immediately tense, hoping everyone is okay.

"Miss Scott, are you all right?"

I nod.

"Mr. Wales, Martin Mills has disappeared. He had a vehicle waiting outside of the exit. We are currently working on tracking him."

Damien pulls me closer to him. "Fucking find him, Bane. We'll need a doctor waiting for us at the house. Alli will need her head looked at. I took her down too hard with all the commotion. I want to get back to the house now. The police can meet us there if they want a statement. Have someone contact Ben and let him know our meeting is canceled this afternoon."

"Yes, sir. I suggest we head that way immediately before the cops get here."

I shudder, thinking about having to relive that moment by retelling it to Bane or anyone for that matter. Damien brings me closer to him.

We leave the room surrounded by security and make our way out of the hotel and into the waiting car. Once inside the vehicle, I lay my head on Damien's chest. I close my eyes, trying to calm down.

∞∞∞∞∞∞∞∞∞∞∞∞∞∞∞

"Miss Scott, all looks good. Take some aspirin for your head."

We are sitting in the formal living room as Dr. Ferguson finishes his examination. Damien is right beside me, watching my every move, not letting any distance in between us.

"Thank you, Dr. Ferguson."

"Anytime, Miss Scott. Mr. Wales, my office will be in touch."

Remaining beside me, Damien doesn't stand as he extends his hand to the doctor. "Perfect. Thank you for coming on such short notice."

With that, the good doctor takes his leave. Dread starts to creep into my stomach, knowing this reprieve is almost over. Damien looks tense and stressed from all the commotion today. Even after arriving home, his tight expression hasn't relaxed. I can almost see all the wheels churning behind those beautiful blue eyes.

Bane takes his seat across from me with that infamous notebook.

Feeling Damien's finger under my chin, he raises my face to meet his. "Alli, before the cops get here, I need you to tell Bane and me everything."

Closing my eyes, I take a deep breath before opening them again. "I needed a taller basket for the table. When I got it, I heard the door close, and I turned around. Martin had locked me in the room with him. He said he had been framed, and he needed to use me to keep you from hurting him. He'd arranged it all through what he called connections. He said he's known for months who killed Rebecca, but he had to unwillingly remain silent."

Bane is writing a million miles a minute, so I stop to let him catch up. Even after all the pandemonium this morning, he looks completely unfazed and perfectly put together. "Please continue, Miss Scott."

After taking a cleansing breath, I say, "He gave me a piece of information for Damien to look into. Once Damien figures it out, Martin said Damien would know how to contact him, like Damien used to when they were in college. Whatever it is, Damien's going to appreciate it, and I think Martin hopes it'll sway Damien to want to help him. Martin also said he was behind the flowers." Glancing over, I think Bane is writing more than I'm actually saying.

Bane stops writing and looks up at me. His eyebrows slightly furrow as he works on piecing all this together. "Did he say why he sent the flowers? What was the piece of information he gave you?"

My head is starting to pound as I think back to this afternoon. "He sent the flowers to spring Damien into action, to heighten security on me. Martin said that Cassandra has slept with more than just him in recent years."

Damien is the first to ask, "Was there anything else about Cassandra or who she slept with?"

Shaking my head, I say, "No. He just said the killer was way ahead of us, and he's targeting Martin and me. Martin said verifying this information will make you want to work with him to expose the actual killer."

Damien blanches at the statement and brings me to him. He's probably picturing my body on the side of the road, just like the way Rebecca's body was found. *I know I am.* With that thought, I feel nauseous.

Damien is rubbing his forehead with his free hand. "Bane, I don't want this to go beyond the three of us on the mere chance that Martin is telling the truth. If there is someone out there, I'm not taking any risks where Alli is concerned."

"Mr. Wales, I will continue digging. Do you have any idea what Cassandra or her sexual habits have to do with this?"

Damien lets out a long breath. "I have no fucking clue. The few times I have seen her in the last couple of years were impersonal and with my parents. She's obviously crazy, but I'm not sure how she fits into all of this."

I don't know how Bane can keep that impeccable posture and even tone of voice all the time.

"Sir, I think we should consider there might be some truth in this. If he wanted to, he could have escaped with Miss Scott before we even got there. However, we should take the utmost caution in case this is a ruse. Until we know more, I suggest we tell the cops that Martin tried to take Miss Scott and failed. Besides the fact that he has an obvious vendetta against you, leave any and all other conversations out of it."

After making another note in his notebook, Bane continues, "If the killer thinks all attention is still focused on finding Martin, it might buy us some time. Until we know more, we do not want this person to feel they need to try and take Miss Scott sooner than their planned attempt."

I can't hear any more of this right now. His words cause the remaining hold I had on my stomach to drop. Running from the room, I make it to the bathroom just in time as I retch everything in my stomach into the toilet. Tears trickle down my face from the intense motion of puking.

Damien is right there handing me a wet washcloth as I sink to the floor onto my knees. After cleaning my face, I look up and see the worry in his blue eyes.

Rubbing my back, he soothingly says, "Baby, we will figure this out. I'll keep you safe and away from this sick fuck. We just might need to change a few things, but we will do this together."

He sits beside me, and I hug him with all my strength.

"I love you," he says.

I inhale his scent, and it calms me. "Knowing you love me is all I need. I'm yours forever."

"Oh, baby, I love you more than my own life."

We sit there, just lost in our embrace.

I love this man, and there will never be anyone else for me.

CHAPTER 28

It's been four days since the Martin attack. I'm eating breakfast in the kitchen while Damien is talking to Bane in the hallway. I pick up my phone when it begins ringing.

"Hey, Sam."

"Hey, how are you doing? Any updates on Martin?"

Sam's been supportive through all the chaos. Same as we've told everyone else, she believes that Martin killed Rebecca seven years ago, and he tried to take me at the hotel due to a vendetta against Damien.

"I'm okay. Security has been increased again, so I'm completely safe. Police are still searching for Martin. It's as if he's disappeared into thin air."

I'm sure he won't be seen or heard from until we figure out his juicy tidbit. The thought of being in his presence again sends my mind to places I just don't want to go to right now.

"I'm glad Wales has increased security, Allison. Martin must have some serious connections." She honks the horn. "Sorry, someone was pulling out in front of me. How's Wales doing with all of this?"

Ugh, I hate hiding things from her. I have to tread so carefully with how I answer her. I want to tell her everything, but I can't. "He's doing as well as can be expected. I think he's still processing."

Deep down, I hope Martin is telling the truth and that he isn't the killer. I think Damien feels the same way. Knowing his best friend was pretending to be his friend all those years would be difficult to comprehend. Knowing your friend also killed your sister would be even harder to grasp.

"I hate he's going through this. Give Wales a hug for me. I'm seeing a friend in Atlanta today, and then I'm going to head down to visit my parents later. Keep me posted. Love you."

"Love you, too."

After I hang up, I overhear Bane talking to Damien.

"Sir, I am still investigating Cassandra's past sexual partners. It has to be done discreetly, so no one knows we are following other leads at this time."

There's no telling what he's going to find. Ugh, she makes me sick.

Damien responds, "Thank you, Bane. Keep me posted."

This morning's paper is on the kitchen island, and a picture of his parents catches my eye. Picking it up, I see his mother and father standing behind a podium. They appear to be giving a speech, and they are all decked out. Cassandra is standing beside his mom, with her arm wrapped around her. *Bitch.*

I read the caption under the picture.

> *The Wales declare, "It all makes sense now. There was always something strange about Martin Mills."*

I'm lost in the image, wondering how in the world Damien could be related to them. They are just so different. I feel a hand on my shoulder and turn to see Damien looking at what I'm reading.

"Mother will never refuse a chance for publicity. By the way, I declined when she asked for our answer regarding this weekend."

"Why?"

Damien's mom, Meredith, wanted us to visit them this weekend to attend a celebration party. *I really don't get them.*

He starts massaging my shoulders. "I know you said you would go, but I don't want to deal with them quite yet. We have enough on our plates, and we can go when it's best for us." The disgust in his voice is evident.

I lay the newspaper back down on the island. "Sounds good. I'm going to finish editing the photos from this week's shoot."

My heart is breaking a little because I resigned from my job. It was a hard decision to come to, but Damien and I would be nervous wrecks if we spent time apart right now, and

I need to put us first. Chris has already found a new photographer, which is good. *I will miss him as a mentor.*

I'm going to start shooting for the football team, and if needed, I might also do some real estate shots for Wales Enterprises.

After giving me a sweet kiss, Damien says, "Ben is stopping by to pick up some contracts in a few minutes. I'll come find you in the den when we're done."

"Sounds good. See you in a bit." After giving him a peck on the lips, I make my way to the den.

cocococococococococococo

Since there was no way I could go back to the hotel after the Martin incident, Chris finished the shoot. I agreed to do all the editing in order to make sure we could still meet the deadline. I pull up the last photo to be edited, and I slightly change the lighting.

When I'm done, I see an email from Mack in my inbox.

From: Mack Presley
To: Allison Scott
Subject: Re: Resignation

Allison,

I wanted you to know that if you are ever able to come back, we will find a place for you. You have a gift, and it has been a privilege to work with you.

Thank you for all your contributions.

Best regards,
Mack

That email alone makes my heart constrict in a bittersweet way. He has been such an incredibly understanding boss.

From: Allison Scott
To: Mack Presley
Subject: Re: Resignation

Mack,

Thanks for taking a chance on me. It means more than
you'll ever know. The last of the photos are attached.
Let me know if you ever need anything.

Thank you for everything.

Allison

Sending the email feels as if one chapter of my life is
closing, and another one is opening. It's harder than I thought.
As my mom always said, *The secret to a full life is to have more
beginnings than endings.* For a few minutes, I just stare at the
computer until I come to grips with what just occurred.

When I look up, I see the man I love watching me from
the doorway. "Hey, how long have you been there?"

"Long enough. You're adorable when you scrunch your
eyebrows while you're working."

"Ha-ha. Yes, a wrinkly ole face is just so adorable." I
cannot help the snicker that comes out.

He pushes off the door frame and walks toward me. "Are
you finished?"

"Yes, I'm no longer an employee of *Do It Yourself Magazine.*
It feels a little surreal."

I can see the concern in his eyes as he sits beside me on
the couch. Immediately, I lean my head on his shoulder as I
focus on the love I share with this incredible man.

"Alli, I'm so sorry that you have to give up something you
love. We'll find this prick."

I take a cleansing breath. "I'm not giving up anything. I
still get to pursue photography, and I'll be with you. We'll
figure out the rest as it comes."

When he kisses the top of my head, I can feel him smiling. The comfort from his touch continues to solidify my decision about my job.

"What would you say to us getting out of here for a while since we've been cooped up for the last four days? I thought it would be nice to have an evening out, so I made a dinner reservation for us if you want to go."

Without even thinking, I jump up. "Oh, that sounds fantastic. Let me go change. What time do we need to leave by?"

When I glance at the clock on the wall, I see it's almost three in the afternoon. I am so glad to be getting out for a little bit. I didn't even realize how trapped I'd felt until freedom was offered.

He laughs at my enthusiasm, and I give him a no-nonsense smirk.

"We need to leave by four. Our dinner reservation is at seven thirty. I thought we could dine on the coast tonight for a much-needed change in scenery."

"Perfect!"

I dash out of the room to go get ready. The security man is jogging to keep up with me as I make my way upstairs. It almost makes me laugh, but I keep it inside. I only have an hour, but I'll be able to make myself presentable by then. Honestly, at this point, I really don't care if I don't look my best tonight. That's how bad I need to get out of the house.

I pull out a deep purple halter-top dress that hits just above my knees. The top is loose and leaves my back bare all the way down to my waist where the material gathers and then hangs loosely around my legs. There's no way I can wear a bra with this. *Hmm, that will make it more interesting and tempting for Damien.*

I go with silver gladiator sandals in case we decide to walk near the water after dinner. For jewelry, I accessorize with silver hoop earrings, a silver watch, and the bracelet Damien gave me for my birthday. I grab my black jacket from the closet in case it gets cooler this evening, and then I practically skip down the stairs.

Damien is standing in the foyer, wearing a white button-up shirt, dark jeans, brown belt, and matching shoes. The shirt is perfectly tailored to fit his body, and his jeans hug him in all the right places. His black hair always has that just-fucked look, and his blue eyes are on fire. By the heat growing in his gaze, I know he is very aware of the fact that my nipples are automatically hard just from the look on his face.

I want him, right here and now. He continues to stare at me intently, and it makes me feel desired.

"You get more and more beautiful every day, Alli."

I smile at him. He is absolutely the perfect man.

"Thank you. I must say though, at this point, I am very tempted to skip dinner altogether."

He smiles his sexy grin and grabs my hand. In a hurry, he ushers us out of the house.

Laughing, I ask, "What's the rush?"

"If I don't get you out of here now, we'll miss our dinner plans, and we need a night out."

I give him my best pouty face, and he chuckles as he leads me to his sports car. Damien loves his cars, but he rarely has a chance to drive them, especially lately. This particular one is a beautiful smoky gray, and it screams luxury with its black interior. It's definitely one of my favorites from his vast collection. I watch as the door lifts vertically into the air. I didn't even know they made cars like this in real life.

"No security?" I ask.

"They'll follow us. I thought it would be nice to have some privacy for once. Plus, it's been a while since I've gotten to drive one of my cars. You'll be safe, baby."

"I always feel safe with you."

He smiles warmly at me and gets me situated in my seat before making his way over to the driver's side. When he sits behind the wheel, I can see his excitement. He's like a little boy on Christmas morning, and the sight makes my heart melt.

"So, dare I even ask what kind of car this is?"

"It's a Mercedes-Benz SLR McLaren."

"I'm guessing that translates to it's just a wicked awesome car."

"Yes, that would be an accurate statement. Actually, it might be a slightly understated assessment."

He's laughing at me for reducing such an awesome creation to a juvenile phrase.

He starts the car, but prior to putting it into drive, he turns my way and hands me a piece of fabric. "I want to keep the restaurant a surprise tonight. I'd like for you to wear a blindfold for the trip there, okay?"

"But I won't be able to see you. Didn't you say we're going to a restaurant on the shore? That'll take a few hours to get there." *What in the world is he thinking?*

"Do you trust me?"

Oh geez, way to pull out the big guns. So not fair. "You know I do. How does that prove I trust you?"

He doesn't say a word as he continues to hold out the blindfold, waiting for me to make my decision. It's not even a choice as I take it and secure it over my eyes. I will give him whatever sign of trust he needs.

My world is totally dark now. I try to sit back and relax as I hear the car shift into gear and feel it begin to move forward. As we hit the highway, the engine roars to life. From that point on, I lose my sense of direction as the miles continue to pass us.

He hasn't said a word since I put on the blindfold. Part of me wants to do something crazy, like show him one of my intimate parts, but I have no idea if someone driving beside us would be able to see. He did say security would be following us, so I can't take the risk of someone seeing me and upsetting him like that.

Instead, I bite the bullet and speak up first. "So, am I allowed to talk on this trip?"

He teasingly answers, "Of course. Why wouldn't you be able to?"

I shrug my shoulders. "Just checking. If you said no, I was going with option B."

Inquisitively, he asks, "And option B was?"

Well, I can't do what I wanted to do, but divulging plans never hurt anyone. Maybe it'll make this trip a little more difficult for him. "Well, I was going to start exposing body parts until I got some sort of reaction from you. It wouldn't take long since I'm wearing little to nothing underneath this dress." My teeny-tiny lacy thong shouldn't even count as actual underwear.

When I hear him groan, I cannot help but smile as I turn toward him.

"That's not playing nice, Alli."

"Well, I never said I played nice, and you did ask after all."

I give a little shimmy in his direction, and he groans again, which causes me to snicker.

"Why the hell did I want to drive us there again? Geez, woman, you're going to cause us to wreck if you don't stop."

Putting my hand to my chest, I produce my best Southern accent as I respond, "Who me? I'm just over here passing the time until we get to our location."

"Fuck. You're going to make this difficult."

The sexual frustration I hear in his voice pushes me forward as I try to drive him mad. Running a finger down the exposed slit in the front of my dress, I reply, "I would never do that."

Hearing him groan is so much fun.

∞∞∞∞∞∞∞∞∞∞∞∞∞∞∞

The car begins to slow and turns right. All of a sudden, the ride gets bumpy. *Where the hell are we?* I want to ask so badly, but I know he wouldn't answer me, and quite frankly, I refuse to give him that much satisfaction.

Mr. Smartass throws gas on my curious fire. "I know you're dying to ask where we are and if we're close…"

He leaves that sentence out there, dangling, waiting for me to bite. Payback serves me right, considering the state I probably left him in after all my sexual innuendos during the ride.

I turn my head his way even though I can't see him, and I just smile ever so sweetly at him. "I have no idea what you are talking about."

I can hear him chuckling in his seat. He knows that I'm lying, which is just as bad as me admitting I want to know where we are, but I refuse to give in.

"I hope I passed all your trust tests," I say.

He doesn't respond…and doesn't respond…and doesn't respond. *Did I say something wrong?*

The silence is deafening, and just as I am about to explain myself further, he finally says, "Alli, it wasn't a test."

That's all he says as the car comes to a stop. We are finally at our destination.

Oh, I wonder if we are having a private dinner on the beach. Eating dinner while listening to the waves crash against the shore would be fantastic. It would be like our first date in Miami, but this time, it would be more intimate.

His car door opens and closes, and before I know it, he's opening my side of the car. He helps me get out of the vehicle since I still can't see.

Well, I don't hear the ocean anywhere.

There are no distinct scents, like flowers, food, or the ocean. If it makes any sense, it just smells like outside. When a breeze blows in this early fall weather, I become slightly chilly. He starts moving his hands up and down my arms to warm me as we slowly make our way to wherever we are going. As we step through grassy terrain, I am so glad I chose to wear flat sandals versus heels. Part of me wants to ask a question, but I'm also enjoying the anticipation.

All of a sudden, I can feel a heat source warming the air around me. As we walk farther to our destination, it continues to get slightly warmer until it reaches a more comfortable temperature. Damien has stopped me now, and he is turning me to face a particular direction. When I hear the whinny of a horse in the distance, my curiosity reaches an all-time high.

Damien takes a deep nervous breath beside me. His fingers brush the side of my face as he goes to untie the blindfold. As he lets it drop to the ground, I open my eyes and wait until they adjust from the complete blackness they have been in for the last few hours.

As soon as everything snaps into focus, I gasp. I cannot believe what I see. We are standing on a hill at my parents' old farm. We're underneath an arbor that has thousands of lights dangling from it with the sun setting behind it. It's surrounded by outdoor space heaters. In the middle of the arbor sits a table for two, complete with flowers and two covered dishes.

"Oh, Damien!"

He's smiling down at me as I look up at him. My eyes start to fill with tears.

He brought me home.

He turns me around to face my old house. When he raises his arm and waves, a golden palomino with a white mane and tail starts trotting our way. It's my horse, the one I grew up with and then had to sell. *I cannot believe Gingersnap is here.* The tears are now flowing freely down my face.

I named her Gingersnap when I got her as a teenager. My mom had made a batch of gingersnap cookies, and the little thief took mine from me. We instantly bonded in that moment.

"Oh, Damien!" My mind is overflowing with all my emotions.

Soon Gingersnap's beautiful trot slows until she is right in front of us.

I immediately start stroking her neck as I coo at her. "Oh, sweetie, I've missed you. How have you been? I'm so sorry I had to sell you."

She continues to nuzzle me.

When I turn around to thank Damien, I find him in all his handsomeness on one knee, looking up at me with his deep blue eyes. My hand goes up to my mouth, and my heart is bursting at the seams as I take him all in.

"Alli, you are my everything. I never thought I would find someone who completes me as you do. You are my soul mate, and I cannot live in a world where we are not together. I never trusted anyone with my heart before, and it's yours for the taking. Will you marry me and be my forever?"

I nod and choke out, "Yes! Yes! Yes!"

Between all my sobs, he stands and slips the ring on my trembling hand. The ring has a large princess-cut diamond, and the band is surrounded with all diamonds that are sparkling in the setting sun. When I throw my arms around him, he lifts me up and spins me in a circle.

"I love you so much, Damien! So, so much! You brought me back to life. You're my forever, too. My heart belongs to you."

He sets me down and gazes at me with such love and tenderness. Slowly leaning his head down, he kisses me as his hands encase my face. There is nothing rushed or rough about this kiss. It is the most loving kiss I have ever received. This is the happiest moment of my life.

When I feel a nudge against my back, I turn and find Gingersnap, seemingly jealous from the lack of attention. Damien wraps his hands around my waist as I stroke her muzzle.

"Thank you, Damien. This means so much to me. How did you get everyone to agree to all of this? I cannot begin to explain how special this moment is to me."

"You don't have to give this moment up, Alli. It's yours forever."

I tilt my head to the side to look up at him in confusion.

He continues, "Gingersnap and the land are all yours again. They're my gift to you. I'd give you the world, baby. I want to be your happily ever after."

With that, my heart officially bursts with my love for Damien. "You are, Damien. You are my happily ever after."

EPILOGUE

Where the hell has that asshole taken Allison? My normal method of keeping tabs on her is not working tonight, and I know he's taken her out of the house. It's as if they've disappeared without a trace. *Fucking bastard.* He better not force her to do anything she doesn't want to do, like he used to do with Rebecca. *That son of a bitch is not going to take her from me. Fucking prick.*

Rebecca would never commit to me for fear of what her brother would do. I'd tried to talk some sense into her about how he didn't matter. Well, we know how that ended…Damien caused her death.

I refuse to let the same fate happen to my beautiful Allison. I know she doesn't really love him. She's in love with me, but she's afraid to tell him, just like Rebecca was. I refuse to let that bastard force her into a relationship.

I stroke her red scarf, the one she gave me to remind me of her when I couldn't be near her. It smells just like her. *Fucking perfect.*

I hope she can hear my mental pleas. I say them over and over and over again, hoping she gets the message.

Just give me time, Allison. I'm working on getting you back. Soon, I'll get word to you that I'm still in love with you. I know you miss me, and you are worried that something has happened to me. Even from a distance, I can see it in your questioning eyes. I felt horrible when your eyes pleaded with me to take you from him, and I couldn't do anything without putting you in harm's way. I'm going to get you back, regardless of the cost. All of my plans are working out perfectly. Just give me a little more time…

I love you.

On the following pages are
three scenes from *Trust Me*
written in Damien's point of view.

Hope you enjoy getting
a little piece of Mr. Wales

From *Trust Me*

The First Time Damien Sees Alli

Hell, it's been a long day. I can't wait to get back to my hotel room for some peace and quiet. Maybe my problem is that I need to find a woman to relieve some stress. I haven't had a fuck buddy for a while. As I've learned the hard way, my lifestyle just complicates things and gives the girl a false sense of security. Then, she starts thinking marriage and babies and shit. *Fuck, that's the last thing I need to deal with.* I shudder at the thought of marrying any of the women I've been with. They've all been beautiful. *Have I ever considered being tied to one of them for the rest of my life? Fuck no.*

At the Miami Beach Resort, I just finished my last meeting to buy some real estate down here. *I need a fucking drink.* I decide to walk away from the deal and have Ben inform them of my decision tomorrow. *No need to waste any more of my time on something that isn't going to work.* I don't do the nice thing just for the sake of it.

When I approach the pool bar, the waiter asks, "What can I get you, sir?"

"Gin and tonic."

"Yes, sir." The waiter quickly mixes the drink and places it in front of me.

As I take a sip, I look out to the pool area. *Maybe I can find a quick fuck here.* My eyes zoom in on the most beautiful woman. She's sitting in a lounge chair, secluded in a corner. My dick instantly goes hard at the sight of her. *I must have her.*

She has dirty-blonde hair and beautiful tanned skin that looks incredibly soft to the touch. I cannot see her eyes from here because of her sunglasses, but I would bet they are absolutely breathtaking. She's toned in all the right places. *Her body was made to be underneath me.* Her ivory swimsuit hugs her body to perfection. *I bet she tastes fucking phenomenal.*

After I get up from my seat, I hesitate and sit back down. *Some fucker is trying to stake his claim on her.* My initial instinct is to go over to the prick and teach him a thing or two for messing with my girl. With how my body is responding to her on an atomic level, I know this girl will be more than just a fuck buddy. That notion doesn't have me running the other direction. Instead, it drives my need to claim her as mine even further.

From the way her mouth is set in a grim line, I can see that she clearly wants nothing to do with the asshole. I smile to myself. Whatever she just snapped at him has him retreating to the pool area. *What a pussy.* It seems like my girl has a bit of a bite, which makes me want to fuck her even harder.

Now is not the time to approach her. She's in complete control of the situation, and she's clearly not open to meeting anyone. I'm going to have to patiently bide my time and run into her some other way. I pick up my phone and call Ben.

"Yes, sir," Ben answers.

"Bring me a shirt and a pair of shorts. I'm staying at the hotel for a bit longer."

"Yes, sir. I'll be there shortly."

After hanging up, I settle in at a nearby table. I position myself, so I can watch her every move. She's eating some kind of sandwich and drinking what looks like a margarita in her lounge chair.

A waiter walks towards me. "Sir, can I get you anything else?"

"Gin and tonic."

"Very well, sir."

Watching her makes me harder by the second. I wonder what she does for a living. At least I know where she's staying if I can't arrange a run-in today. I'm going to meet this woman one way or another. *She will be mine.*

She stands from her seat. *Fucking hell, she is beautiful.* When she removes her matching swimsuit wrap, I can see more of her gorgeous body. As she takes a quick dip in the pool, I think I'm having heart failure. I'm forcefully restraining myself from diving in after her. I feel some strange need to haul her off somewhere to protect her from all these gawking eyes. Every jackass here is watching her, thinking the same thing, but what they fail to realize is that I will be the only one to succeed in making her mine.

Shit! She's grabbing her stuff and heading for the hotel. I want to make a move, but she is sending off such strong vibes to leave her alone. I know I'll blow it if I approach her now. *Shit. Shit. Shit.* She stops a couple of tables away to talk to a waiter as he's wiping off a table. *She's so unbelievably gorgeous.*

"Excuse me, what time does the sun set here?" she asks.

Her sweet voice makes my dick get even harder.

The waiter stands up from his crouched position. "Right before eight, ma'am. If you're thinking about catching it, I suggest coming down around seven thirty. Make sure to bring your camera if you have one."

She gives him a warm smile. "Thank you. Have a good day."

"You too, ma'am."

When she walks away, he stares at her ass. I want to smack the shit out of him. I look at my watch. *It's going to be a long fucking day of nothing but waiting until sunset.* Patience is not my strongest suit, but I have to have her.

∞∞∞∞∞∞∞∞∞∞∞∞∞∞

I set up shop to work in a nearby corner of the hotel lobby. I need to ensure that I can see whatever way she decides to leave the hotel. Ben is on standby, so he can come in and gather my things as soon as she starts to get on the move again. This mysterious woman is about to meet her match, and even though she doesn't realize it yet, I'm going to claim her as mine, regardless of what it takes.

From *Trust Me*

Alli and Damien Together In the Truck

Fuck me. I grab Alli and lead us to the car. I am fuming with irritation after what that dickwad, Brad, tried to do with her. When she came alive on the dance floor, there wasn't a guy in there who wasn't looking at her with complete lust in his eyes. *How the hell has she not had a guy capture her attention?* For the millionth time over the last week, I just thank my lucky stars that it was me she said yes to. I don't give a shit if I had planned our accidental run-in. She's mine, and I'm never letting her go. I don't think she has any idea how important she really is to me.

I place her safely in the passenger's seat. This strapless turquoise dress is going to be the death of me. When the fabric shifts just right, I keep seeing hints of her nipples. As I get in the car and look at her, I see them again. They're perky and ready for my mouth. It is taking every ounce of willpower not to haul her onto my lap.

I need to get this evening back under control. If she will have me, I want to make love to Alli tonight. I will wait until she's ready, even if that means waiting forever. I just want to have the chance to eventually get to have her, but at the rate I'm going, I'm sinking any chances to be with her. I'm acting like a total asshole. I don't want to be that way with her, but I feel so possessive when it comes to her. The thought of anyone else even looking her way makes me furious. Those looks come with want, and then she could be in danger.

She glances over at me. "I had no idea Brad would be that way."

I squarely look back at her. I need fucking details on how she knows that prick. "How long have you known him?"

"Maybe six months or so. I'm not sure. There's nothing between Brad and me. There never has been and never will be."

The relief that floods my system is immeasurable. "I know you're not interested, but he is definitely going to be a problem. He wants you badly." Just thinking about the look in his eyes makes me want to go through the fucking roof.

"His ego was doing the talking. He's with a different girl every week. He was just trying to irritate you."

It's adorable how clueless she is about her beauty, but it also scares the shit out of me. Being naïve about how guys feel about her could hurt her.

"I disagree. I don't want you around him if I'm not around."

"Damien, don't be unreasonable. He's at a lot of events Sam goes to. You can trust me, you know."

Images of him watching her from a distance, waiting for his chance to try and move in, have me gripping the steering wheel in a death clutch.

"This is not a matter of trust, Alli. This is a matter of me protecting you. If he's around and I'm not, I want you to call me. I don't think you understand what I saw tonight. Every guy in that joint was watching your every move, and that was before you danced. After that…fuck, I don't want to think about it or I'll turn around and it won't end pleasantly." My voice ends up colder than I intended.

With the way he was eye-fucking my girlfriend the entire night, I know this is not the last we will see of that asshole. I need to calm down before I get too irate from thinking about it. I'm going to have to protect her so fiercely, which is going to piss her off. If it keeps her safe though, we will deal with it because losing her is not an option.

I glance over and see her looking stressed and unsure. *Shit, I need to turn this around.* I'll go the back way to my place, pull over, and hopefully I can get this situation under control.

She warily responds, "I'm not sure what you are talking about, but I really don't understand why you are being so cold right now. I don't know what I did. I was there with you, and I danced with Sam."

Fuck me. I've screwed this night up. It's not even about the sex. I don't want us to fight the entire time we're together. I've had so little time with her, and I just want to enjoy being with her. Plus, I need things okay between us before we get to the house. I don't want her to feel like she has to do anything she doesn't want to do, especially with the preparations I've had done in my room. I want her to feel comfortable to voice her opinion with me. I turn on the dirt road that lines the back of my estate and pull off to the side of the road.

The glow from the dashboard causes her eyes to dance, and I am frozen for a second at her breathtaking beauty. "You did absolutely nothing wrong. You have no clue what you do to the guys around you. I can see their faces, and I know what they are thinking. Knowing some prick is waiting on the sidelines for me to get benched drives me fucking mad. I'm staying in the game, Alli. You are not getting rid of me."

I cannot live without this woman. It seems crazy, especially considering I classified my most serious relationship as a long-standing fuck buddy. In less than one week, Alli has totally captured my heart. Giving someone so much control over that part of me scares the living shit out of me. When we were in her hotel room, I knew I loved her the moment she fell asleep in my arms. I tragically lost someone in my life once, and I cannot bear to lose someone as special as Alli. There will never be anyone like her again.

Without any warning, she unbuckles her seat belt, crawls over onto my lap, and straddles me. *Fuck me.* I look down, and her skirt is riding high on her legs. Her breathing is erratic, and her berries-and-cream scent completely seduces me. I want her right now.

She solemnly says, "I only want you. No one else."

I have to taste her right now before I explode. I cannot help myself. I devour her mouth and yank her hair out of whatever clip thing she has it in. She tastes of something sweet, and I love her hair down. She looks like a goddess.

Her hands have moved to my shirt, and she's trying to get it unbuttoned. Our need for each other is the most indescribable feeling. I groan into her mouth as she rips my shirt apart, sending buttons flying through the car. Her fingers graze my chest, and her touch cements my feelings for her. *I'll never let her go. She's mine.*

I have to remind myself that I'm not going to take her for her first time in a fucking truck. However, I can give us both a little taste of what's to come. I move my hands from her hair and begin caressing down her neck to the top of her sleeveless dress. I have spent the entire night loathing this dress because of all the attention it garnered, but right now, this is my most favorite dress in the world.

Her body naturally responds to my touch as she unconsciously shifts toward me. We are made for each other. I pull down her dress, leaving her perfectly perky breasts bare for me to feast on, but I cannot break away from her mouth. They fit perfectly in the palms of my hands. When I start to tweak one of her nipples, she breaks the kiss and leans back onto the steering wheel.

Fuck, she's beautiful. My other hand is at the hem of her dress, and I slowly move it up to the middle of her thigh. Her skin is as soft as I thought it would be that day at the hotel. Her eyes are closed, and part of me wants to suck on one of her breasts, but I want and need to see her come from my hands for the first time.

I need to tell her what I am going to do. I want her to feel safe. "Alli, I am going to make you come hard and fast, and then I'm taking you home and claiming you as mine." *Maybe I should say something else because that came out as more of a demand.* I just can't help this possessive nature she brings out in me.

"Please, Damien…it's throbbing."

I smile at her needy little body. She wants this so bad. She probably does not even comprehend much of what I am saying. I finally reach the entrance to her sex, and from feeling how wet she is, I cannot help the groan that escapes me. Her panties are completely saturated. *I cannot wait to taste that sweet goodness.*

"Oh, baby, you are so wet."

She moans as I slip one finger inside her. *Shit, she is so fucking tight.* Her walls clench around my finger. I'll have to be sure to loosen her up more before I go inside her. There's no way I could live with myself if I hurt her. I've barely moved my finger when she starts bucking her hips. She's so desperate for the friction. I want to give it to her, but I need to stretch her a little more. My dick is so hard at this point because I know how good she's going to feel around me.

Using my thumb, I stroke her clit. I can feel her walls starting to squeeze around my fingers. "Let go, baby."

Just like that, her body orgasms, and her skin slightly flushes from the pleasure. It is the most beautiful sight I have ever seen. Her eyes are closed, but I can tell she is pleased. Trying to give her every last bit of pleasure, I start sucking on her breasts as she starts to come down from her high.

Her pleasure is my number one priority. "Was that good, baby?"

"Mmhmm." She starts to open her eyes, and she's smiling that drug-induced-type smile. "I hope you live close by here," she replies in a raspy voice.

Pulling back, I sever the connection between us. I need to make it clear to her that we don't have to do anything else if she doesn't want to. I don't want to fuck this up. "We are at the back edge of my estate. Are you sure you are ready for this? We can take this slower."

"Please."

I cannot help the grin that spreads across my face. She's so sure and confident of what she wants. I cover her up and give her space to crawl back into her seat. Instead, she leans forward and starts kissing and sucking on my neck. *Oh fucking hell.* She's making it so hard not to take her right here and now. The way she's touching my body has me worked up to an all-time high.

"Alli, you need...fuck."

Her hand reaches my dick, and I don't have the willpower to make her move. I'll just have to be extra careful with her. I start driving the car back to the main entrance. Part of me wants to take down a fence and drive straight up the property to the back entrance.

She presses herself against me. As she moves up, her dress falls off, and I can feel her breasts against me.

I murmur, "Oh fuck, you feel fantastic."

I have never been this hard in my life. I'm about to explode like a fucking adolescent when we finally pull up to the front of the house. I planned on showing her around to make her feel comfortable in her surroundings, but we can do that some other time. I just need to get her to my room as quickly as possible.

From *Trust Me*

Alli and Damien's First Time Together

I gently pull her entwined limbs from me as we make it into my bedroom. She hasn't even noticed all the candles I lit in anticipation of making this the most special night of her life. I want to ease all her worries. She deserves nothing but the best, and I'm going to be the one to give it to her.

I put my finger underneath her chin to make sure she's listening to me, and she looks up with lust-filled eyes.

"We are going to take it slow tonight and enjoy each other. If it gets to be too much, we can stop this at any time. All you have to say is stop. I have condoms. I'll be safe with you always, regardless of how worked up we are."

She looks at me nervously. "Are you clean?"

"What?"

"I assume you have been sexually active, and I am asking if you're clean." She looks a little embarrassed.

I need her to feel safe with me. It's important. "Yes. I would never make love to you if I wasn't. I have always used protection with no exception."

She's making a decision on something. I can always tell because her hand automatically goes to her hair as she starts threading strands through her fingers quickly. I don't even think she knows about this telling sign.

"I'm on the pill due to irregularity, and if you're clean, you don't have to wear a condom."

Did she just say what I think she said? Could I be that lucky to have her bareback for the first time?

Damn it. I haven't responded, and she seems really nervous. I just never imagined her offering herself up to me like this.

"I mean, you don't have to. I didn't mean to assume. I understand. It's not a big deal." She's talking faster and faster.

I'm just completely stunned. "Are you sure?"

She flushes. "Yes, of course. I would never force you to go without a condom. I don't want you to do something that would make you feel uncomfortable."

As my brain starts to fire on all cylinders again, I cannot help the small chuckle that escapes me. She thinks she's pressuring me to do something I don't want to do. *Does she not know she just offered me the one gift I would never ask for?* Before her, I would have never even considered it. "Alli, I'd like that more than you know. I swear I am clean, and I have never been with a woman unprotected. Are you sure?"

"Yes."

I cannot believe it. I need to slow down and make sure she enjoys this. I want this to be more incredible than she has ever imagined. I grab her shoulders and turn her around to face the room. I hear a gasp as her hand goes to her face. I know her surprise is not from the luxury I live in but from the romantic setting of the fire and candles that give the room a romantic feel.

I put my lips right next to her ear. "Baby, do you like it?"

"Oh, Damien…" She turns to face me and brings my lips down to meet hers.

I will never tire of her kisses in a million years.

"This is unbelievably perfect," she says.

"Alli, I…" What the fuck? I almost told her I loved her.

I know she's opening up again for the first time in a while, and that would be the surest way to scare her off. I just start kissing her again in order to hopefully make her forget about what I was going to say. I begin to slowly back her up to the bed as I taste every inch of her mouth. When we reach the end of the bed, I step back to memorize this moment. *She's so beautiful, so perfect, and mine.*

I reach for her belt as she stares back at me with her sparkling blue-green eyes. I've noticed the dominant color in her eyes switch. It's as though they are reflecting my blue ones. I remove her belt and discard it off to the side. She looks amazing with her recently messed up hair. Next, I move to where my lips are almost reaching hers. We are breathing each other in as I slowly unzip her dress and release it. *Unfuckingbelieveable.* She's wearing nothing but her lacy boy shorts and cowboy boots. I am gawking at her beauty.

Without even thinking, I say, "One day, we are going to fuck in nothing but your cowboy boots." *Fuck, that was the furthest thing from romantic.* I quickly add, "Tonight, I'm only making love to you."

Stepping back, I look at her and savor her beauty. "Alli, I am the luckiest man alive to have you here in my room."

My words affect her as she squeezes her thighs together. I need to make her come one more time. I lift her small body onto the bed and slide one boot off at a time. I take her panties off last. My body is screaming for me to pound into her, but there's no way I could hurt her like that. I move my body on top of hers and begin kissing down her neck, memorizing her body's response to my touch. It's unbelievable how responsive she is. I take another taste of each of her breasts, working her into a frenzy of need. When I continue kissing down her flat stomach, I feel her go rigid beneath me.

I immediately stop. "What's wrong? Do you want me to stop?"

"No, no. I just...I, um...well I..." She looks so nervous, and she's squirming beneath me in a self-conscious sort of way.

"Alli, you are perfect, absolutely perfect...more than perfect. But, baby, I need you to orgasm one more time for me in order to make it as painless as possible when I enter you. Okay?"

She nods as I start kissing her stomach again, and I feel her get more relaxed. I continue moving until I reach her sex, and then I slowly lick upward because I need to taste her sweet nectar immediately. *Holy fucking shit.* It's the most addictive taste I have ever had in my mouth. I start sucking on her clit while I insert a finger into her tight heat, stretching and preparing her. When she bows off the bed, I bring my hand up to hold her in place in order for her to absorb more of the orgasm. I'm lost in her.

I murmur, "Nothing can even compare to you."

Just like that, she's gone again as I take everything she gives me.

My dick is as hard as granite after watching her come apart on my hands twice. I jump off the bed and remove my clothes in record time. When my dick springs free, her eyes get as wide as saucers.

"We'll fit perfectly. Do you trust me?" I ask.

She nods, and I bring my body on top of hers. I'm careful not to crush her as I begin kissing her again. Her two tastes create the headiest combination. My erection is throbbing as I scoot us both farther up the bed. I move my body down and poise myself at her hot entrance. It's as if it wants me inside just as much as I want to be there. She is about to give me a once-in-a-lifetime gift. No one else will ever have this with her. Actually, no one will ever have her besides me.

I need to check one more time. "Are you ready, baby? You are so gorgeous."

She nods. My body is clenched so tight in anticipation.

"This is going to hurt. I am going to go as slow as I can. Tell me if you need me to stop."

She gives a small smile as I slip inside her. *Fuck! She feels unbelievable.* I'm going to come in no time at all. She is so incredibly tight, and she fits around me so perfectly. When she stiffens beneath me, I know it's because she's adjusting to my size.

"You've got to relax, baby, and stop fighting me. Breathe, Alli. Trust me."

She follows my command and starts to relax slowly.

"I'm going to go in a little deeper."

I hate it that I'm barely in, but I slowly move a little deeper. Her warmth envelops me completely. I then move out and slowly back in several more times. *She's so incredibly perfect.* Finally, I am in to the hilt. *I could stay here for the rest of my life.*

"I'm all the way in, baby. You feel so incredible. Nothing has ever felt this perfect. I'm going to start moving now."

She nods as I begin to move. I can tell the moment her discomfort changes to pleasure. She starts meeting my movements as her body takes over, seeking that high.

"Alli, you're mine. No one else is ever going to have you."

I continue to thrust faster and faster, giving her the friction she wants.

She responds, "Yes, I'm yours. I'm all yours, Damien. Please. Please. Faster."

I move my hips one more time. I feel her clench around me tightly, and I erupt inside her, marking her as mine in the most animalistic way known to man. I am now a part of her. I slowly pull out of her and immediately miss the feeling of being inside her. I would love to stay inside her longer, but I don't want to make it days before I can have her again. It's going to be hard limiting myself with her for a while since she's not used to having sex yet.

There is no going back from this perfection. No one will ever compare to her. This woman is going to be mine forever.

LOVE ME

*Damien and Alli's story continues
in the Trust Series sequel.*

WILL DAMIEN BE ABLE TO FIND REBECCA'S KILLER BEFORE IT'S TOO LATE?

WILL DAMIEN AND ALLI SURVIVE HIS PAST?

OR WILL THE TRUST THEY'VE BUILT BE DESTROYED?

Hopefully, their love will be enough...

AVAILABLE
NOW

Ripple Effect

BOOK ONE OF
The Effect Series

COMING OCTOBER 2014

THANK YOU

First and foremost, I want to thank my husband, Paul, for all his patience and support throughout this entire process. You are my rock, and I love you dearly. You truly are my happily ever after, and I am so blessed to have you by my side, day in and day out.

To my daughter, Makaela—You are so incredibly special to me, and I love you to the ends of the Earth. Right now, you're too young to remember this journey, but since you were born, your smiles, hugs, and unconditional love have made my world a brighter place.

To my dad, Gehrig—After all the endless hours I spent reading over the last couple of years, thank you for putting the idea to start writing again into my head. I am so incredibly lucky to have a father like you. I will always be Daddy's little girl.

To my stepmom, Janet—Thank you for going on the various journeys with me this last year as I researched everything that was needed for this book. We had so many good times filled with laughter, and I will never forget them. As you would say, "We definitely made some memories."

To my mom, Kathy—You have always been there for me and supported me in all of my life's ambitions. I have you to thank for my drive and never-ending desire to make the most of everything I do. All the quotes from Alli's mother remind me of things you have said to me. I could not have asked for a better mother.

To my stepdad, Tim—Thank you for always being there for me. I am so fortunate you came into our lives all those years ago.

To Harper, Harper, Harper—I heart you sooo much! Thank you, thank you, thank you for all your time and feedback during this journey. You've kept me grounded throughout this ride, especially when things seemed to spin out of control. I'm so thankful that you came into my life with your brilliant personality and smile. We have laughed a lifetime's worth during our friendship, and I cannot wait to share another lifetime's worth in the coming year. You've been with me since the beginning, and I cherish the memories we have made. When I see the bracelet on the book cover, it will always remind me of you. Also, Damien and Alli thank you for all your wardrobe advice.

To Jovana Shirley—You are my Fairy Edit Godmother. You have an incredible talent of editing books. I feel honored to have you as my editor. I am thankful beyond words that I found your name in a book I was reading. When I read some of your editing samples, I knew you were worth the seven-month wait. I feel blessed to have you in my life as a friend and editor. Thank you from the bottom of my heart for your hard work. I heart you so much and cannot wait to meet you one day.

To my beta readers: Maren, Heather, Nikola, Lori, Brandy, Leanna, and Kim—I am so thankful for each and every one of you guys. Your friendship means more to me than you will ever know. You are the best beta readers a person could ever ask for. I heart you all!

> To Maren—I'm so glad we found each other in Mexico when we lived there in college. Since then, we have become the best of friends. Mexico will never be toured as fast and furious as we did it that summer!

> To Heather—Through this experience, one of the many wonderful things that has happened to me is meeting you. You're my own personal cheerleader. Thank you!

> To Nikola (You'll never be Nikki to me.)—You are one in a million, and I'm so fortunate that I met you all those years ago. With your energy and charisma, you light up a room when you walk into it.

To Lori—Girl, you have always been there for me. Thank you for your mentorship through the beginning of my career, and thank you for always keeping it real. I love all of our pedicure dates.

To Brandy L. Rivers—I will cherish all our late-night messaging chats. Thank you so, so, so much for the advice you have given me. It has made all the difference in the world. And because you know I have to declare it as much as possible…Slater is *mine*!

To Leanna—Thank you for all your feedback, friendship, and for taking the photograph on the cover. Your work is beautiful.

To Kim—Thank you for all the time you spent chatting with me about the book. Damien also wanted me to tell you thanks for keeping the red and gold out of his bedroom.

To Kelly Elliott—Your friendship has meant the world to me over these last few months. When I started this journey, you were one of the first authors I reached out to. Your kindness knows no ends. It's amazing what a few chats here and there can turn into. Thank you for everything! Many, many congrats!

To Stacy Borel—Thank you for all your advice and encouraging words. It's wonderful to have a friend like you. The jokes we have made will always bring a smile to my face. I cannot wait to be your table buddy at the signings we are doing throughout the next year.

To Chris—Thank you for creating the cover design to my book. It's beautiful, and it's just what we discussed. Love it! Thank you for being such a wonderful uncle. I will never forget bunt ball games in the basement, my first pet turtle, the surprise look, and the many other memories we made as a family.

To Jessica—You're my favorite ninja of all time. Thank you for your never-ending friendship and laughs. You mean the world to me! Fish sticks and oranges will always be our story! Let's not forget "Evacuate the Dance Floor" and "Drop It Like It's Hot."

To the Misery Ladies—I will treasure all our group messages, conversations, and friendships for life. It's amazing what came out of one little weekend. I love each and every one of you guys. I cannot wait until we have our next vacation together. You guys make me chortle so much. Who would have thought Nutella could have so many meanings? As I sit here writing this acknowledgment, my phone is currently going crazy with Voxers. We sure do know how to chat. Love you all!

To Kendall—You have done so much for me, and I truly appreciate it! Sending you a huge, huge hug across the Atlantic, my sweet friend! It has become my mission to one day give you a huge, huge hug in person. You mean the world to me.

To Mayer's Trusted—You guys are *ah-may-zing*! Thank you for everything you do! Getting to know you all has been fantastic. Like I've said over and over again, the best part of this journey are the newfound friendships I have made. Thank you!

To Allison—It's amazing the friendships that blossom from just a simple inquiry. Thank you for your encouraging words and all that you have done for me.

To Mandy (Santa)—Thank you for sharing so much with me. I cannot wait to meet you this December.

To Rochelle and Tarnya—Your designs for the swag are absolutely breathtaking. Thank you!

A special shout-out to Joy, my BRP—Thank you, girl. You're the best.

To Jason, aka The Jefster—Thank you for your friendship and guidance through the years. It's an honor to call you one of my close friends. Pssst…each comma in this book was made with you in mind. Imagine a duck-call sound right now! Ha!

To Linda—You have always been there for me and supported me through the good and bad times. Thank you, thank you, thank you! One of my most treasured trips is when we went to Portugal together. I have never laughed so hard in my life. Geez, I will never forget the wake up call you gave me that first day in Lisbon! I love you to the bottom of my heart!

To all the amazing friends and readers that I've met and will meet along this journey—Thank you for all of your encouraging words, support, and friendship. Each and every one of you is incredibly special to me. Thank you from the bottom of my heart.

Hope you have enjoyed Damien and Alli's story as much as I enjoyed writing it.

CPSIA information can be obtained at www.ICGtesting.com
Printed in the USA
LVOW11s1534110814

398587LV00001B/73/P